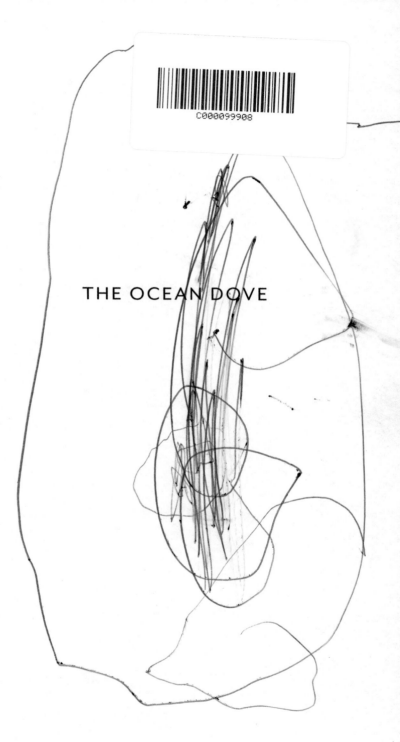

THE OCEAN DOVE

THE OCEAN DOVE

Carlos Luxul

Matador
9 Priory Business Park,
Wistow Road, Kibworth Beauchamp,
Leicestershire. LE8 0RX
Tel: 0116 279 2299
Email: books@troubador.co.uk
Web: www.troubador.co.uk/matador
Twitter: @matadorbooks

ISBN 978 1838594 008

British Library Cataloguing in Publication Data.
A catalogue record for this book is available from the British Library.

Printed and bound in the UK by TJ International, Padstow, Cornwall
Typeset in 11pt Adobe Garamond Pro by Troubador Publishing Ltd, Leicester, UK

Matador is an imprint of Troubador Publishing Ltd

ONE

'You must help me, Captain! There's a dhow in the water. It's been drifting. I don't know how long. They're fishermen, I think. Some men, a woman and child. They're so weak. I've got medicines but I need more – bandages, antibiotics, other things. And saline, do you have saline? Over.'

The voice on the radio was anxious, speaking quickly. Captain Pedersen looked up through the bridge windscreen and pressed reply.

'We wondered why you'd stopped. Okay, there's plenty of stuff on board and we'll be with you in twenty minutes. Over.'

'Thank you, Captain. Thank you. I'll send the mate to you. Over and out.'

The *Ocean Dove* was four miles ahead; it was a ship Captain Pedersen knew. He had been behind it, following the same course for the past week. Now it was turning, swinging round to face him. A small boat lay in the shadow of its hull but he was still too far away to pick out any detail. He reached for his binoculars and stepped out to the observation wings, steadying his elbows on the guard rail and glancing up at the sun as the hot steel began to sting.

It was 16.10, Saturday 5 December, four hundred miles north of Madagascar, summer in the Indian Ocean. The temperature was forty degrees. Pedersen was hot, tired and behind schedule. And these men in the water? They were only fishermen, but they were still fellow seamen and they needed his help. Captain Mubarak of the *Ocean Dove* had not hesitated and he knew he must do the same. It was the code of the sea.

He told the ship's mate to gather what he could from the medical station and to rouse the crew. There were just eight on board. The *Danske Prince* was a small ship plying a specialised trade.

1

'Okay, guys,' Pedersen said when the last of the men arrived on the bridge. 'We do what we can and then we get going again. We can't afford the time,' he added, conscious of the delays suffered on the voyage already.

'Take a look,' he said, handing his binoculars to the chief engineer.

They were now within a quarter of a mile of the *Ocean Dove*. Its port side faced them, lit by the sun low in the west. The ship was similar to their own but larger, five thousand tonnes, a hundred and fifteen metres long. On the funnel were the shipowner's colours: a blue bird silhouetted against a yellow shield.

At the waterline was the sleek outline of what appeared to be a typical Indian Ocean dhow. There was no sign of masts or sails. Yellow hard-hats moved about in the dhow. A crewman in yellow overalls climbed a scaling net. On the deck, more yellow overalls stared down from the ship's rail, gesticulating, walkie-talkies held to ears.

'What do you think?' Captain Pedersen said.

The engineer sucked in a breath and shook his head. 'Looks a fucking mess.'

The *Danske Prince* stopped seventy metres from the *Ocean Dove* in dead flat water. Flags hung limply. Funnel smoke eddied blackly in the heat shimmer. Pedersen trained the binoculars back on the dhow. He could hear shouting, see shadowy figures stretched out, *Ocean Dove* crewmen crouched over them. The fishermen looked in bad shape, their clothes in tatters, makeshift bandages. One raised a hand limply before it fell back. Another spluttered when a bottle was put to cracked lips.

'For Christ's sake ...' Pedersen sighed as a child's head bobbed up behind a pile of nets and a voice rang out across the water.

'Captain, Captain!'

Pedersen recognised the voice. 'I'm here!' he shouted back, raising his arm.

'I'm sending the mate in the small boat!'

A dinghy swung over the *Ocean Dove*'s side. Two figures in yellow and one in white started down the ladder, rucksacks on their backs. The yellows took an oar each. The white sat at the back.

Minutes later the man in white and one of the yellows were climbing up to the *Danske Prince*'s rail. Hands reached out to pull them on board. First on deck with an agile spring was a tall, rangy crewman in yellow, followed by the mate, in white.

Pedersen met a pair of clear, alert eyes and shook a hard-skinned hand. The guy before him was around thirty, powerfully built, a shade over six feet.

'I'm Choukri,' the mate said, turning and gesturing to his own ship and the dhow languishing at its side. 'My God ...'

'This way,' Pedersen said. 'We've got some things ready. Just tell me what you need.'

He led them along the walkway, his own mate and chief engineer behind him, climbing the stairs from the main deck to the bridge and stepping through the open door. On the far side, the chart table was piled with pharmacy bottles, packs of bandages and cases of drinking water.

When he reached the table, Pedersen heard two dull thuds behind him, followed a split second later by two more. They registered in his subconscious as distantly familiar but out of context. A gasp, a scuff of a boot and he was still unable to make the connection. In the corner of his eye he saw the *Danske Prince*'s mate stumble. Instinctively he thrust an arm out but was too far away to catch his crumpling friend. The last thing he saw was his chief engineer pitching to the floor, bewilderment etched in his face.

~

A blink of an eye: three men dead. The yellow-overalled crewman stood over the bodies, making doubly sure with a bullet in each of their heads. They were hollow-point shells, expanding on impact for greater shock and stopping power. After nine bullet wounds, blood pumped in uniform channels along the floor's grooved rubber matting, shifting one way and then the other as the ship rocked gently.

Choukri turned on his heels and sprang back to the doorway. He reached in his rucksack, swapped his silenced Glock pistol for another and reloaded the used gun, his practised fingers moving with speed as he changed the clips.

'Five more,' he said, his eyes darting around the bridge.

Edging his head out of the door, he looked along the ship. The remaining crewmen were at the guard rail thirty metres away, absorbed in the activity on the dhow. One of them turned in his direction. Choukri raised a hand, the gesture immediately returned with a friendly wave. It reassured him the crew of the *Danske Prince* had seen and heard nothing. Barely two minutes had passed. They would assume their captain and colleagues were sorting out supplies on the bridge with the guys from the *Ocean Dove*.

Choukri turned back to the bridge, his eyes flaring at the sight of his motionless accomplice staring down, apparently fascinated with the shattered skulls on the floor.

'Assam, get fucking real!' he hissed, pointing to the far door. 'Round the port side, now. And wait out of sight at the bow.'

The ship's hatch stretched away from the bridge, rectangular, forty metres long. On either side was a narrow walkway, the guard rail to the outside, the hatch covers and the top of the hold walls to the inside. If the crew got wind of what was happening and backed away towards the bows, they could only meet Assam.

He watched Assam go down the stairs and along the walkway, the *Danske Prince*'s crew unaware, their backs to him on the other side of the hatch. When he turned the corner at the bow and disappeared from sight, Choukri slipped out through the opposite door. At the foot of the stairs he balanced his rucksack on his two guns as though he was carrying it in front of him, full of medical supplies.

Three of the crew were shoulder to shoulder midway along the rail. With the *Ocean Dove* to the west and the sun dropping fast to the horizon, they were shielding their eyes from the glare and focusing on the dhow. One turned, saw Choukri and started towards him as if to offer help. At five paces Choukri let the rucksack drop and put two shots in the man's chest, then one more as he stepped over his fallen body without breaking stride.

The next two straightened and turned, without obvious alarm, as if to assist a colleague who had stumbled.

Two rapid shots. The nearer crewman fell instantly, almost silently. He clearly weighed next to nothing, looked so young. Choukri strode on, his right boot stamping down on the boy's fingers.

The heavily built man next in line crumpled against the hold wall, bent double by two bullets from the gun in Choukri's left hand. The pistol in his right whipped the slumped head aside, sending a lifeless arm flailing and shattering a watch glass.

He bore down on the final pair. Only now were subliminal messages translating rapidly into stark, conscious terror. The crewman's head jerked, his eyes staring at the two Glock pistols held chest high in extended arms. His mouth opened but no sound came out. Spinning round towards the bows, the only line of escape, he crashed into the back of his colleague, bringing them both down in a tangle. Neither had time to look up before bullets ripped into them

Choukri gulped a breath. 'Assam!'

At the sight of a boot appearing around the side of the hatch, his shoulders dropped, the pistols hanging dead weight in his hands. Sweat ran down his forehead, stinging his eyes as he panned up and down the ship and across to the *Ocean Dove*. The activity to help the fishermen on the dhow was continuing unbroken. Exactly, he thought. The training was working.

Assam ran along the walkway, vaulting the two corpses blocking his way with scarcely a glance. He gripped Choukri's arm, his eyes excited.

'Make sure,' Choukri said, shaking him off.

Blood was drying quickly on the walkway, vivid crimson turning dirty brown. A cheek, the back of a hand, the leg of the boy in shorts scorching on the hot steel, all past caring.

Assam turned and stood over them, his Glocks held sideways, lowered close to their heads. He put a bullet in each, taking his time, working his way along the walkway, alternating between the two guns. The last victim he shot full in the face, straddling him, motionless, looking down with detached curiosity.

Watching from the ship's rail, Choukri stepped up silently behind him, the barrel of one of his Glocks in his hand. He waited a second, then a second more, before lashing out with the butt of the gun. Blunt metal rapped Assam's skull, his neck compressing as he snapped from his reverie and spun round.

'Concentrate!' Choukri barked, peppering him with spittle.

Satisfied with Assam's head bending in submission, his angry eyes lowering to the deck, Choukri turned and stepped back to the rail. Holding his guns high, he stretched his head back and bellowed across to the *Ocean Dove*.

Activity froze. Eyes lifted. Everyone leapt to their feet, including the injured fishermen, their fists pumping the air as Choukri's triumphal roar echoed across the lifeless water between the ships. Yellow overalls sprang up scaling nets and ladders to the *Ocean Dove*'s deck. Fishermen in the dhow shouted up to the ship. Guide ropes were thrown to them. A motor coughed into life and the dhow slid across to the *Danske Prince*.

Choukri's narrowed eyes darted about with satisfaction as three fishermen in bandages and castaway rags climbed the *Danske Prince*'s ladder and heaved mooring lines up, hooking them over bollards. Winches turned on the *Ocean Dove* and the two ships edged towards each other.

Fishermen dragged the bodies of Captain Pedersen, the mate and the chief engineer from the bridge, their heads bouncing on the stairs, their final expressions unchanging. They were dumped in a heap on the walkway with their crew and upended one by one over the rail into the water, where they were boat-hooked and hauled onto the dhow.

Fenders were lowered as the ships inched together. A gangway was laid between the two decks and the *Ocean Dove* swung its cranes out over the *Danske Prince*. A crewman in yellow started the hatch motor. The screech of steel rollers cut through the air, the hatch panels inching along, rising in symmetry before hitting their stoppers with an echoing boom, revealing the *Danske Prince*'s hold below.

Four wooden packing cases were stowed in a row, each about six metres long. Next to them were twelve shipping containers. The crew worked quickly with bolt cutters, slicing through the lashing straps holding the cases in place. A crewman above the hold looked down and guided the *Ocean Dove*'s crane operator by walkie-talkie. Slings were attached and the first case rose into the air. At the other end of the hold, the *Ocean Dove*'s second crane repeated the process.

A packing case emerged from the *Danske Prince* into the sunlight, swinging over the ships' rails before being lowered into the *Ocean Dove*. Choukri stepped across the gangway to the *Ocean Dove*, jumped to the deck and made his way down to the hold. The first of the packing cases and two containers were there already. Another was above him, the crane slewing it into place, throwing a shadow across the floor.

He edged to the side and grabbed a crewman by the arm.

The guy grinned, hopping from one foot to another as if about to break into dance.

'You've done it!' he gushed.

'Not yet,' Choukri snapped. 'Tell Snoop to get the explosives.'

~

Twenty-five minutes after Choukri first set his boots on the *Danske Prince* he took a swig of water, pouring the last of it over himself, closing his eyes as the coolness ran down the back of his neck. Shaking sweat and water from his head, he glanced along the walkway where Captain Mubarak's crisp white shirt was bent over the rail.

Throwing the bottle aside, Choukri strode up to his side and looked down. Below them at the waterline, the dhow was tied to the foot of the hull ladder.

A crane boom swung out and lowered a wooden pallet. Fishermen heaved the *Danske Prince*'s crew onto it. Distinguishing one body from another or working out which tangled limb belonged to which twisted torso was impossible. Bloodstained clothes were darkening quickly in the sticky heat, shattered skulls lolling pathetically as the dead were manhandled and dumped in a heap without ceremony.

Mubarak brought his hands together and looked to the sky as the corpses swung past and disappeared into the hold, where they were stuffed into a bright orange container.

'It troubles you?' Choukri said, his face set hard, suspecting Mubarak was unaware he was at his side.

'Sometimes it does,' Mubarak said without turning. 'Not our destination, just some of the roads we take …'

Choukri ran his eyes up and down the captain's profile for a moment before glancing at his watch and barking into his walkie-talkie.

'Snoop, where are my explosives?'

Without waiting for a reply, he made his way back down to the hold and crossed to the far side, stopping by the open doors of a container. Inside it, Snoop was crouched at a packing case lifting its lid, the gold chains around his neck swinging free and chinking against the hinges. In the case was a nested row resembling oversized shoeboxes, the writing on them a mix of Cyrillic and Arabic. Adjusting his grip, he braced his knees against the side, lifting carefully.

'Easy …' Choukri said, from behind.

Snoop's pockmarked face turned. He checked the floor of the container for obstacles before edging backwards. A personnel transfer basket sat by the container doors, its gate open and facing him. Placing the first package in it carefully, he turned and repeated the process. Moments later there were five identical mines in the basket, but there was still one more package, and it was quite different. Two transparent canisters were filled with a crystalline powder, woven together with tape, wires, a junction box and a timer – an improvised explosive device.

The IED was too heavy for one man to lift. Choukri stepped up to the side of the case and took a firm handhold.

'Ready?' he said.

Snoop nodded.

High above the hold, the crane operator signalled from his cabin. The slings tightened, taking the weight of the mine-filled basket. Choukri watched it rise before beckoning to Snoop.

'Get Assam, Faisel and Tariq and meet me on the *Danske Prince*.'

Choukri went up to the deck and crossed the gangway between the ships, descending to the *Danske Prince*'s hold. Snoop and Assam came through the door first, followed by Faisel, the *Ocean Dove*'s second officer, efficiently kitted out in safety glasses, hard hat and gloves. Tariq trailed behind them, his face flushed from the heat and the extra pounds he carried on his waistline.

'You know where to put them,' Choukri said, nodding at the explosives. 'I'll be at the bows with Assam. Radio me when you're done.'

They split up. Choukri's earlier instructions had been clear. Faisel and Tariq were to head down to the engine room and put a mine on either side of the hull, below the waterline. Another was to be placed at the end of the propeller shaft where it exited the hull, to blow the seals out. Snoop was to make his way below the hold, down among the ballast and fuel tanks in the bowels of the ship.

Choukri and Assam lifted the IED from the basket and shuffled sideways in tandem. The hold door was narrow. Sweat ran into Choukri's eyes, his grip clammy as they pivoted. He looked over his shoulder along the cramped, ill-lit passageway, its floor slippery and stinking of fuel oil.

They edged towards the bows, checked their position, and set the IED down. Choukri studied the shape of the hull and made a mental calculation of where, on the other side of the hull, the waterline divided sea and air. The blast had to be concentrated on an area just on and slightly above the waterline. When he was certain, he marked the spot and slid the package across the floor.

Assam stiffened at the sound of scraping along the hull.

'It's okay. It's the dhow,' Choukri said.

They listened, their ears to the hull walls. Coming from the other side was the murmur of voices.

'Yeah, they're right on us, exactly,' Choukri said, nodding in satisfaction.

Captain Mubarak's voice came over the walkie-talkie to confirm trans-shipment of the *Danske Prince*'s cargo was now complete. Then Faisel reported in and, moments later, Snoop. Their mines were in position.

'Okay, everyone. Set for 17.20 and wait for my mark,' Choukri said, punching 17.18 into the IED's timer.

He checked his watch. It was 17.13. Five minutes to get off the *Danske Prince* and back the *Ocean Dove* away to a safe distance.

'Three, two, one, set!'

With Assam behind, they scrambled back along the passageway and into the hold, securing the door open before climbing the steps to the main deck.

Choukri sent Assam aft to check while he went forward. The others were already back on the *Ocean Dove*. They met again at the gangway.

'Go,' he said, looking up and down.

Along the walkway were assorted items the fishermen had gathered from the *Danske Prince* – lifebelts, a hard hat, the captain's binoculars case, a shirt, a cushion, a cooking pot, a coil of rope and a bucket.

Had anything been forgotten? It was too late now. He unhooked the mooring lines and threw them over the rail, jumping across as the *Ocean Dove*'s funnel belched smoke.

The crew were at the rail, quiet, still, their expectant eyes fixed on the *Danske Prince*. Water lapped at the hull, the sea between them motionless. Only the throb of the main engine broke the eerie silence as it ticked over.

Choukri turned to Mubarak.

'Make the first entries.'

They stepped back to the bridge. Mubarak sat at the chart table with Choukri standing over him, watching the captain's familiar routine of writing the daily log in a notebook, in Arabic, before he would type it in English on his computer the next morning. In Arabic he wrote:

16.50.   *Smoke vicinity D.Prince. She's stopped. Hailing her. No response.*

16.55.   *Still no response. Turning back.*

17.18.   *Explosion. Sent Mayday.*

17.20.   *Explosion. Repeated Mayday.*

'Exactly,' Choukri said, nodding to himself.

Mubarak put the log away and they both stepped outside, scanning the horizon, looking for an elusive dot. Somewhere out there was the small RIB – rigid inflatable boat – they had slipped over the side of the *Ocean Dove* when the trap was set for the *Danske Prince*. A duplicate set of the *Ocean Dove's* positioning, datalog and communications equipment was fitted to it. At Choukri's signal, the dummy kit had been switched on as Mubarak turned the *Ocean Dove's* off, with the RIB powering away at the same twelve knots the *Ocean Dove* had been making, on precisely the same course and heading. To the world's monitoring systems, it looked just like the mother ship continuing on its unbroken course, while the *Ocean Dove* became a ghost.

The *Danske Prince* was hailed at 16.50 – when the *Ocean Dove* had supposedly seen smoke. The RIB turned at 16.55 when no response was received, carefully copying the wide turning circle of a ship. And at 17.18, just as Mubarak had recorded in the fictitious log, it would send a Mayday and repeat it at 17.20 when the gap between itself and the last known location of the *Danske Prince* had closed to twelve miles.

All the signals and data would be picked up by other ships, by monitoring stations and by the relevant authorities. They would all plot position, speed and heading. All would confirm the *Ocean Dove* had been nowhere near the *Danske Prince* at the moment of its disappearance.

Out on the wings, Choukri looked at Mubarak, then across the shimmering water.

Seconds later the IED tore through the hull of the *Danske Prince*; it bucked, and a thunderclap echoed between the ships as the dhow shattered, hurling debris into the air and showering down, the water in turmoil, a bow wave surging towards them.

Instinctively, the watching crew ducked. As they straightened, they turned as one and lifted their faces to the bridge, punching the air and chanting Choukri's name. Moments later, jubilant voices were drowned by the successive detonation of five mines.

The *Danske Prince* shuddered as though a giant hand had picked it up and slapped it back down to the water. Flames shot from vents and a pall of smoke rose. In minutes the ship began to sink, the stern flooding and the bows rising to reveal a hole in its side big enough to drive a car through. The bows were almost vertical when it slipped below the surface, a whirlpool fanning out in an increasing circle of foaming water.

At walking pace, the *Ocean Dove* edged across the debris-strewn water. Fuel from the *Danske Prince*'s ruptured tanks was spreading in an oily slick around dead and stunned fish. The ship quartered the area systematically, the crew scanning the water. The search had to be methodical and thorough. It took an hour. Things they didn't want to be found would be pulled from the water. Nothing else would be touched. It needed to be left as it was for the authorities to deal with.

'There,' Choukri said, pointing to a speck in the distance, low in the water to the north-east.

'I'll make the entry ...' Mubarak said.

18.20. Arrived on location. One hour after second explosions.

The RIB cut its engine and glided to a halt, nestling into the hull. Choukri looked down from the rail. It appeared unmanned, its crew of two dressed in black and blending in. He checked that both Mubarak and the RIB's crewmen could see him before he signalled: the RIB's phantom communications were switched off and the *Ocean Dove*'s turned back on.

'No complications?' Choukri said.

'Textbook,' the RIB's driver replied, climbing the ladder and handing him a bag containing copies of the communication and positional data.

'Then get your people and go.'

The dhow's fishermen were on deck, ready to climb down and melt away into the dusk, leaving the *Ocean Dove* with its regulation crew and the illusion of normality.

Faisel was at Choukri's side. Below them, in the hull's shadow at the waterline, the RIB bobbed – predominantly matt black, with random patches of grey and off-white.

'It's uncanny,' Faisel said, shaking his head. 'Even from here it looks like the real thing.'

Choukri smiled. 'Exactly. Let's hope others see it the same way.'

He made his way back up to the bridge, where Mubarak was busy on the radio with ships responding to the Mayday. He spoke in English with the *Topaz*, a Thai freighter, and in German with the *Stadt Hamburg*. The *Topaz* said they were altering course and would be on station around 21.00, the *Stadt Hamburg* an hour after that.

Choukri's ears were pricked, listening intently. His fingers were at his collar working a small, smooth disc between them that was hanging from a chain around his neck. Two minutes later he pumped a fist.

'Yes!'

Turning to the others, he waved his hands up and down to suppress any noise. A French navy vessel, a *La Fayette* class frigate, was coming over clearly on the speaker, advising the earliest they could get there was first light on Monday morning. He and Mubarak had plotted other ships' positions throughout the previous week, accepting a clandestine naval vessel, running dark with its identification systems switched off, might well have been in the vicinity. It was a calculated risk they had to take.

He called the crew together. 'We clean the ship from top to bottom. The French will be here and we must impress them, and we don't know what they'll want …'

'They'll just want *café et croissants*,' Snoop drawled.

Some laughed, but not Choukri; his face was devoid of humour. He prodded Snoop's chest, his eyes sweeping around them all. 'We've achieved nothing yet, and it'll all turn to shit if some idiot shoots his mouth off.'

~

Just before six o'clock on Sunday evening, Dan Brooks shuffled the supermarket bags in his hands and slipped a key into the lock of his first-floor flat in Shepherd's Bush, London. There were three of them living there now and it was starting to feel cramped, but a tube link to Westminster was a five-minute walk away and it wasn't the time to take on greater financial commitments while he was still trying to find his feet at MI5. Government pay wasn't generous anyway.

Julie was at her laptop, her long legs stretched out under the kitchen table. Up against the wall their daughter, Phoebe, was thrashing around unhappily in her cot.

'I think she needs changing,' Julie said, looking up as Dan kissed her. 'I've got to finish this for tomorrow.'

'Great,' Dan said, glancing around for the nappies. 'What is it – some MP and an underage hooker?'

'Not this time,' Julie said, rubbing her temples as she stared at the screen.

She was a partner in a small PR firm, working in the political field. They had put all their money into it. While it gave her some flexibility on time and the chance to work from home when necessary, it was only providing a meagre return.

'Come on, baby,' Dan said, picking his daughter up and rubbing noses with her, though it failed to raise a smile. He opened a window and started to change her on the worktop. It was cold outside; the sash rattled; the papers next to Julie's laptop rustled.

He lifted his daughter's legs and recoiled with a grimace. 'Perhaps I should use my tongue? I'm getting good at arse-licking.'

Taking a deep breath from the open window, he pondered the smeared mess before getting stuck in at the business end. In moments the nappy was bagged and binned with a flourish.

'Who's a lucky girl then?' he said, smiling as he cleaned her up. 'Big handsome Dad, navy hero, ship's captain, secret agent, licensed to kill anyone who disses me. But fortunately for you I'm in touch with my feminine side, a real new man – as your sexy mother will confirm. And now, best of all, I'm an arse-licking junior clerk. You lucky girl!'

Julie turned. It was the second time he'd said 'arse-licking'.

'Nice try.' She smiled. 'But you forgot boneheaded. And you aren't handsome – though it gets easier for me with wine.'

'And I'm fantastic in … the kitchen.'

There was cold meat in the fridge and an open bottle of Chardonnay. He put some potatoes in the oven to bake, poured a glass of wine and took a beer out for himself.

Julie shut her laptop, pushed it away and got up from the table.

'What about the Monday meeting?' she said, wrapping her arms around him from behind, her chin on his shoulder.

'Dry ... I suppose,' he said, knowing she understood what Mondays were beginning to mean to him.

'It'll get better.'

'Is that a promise?' he said, turning and brushing stray hairs from her eyes, the back of his finger stroking a sharp cheekbone. 'You remember the selection process – a major impact. They said major.'

Julie would have remembered it only too well: her own background vetting, interviews, home visits. The intrusion had been disturbing for both of them, though she had told him that what they knew about her already was more so.

Necessarily, the details of what Dan would do at the agency had not been disclosed to her, while he barely knew more than the grade he would start at and the broad scope of how his specialist knowledge would be brought to bear on the nation's security. But he had pinned his hope on the major impact.

'The only major impact I'm having is on Jo Clymer's networking,' he said. 'I'm not going to change the world, I know that, but I also know that everything the agency faces now comes out of the left field. It needs exceptional people, big hitters, and definitely not political careerists. And I don't know if I'm one of them.'

'One of *them*, or one of the exceptional people?'

'Good question.' He shrugged, turning away as his phone rang on the worktop.

'Lars. How is it?'

'Total shit. Eight crew. Wives, children. One was turning eighteen in two days – a trainee doing his experience from the nautical college. A fucking kid, you know? I just seen his mother on the local TV news. Total shit.'

'I'm sorry,' Dan said. 'It's terrible.'

'Yeah, total shit.'

Dan was plugged in to newsfeeds and alerts on duty and off, so the fate of the Danish ship had reached him late on Saturday evening. Lars had been his first thought; he had been his first captain after leaving the Royal Navy, on the *Astrid*, a commercial ship. Now, like Dan, Lars was behind a desk, based at Denmark's Maritime Authority in Copenhagen. He would be heading up the enquiry into the *Danske Prince*'s disappearance.

'Do you know any more?' Dan asked. 'I've been following the news, but …'

'No, nothing. Some guys from the shipowner were here today with all the manifests, packing lists, stowage plans and shit, but they don't tell us anything. It's all correct. These guys know what they're doing, but I just don't get it …'

'And the shippers?'

'Yeah, we're checking. They could easy fuck up.'

'And there was a ship near?'

'Yeah, the *Ocean Dove*, but too far away. It's heading to Bar Mhar now for maintenance. It's an old Claus Reederie vessel, like our *Astrid*, but run out of Sharjah now. I spoke to some guys in the market. Good operators, they say. Anyway, that's it. Total weird. Total shit.'

'And you know the shipper is British-owned. Can you send me something?' Dan said.

'Yeah. End of the week?'

'Thanks. And thanks for getting back to me.'

'No problem. Look, I gotta run. Say hi to Julie for me.'

Dan put the phone down and gave Julie's shoulder a squeeze. 'Lars says hi.'

He thought about the shippers – the cargo suppliers. It wasn't glamorous work in the despatch department of a large corporation, usually low paid and undervalued. Lars was right. The *Danske Prince*'s owners and crew knew the ropes. They carried dangerous cargoes but they were experts. Legislation had tightened and accidents had become fewer. When something did go wrong it was usually traced back to the supply chain, inadequate training, misunderstandings and the bottom line.

Total weird. Total shit. *It's definitely both*, Dan thought, remembering Lars's words and the baffled, exasperated tone of his voice.

And who was going to care about the deaths of some foreign seamen in an accident far away? They weren't tourists being deprived of a dream holiday, the recurring nightmare running through the DNA of the security services. The point had been pressed home during his induction. Nothing inflamed public opinion more. A mining executive could be murdered by Boko Haram in Mali and it was their own fault for being there. But a husband and wife murdered on holiday in Egypt was our guardians' fault – and pray God he wasn't a teacher and she wasn't a nurse.

It had disturbed him at first, but within a few months he'd seen it was no exaggeration. This was one of several uncomfortable aspects of the job he was having to come to terms with. Worst was not being able to chew the problems over at home. Then there were the friends he had to tell, in the vaguest possible way, that he was a civil servant attached to the naval section at the Ministry of Defence, dealing mostly with policy administration. It was routine stuff, he'd say, before apologising for being bound by the Official Secrets Act and assuring them he couldn't see any reason why it applied to his own mundane workload.

'What's terrible?' Julie asked, taking a sip of wine.

'A Danish ship disappeared yesterday afternoon. All the crew lost. I got the alert, you know.'

'Not nice,' she said, lowering her eyes without pressing for more.

The *Danske Prince*'s fate was public knowledge, though unreported in the mainstream media, so it was okay to skirt around it with small talk without details, without him disclosing if or why the security services had an interest in it. He was grateful that Julie understood politics in all its hues, Westminster, corporate or institutional. She'd studied it at university, joined the BBC and moved on to *The Times* as a parliamentary reporter before setting up the PR company with former colleagues. Now and then it was prudent for her to keep aspects of her own work to herself, and as a quid pro quo in their relationship, he respected the fact that it helped to balance his sealed working life.

After supper, with Phoebe sleeping soundly in her cot, Julie turned in for an early night. Dan reached under the sofa and pulled out a small wooden box. Inside were papers, card and a wrap of weed. He rolled a one-skinner, set the music on his phone to shuffle and sat back, the sound of old reggae clear in the headphones.

Ten drags on a small spliff. Eyes closed. Feet on the coffee table. Julie warming the bed. Phoebe soundly asleep.

Twenty minutes later, with his mind drifting in the Indian Ocean, he opened an eye lazily as Dennis Brown's sweet voice faded away, plaintively denouncing the world's many and varied cheats. Then his other eye opened sharply. He sat up and pressed pause. Was it the weed or was there a spooky significance in the random shuffle that had just played 'Ordinary Man', 'Lonely Soldier', Too Late' and 'Cheater' – in that order? He shook his head, smiled weakly in denial and tapped resume.

The next track was Errol Dunkley, 'Created by the Father'.

'Fuck,' he said out loud, yanking the headphones off and sitting up sharply. Okay, he thought. He got it. He was out of his depth, but it didn't stop the resentment rising, the subliminal message being shoved down his throat.

Created by the father? Was that Mick Brooks, the chancer from Dublin, or was it the only real father figure he'd known: Dalton, his mother's long-term boyfriend after her short-lived marriage. Dalton, the market-stall dealer in early reggae who had introduced Dan to the music. Dalton, shot dead on the estate, a casual drive-by, a casual case of mistaken identity, casually investigated by the local police and casually dropped.

He slipped the box back under the sofa and thought of Julie, who would turn instinctively in her sleep when he got into bed. There was a choice: dwell on work, doubt, the prospect of the Monday meeting and the apparent significance of randomly shuffled song tracks; or there was the comfort of Julie's breath on his back.

TWO

A party of a dozen climbed the ladder to the *Ocean Dove*. Lieutenant Boissy looked about, pleasantly surprised as he checked his tropical whites for grease stains. He was impressed once again when he exchanged handshakes with the smartly turned out captain and mate, both cleanly shaven, in fresh white shirts, gold braiding, badges on their chests with name and rank under the company logo.

His frigate had arrived on station at six o'clock on Monday morning, four hundred metres off the port beam. It had been a busy and pressured time for Lieutenant Boissy as the frigate steamed at full speed towards the *Ocean Dove*. He'd fielded a stream of communication flowing between his ship and headquarters, which was coordinating between the *Danske Prince*'s owners, the cargo owners, coastguard stations, InMarSat, the AIS and a host of other parties with a stake in understanding what had happened. Government security agencies had begun to sniff the air, their noses twitching for a scent of incongruity. It had put Boissy on his guard, wary that his own conduct would be under scrutiny.

But one significant fact had relieved the pressure. All the data established that the *Ocean Dove* had clearly been miles from the *Danske Prince* when it disappeared. He had received precise confirmation. The *Ocean Dove* was under no suspicion.

'These are very good,' he said, brushing crumbs from his lips, enjoying coffee and cakes on the bridge.

His eye caught a framed certificate on the wall, some familiar capital letters drawing him in. CMA CGM, a French container line, had awarded it to the ship for one hundred and eighty days of accident- and injury-free service.

'We were on charter to them last year. A first-class company,' Mubarak said.

'Very good,' Boissy nodded, the last shreds of scepticism evaporating. 'Now, Captain, I need copies of your AIS and VDR, and your written report in say, twenty-four hours?'

'No problem,' Mubarak replied, glancing across to the equipment that recorded the ship's voice and positional data. 'We'll make some copy disks and I'll send you the report this evening. Our VDR is limited to twelve hours, so that's only since six last night, I'm afraid.'

'That's okay.' Lieutenant Boissy nodded; he knew the relevant maritime regulation.

The Automatic Identification System transmitted a ship's name, speed, course, destination and other data constantly. Other ships, land-based transmitters and satellites repeated the transmissions so that every vessel afloat could get a clear picture of others around them and where they were going. Shipowners, port authorities, pilots and marine authorities were able to plot movements on their office computers and manage operations in real time. Naval ships had AIS too, but often switched it off to conceal their presence.

And the Voyage Data Recorder was a ship's black box, performing the same function as a commercial plane's, logging technical information and recording what was said on the bridge.

'Can I see the ship's log please?' Boissy said.

'I write it in Arabic before entering it in English in the computer,' Mubarak said, handing a book across.

It was incomprehensible to Boissy, but he could see it was neat and ordered. Mubarak showed him the computer version, reading entries from the book and pointing to their duplicates on the screen.

'We saw on the monitor that the *Danske Prince* had stopped – and why not?' Mubarak shrugged. 'Ships stop all the time ...'

Boissy nodded. He knew it was so.

'Then my cook was on the wings having a cigarette. He saw smoke on the *Danske Prince* behind us. The duty officer hailed them but received no reply. We continued to hail them. The smoke was increasing so we turned and steamed back at full speed. I roused the crew and prepared the emergency and firefighting equipment. Then there was the first explosion. Then a few minutes later a series of explosions, four, maybe five, I think, all very close to each other. We were still an hour from them and by the time we arrived, well, there was just nothing.'

Mubarak clasped his hands together and looked down in reflection.

'We have the cargo manifests,' Boissy said, breaking the silence. 'It was mostly hazardous cargo and some explosives. But to go just like that ... and there's nothing useful from any other ships, and nothing from the *Danske Prince* itself. You're the only witness.'

'I wish we could have done more,' Mubarak said.

'You did everything you could,' Boissy said. 'I'll note that in my report. And now, Captain, you might as well resume your voyage. Time is money and I think we both know we aren't going to find any survivors.'

Mubarak looked out through the bridge door, sighed, and turned back to Boissy. 'No. I think you're right.'

'Thank you for your help, Captain,' Boissy said. 'And if I may say, you run a very smart ship.'

'You're very kind.'

Above them the frigate's helicopter circled. Dinghies in the water were taking samples, photographing, gathering anything on the surface into nets. Every item would be tagged, logged and taken on board the frigate, pending the investigation.

A French sailor stepped onto the bridge and went across to Boissy. 'There isn't much out there, just some lifebelts, a hard hat, a binocular case, a cooking pot and some other stuff. And there's a lot of wood,' he added.

'Wood?'

'Yes, wood. We're bundling it all up.'

'Okay.' Boissy nodded.

The Frenchmen stepped from the bridge, their hands full of data disks, clear plastic wallets of photocopied documents and doggie bags of pastries. Choukri ushered them down the stairs to the main deck where Boissy shouted across to some marines lounging on the hatch smoking cigarettes, contentedly gazing out to sea, their backs leaning against the shaded side of a bright orange shipping container.

~

'So, let's kick off, guys.'

The weekly meeting started punctually at ten o'clock on Monday morning, led by Jo Clymer from MI5's Executive Liaison Group. Her sharp voice cut through the chatter of a dozen people, each representing a specialist field with an emphasis on potential connection to terrorism, the focus of more than eighty per cent of the agency's resources.

The first item was the usual update. Clymer went round the table, checking the progress of open files, asking what was new, her eyes probing the room under a haircut that other women considered 'practical'. It had come with her from McKinsey, the global consultancy, where she had specialised in the qualitative and quantitative analysis of management process. After her fast-track entry to the agency, she still preferred the consultant's uniform of a sober blue suit and modest cream blouse, set against an idiosyncratic taste in shoes.

Her eyes came to rest on Dan Brooks.

'There is something new but it's a bit early to say how it might develop,' Dan said, keying his laptop and putting a photo of a ship on the meeting room screen.

'The *Danske Prince* sank in the Indian Ocean on Saturday afternoon. It carries the stuff the mainstream ships can't or won't – toxic, military, flammable, explosive …'

Dan was one of a three-man team monitoring everything moving in or out of the country by sea, air and land – materials and people. If something was unusual, suspicious, or suggested potential to develop into a threat, they investigated and passed their findings into the wider intelligence community, linking mostly with the Special Branch Counter Terrorism Unit. The work was mainly analytical and acting on it in the field was in the hands of others. They had no powers of arrest and they didn't carry guns.

He clicked another slide: a map of the Indian Ocean with the ship's positions marked, followed by another one, the *Ocean Dove*.

'This was the nearest ship, ten or twenty miles away. It turned to help but the *Danske Prince* blew up and sank before it could get close.'

'So, going forward, where's the relevance?' Clymer said.

'We could be involved. The main cargo was four Bofors guns and forty thousand rounds of ammunition for some new destroyers the Indian navy are building. As you know, Bofors is Swedish but it's owned by BAE.'

Some eyebrows around the table lifted. BAE Systems was an independent British company, but its links to national defence were so close that it was practically an arm of government.

'What do we know about this *Dove* ship?' Clymer said.

'Seems legit.'

'So it's just something for the insurance companies – pay up and move on?'

'The information's thin. A French frigate was on the scene this morning and the ship's Danish flag, so they'll lead the investigation. I know the guy there. The insurance for the ship and cargo was underwritten in London, and the Indian navy is seriously unhappy at the loss of its guns.'

At the mention of India, Clymer's eyes switched to Vikram Mehta, who did not meet them. Vikram was ex-British Airways. Sitting next to him was the third member of the team, Richard Nuttall, who had previously been with DHL's European land-transport network. They had both joined the agency shortly after Dan – the trio constituting one of Clymer's initiatives to manage threats from the sea, air and land.

'And these guns are what, exactly?' she said, turning back to Dan.

'They fire four computer-guided shells a second, range up to ten miles.'

'And this will all be verified by the salvage operation?'

'It's six thousand metres deep there – almost impossible.'

'And the French are inspecting this ship?'

'No.'

'No?'

'It's the open sea. No jurisdiction.'

Clymer frowned. 'So, we've got four guns and forty thousand rounds of ammunition – probably at the bottom of the Indian Ocean?'

'That's about it.'

'And why is this your concern – or mine?'

'I'm just flagging it up. I'm not sure it is yet.'

'Evidently.'

Clymer knew that 'evidently' referred to the second part of his reply, that he wasn't sure, rather than the first – the flagging up.

'As I said, I'm just flagging it up. In the wrong hands these guns …'

'But why assume they're in the wrong hands?' Clymer cut in, her voice rising around the quiet table.

'I'm not assuming anything,' Dan said. 'I just want to flag it up and monitor it. These guns are dangerous in the wrong hands.'

'Thank you for the *expert* analysis, but I really don't see why you or I should have an interest. It's the middle of the Indian Ocean. It's an international incident and, if it's for anyone, it's for MI6. Going forward you really must focus on domestic security – that is key. And remember the budget,' she added, making a note on her iPad before moving summarily to the next update.

The meeting wrapped up punctually at eleven. Clymer stayed in her seat, glancing away from the window as the sharp winter sun reflected from the river, pondering the prospect of four Bofors guns not lying on the bottom of the Indian Ocean, trying to connect it with any intelligence she had picked up.

It was her job to sift information from the group and take action when she saw fit, linking with section heads internally and a network of outside agencies. Nothing came to mind. *It's just an accident at sea*, she reasoned, far away and someone else's problem. She opened her iPad and made a note: *'Dan. Future? Tendency matters outside remit – irritating. Focus, team priorities, network, influence!'*

~

As he crossed the road with Vikram and Richard Nuttall, Dan looked back over his shoulder at Thames House, MI5's head office. It was the former headquarters of ICI, once a global powerhouse of the chemicals business. Overlooking the river, one bridge upstream from Parliament, it was still outwardly grand and hinted of empire, though the building had been toned down internally to reflect a more democratic age.

Their team's office was a five-minute walk away in Bell Street, shared with another twenty or so who couldn't squeeze into Thames House. They had been left to organise it much as it suited them, but it was an overspill, not head office.

Nuttall broke the silence.

'What does JC fucking know, eh?' he said. He turned to Dan before raising an eyebrow to Vikram.

'She knows the system,' Vikram said. 'And we don't, yet ...'

'Yeah, and fuck all else,' Nuttall said, giving him a prod in the back.

'Okay. I don't like it.'

'Easy there, Vik. You don't want to fall off that fence, mate. She's just using us. It's all about her.'

Vikram carried on walking ahead of them with a light shrug. 'I guess you're right.'

'Course I'm right. She's full of shit. "I'm a team builder – it's what I do ..."' Nuttall added, mimicking Jo Clymer. 'If anyone has to tell you what they do, you can be sure they don't fucking do it. And you shouldn't take that bollocks from her. I wouldn't. My old boss is ringing me every week.'

Dan ignored him.

Nuttall started up again. 'But I don't get it. You don't back down. What about the Queen's, eh?'

The three of them often had a beer on a Friday night in the Queen's Head to chew over the week before heading home. A month ago, Vikram had accidentally bumped into some guys from a local building site. Drinks were spilled and they had needlessly taken offence. When it looked as though things were about to escalate, Dan had stepped between Vikram and the ringleader, raised an eyebrow and said, 'Don't be fooled by the suit, mate.'

Dan shook his head at the memory. He eyed Vikram's narrow shoulders, his thin wrists and small hands swinging without natural rhythm, unable to imagine anyone less inclined or more ill suited to a meaningless pub fracas. He would have been cleaning his glasses on his neatly folded handkerchief before he literally would have known what had hit him. 'I didn't know those guys and it was nothing to do with work,' Dan said.

Nuttall shook his head. 'Don't see the difference. But doesn't JC fuck you off?'

'Let's just leave it out.'

'We'll trot on then,' Nuttall said, turning and striding ahead, his shoulders bulging in a tight suit, thick neck hunched against the chill wind coming off the river.

'What do you think?' Dan said, letting Nuttall get ahead.

Vikram looked up from his apparent study of the pavement.

'You're right not to rise – which I think is what you mean – to either of them. Your case holds water.' He paused. 'Sorry, no pun intended. I'd have flagged it up too.'

'Really,' Dan said, hearing the lack of conviction in his own voice.

'Stick to your guns,' Vikram said, realising his second pun and raising his hands.

'Yeah, but same old Monday morning. My balls in the mincer. She doesn't like me and I don't like her. And him,' he added, nodding along the street, his nose twitching at the cheap aftershave gusting back on the wind.

'Do things your way. He's got his own style.'

'Yeah, *sarf* London.'

'Aren't you the same, but *norf?*'

An innocent comment, made without pretext, but it still hurt if he acknowledged it wasn't far from the truth. Nuttall wasn't made of the right stuff for the service. And if Dan could see it, then by definition – or association – he too must also be the wrong stuff. Vikram had meant no harm, so he ignored it.

'He's all bollocks. And no bollocks when they're needed. Slow out of his chair in the Queen's when it all kicked off. I saw it, and he knows I saw it.'

'I wouldn't know,' Vikram said quietly.

'Good for you.'

At the bottom of Bell Street was an Italian café, old school, no Wi-Fi. The coffee was good, the prices fair and the owner, Alfredo, looked after them.

As they turned the corner, Nuttall was waiting. 'Alf's?' he said. 'I'm buying.'

They took a corner table, passing the sugar shaker around and spooning chocolate-speckled froth absently, waiting for someone to make the first move.

'Must be my face,' Dan said. 'Doesn't seem to fit.'

He glanced across at Vikram.

'I don't feel it ...'

'It's like in the navy,' Dan continued. 'At officer training the others were all shoo-ins from smart homes, the right schools, the right stuff.'

'Posh wankers,' Nuttall said.

Dan's eyes remained on Vikram's.

'They're not that different – just from a different world.'

'Like how?' Nuttall said.

'Like at weekends. They'd go to each other's places, big spreads, and they'd invite me, and they had these girls with names like Verity and Venetia – I'd never heard of names like that. But I couldn't enjoy it and I couldn't exactly invite them back to my place.' He paused, opening his hands. 'My mother's flat was on an estate all right, but the wrong kind of estate. And there was plenty of shooting, but the wrong kind of shooting.'

'Them posh birds,' Nuttall said. 'Do any good?'

Dan's eyes switched between the two of them, inwardly correcting 'them' to 'those'. It grated, mainly because it reminded him of his younger self.

'No chance,' he said. 'But that's not the point. It's the—'

'I had a posh bird once,' Nuttall cut back in. 'Fucking filthy she was.'

Vikram stirred his coffee, his eyes alternating between his cup and Dan.

'The difference – it's politics?' he said.

'At the officer college I had no problem with the physical, the practical, and I was surprised they didn't get ahead of me in the classroom. Some were bright but plenty weren't, and by the end they were leaning on me, and the instructors knew it. But I never felt I fitted in.'

'Because of – background?' Vikram said.

'Suppose. It's the difference in the backgrounds. Same here. Look at them, the top universities, the intellectual set.'

Vikram raised an eyebrow. 'The game players. Our best minds against the best the enemies of the state can offer, continued long into the night in the clubs, debating with their mandarin contemporaries from the other establishment pillars ...'

'You put it better than me.' Dan smiled. 'And then you've got your Clymers, the manager types from Cambridge and McKinsey. And I'm none of them.'

'No, you're like me.' Nuttall laughed. 'The cunt who does all the work.'

Dan turned, his eyes hardening. 'Call yourself a cunt any time. But never me.'

Nuttall shifted in his seat, raising his hands and sitting back.

Vikram broke the silence. 'You make too much of it. This right stuff? I'm not sure I know what that is, but I don't see any of the wrong stuff.'

'Maybe. But that's not my point. It's just that here, and in the navy, there's a type that fits. Doesn't matter what you are, it's just who you are – someone that fits or doesn't fit.'

'I don't feel this,' Vikram said. 'The recruitment process was clear. It's open to anyone and it's simply a matter of taking it. I just don't get your reluctance. From where I'm sitting there's no lack of talent – it can only be a matter of perception.'

They'd been over the ground before and Dan didn't answer. Vikram had made it clear he felt Dan had to know this, finding it difficult to understand why he was wary of acknowledging it, as if accepting that this was the game would be evidence of a flaw. They knew that MI5 answered directly to government and they knew that ministers wanted people they could do business with, people who would run the service on corporate lines and present the public with an organisation that appeared to be accountable. The rewards would not initially be financial, though that might come later through networking and the prestige of awards, and Dame Jo Clymer would no doubt find lucrative sidelines in later life, perhaps on the supervisory board of Goldman Sachs or BP, or back at McKinsey. And as Vikram had said, 'In twenty-five years I might be Sir Vikram Mehta.'

Alf held the door open for them as they left, nodding his usual, 'Grazie.'

Walking up Bell Street to the office, Dan's mind was drifting back to when he joined the navy as a junior rating at sixteen. Later, the promotion board encouraged him to try for his commission at the staff college. With officer's braid on his shoulders he'd served on patrol boats, frigates and destroyers, rising to the rank of lieutenant commander. On the verge of further promotion and, to the navy's great irritation, he opted not to extend his commission. 'You're switching to *commercial* shipping?'

He'd started on a multipurpose ship, the *Astrid*, captained by Lars. Then he switched to a container line before moving on to his first command: a bulk carrier in the Atlantic grain and steel trades. Now, with a wife and baby daughter and his thirty-seventh birthday approaching, he felt it was better if he was closer to home.

It was as easy to have doubts at MI5 as in the navy, doubts he hadn't felt for years. He held fraught memories of transiting from the ranks to the officers' college – the etiquette, the chat, that he'd left his comprehensive school at sixteen, wasn't good with table cutlery and countless other things it was mutually understood that he didn't understand. When he left the navy for commercial shipping, the switch had been frictionless. Now, those distant concerns were rekindling and, despite his efforts to make himself acceptable at MI5, he feared he had entered another world that held barriers.

Bell Street was not without its attractions. There were mature trees, bare at this time of year. Midway along, a small garden was set to one side. The original buildings were mostly on the cusp of Victorian and Edwardian, with notable exceptions due to bomb damage from the war. One of them was MI5's overspill office, a charmless example of 1950s austerity and expediency.

The office's lower floor was occupied by Gold Star Cars, a minicab firm staffed mainly by Ghanaians. Some of the drivers may have held dubious residency or work permits. If they were hiding in plain sight, they were of no concern to MI5, which was one of its valued customers for non-sensitive trips.

A street door opened on to a cramped hallway and steep, narrow stairs leading to the upper floors. Their office was really only big enough for two. The ceiling was low, the walls crammed with filing cabinets, shelves, charts and Post-it notes. A threadbare set of carpet tiles lined the floor. Three desks were squeezed in; Dan, the team's first recruit, had taken the one by the window. Being close to fresh air was an advantage, with Richard Nuttall's predilection for farting, each one proudly announced with 'Bingo'.

Lunch was a sandwich from Alf's. Dan ate it at his desk and checked the online shipping news sites. *Lloyd's List* was giving prominence to the fate of the *Danske Prince* and praising the efforts of the *Ocean Dove*, but there was little solid information. *Tradewinds* had nothing new to add except a quote from Bulent Erkan, CEO of OceanBird, the *Ocean Dove's* owners. 'My ship has done all it can in this terrible tragedy. I've told my captain and my crew to give their full support to the international effort.'

Nice words, Dan thought. But is it all about you, Bulent? 'My ship, my captain, my crew.' What about the eight missing Danes?

Both the *Danske Prince's* and *Ocean Dove's* owners had websites, though he knew the Danish company already: a respected operator with their fleet all named after kings and queens and other noble ranks. The *Ocean Dove's* owners were new to him. Their site, oceanbird-marine.com, was professional and open with its information.

The 'About us' section had a biography of Bulent Erkan – Turkish, commercial maritime degree, trained in an Istanbul shipowner's office, five years in Hamburg, four in Rotterdam. *So*, Dan thought, *you learned your trade, made the right contacts, sweet-talked some backers and went your own way with some second-hand ships from good homes in Germany, from people you no doubt knew.* It all rang true. There were also contact details on the site for OceanBird's partners around the world, including their London brokers, a well-known firm.

After closing the site, he ran Bulent Erkan through the internal systems. Nothing.

Initial information was sketchy and there was little to go on. It was difficult enough to justify his interest to himself, let alone to Clymer. She had made her position clear, and Richard Nuttall's words came into sharp focus as he recalled his last assessment.

'I'm a team builder, Dan. It's what I do ... I need team players, Dan. Is that you?' Clymer had said.

He clearly remembered holding her eyes and replying, 'Absolutely,' before she looked down and ticked a box on the form in front of her.

And Nuttall, he thought, though usually full of piss and wind, was on the money: 'If anyone has to tell you what they do, you can be absolutely sure they don't fucking do it.'

Dan logged into the AIS site and plotted the voyage record of both the *Danske Prince* and the *Ocean Dove*. The AIS was only concerned with ships' positions and routes, so there was no mention of cargo.

Bar Mhar was listed as the *Ocean Dove's* destination, a place and name he was unfamiliar with. Last night, its identity and location had failed to register when Lars mentioned it. He made a mental note to check.

He sat back and turned the information over, distracted by the ringing of his mobile, the caller unidentified on the screen.

'Good afternoon. Salim Hak, MI6 Pakistan desk,' a cultured voice said. 'I recall a Daniel Brooks when I was up at Sidney Sussex – a Trinity man, if memory serves?'

'Another Dan Brooks I'm afraid. I was Dartmouth.'

Up was the key, which Dan had quickly learned to recognise, always accompanied by an archaic sounding name – Gonville & Caius or Brasenose. This time it was Sidney Sussex, and his stock reply of 'Dartmouth' was shorthand for an alternative route, a leading military college rather than Oxford or Cambridge: a choice, not an impediment.

'Oh, very good,' Hak said, credentials established and accepted. 'Got his blue for boxing, I think ...'

'What can I do for you, Salim?' Dan said, keying MI6's directory on his screen.

'My boss suggested I call you.'

'Nick Pittman?' Dan said, his eyes scanning the listing.

'No, the big boss.'

'I see,' Dan said, checking the screen again. 'Didn't know he knew me.'

'I think LaSalle told him.'

'Edmund LaSalle?' Dan said, surprised.

'Is there another?'

'Guess not. But I didn't think he knew me either.'

'There's not much LaSalle doesn't know,' Salim Hak said. 'Look, I've got something to discuss with you. Can we meet?'

Dan put the phone down, opened a new file and logged it into the system. But then he hesitated. The file name he'd chosen was *Danske Prince*, but it was a dead ship so he pressed delete. It was the *Ocean Dove* that was still alive.

Vikram and Richard Nuttall had both left the office for appointments. With the place to himself it was an opportunity to work through some of his backlog. There were over fifty thousand cargo ships on the world's seas and another fifty thousand lesser vessels – fishing boats, harbour launches and so on – and about a hundred and twenty commercial ports in the UK. He was one man and the word he heard most was 'budget'.

By four o'clock it was dark outside. He tried to concentrate but his attention was drifting. Standing in the corridor and shoving a plastic cup in the coffee machine, his mind was in the Indian Ocean. I can see you, *Ocean Dove*, in the shadows, ploughing your steady course. And when you get there, what are you going to do? There's something about you, *Ocean Dove*, I don't like.

~

Early that evening in Sharjah, United Arab Emirates, Bulent Erkan was making calculations at his desk in OceanBird Marine's office. The *Ocean Dove* would arrive in Bar Mhar shortly and he needed to get it working again, earning money.

Sharjah was in the middle of a conurbation. Its more glamorous neighbour, Dubai, was joined to its hip on the west, with Ajman to the east. There were no apparent borders or boundaries. Each merged seamlessly with the other, though Sharjah was independent with its own absolute ruler and constitution, just one of the seven Emirates that made up the UAE.

OceanBird had a suite of rooms on the top floor of a respectable building in the industrial district, close to the port. In the reception area were scale models of ships in display cases. Arranged neatly in a symmetrical block on one wall were chrome-framed photographs and ISO certificates for quality, health, safety, environment and all the other pertinent accreditations of an efficient company.

The office was mostly open plan, with two separate meeting rooms, a reception area screened with plants, and Bulent's private room. From his desk he had a view of the creek, the distant sea, and the car park where his Porsche SUV was being washed. They were a small team of about a dozen. Bulent took care of the commercial side, assisted by a chartering broker, and there were a few technical, operations and accounting people.

Bulent keyed a button on his desk phone. The display said the call was from a local shipbroker.

The voice on the speaker said, 'I can't get him higher than three-seventy-five thousand, lumpsum.'

'Okay,' Bulent said. 'Fix it and send me the recap. And tell Bill he has to let me win at tennis next time.'

'I'll tell him. Get back to you.'

Bulent's calculations had shown his bottom line was three hundred and fifty thousand, so getting an extra twenty-five thousand dollars was satisfying. The broker would confirm it with the client, the marine supervisor at the local Halliburton office. He would joke about the tennis and draw up the charter party.

The cargo was fixed, shipping-speak for a contract. *Good job*, Bulent thought; the local broker was doing a good job with Halliburton, the giant American oilfield services company. OceanBird were getting closer to them, building the relationship. This was their third Halliburton cargo – a valuable name to drop when he spoke to other multinationals, especially in the lucrative oil-and-gas market.

The contract was for oilfield machinery to be shipped from Dubai to a project in Indonesia. It was lucrative work for the ship, unlike its current voyage. It would bring in real money. Freight rates were on the floor and the Emir always demanded money.

Cement from the UAE to Mozambique was not a money-spinner. Neither was ballasting an empty ship back from Mozambique to Pakistan where it would sit for nine days of repairs and maintenance work, and then Bulent would have to dig deep to make the payments to the shipyard.

Fuck it, he thought. At least I can soften the blow by showing them it's now earning proper money from a proper charterer. The Emir would also relish the irony of working for Halliburton. He could hear his childlike, almost girlish giggle. He'd heard it once before, when he'd told him they were contracted to Bechtel, another American company, the world's largest builder of oil and gas processing plants and the CIA's favourite conduit of the gossip from global energy boardrooms.

THREE

On Tuesday evening, Dan took the underground to Monument station and walked up Lime Street to Lloyd's. Lights cloaked the building in a blue haze, hanging around it like a shroud and reflecting from glass and stainless steel to its neighbours in the cold wintry air. As he crossed the underwriting room to the lifts, he passed the Lutine Bell and wondered if it had tolled for the *Danske Prince*.

The lift rose through the cavernous atrium to the 1688 room, the name commemorating the foundation date of the original Lloyd's coffee house. Here, the American Bureau of Shipping was holding its reception. He handed his invitation in to the desk clerk, pinned a name badge on and walked into the room. The ceiling was low, clad in steel with glass down two sides, and views of the blue shroud beyond. About four hundred people were making a lot of noise. A woman from ABS greeted him and glanced at his badge.

'Hi, Dan. Welcome,' she said, offering her hand. 'Come and meet some of the guys and let's get you a drink.'

She led him over to a dark-suited group and beckoned to a waiter. Introductions were made – ABS people, underwriters, brokers, agents.

'You're with the ministry?' an underwriter said, his well-lunched jowls folded into the collar of a worn but handmade shirt under a Charterhouse school tie. He ran his eye over Dan, checking for hints and prompts – his tie: neutral, his bearing: tall, broad shouldered and straight backed.

'So, lieutenant commander on destroyers, then a container ship, then the MOD. I say.'

'My first ship was a multipurpose – and that was my favourite.'

'Multipurpose eh? Not my type. You should talk to Hugh Pinchon from BDN, the loud one in the chalk stripes making all the noise over there,' he said, pointing to a group across the room.

BDN, Dan thought, OceanBird's London brokers, remembering it from their website. He shook some hands, swapped business cards, made small talk and worked his way around the room. Psychometric profiling had been part of his induction training at MI5, how to read people, what they said and didn't say, their body language and tics. Instructors started by dismantling the inductee, exposing their 'tells' and remodelling them into something that made all the right impressions but gave little away. The training concentrated on individuals and groups. In this setting he could read the room. He knew where the power was, who had something to hide, and who was trying too hard to show they had nothing to hide.

But this was a reception at Lloyd's, not a terrorists' convention. Even here, however, some things were better left hidden – the dubious tax returns, the understanding ladies in Paddington who spanked bottoms and told them they were naughty boys, the sixes scored as fives at the golf club.

Hugh Pinchon was indeed loud and in expensive chalk-striped cloth. He was also approachable, wanting to be approached, paying close attention to the group he was with but keeping an eye and ear roaming beyond it as well. His posture was open, one leg planted at an angle, allowing an opening, his hands active and visible, his voice loud, beckoning you in, wanting your attention. But Dan didn't accept the invitation.

On the other side of Pinchon's group was a tall, elegant woman displaying the same characteristics. Dan approached her but not until at least five minutes had passed since the underwriter made the suggestion. It wouldn't do to have anyone think there was some kind of necessity.

The woman was a partner at one of the big shipbroking houses. They chatted for a while, a couple of others at their shoulders joining in, intrigued by the ministry, breaking the ice with the usual well-intentioned jokes about Walther PPKs.

She made the introduction to Pinchon, whose antennae had already picked up buzzwords.

'I was first officer on the *Astrid* for Smit and Vermeulen,' Dan said.

'Oh really! We fix S and V often,' Pinchon said, his sausage fingers crushing a vol-au-vent and bringing it up to his cavernous mouth.

'And how's the market now?'

'Dire,' Pinchon said.

'Is the multipurpose size worth it? BDN's a big operation.'

'Yes and no. There's less money in the smaller types, but from little acorns ...' He smiled. 'Funnily enough,' he continued, 'some time ago we took on an outfit from the Emirates who'd just picked up some ships from Claus Reederie, very similar to your *Astrid*. OceanBird's their name. Sharjah. Run by Bulent Erkan who was at Claus for a while. Do you know him?'

'I was in their office a few years back – the tall skinny guy?' Dan said, a punt to draw information.

'No!' Pinchon laughed, gesturing to about five and a half feet with the flat of his hand. 'Short and fat. All Armani and Gucci and giant Rolex. But a great guy.'

Dan smiled. 'I think I might have remembered him.'

'Anyway, terrific little outfit. I knew Bulent when he was in Hamburg. Very sharp cookie. Very interesting company all round. One of their captains is a high-class backgammon player. Spends most of his leave at tournaments in Monte Carlo or Rimini. Anyway, we helped with a few things in the early days and now we represent them here. They're doing very well, you know. I wouldn't mind betting they make quite a name for themselves one day.'

'Perhaps they will,' Dan said. 'The name OceanBird rings a bell.'

Pinchon grimaced. 'You're thinking of that dreadful business in the Indian Ocean over the weekend.'

'Right ... I knew I'd heard the name.'

He spotted some familiar faces from one of the big ferry companies, excused himself and made his way across, speaking with them about their work together for a while. Earlier he'd bumped into a contact from a container line whose ships were in and out of

Felixstowe every week. Container security was another of the files on his desk.

Once or twice the *Danske Prince* was mentioned in memoriam. The information about OceanBird had been a bonus and, though nothing emerged concerning shipyards in Bar Mhar, it was not a complete disappointment. Events such as these always offered a little something here and something there. They helped build clearer pictures, with snippets of information, names, contacts, all of which were useful.

It was eight o'clock and time to go. Julie was having a drink with the press officer from an American-based think tank that was promoting liberalism and democracy in the former Soviet Union – though she was finding it neither liberal nor democratic about settling its bills. Dan had said he'd swing by the bar and they could go on somewhere to eat before the babysitter curfew.

Julie was alone at a table when he walked through the door. She looked up and smiled, but without enthusiasm. From ten metres away he knew there wasn't a bank transfer slip in her bag.

'Next week,' she said, her brow furrowing.

Dan put his hand on hers. 'They're not getting my donation.'

~

Fish was on the menu in the *Ocean Dove*'s mess. Lines trawled over the stern had hooked some wahoo, fresh and gleaming, untainted by the slick from the *Danske Prince*'s ruptured fuel tanks hundreds of miles to the south.

The mess was rectangular with bench seating along one side and one end, and a large table dominating the space. A cool evening breeze drifted in from an open porthole. There were eight for supper; the other six were either on duty or in their bunks.

In the corner of his eye, Captain Mubarak saw Assam push his plate away. It was barely touched, mainly due to the khat habit Assam had picked up in Somalia. He sighed inwardly, reflecting with distaste that, though in the short term chewing khat leaves brought alertness and euphoria, in the long term it only resulted in loss of appetite, psychosis, and darkened, greenish teeth.

Next to Assam was Snoop, the gold chains around his long neck spilling out over one of the Snoop Dogg T-shirts he always wore.

'How many did you kill?' he said to his neighbour.

'Just one on the bridge.' Assam shrugged. 'But I busted them all to make sure. One was just so cool – his head exploded like a melon.' He shaped his fingers into a gun. 'Poooof, amazing.'

'Mad, yeah.' Snoop nodded.

'The boss did seven,' Assam added, glancing up the table to where Choukri was loading his fork with a wedge of grilled wahoo.

He put it down and looked at the faces that had turned to him. 'Not at the table,' he said, glancing up to Mubarak before returning to his supper.

'Is it true you met the Emir, yeah?' Snoop Dogg said.

'Where was this?' Tariq added.

The table quietened as Choukri's knife and fork clattered down on his plate.

'Don't ask. You don't want to know.'

Snoop's chastened eyes dropped. Tariq shifted uncomfortably in his seat.

'Who is the Emir? What is the Emir?' Mubarak added, raising a finger and pointing sharply at each of them in turn, his voice challenging, as if dispelling a foolish myth. 'If he exists at all, he's everybody and nobody, everywhere and nowhere. Like our Network.'

He gestured irritably for a dish to be passed to him, signalling the subject was closed. The crew settled, making conversation among themselves. They knew only that they worked for the Shabaka – the Network. Two more things they understood were that discussing the Network was not encouraged and speculating about the Emir was not permitted.

Mubarak spooned some lentils and okra onto his plate and glanced around the quietened mess. Across the table from him, Tariq Al Bedawi took a swig of beer. There was always alcohol on the *Ocean Dove* and he knew that Tariq had grown up with it in Birmingham, with the more prosaic name of Darren Hussein – Daz to his mates. And he understood how he had been much like other young guys, cruising the clubs, smoking weed, snorting whizz and hosing premium lager while scoping for girls with potentially loose knickers.

Drink and drugs, porn and whoring, and un-Islamic behaviour of various kinds was tolerated if it deceived the authorities. In customs and immigration inspections, a ship without a suggestion of one or all of them was odd. The *Ocean Dove* needed to go about its business as a working ship, not as an annexe to a mosque. The imam's beard was discouraged, as was ostentatious prayer, though few of them were especially religious and knowledge of the Qur'an was an ideal that many found difficult to attain. Now that they were far away from propagandists and proselytisers, the Network found it prudent to grant them a little leeway – a policy he did not wholeheartedly agree with but accepted for expediency.

His crew could conceivably all have shared the same pedigree as Tariq. It could have been an all-British crew, or a cocktail of any number of EU passport holders. He knew all their backgrounds; Mehmet, sitting next to Tariq, had been born and raised in Mannheim, Germany, to third-generation Turkish parents, and was now Faisel Ibn Bhakri, the ship's second officer.

The crew list was more fiction than fact. They sailed under assumed identities, though their documents – passports and seamen's books – were real enough. Why use forgeries when well-placed friends and sympathisers could supply the genuine articles? Only Choukri and himself were who they said they were. It helped the cause to have certain people in plain sight but under the global security radar.

They passed for a good crew. They were professional. Here, no one was concerned about former lives and lifestyles, youthful indiscretions or felonies, once they had seen and accepted the light. As a company, OceanBird was building a reputation, which allowed its ships to come and go as they pleased, all over the world.

~

For Choukri, the matter of the Emir was not closed. Injudicious questions had stirred his memory. In his mind's eye he was back on a flight to eastern Saudi Arabia, checking into a hotel and waiting.

Three men had come for him mid-evening. A car drove out of town, heading west into the desert. After an hour they stopped in scrubland. Choukri knew the routine. He stripped naked and handed over his clothes. His pockets were emptied and the contents put in a bag with his watch, shoelaces and belt. When he was dressed again, his hands were tie-wrapped behind his back and a hood pulled over his head. They drove for another three hours, changing cars twice, always with three men in the car and Choukri trussed up in the boot.

He listened for telltale sounds, to the traffic on the highway, the tyres whining on tarmac or muffled on sand as dust seeped into the stifling air around him. Sometimes he registered a slower speed and the commotion of towns, but no singularly identifiable sounds. Disorienting circling at roundabouts – or perhaps not at roundabouts at all, just diversionary manoeuvres to confuse and deceive – before more open highway.

When they finally stopped and the boot opened, his aching legs stood on solid ground. He was led away, his footsteps echoing in the still night as if they were in a high-walled yard.

Then he was in a building. They took his hood off in a dark corridor and showed him through a door, alone. The room was hot and airless. A glimmer of light came from a single candle in a corner. A man was sitting on a low divan. He gestured to a chair opposite before picking up a slender metal pot and pouring two small glasses. Choukri could smell mint, the thought of home flashing through his mind.

The man said, 'As-salamu 'alaykum.' *Peace be upon you.*

His accent reminded Choukri further of home.

'Wa 'alaykumu s-salam.' *And upon you, peace*, he replied.

The accent suggested its roots were in Algeria's Ghardaia region, close to Choukri's childhood village in the M'zab valley. Perhaps it was from Ghardaia itself, the hilltop desert town three hundred miles south of Algiers where sugar-cube houses in white, pink and ochre climbed the slopes. Under his feet could have been a Mozabite rug, though it was difficult to tell in the gloom.

Choukri was thirsty. He drank his mint tea, gratefully accepting another, careful not to touch the long fingers offering the glass, conscious of observation, conscious of avoiding small talk and any suggestion he might have recognised the accent or may share some kinship with the man. Sitting across from him, he assumed, was a man with no name, unknown to him personally, known only as the Emir, the Network's leader.

'Choukri,' the man said, leaning forward. 'I watch your career. You've come a long way from the banks of the M'zab, but are you becoming too ambitious?'

'It will work,' Choukri replied, beginning to pick out the Emir's features in the half light: the high forehead, the sharp eyes that seemed not to miss a detail.

'This I believe. But at what cost? And I don't mean financial. I must think of a bigger picture than you. And I must be cautious. It is not the act I fear, but the aftermath.'

'Do we not want to take it to another level?'

The Emir scoffed. 'Another level?' He looked away for a moment before turning to fix his eyes on Choukri's. 'And you are impatient. There is always a status quo, and for good reason,' he added, prodding the air with a bony finger, his voice quietening to a whisper. 'Be careful what you wish for, my young brother. You are brave and strong, perhaps wilful – or maybe I should be more generous and just say you are dynamic.' He paused, looking across intently. 'Or is it that you imagine they will speak your name in a thousand years in the same hushed tones they use for Saladin?' He left the point to settle before bringing his fingers together around his nose, under his probing eyes.

'Or perhaps you seek to replace our protégé, Bin Laden?' he continued, his mouth twisting with distaste, before a shake of his head. 'God rest his soul. Our poor little rich boy, idly disaffected, searching for a cause. We amplified the propaganda. We fanned the flames and the public warmed their hands on his downfall. And the security services congratulated themselves. They thought the head of the beast had been removed and the body had splintered into factions – Al Qaeda was now DAESH, ISIL, ISIS, Al Shabaab, Boko Haram, Abu Sayyaf and any number of names and allegiances in distant places. And they perceive we are isolated and weak, lacking cohesion and a common purpose.' He paused, looking questioningly at Choukri. 'But what has changed? Nothing has changed. I ruled over it then as I do now, and having that self-appointed cliché as a figurehead was the perfect cover.'

With an eyebrow raised he sat back and rearranged his cushions. 'So, your plan, once again. And take your time.'

Tapping a fingernail on a tooth, the Emir listened, asking no questions, making no notes, his face set in scrutiny.

When Choukri came to the end, he thought he could hear a muezzin calling early morning prayers in the distance. The room had no windows and he could only estimate the time: around dawn. He cleared his dry throat. 'September 11? That was just two buildings. This will be thousands and …'

The Emir raised a hand. 'This I know,' he said quietly. 'I will give my answer in a month.'

Choukri's memory of the meeting was clear, but not of the man. Should he ever be taken by the security authorities, he knew he would truly be unable to help them identify the Emir. But then again, the authorities weren't looking for the Emir. They were not even aware of either him or his organisation.

He had gone deeper underground, thinning his personal retinue while tightening overall control. The command structures were hidden, but the operations moved out to the high street, the business park and the financial communities. They filed their returns, paid their taxes, fronted by people with clean backgrounds who simply did not register.

The Network's public face was manipulated to express chaos and nihilism, strong hands and second-rate minds. Its private actions were directed corporately to finance, IT, secure communications, management systems, human resources and the development of people who could influence outcomes. It was enriching itself. Money was power. Though its operations had become more sophisticated, it didn't turn its nose up at cash from the street. Across the Islamic world it controlled the drugs trade, human trafficking, money laundering, and lucrative scams in bogus charities and creaming off foreign aid. Attacks and atrocities might seem random, but they were usually built around sophisticated market plays by their specialist financial teams in Switzerland and Dubai. Fortunes could be made during the hiatus from the swing of a percentage point.

Prized above all were the executive cadre, those with a growing sense of disillusionment who were distancing themselves from the Western mores that had once held so much appeal, but no longer seemed to offer fulfilment. They felt keenly how that lifestyle clashed with the ideology of their upbringings and were drawn back to those early simplicities, propelled by a seething resentment at Western interference and a deeply held belief that injustices were being done to their culture and people.

They might already be in positions of influence in corporations or government bodies and might be encouraged to stay there as sleepers. Or they could be transplanted into some other enterprise controlled by the Network. Their faces were plausible, likeable; they were the guy who organised the fun run at the shipping conference, the Rotarian, the charity fundraising businessman, the nice guy who had just moved in next door.

The truth was, it had always been a network, *the* Network. And now it had never been stronger, more sophisticated or harder to identify. As those at the mess table had said, it was everybody and nobody, everywhere and nowhere, everything and nothing.

~

Mubarak looked up from his pudding, aware of Cookie standing patiently at Choukri's shoulder.

'But Choukri, it's your favourite,' Cookie said. 'Mangoes and ice cream. And you did not answer me. You were away with your dreams.'

Choukri glanced round. 'I was.'

'You were back in Algiers with your loved ones.'

'Something like that ...'

'It's the last of the fresh mangoes.' Cookie sighed. 'But there's still plenty of ice cream in the freezer.'

Across the table, Faisel stirred in his seat. 'Choukri,' he said, 'can I ask you something? Doesn't the Qur'an say it is forbidden to harm women and children, and civilians?'

'That's right,' Tariq added. 'We were wondering.'

Mubarak caught Choukri's eye and took the question up. 'You are correct,' he said. 'But the book is also very clear – if you are transgressed against, you are entitled to turn that transgression on the transgressor. You don't start it, but if they do, you are permitted to do the same to them.'

'And who started it?' Choukri added, stabbing the air with a spoon dripping ice cream. 'The West, that's who. Look at our cities, our women and children, our old people. Look at their suffering.'

Heads nodded as they pondered. It made sense and the Qur'an justified it, but they turned their attention at the sound of Faisel's voice again.

'But aren't they only civilians? Is it not just the military and government we should target?'

'And who empowers the government and the military? Those same civilians,' Mubarak said. 'Are they not complicit? Are they not truly the guilty ones in their so-called democracies? Why aren't the governments the innocent ones – are they not mere servants of these civilians?'

'Exactly,' Choukri said. 'Look at America. Look at this Trump. Look at their world.'

'And many Americans will die?' Assam said, his tongue circling his lips.

'Many,' came Choukri's eventual reply. 'Many thousands.'

Eyes lowered and the mess quietened before a new voice broke the silence.

'Choukri and the captain are right,' Cookie said. 'Hear their words. America and its lapdogs,' he spat.

Mubarak saw the faces turn to Cookie, leaning against the door frame, his burly, burn-scarred forearms folded across his chest. He was someone to listen to, older and more experienced. Snoop and Assam turned too, partly in respect for his opinion, but mainly because he cooked well, though Assam's growing khat habit was killing his appetite.

Mubarak considered the pair of them, his eyes coming to rest on Assam, sitting in profile in repose, his mouth open and lower lip jutting. In repose, he felt, a mouth should be closed. An open mouth and jutting lip rendered a face lumpen and stupid. It irked him. It also worried him that he should worry about such things, or about Assam.

'Your head. It's all right?' he said, his voice lowered, leaning across with a look of apparent concern, though his greater interest lay in turning the conversation.

Assam's hand dropped from where it had absently been probing the back of his skull.

'It's nothing,' he said sheepishly. 'One of those doorways on the *Danske Prince*. You know, it was low, it was dark – doh ...'

'Do you need me to take a look?'

'No, no. It's nothing,' Assam said, his eyes flitting in the direction of Choukri, whose attention appeared to be focused on a second helping of mangoes and ice cream, though Mubarak knew that when Choukri's eyes were in one place, it did not mean his ears were there too.

'Okay,' Mubarak said. 'If it doesn't settle, you come and see me.'

He had seen a bruise the size of an egg in Assam's short hair when he passed behind him to take his seat at the table. And on Saturday afternoon, through his binoculars, he'd seen Choukri inflict it with the butt of a pistol.

Just along from him, Tariq returned to the ethical discussion. He'd seemed satisfied by his captain's explanation but something was still troubling him. He turned to Faisel. 'So, it's okay then?'

'Yeah, definitely.'

'But why are the civilians the guilty ones?'

'Because they vote for the governments that have the policies they agree with.'

'I see ...'

'Isn't that how you voted, in England?'

Tariq looked up. 'I never did.'

'What, vote for the ones you agreed with?'

He shook his head. 'I never voted.'

In the rumble of voices and chink of cutlery, Mubarak was close enough to follow their discussion, his understanding strengthened by Tariq's puzzled expression and Faisel's evident consternation. He knew the sense of dislocation they'd felt in their earlier lives, before they had joined either the Network or his crew; they were no different from the rest. They had all been drifting, with neither a sense of belonging nor purpose. Often thwarted in their ambitions, regardless of whether or not those ambitions had been realistic, the resentment they'd felt was real enough. Now they had camaraderie and excitement. They belonged and had something to believe in. They were strong on the ship and could hold their heads up. For the first time in their lives they no longer had to avert their eyes and stare at the ground in apology for their intrusion.

Mubarak's thoughts about political awakening and inner-city youth were broken by Cookie attracting his attention from the doorway.

'The rattler?' Cookie said, putting the ship's backgammon board on the edge of the mess table. It was made from light boxwood and named by the crew for the clattering sound of the dice and counters that echoed about.

'Sure, why not. I'll be in my quarters,' he said, as Cookie began clearing plates away to the sound of chairs being pushed back.

In the quiet of his cabin, Mubarak saw Cookie's eyes light up at the six and one he had thrown, but his attention was broken by the bark of a familiar voice in the corridor.

'Assam! Snoop!'

Cookie raised an eyebrow. Mubarak met his eyes as the last echoes of Choukri's voice faded away.

Cookie grinned. 'What have they done now?'

'Or not done.' Mubarak sighed, pushing up from the table.

Along the passageway, Choukri was in his cabin doorway flashing a torch.

'Look at it,' he said as Mubarak arrived at his side. 'The fuckers didn't dirty the heads up.'

Mubarak stepped through the doorway, his eyes following the torch beam darting over the panelling at the side of Choukri's bed. Behind it, the ship's small arms were hidden in a concealed chamber. Assam and Snoop had put the guns away on Saturday night after the hijack, and, he remembered, Choukri had told them clearly to dirty the screwheads.

Scowling at the glinting reflections, Choukri crouched down, ran his fingers along the crack where the floor met the wall and scooped up some dust. A little bit of spittle held it in place as he worked his finger over the screws. He stood back, checking them in turn, flashing the torch at varying angles until he was satisfied the panel appeared as if it had been unmolested for years.

'I told them ...' Choukri muttered, his eyes narrowed on the offending wall.

Mubarak nodded, edging past him to the door. 'Well, deal with it.'

Returning to his cabin, he had just managed to close the door and resume his place at the table by the time two sets of feet came down the stairs.

'Your move,' Mubarak said, his eyes settling on the board and studying the options, trying to ignore the muffled though clearly agitated voices along the corridor. 'And don't be so bullish. It's better to walk past. There's a forty-seven per cent chance I'll hit that. Go for the seven – that's only seventeen per cent and it's eighty-nine per cent sure I'll get back in.'

It was good advice. The aggressive choice would leave a counter exposed.

'Shit,' Cookie rued, moments later, the side of his mouth screwing up as Mubarak moved his man to the bar without ceremony.

Cookie had been on the ship from the start, though it was curious, Mubarak thought, that they had shared few words. Time at table, cramped in the mess with his crew, he'd seen them all from a different, a more personal perspective, away from their duties. He knew them as sailors: some bright, willing and dutiful, some sloppy and slower minded. Most he knew as individuals, but not Cookie, who never ate with them. Though they whiled evenings away on the rattler, he concentrated his attention on feisty tactics and didn't linger when the board was folded at the end.

Why was Cookie here? He was well liked, though shyly caring for his own company more than that of others. And as with most of them, there was that familiar something that hinted at a void, some inner disappointment that had driven him to look for solace. Perhaps more than others, he'd found it, through purpose, place or people. Whatever it was, he seemed to have arrived at some form of contentment or equilibrium.

It buoyed Mubarak to enrol a colleague as a kindred spirit, to place another in his camp, whose motives were considered, on a higher plane and justifiable according to belief and doctrine. History would judge them. More than anything he wanted his legacy to be interpreted as an intellectual and spiritual act of faith. It was the inner demon of his doubt that it should be dismissed as mania, in the company of other maniacs.

FOUR

Late on Thursday afternoon, Dan was updating his casework. Jo Clymer would review it over the weekend in preparation for the Monday meeting. His personal dashboard had to be completed – a graphic display of all his files culminating in a summary of timescales and trends. It was a useful tool for both the individual and the manager, where each could see progress and effectiveness, but Dan was beginning to feel that Clymer was too quick to recommend the dropping of files that weren't displaying the right kind of key performance indicators. The trajectory had to point north, with fast files, results and demonstrable inter-agency coordination.

He breathed a sigh of relief, clicked the dashboard shut and checked his inbox. There was an email that needed dealing with. He'd received it late last night from Clymer.

'*Speak to Salim Hak at 6 about Bofers,*' it said – Bofors misspelt, no greetings or regards, cc-ed to her boss and a string of other people whose names he knew only vaguely but were no doubt high-ups. LaSalle's name, he noted, was not one of them. But he did wonder why she had become interested at close to midnight in something she'd so recently dismissed as inconsequential.

He typed a reply as a new message arrived in his inbox. It was from Lars Jensen. Checking it through, his eyes widened. It was all there – voyage schedules, cargo manifests, packing lists, stowage plans, statements from the shipowners, crew lists. He sent a quick thank you and started to read. The last attachment was the crew list. It wasn't the usual stark register of names and ranks. This time the shipowners had included photos, ages, marital status, children and so on. Scrolling through it felt uncomfortable, as though he was prying, voyeuristic.

The names were personal: Morten (Pedersen, the captain), Troels, two Jacobs, a Mogens, Henning, Anders. Last of all, there was Mads. As Lars had said, Mads was supposed to have celebrated his eighteenth birthday the day before yesterday.

Under a shock of red hair, bright blue eyes stared from the screen in a nest of freckles. His mother would be weeping at a memorial service before long, a Lutheran church, no body to bury, just some words, perhaps magical from Hans Christian Andersen, perhaps philosophical from Soren Kierkegaard.

After closing the file with the lightest of clicks he sat back in his chair, reflecting on a kid's face and how difficult it was for a ship to vanish. *And how easy, if someone wanted it to.*

His mind was drifting in the Indian Ocean when the phone snapped him upright with a start.

'So, have you touched base with Salim Hak yet?'

'Hello, Jo. Yeah, I have.'

'Who initiated contact?'

'Actually, he did.'

'When was that?'

'He phoned on Monday afternoon.'

'Okay,' she said.

The line cut summarily. Dan pulled the phone away from his ear and looked at it quizzically. *What's her angle now?* he wondered. *One minute she's stone cold on the subject and the next she's hotly chasing me?*

Bell Street was quiet as he walked south. The more he delved into his suspicion of the *Ocean Dove*, the less precise it became. More facts, more possibilities. Simply adding multiple scenarios and driving him further away from anything resembling a conclusion. One step forward, three steps back, he thought, reaching into his pocket for his mobile.

'Lars, it's Dan. How are you?'

'Fine, and you?'

'Everything's good here, thanks, and—'

'Sorry,' Lars cut in. 'I'm at my mother-in-law's right now. We got a family thing, you know.'

'Okay, got you, I just wanted to catch you away from the office.'

'Oh yeah ...'

'There's something I want to talk to you about. I can come over to Denmark any time.'

'No need,' Lars said. 'I'm in Hull next week.'

Dan slipped the phone into his pocket and walked on, pleased to have caught Lars – doubly so at his plans to be in England.

~

It was a traditional London pub, tucked away in a side street off the King's Road, Chelsea. Dan hadn't been in it before. He cast an eye around the large high-ceilinged room with its cream walls and ornate iron pillars spread uniformly across wide floorboards. The bar was three sides of a square, jutting out like a peninsula from the back wall. At 6.30 the early drinking crowd were making noise and keeping the bar staff busy.

That must be him, Dan thought, setting his pint down as a guy stepped through the door, his eyes checking left and right briefly before starting across the floor. He was about six feet two, clearly Asian, with about three days of stubble on his face. His hair was long and dark, swept back behind his ears. There was a bohemian air about him, Dan thought, with the dark roll neck under a herringbone coat, the collar turned up. He strode over with purpose but without drawing attention. His gait appeared athletic – at first. Then Dan noticed an unevenness.

He smiled, said, 'Salim Hak,' and offered his left hand. 'How do you do?'

Dan shook it, awkwardly, with his right, which he had already extended.

'Sorry,' Hak said, glancing down and turning his right hand over in what seemed to Dan to be half apology and half incredulity.

'What can I get you?'

'Merlot,' Hak said, nodding to the far end of the bar where there was an unoccupied space.

Out of the corner of his eye, Dan saw Hak's wine barely touch the sides of the glass before he caught the barman's eye, ordered another large one and a pint of Guinness for Dan.

Hak smiled conspiratorially. 'An imperfect Muslim. Deceptive, isn't it?'

'We're told to be open-minded at MI5.' Dan smiled back.

'By Jo Clymer?' Hak said dryly, his eyes wandering around the bar. He turned back, raised an eyebrow and added, 'So, what time does the fight start?'

Evidently, gossip about minor disturbances in backstreet pubs travels quickly within the services, Dan thought. 'Just let me know when you're ready.' He smiled, before adding, 'That's if you're up for it?'

Hak acknowledged with a nod. They chatted for a few minutes, breaking the ice, referring to the recent initiatives to foster greater cooperation between the services.

At a lull, Hak reached into a pocket, handed some papers across and excused himself. Dan watched him cross the floor, identifying the tic in his walk as a drop of the right shoulder with every other step.

When he disappeared from view, Dan turned to the first of the documents. It was a presentation from the shipyard in Bar Mhar: six PowerPoint pages about the yard's capability. They didn't have a dry dock, so all work was carried out afloat. From the photos it appeared their clients were from the lower end of the market – mainly coasters, fish-factory ships and so on. But there was a photo of work being carried out on one of the *Ocean Dove*'s sister ships. There were also the names of the yard's directors.

The other document was a mining consultant's report, setting out the prospects for reopening the local mine, commissioned by the local enterprise board and dated nine years ago. There had evidently been no takers and the mine was indeed played out.

'Do they tell you anything?' Hak said on his return, catching the barman's eye again.

'My round,' Dan reminded him, folding the papers and slipping them in his pocket. 'Nothing specific,' he said. 'But it's all useful.'

'Well, it's not every day India loses four Bofors guns and the nearest ship is heading for Pakistan, so we had to do some digging.'

'How deep does that go? I'm not clear on the procedure,' Dan said, acknowledging that Hak had experience on his side while he was still new to the service. Hak might be behind a desk now, but from some of the things they had discussed, it seemed evident he had also known the sharp end. He wished he'd done his research – as he suspected Hak had.

'Everything checked – the mine, the shipyard, the personnel, everything in the documents – all cross-referenced. And all clean,' Hak said.

'I see. And your people there, there's no, how can I say ... compromise?'

'Insha'Allah ...' Hak said, with the hint of a yawn in his voice.

Fair enough. Hak was no doubt bored with the assumption that cooperation from Pakistan was probably flawed, distorted by split loyalties, one side loyal to traditional Islam *and* a Western sense of global propriety, the other only to radical Islam.

'Sorry.' Dan shrugged.

'Not at all. It's no secret we took a sharp knife to the section last year and, since then, treasure, lots of it!' Hak said, a glint of pleasure in his eye. 'But Pakistan? There's only one thing to trust – its untrustworthiness. It's just the way it is. But hey,' he added, 'the weak link could be here. Could be me. Could be you? And we're more than alert to that. Especially you,' he said, leaning in with emphasis and no suggestion of irony.

'Thanks, that's good to know,' Dan said lightly, though he was disconcerted by the intense, probing black eyes. When Hak spoke, he looked directly at him. When he listened, his eyes dropped obliquely to the floor. First impressions can be deceptive, he thought. There's little jazz-cool about him; he was edgy but not manic, but too wired to be playing double bass in a smoky cellar bar.

'So what happened out there on the sea?' Hak said, focusing on Dan once more.

'I can't say for sure,' Dan said, taking a long swig from his glass and looking across the room before turning back to him. 'It's all scenarios. And none I can prove.'

'But you have an instinct, and it's less than positive.'

'Just a feeling.'

'Hmm,' Hak mused, chewing it over for a while. 'Look, we can be of use to each other. We don't know about ships, and the boss needs your help.'

FIVE

Faisel and Tariq had a passage from the Qur'an on the screen in their cabin and were reflecting on the recent discussion at the dinner table.

'There,' Faisel said. 'If you are transgressed against …'

'The captain's right,' Tariq said, nodding to himself and running a finger under the relevant lines.

'Course he's right.'

'And what Choukri said, that's so true.'

'I felt sure I'd heard the same thing in the mosque at home,' Faisel said.

'At home in Mannheim?'

'Do you know it?' Faisel said.

Tariq shook his head. 'Is it near Paris? I went to Disneyland when I was a kid.'

'Not really,' Faisel said, tilting his head to one side, feeling the engine revs drop and the ship's vibrations settle. He glanced at his watch. 'I think it's Bar Mhar. I'll wake the others.'

The ship was due to arrive there just before midnight, when the crew rota also switched.

He stepped along the passageway to the next door, knocked and opened it. In the half light, Snoop Dogg was on the lower bunk, asleep, his mouth opening and closing rhythmically. Above him, on the top tier, Assam had his laptop propped against the bulkhead, his cock out, bony fingers tweaking his nipples as he watched a muscular black man arse-fuck a skinny teenage blonde.

Faisel's eyes rolled as he looked away, but he said no more than, 'It must be Bar Mhar.'

'Must be …' Assam said, slipping down from the bunk, a free hand patting down his erection.

Mubarak's door opened just as Faisel raised a knuckle to it.

'I know,' Mubarak said. 'It woke me.'

Faisel smiled; a change in the ship's equilibrium was more effective than the alarm clock at his captain's bedside.

~

At first light they brought the ship in. The morning sun was rising slowly over India to the south-east, creeping above the headland in shards as pale as sandstone, the shadows on the coastline beginning to recede. The *Ocean Dove*'s bridge caught the first of the glare, then the lower decks and hull, until the ship and the bay were awash with light.

Choukri shielded his eyes. The bay curved in front of him, five miles across, a mile deep. On its eastern fringe was an old gypsum terminal, now converted into the shipyard. Facing it across the bay was a village with low indistinct buildings sheltering under the cliffs. It had sprung up to house mine workers and was now mostly abandoned. Just a few people remained who found intermittent work at the yard, along with the elderly who had nowhere else to go.

Jagged cliffs stretched in both directions, mottled greys, stone and dust, with no hint of green or trees, no mangroves at the waterline. There was a cleft in the shoreline behind the yard where a railway had once run down from the mine a dozen miles inland. Between the old gypsum mine and the shoreline was the main east–west coastal road.

This was the western end of Pakistan, the Makran coast, close to the Iranian border. The land was barren, the rains sporadic and the heat unrelenting. The nearest towns with industry, with work, were many miles away. Bar Mhar was forgotten.

The shipyard sprawled over forty acres of dust. Under the cliffs were warehouses, sheds and workshops in uniform sun-bleached paint. At the back, commanding a view across it all, was a three-storey office building of faded concrete panels. A jetty stretched out from the shore and turned through ninety degrees to create an artificial harbour. Smaller ships like the *Ocean Dove* were able to berth on its inner wall.

The bulk carriers that once loaded gypsum had used the seaward side where the water was deeper.

Just after eight o'clock, Choukri and Mubarak walked up the jetty and across the yard. A clerk showed them up the stairs to Hassan Khan's office. Choukri stepped through the door, his eyes roaming around a large airy room with faded red lino on the floor and white painted walls. Broad metal-framed windows lined one side, overlooking the terminal. Khan's desk was at the back. In the centre was a meeting table, with a pair of drawing-office tables to one side covered in blueprints and fluttering under a fan.

Khan got up to greet them, a tall, slim, fine-featured man of about forty with a neatly clipped beard that wasn't showing any grey. Over a shirt and tie he was wearing an engineer's coat, with pens, pencils and a micrometer in a breast pocket.

'Please,' he said, extending a hand to the meeting table before telling the clerk to bring coffee.

'What about security? I didn't see anything,' Choukri said, sitting down next to Mubarak, facing Khan across the table.

'They saw you,' Khan said, his eyes moving left and right between them. 'I've got people on the yard and up in the cliffs. We do it ourselves, round the clock.'

'And the village?'

'They're not involved. We give them work when we can, but nothing important,' Khan said.

'Exactly. Keep it that way.'

Choukri got up and stepped across to the windows, leaning down and resting his hands on the sill, a pendant on a silver chain slipping from under his shirt. It swung free for a moment before he steadied it, working the small disc carefully between thumb and finger, looking out over the terminal before turning and gesturing with a hand.

'Okay,' Mubarak said, glancing across to Khan.

The two of them began to go through the list of steel repairs to the floor of the ship's hold and some of the fuel and ballast tanks. Khan clarified points for accuracy, making notes and cross-referencing with the scope of work from OceanBird's technical department.

Choukri followed the discussion closely but made no comments. The repairs were not complicated and there was a genuine need for them, unconnected with the guns. After a concluding lull, Mubarak turned to him and he stepped back to the table.

Resuming his place opposite Khan, Choukri opened a slipcase and passed him a hand-drawn schematic.

Khan studied it for a minute before pushing his chair back.

'Come. I have it here.'

At his desk, he clicked a file on the computer. A three-dimensional, multicoloured CAD animation filled the screen, rotating to provide viewpoints from every angle. He stood back as Choukri's eyes darted around the images, narrowing in concentration on one point and then another. The guns were lined up in a row along the floor of the *Ocean Dove*'s hold. The first one was placed at the back of the hold, facing forward. A few metres ahead was the next, also facing forward, then the third and fourth. The fourth and last was far enough back in the hold to allow sufficient angle to fire and clear the forecastle at the bows of the ship. The ship's hold was shaped like a shoebox. All it needed was to lift the hatch and open fire, virtually unseen, except from a bird's eye.

Khan cleared his throat. 'There's more.'

Another simulation played, showing each gun traversing. The available angle of fire was superimposed in triangulated shading, with the barrel raised, lowered and panning left and right. The sharp point of the triangle was at the barrel tip, the shading expanding as it cleared the hold to the open air.

'And the last,' Khan said.

Choukri's head lifted with a gasp. He said nothing, leaning back down to the screen and reaching across to grip Khan's forearm.

Superimposed on a map, the *Ocean Dove* was moored at a jetty. Fanning out from the ship was red shading – the effective range of the guns. Numbered dots on the map corresponded with a list of specific targets.

More than once Choukri lifted his head from the screen, but each time he was drawn back by another detail. Eventually he pulled away. 'Where did you learn this?' he said.

Khan shifted his feet. 'I trained as a naval architect and marine engineer. For ten years I was at the Gulf Arabian Shipbuilding and Repair Yard. Then I returned to Karachi and worked on the Zulfiquar-class frigates. I was responsible for all the gunnery installation.'

December was winter in Pakistan, freezing in the northern uplands but mild on the coast. The air was warm when they stepped from the office building. It refreshed Choukri. He felt the tension falling from him as his purposeful march eased to an amble and the muscles in his face relaxed. He turned to Khan. 'It's good, very good,' he said, allowing the suggestion of a smile to play in his eyes. 'I had hoped, but ...'

'Thank you,' Khan said, nodding his appreciation before pointing across the yard to the warehouse buildings. 'We've got everything we need here. The mine had a machine shop and I've updated it with a CNC milling machine so we can design in CAD and make anything we need. The ammunition cassettes on carousels are my idea. You can fire continuously without the need to stop and change cassettes.'

Khan opened the door of a sprawling building. It was high-ceilinged and cool inside. Swifts darted in the eaves, their shrill cries echoing. 'This was the railway shed,' he said.

Choukri hesitated as Khan moved on. 'Oh, I nearly forgot,' he said. 'We've got eight bodies in a container on deck.'

Khan stopped and looked back hesitantly. 'A container ... we can bury it too?'

'We don't want it back,' Choukri said, surprised.

'Right,' Khan said. 'I guess not.'

He led them from building to building, his pride in the facility evident to Choukri, who approved of the order, the cleanliness and the general sense of improvement. The outside may have been shabby but the content was sharp. He knew where the initial funds had come from, but the yard had to survive on its own in the world now, and Khan's skill and dedication was making it happen.

A breeze kicked up dust in the yard as Choukri stood and looked around, taking in the layout and putting Khan's explanations into context. Khan offered lunch in the canteen, but Mubarak excused himself.

They took a table to themselves at one side. Scattered around the room were about thirty men and a handful of women. Some wore office clothes or engineering coats. Some were in green-and-white overalls, the colours of Pakistan. The tables were Formica, the seats plastic, with the same red lino on the floor as in Khan's office, Choukri noted.

'All our people,' Khan said, gesturing to the other tables. 'They're quiet today. They know who you are.' He smiled. 'The woman with the red ribbons – that's Bashira, my wife. She's Palestinian.'

'Hamas?'

'Hezbollah. But she's clean now. Got a US visa last year, no problem. She comes with me when I'm in the States on my multi-entry visa.' He smiled again.

'Bashira – the bringer of good news?' Choukri said.

Khan raised an eyebrow. 'Not always … And you?'

'I have a wife and baby girl in Algiers.'

'That's good,' Khan said, nodding. 'And over there, the little guy at the end, he was wasting his time mending pickups in Syria.' He shook his head. 'He's an electrical engineer, and a good one. Worked for Siemens in Germany on turbines and generators. Pickups, eh?'

'What about the Russians?' Choukri said, conscious of the effort it had taken him to force the final word out.

Khan bent his head closer. 'I don't know. The Emir sent them, so …'

He glanced across nervously, as though he might have spoken out of turn. People rarely met the Emir more than once and they were not allowed to discuss it. No mention was ever made of where the meeting took place, what he looked or sounded like, or any speculation about his background and who he might once have been.

'Don't worry. The Emir knows what he's doing,' Choukri said. 'I'll see them after lunch.'

Food was brought over and set before them, but Choukri's mind was on the Russians. The guns were computer controlled, and he didn't have the codes. Their contact in the Indian navy worked in the logistics section and knew everything about delivery from Sweden.

But the computer codes were always sent to another department after each shipment.

'And they'll build a new system?' Choukri said.

'All controlled by a laptop.'

'And no fuck-ups?'

Khan shook his head.

Choukri sucked at a knot of food caught in his teeth. 'I don't trust the …'

'Don't worry,' Khan said, leaning across. 'It's not that complicated. We could do it ourselves. Don't forget, we built all the AIS and VDR equipment for the RIB, and in many ways that's more technical. But anyway, these guys are pros.'

'So I'm told. Russians …'

'It's preprogrammed,' Khan continued. 'All we need is the exact location of the ship. You just push the button and …' He peered across, his mouth pursed. 'Will you get the time?'

Choukri stretched out his fingers, pulling them back into fists. 'I think so. In all the confusion, why not? No one's going to be looking for a ship.'

Khan nodded. 'And the list of targets?'

'I'm working on it,' Choukri said.

Identifying specific targets was not a problem. Everyone and everything had a website these days. It was all available to him at the click of a mouse, with details, maps and schematics. Grey areas could be clarified by comparing incomplete information with online maps, Google Earth and GPS coordinates. And he was, after all, an expert navigator. Degrees, minutes, seconds and their fractions posed no difficulty whatsoever.

There wasn't a problem with information about targets. The problem was the overwhelming mass of it. He had time on his side and one by one the targets would be researched and added to his file, the wish list.

And now Choukri had a clear picture in his mind of where he needed to position the ship. The choice was narrowed to a defined zone. It also influenced how they must approach getting the ship in the location in the first place. The location had to offer a degree of privacy and they needed a legitimate reason to be there. This was paramount.

~

Darkness came down shortly after six. Choukri ordered the arc lights on deck to be turned off. They would unload with just the hold lamps. The motors were switched on and the ship's hatch opened slowly.

'Easy,' he barked into his walkie-talkie at the crane operators, the men in the hold and those unhooking the cargo on the trailers, though he could see in their faces they felt the same way he did. This was the end of the first phase. They all wanted to get the guns ashore safely. One by one the packing cases and containers were lifted from the hold. Trailers ran along the jetty to the warehouse then back again to the ship. It was slow work, waiting for each trailer to return before it could take another load, but they were not pressed for time and the cargo needed to be handled carefully.

'When the Danes come off the ship, you three go with them,' Choukri said, glancing in turn to Faisel, Snoop and Assam. 'And if the bodies are found, I'll bury you with them.'

Slings were hooked on to the orange container. It rose into the air, swinging over the ship's rail to a trailer. On the quay, the truck driver turned the locks to secure it as Assam, Snoop and Faisel climbed into the back of a pickup.

Choukri went up the stairs to the bridge. Through the far door, he saw Mubarak's shoulders hunched over the rail on the wings.

'Went well,' Choukri said, stepping out to join him.

A stony face turned. 'Did it? No service. No words. A container for a coffin, a trailer for a hearse, a pickup truck in attendance. Not much of a send-off for the *Danske Prince*'s crew …'

'Not much,' Choukri conceded, remembering the day of the hijack and the unceremonious manhandling of the bodies below the rail of the *Ocean Dove*. But he was pleased the guns were now safely ashore, doubly pleased they had reached such a milestone, and reluctant to spoil the moment. 'Remember the destination, not the road,' he said quietly.

Mubarak nodded. 'It's in here,' he said, tapping a finger to his head.

~

The men were back at work at seven o'clock in the morning. Yard technicians inspected the steel plating in the hold and discussed the processes. On the jetty, a trailer drew up with equipment and materials. Safety checks were carried out. Fire was a hazard during cutting, burning and grinding. Khan was there, talking to his foreman. The work they were doing was necessary to keep the ship in good working order and to comply with maritime regulations, but it was also preparatory. What they did now could not be allowed to affect the eventual fitting out.

Welders were marking cut lines in chalk on the floor. The ship's cranes hoisted materials into the hold: steel plate, trolleys with acetylene bottles, cutting torches. The sun crept over the bay, its shadow receding in the hold. In a few hours it would be overhead, the hold a steel box radiating heat where men were working with burning equipment.

After lunch, Choukri was drinking coffee on the ship's wings when a pickup truck appeared at the end of the jetty.

'Come on,' he said, wagging a finger at Faisel. 'Our ride's here.'

Around the back of the office block they picked up a service road running alongside the railway. The track climbed steadily, passing through a divide in the cliffs, the valley rising steeply to either side and snaking ahead into the distance.

'Hey, slow down,' Choukri barked, giving the dashboard a slap as the pickup jolted on the rough track. 'I want to see it.'

After a few miles they passed under the Makran highway bridge; the railway ran through one gap in its pillars, the track through another. A slip to the highway branched up to one side. The valley was a bowl of mottled greys, pinks, apricot and chalky white, the pale blue of the sky ahead in the distance.

The ground levelled on the southern tip of the Balochistan plateau. Mountains rose in isolation from their neighbours, separated by plain.

Some were rippled with soft folds as if sculpted by a caring hand. Others were wilfully irregular, the colours unchanging – cream and grey and white. Fingers of rock stood like towers, some solitary, some in clusters, interspersed with smooth-faced monolithic slabs stretching laterally over the ground. The landscape competed with itself for incongruity – illogical and eerie. Choukri knew the desert and the corruptions of time and erosion, but this was unlike anything he'd seen before.

He turned to Faisel. 'Beautiful, eh?'

'It's not at all like Mannheim,' Faisel said cautiously.

Choukri sat back, looking contentedly at rock, his open hand stretched from the window in the cooling breeze.

A puff of dust kicked up at the side of the track under a stunted tamarix bush. Disturbed from its slumber, an animal shape scuttled away, dark eyes glaring indignantly over a rolling shoulder.

Choukri looked inquisitively at the driver.

'A honey badger.'

They took a long curve around the side of a towering rock, its shadow cast across the dust. The track straightened ahead of them, dipping to the mouth of a pale chalky crater, an amphitheatre a mile across. The ground was scarred with regular lines, the evidence of machinery – a smooth face here, a spiralling track climbing the walls there.

'Stop,' Choukri said as they neared the centre.

The driver crouched at the side of the pickup, shielding his eyes from the sterile glare as Choukri walked across the pit. Under his feet the ground was compacted by the studded ridges of caterpillar tracks. He looked about him across to the distant walls. The criss-crossed lines gave no indication of what kind of work had been carried out, or precisely where. To one side, under the lee of the crater lip, was a heap of spoil the size of an office block. It may have been there a day, a month, or some years. Perhaps the container was beneath it, or maybe it was a couple of hundred paces away, but he couldn't really tell in the mass of uniform tracks.

On the far side was the old railway, some of it under rock and dust, some still above ground, an indistinct line of russet stretching into the distance. In a spur to one side were battered freight wagons, a fuel bowser, and the remains of a crushing plant, its paint yellowed and peeling.

'Good job,' Choukri said, squinting down in the harsh light and kicking at a loose gypsum rock. 'And the bulldozer?'

'Khan's men picked it up this morning.'

'Good job.'

They made their way across to a zigzag path in the corner of the pit. It wound its deliberate way to the rim of the bowl. At the top, Choukri wiped the sweat from his forehead, taking in the silence and isolation, his eyes panning the horizon. Beyond the mine, in the distance between gaps in the mountains, the blue of the Arabian sea stretched away.

He motioned to Faisel to sit. Faisel's feet shuffled in the dust as he struggled to make himself comfortable, though the rock was quite smooth, the right height, and almost like a bench.

'Are there snakes?' Faisel said, looking around distastefully and swatting at the flies circling his perspiring head.

'Probably,' Choukri said; a beetle with an electric-blue shell scuttled away from under his feet.

The burying of the container was important, but it wasn't the main reason Choukri had come here. From the ship, the hinterland had beckoned. It reminded him of home, the desert's solace, a place to think. Mubarak had said he'd like Khan, and that, he had to agree, was proving to be true. Khan's plans were comprehensive, his thoroughness impressive, with modelling of every scenario to identify the ideal operating conditions.

Choukri had no doubt that Khan knew what he was doing, but he wasn't going to be there on the day. So far it was only theoretical. They could test, but the tests would be dry runs. The mechanical side of it, Khan's side, held water. The electrical side, the command and control, was in the hands of the Russians.

Subconsciously his fingers crept inside his shirt, turning the pendant over and over. As he sat on the rock idly picking up pebbles and flicking them away, the dinar pendant between his lips, the chain hanging in an arc, the same thing was turning over and over in his mind – what if he pushed the button and nothing happened?

'My father used to take me into the desert in the evenings,' he said, breaking his own silence. 'I had to listen out for wolves. Of course there weren't any, but he would promise me a dinar if I heard one before him. Sometimes he gave me the money anyway, but usually I went home no richer.'

'And he's there now, at home?'

'Afghanistan. I was put to bed one evening and the next morning he was gone. I was six.'

'What does he do there?'

'Nothing. He's dead. Russians …'

Choukri pulled the chain up from around his neck, studying it for a moment before handing it across to Faisel.

'Is it still the dinar in Algeria?' Faisel said, turning the silver chain, looking at the coin, careful not to touch it.

Choukri nodded. 'Then my mother took us to Marseille where her sister lived. My French was bad, and now it's better than my Arabic. I went to school, where they tried to teach me to be a good Frenchman.'

'And then the navy, the French navy?'

'Better than prison … just. The police rounded us up when there was trouble and the magistrate said prison or the military – make your choice, boy. They're just cleaning out the estates.'

Choukri was staring straight ahead, but he felt Faisel's glance at him.

'What about your community leaders?' Faisel said.

Choukri turned. 'You kidding? They're in on it, the corrupt fuckers,' he said, before adding a punctuating jet of spit. 'I keep a special kind of hate for them.'

'We had the Deutschmark,' Faisel said, handing the chain back. 'I was just beginning to understand money and then we got the euro. My parents were proud to name me Mehmet, but then …' he added. 'I was taught to be a good German and I looked and sounded like one until someone asked my name. By the time I was ten I understood the looks on the faces of my friends' mothers.'

The chain was in Choukri's hand, his fingers turning the coin worn smooth with time. He looked at Faisel, understanding the lost pride in his name, knowing it meant Mohamed in Turkish; the good little German, the dirty little Turk, the cracked mirror of his own experience. 'Forty thousand shells ...' he said quietly.

Faisel turned. 'But when?'

Choukri let the suggestion of a smile on his mouth speak of one thing but left his narrowed eyes to say another – don't ask, don't push.

'Soon,' he conceded, tapping a finger on his forehead. 'The date's here, and soon it'll be our day.'

'At dinner on the ship you said many thousands will die. Can it really be so?'

'Forty thousand shells ...' Choukri repeated.

'And soon it will be our day.' Faisel nodded.

~

The next morning, a minibus was on the jetty before breakfast, Sunshine Tours painted cheerfully on its sides. Karachi airport was around three hundred miles away, a journey of six hours, considerably shorter than the two days it had taken before the construction of the Makran highway, the new east–west coastal road.

All the crew were going on leave, including Mubarak. The chief engineer and Choukri were staying an extra day. They had things to attend to with the technical superintendent from OceanBird's office, who was stretching his legs on the jetty and looking up at the ship, having just arrived with the minibus from Karachi.

Within reason, the crew could go where they pleased, which usually meant the fleshpots of Thailand or the Philippines. They had identities that would stand most forms of scrutiny. Home, however, was off-limits. Listed as missing under their former names, their families and communities being watched, they were effectively displaced.

The bus driver packed the luggage away while the crew milled around, calling to each other, arguing over seating plans. Faisel was dressed sensibly, mostly in beige. The morning wasn't yet hot but he was wearing an anorak, also beige. Rap music was coming from the cans hanging around Snoop Dogg's neck. He looked like he was ready to hit the clubs. Assam was all tough guy in gangsta black, tapping the beat with a finger on Snoop's chest and cutting some dance moves, pirouetting on the ball of a foot and striking a balletic pose before going through a flurry of shadow-boxing. 'Ready to chill, thrill and kill,' he said, a leer spreading over his face.

Mubarak checked the ship's emails before going through to breakfast. The frigate had arrived in Toulon ahead of schedule and there was a message from Lieutenant Boissy. It said that everything they had collected from the accident location would be handed over to the authorities and that he was going on holiday. In closing, he wished them good sailing and a happy Christmas.

His reply thanked the lieutenant and explained they were all going on leave as well. He put his private email address in open cc, and Choukri's, and suggested that if Boissy needed any further information he should feel free to contact either of them directly. After his best regards, he wished him a happy Christmas too.

When Mubarak stepped into the mess, Choukri was attacking a plateful of eggs on waffles with lashings of maple syrup. He poured himself a cup of coffee and sat down, smoothing his crossword out on the table. Five down was giving him considerable trouble: 'Huge Greek pastries back plan, 9, _ T _ A _ _ _ _ _'

Each week he printed *The New York Times*' Sunday magazine puzzle and the Everyman from London's *Observer* newspaper. They went everywhere with him. He struggled with some of the more culture-specific clues, but enjoyed an advantage with anything involving Egyptian mythology, which often featured.

His concentration was broken a minute later at the sound of Choukri's voice, a familiar 'Exactly.'

'What is?' he said.

Choukri looked up. 'I was thinking to myself, out loud ...' he said, smiling self-consciously. 'How are you? You're all ready, you're all ready?'

'As I'll ever be,' Mubarak said, sensing an unfamiliar atmosphere. It could be, he thought, that Choukri recognised this was the last time they would part from each other in this way, returning home, leaving what was effectively their second home, their second family.

They exchanged enquiries about flights, the minibus, the road to Karachi and the airport, though Mubarak steered clear of what was at the front of his mind: the parting from the ship.

'I think I might make Faisel some sort of acting captain when we get back,' he said.

'Why not. Do him good,' Choukri said.

Faisel's exam results were due. It was a foregone conclusion that he would pass. He would have his master's ticket.

'It will help him come out of his shell,' Mubarak said, glancing towards the mess door at the sound of footsteps in the corridor. He turned back, catching Choukri's eye. 'So how will it be for you, at home?'

Choukri's gaze dropped. 'Fine,' he said. 'I'll just act the same, I guess. Nothing any different from any other time I go home. And you?'

'The same.' Mubarak shrugged. 'I'll see my daughter for the first time in two years, but as usual we won't get on. I'll put fresh flowers on my wife's grave, and at the end I'll tidy my apartment and pay the landlord the usual six months' rent. I've had that apartment for twenty years. Nothing has changed. Not the landlord, not the furniture, not the way I live. Only the world has changed.'

'My wife is excited about a new apartment. I'm supposed to go and see it when I get back. She's choosing the curtains and things. What can I say?'

'The district's changed though. There's a Starbucks on every corner,' Mubarak added.

'I don't like the district,' Choukri said.

'No, nor me. I used to.'

'No, in Algiers.'

'Sorry,' Mubarak said, realising they had each been in their own worlds, talking to themselves rather than the other person.

'So you'll leave everything just as you normally would?' Choukri said.

'Yes. See my friends from the Brotherhood. Say my goodbyes. Maybe they'll feel something different in me this time. Maybe they'll think it's just me.'

'They mean a lot to you.'

'I've known them all my life, but I think it's more valuable that they've known *me* all my life. There's no room for pretence. You can't fool people who've known you since you were a child.'

Choukri looked away, the heels of his boots grinding together. 'Oh yeah. I nearly forgot. You saw the news, Madrid last night?'

'I did,' Mubarak said, the side of his mouth screwing up. 'Did it have to be kids?'

'Not my decision – but an efficient operation,' Choukri said, gathering his things together and pushing up from the table.

Evidently, Mubarak thought. Yesterday evening, outside a Justin Bieber concert in Madrid, a truck had ploughed into the queue – mostly kids, girls with their mothers. The news was still fresh, the details patchy, but there were already reports of fifty-two dead and over two hundred injured.

Moments before, they had shared heartfelt thoughts: the pain of home, of family and parting. Pain and doubt shared, like brothers. But how quickly it had turned to the efficiency of mowing down Spanish children. Madrid could now be added to the Ohio baseball game, the Amsterdam nightclub, the Toulouse fair, Munich's Christmas market and other efficient operations still to come.

God, he thought, lifting his eyes, both you and your faithful servants on this earth do sorely test me. Please send me a sign. My mind is strong but my stomach is weak. Or do I just flatter myself that my sensibilities are finer, while secretly glorying in the carnage? Perhaps it is only hypocrites who relish their own regrets. Good men *can* kill.

It was all well and good to support something on an intellectual level, as it was to be an intellectual itself. It was also a self-justification he was struggling to accept. At times like these he wished he could find some of the crew's blind acceptance or Choukri's unblinking determination. He looked at the empty place along the table, at the soiled plate of waffles. Shrewd he may be, quick-witted and determined, but unhindered by a capacity to pause and weigh a philosophical balance. Mubarak envied him that, especially now.

He'd slept badly, weighing a private philosophical balance of his own, troubled by the recurring dream of his wife's face in her bed at the Anglo-American hospital in Cairo. She was staring blankly, not recognising him, a doctor at her side who recognised Mubarak only too well, waiting with what seemed a detached impatience for his consent to switch off her life support – her young life.

SIX

Dan arrived at five o'clock on Wednesday afternoon. He'd caught an afternoon train to Hull's Paragon Station. From there it was a short walk to Lars's hotel overlooking the marina, where he had also booked a room.

There was nothing unusual in a business trip to Hull. He had signed out, logged his destination as he was obliged to do, and arranged a meeting with the head of operations at the ferry terminal for the following morning. Lars hadn't been mentioned in his itinerary.

Apart from the problems of contraband and people-smuggling on the ferry services, an additional threat was gaining traction within the security services. The ferry systems throughout the UK were potentially vulnerable to terrorist attack. Intelligence and chatter indicated an increase in attention. Security needed to be tightened. Dan had worked with the ferry companies and ports and introduced new protocols and methods.

Hull and the Humber were familiar territory, though he was more used to arriving and departing by sea. The train had been a welcome change, especially when it branched along the estuary, the last of the wintry sun low on the horizon picking out the Humber Bridge's towers in silhouette.

Nothing appeared to have changed much, especially the weather, he thought, getting his bearings outside the station. A biting wind was gusting up the street leaving a taste of salt on his lips. He wrapped his collar tight and set off. Had he not known where he was going, the clatter of halyards whipping against masts in the marina would have guided him.

He checked in, went to his room, called Lars on the internal phone and arranged to meet in the bar. Dan got there first, ordered a beer and checked his phone for messages. A minute later, in the corner of his eye he recognised the shambling gait of a burly man approaching him. He turned to meet a warm smile and an outstretched hand.

Lars Jensen was in his late forties, his hair steel grey, thick and cropped short. A pair of reading glasses were hanging from his neck on a cord.

Dan smiled. 'Good to see you, Lars.'

'You too. Been a long time.'

'Too long. A beer?'

They stood at the bar, catching up with the news and laughing about the old times, comfortable in each other's company. At sea, it didn't take long to gauge a man. You either rated him or you didn't.

Their attention switched abruptly to the TV screen across the bar, where a camera was sweeping along a Madrid street, an anchorwoman sombrely announcing the death toll had risen again.

Dan shook his head. 'Give it a few years and that's Phoebe and Julie, or me, holding her hand in the queue.'

Lars sighed. 'Don't. Makes me think of my Pernille.' He blew his cheeks out as the TV piece ended and turned back to Dan. 'So, why is it you come up to Hull to see me?'

The bar was filling for the early evening session.

'Can we go up to my room?'

Lars looked at him before draining his glass. 'Sure.'

Dan's room was at the front of the hotel looking out over the harbour. The wind had calmed; lights twinkled, reflected in the still water. By the large window was a coffee table with two easy chairs. Dan gestured to them and opened the minibar.

He pulled a bottle of Carlsberg out and handed it across. 'I'm glad you're here,' he said, lifting his hands, his fingers spread. 'I've got a problem.'

Lars took a mouthful of beer and raised an eyebrow.

'You know I work for the government,' Dan continued. 'Well, it's a bit more complicated than that – national security, you know.'

'I think so.'

'You can't discuss this with colleagues or anyone. If you don't want me to say anything, I won't. We can just have a drink and dinner like friends, and that's it.'

Lars pushed the curtain aside, casting an eye over the marina for a moment before turning back. 'Why me?'

'Because you know the sea and ships. And because I trust you.'

Lars's head tilted back. 'And I can't use this, and we didn't meet here today?'

'Maybe you could. If it was your own idea. If it never came back to me.'

'I see,' Lars said, looking away, and back to his empty glass.

Dan got up and went back to the minibar. He opened two more bottles and tossed a bag of nibbles across. Lars pulled the bag open and tipped a few into his hand.

'So, okay, you tell me, then we decide what we do,' he said.

Dan sat down. 'Do you have any suspicions about what happened to the *Danske Prince*, or do you think it's just technical and procedural – procedures that went wrong …'

Lars's head rocked gently as if he was weighing up his answer. 'Suspicions? Not really.'

'Just an unfortunate accident?'

Lars's chest filled. 'It's all total shit. We got a hundred questions and no real answers. But I don't have that kind of suspicions – like you suggest.'

'Did you know, on the second Bofors voyage in July on the *Danske Queen*, the *Ocean Dove* followed her for about two weeks.'

Lars sat back. 'No. I didn't know that.'

'It's in the AIS archive. I plotted it all out.'

Lars scratched his chin and took a swig of beer. 'But it doesn't mean anything.'

On that I disagree … Dan thought, but he left the comment to ride as he sifted through other details in his mind. Last week, when Lars had emailed the *Danske Prince*'s voyage information, the shipowner's statement had added something new: the sale of guns to the Indian navy hadn't been a separate contract. Bofors had sold twelve guns in total. Four were shipped in March, four in July, and the last four loaded in November – on the *Danske Prince*. All three shipments had been contracted for by the *Danske Prince*'s owners. The two earlier voyages had delivered the cargo without incident and, during the July shipment, the ship also called en route at Port Elizabeth.

'What do we know about the *Ocean Dove*?' Dan continued. 'Based in Sharjah. Run by a Turk. Egyptian master. Muslim crew.'

'Yeah, but they got a good name. The master was on it when she was a Claus Reederie ship. He's one of us, for fuck's sake. Isn't he? I asked around. They're good operators, a good crew, good guys.'

'Are they? The 9/11 guys all had pilot training and everyone said "But they were just like us." We don't know, do we? Terrorists aren't just picked up off the street any more. They've got relevant backgrounds, skills, education. They blend in.'

'Terrorists. Who's saying terrorists?'

'No one's saying it. But who else would want four Bofors guns and ammunition? I ran all the *Ocean Dove* crew names through our systems and none of them registered, but I didn't expect them to. And where did the *Ocean Dove* go straight after the accident? To the shipyard at Bar Mhar. The boss there is an expert in naval weapons installation – it says so on his LinkedIn page.'

Lars's forehead creased. 'LinkedIn … is that what terrorists do now, put their CV on LinkedIn? Are you serious?'

'The *Ocean Dove* was there. Twice.'

Lars looked down, tapping his pockets and pulling out a tobacco pouch. He started to roll a cigarette in silence.

'Look, the AIS says they were not there,' he said after a while, putting his part-rolled cigarette down again. 'At one time she was eighteen miles ahead when the *Prince* was just sitting there. Then she turned and was twelve miles away when the screen went, you know, finished. All the timings add up. The AIS on both ships and the InMarSat beacon on the *Prince*. It all adds up.

'And one more thing,' he added, picking up his paper and tobacco before putting it down again. 'This you don't know but we checked everything. We got help from the AIS guys, from InMarSat, and the Danish navy, and they got help from the American navy – you know they got all kinds of satellite stuff. So, we analyse all the sats. We plot all the ships. And there's nothing in the area any time, just the *Prince* and the *Dove*. Okay, the American sat isn't always clear and doesn't cover the exact area, but it covers the next areas, so when there's a gap there's no time for a ship to be there before the gap closes. So we know there were no ships there, just those two, eh?'

Dan chewed it over for a moment. 'Did the Americans or your own security services say anything unusual to you, ask any strange questions?'

'Nothing,' Lars said, opening his hands.

'Well, I'm glad you did that,' Dan said, 'but I never thought there was a third ship, and I don't believe the data just because that's what it says. It's just computers.'

Lars looked up from kneading his tobacco. 'But there was nothing funny this time. We checked, all systems working, nothing funny. Okay?'

Dan weighed it, noting the rising frustration a few feet across from him. 'I don't doubt the explosion, just how it happened,' he said, willing a conciliatory tone to his voice.

'No,' Lars said, 'and we weren't there. We don't know what the crew was doing at that moment. Maybe someone sees something, they hear something, smell something. Maybe they're checking and then … It's always total shit, you know that. Things start small, something stupid, and it just goes from there.'

'A chain reaction.'

'Yeah, a chain reaction.'

Dan left it to settle before saying, 'You going to smoke that?'

'We can go out – fresh air?'

'No problem,' Dan said. 'I'll just open the window a bit.'

In its reflection he saw Lars get up and head to the back of the room, to the bathroom. Dan thought about what he had learned. Not much so far. Though what Lars had said about the satellite analysis had been pertinent. InMarSat, the International Maritime Satellite Organisation, though now a private communications provider, had its roots in the maritime world. Its privatisation charter demanded it maintained its distress assistance to the world's ships and planes, which it tracked through beacons – or blips on a screen. AIS was also just blips on a screen, but both AIS and InMarSat provided accurate data. More valuable perhaps was the eye-in-the-sky technology of the US military, which gave real imagery of real things. The middle of the Indian Ocean was nobody's idea of a global priority, so resources were not thrown at it. As Lars had said, the satellite had holes in its coverage. But if something, a ship, had been in such a hole, then it stood to reason that at other times it must have been on another side of that hole, and this, as Lars had said, they had proved was not the case. If something wasn't somewhere at a certain time, it was impossible for it to be somewhere else at another given time. Ships were large and ponderous movers. They couldn't jump around and dodge satellites at will.

'I don't like it. I mean this whole thing,' Lars said, emerging from the bathroom. He went over and stood by the window, searching his pockets for a lighter. 'Terrorists?' he added, shaking his head. 'Shit, they're just seamen, good seamen. They went to help. You know it.'

'Another thing,' Dan said. 'What about the salvage? That would at least tell us if the guns are at the bottom of the Indian Ocean – and maybe the crew.'

Lars was slow to reply, exhaling smoke heavily at the window.

'There's not going to be salvage,' he said quietly. 'Too expensive and no budget. Only two or three companies can do it that deep and they're busy. We got a rough price – eight million dollars, and then more,' he said, looking back out into the darkness.

Dan turned to the window as well, to the darkness, but the real darkness he was seeing was at the bottom of the Indian Ocean in its deepest trench.

'Six thousand metres. Convenient it's so deep there, but in other parts quite shallow …'

Lars's face coloured, his voice rose. 'I hear you, for fuck's sake. But if you think I'm gonna do it for you, or Denmark will,' he shook his head, 'think again. We're a small country. We don't have all your … you know. I don't want to know about this any more, and Denmark doesn't want to know about it, you got it?'

He looked at his watch, at the door, and was through it in seconds without a backward glance.

Dan finished the last couple of inches of his beer and stared down at the empty bottle. *Went well,* he thought, shaking his head softly. *Nice bedside manner, Dan. Well done. But that's not the Lars I know.*

SEVEN

Bulent Erkan was waiting behind the ropes as Choukri came through the doors from the immigration hall.

'Hey,' Bulent called, raising a hand and ducking behind the crowd to meet him. 'Good flight?'

'Fine. No problem.'

'You hungry? Let's get dinner.'

'Somewhere quiet,' Choukri said.

They stepped through the doors, exchanging air-conditioned marble for concrete that radiated the day's heat, a cloying humidity refusing to move in the still air.

'Here we go,' Bulent said as a valet-parking guy pulled up to them, the quiet disturbed by the roar from a powerful engine.

They turned from the airport road on to the Al Ittihad Expressway that ran through downtown Dubai to Sharjah. Bulent accelerated hard.

'Like it?' he said.

'It's fine,' Choukri said, glancing around inside the car. 'What is it?'

Bulent looked across. 'Porsche Cayenne.'

'Oh … can we get pizza?'

'Sure,' Bulent said, without enthusiasm.

He knew better than to press it. Ideologically there was little between them, though they set about it from different ends. He was also aware that sometimes he was prone to forget that the shipowner answered to the ship's mate.

The restaurant was behind a petrol station close to the Sharjah Expo centre. He had brought Choukri here before and knew its plainness met with his approval: a functional, modern building, but the lights were low, the tables well spaced and the Filipino staff attentive.

Choukri ordered a Pepsi and Bulent did the same. This was Sharjah, a dry state. He would have to wait until he was home before he could have a cold beer.

The waiter brought the drinks and some snacks. Bulent watched him put them down and walk away before he shifted his eyes to Choukri.

'So what happened … The *Danske Prince*?' he said.

'There isn't much to tell.' Choukri shrugged.

'But how did it go?'

'As we planned. In minutes we had the ship.'

Bulent looked across the table, his eyebrows raised.

'We trans-shipped the guns,' Choukri continued. 'It was a good trans-shipment. The crew did well. Then we laid the charges and it sank quickly.'

'And the crew?'

'Like I said, they did well,' Choukri said, scooping some hummus with his bread.

Bulent shook his head. 'Not ours, *theirs.*'

'Oh,' Choukri said absently, his mouth full.

Bulent waited while he chewed half of it, making room to speak.

'Buried at the mine in a container,' Choukri eventually said before looking up. 'You're down a container, but don't worry. I amended the asset inventory on board.'

It evidently didn't disturb Choukri. In the silence Bulent wondered if it disturbed him. He'd spent years with Europeans, got on well with Danes, and knew that individually the crew of the *Danske Prince* would have meant no harm. But any faith in people was one thing and entirely separate from the collectivity of states. In Germany he'd simply been a Turk, their Turk, their good Turk, who did their bidding. He dealt with difficult Turks in Turkey for them, difficult Arabs in Arabia, difficult Egyptians in Egypt, steering negotiations into a shape and outcome that benefited the German way of thinking. He earned their approval and no little amazement that he was actually capable of doing things the right way, their way, given that he was a Turk, a Muslim, and an altogether inferior being.

The waiter cleared the dishes away and brought the pizzas and more drinks. Choukri was eating quickly, in silence, concentrating on his food, his eyes lifting only when someone passed in or out of the door. Eventually he pushed his plate away. 'Khan showed me the firing scenarios. It has to be Moritz. In the morning we meet Rashid.'

'I think Rashid is busy,' Bulent said.

Choukri's eyes narrowed. 'Then make him un-busy.'

'You know they don't like Moritz,' Bulent said, opening his hands and looking across, his head tilted, his eyes requesting reasonableness.

The eyes across from him only hardened. 'I know, and we both know why. The old man wouldn't hesitate, but Rashid ...'

Bulent understood. Moritz would drag STC in as well. In addition, there was a vocal lobby that said it was a sacrifice too far. Rashid's father was an ideologist, not far from death and keen to go out in glory. Where he stood was clear, while Rashid enjoyed the trappings of wealth and a privileged future.

'And what will you do?' Choukri said, his tone unconcerned, and, as it seemed to Bulent, even mocking.

'Disappear,' Bulent replied casually. 'We all will. And then who knows?'

'And you're ready to give up all this?' Choukri said, reaching across and tapping a finger on the Rolex dangling from Bulent's wrist.

Bulent looked away but turned his eyes back to meet Choukri's.

'I might not be sacrificing as much as you,' he said, with a thin smile and an ironic shake of his watch. 'But I keep my end up.'

'Exactly.'

The smile on Choukri's face seemed to signal he was content to have got a rise from him, which Bulent acknowledged with a nod and a raised finger. 'And,' he said, 'don't push it. Don't push it with STC. Don't go in there swinging your muscles around. There's plenty of people wishing you'd never come up with this.'

'True. But not the Emir.'

'Who's changed his mind before,' Bulent said.

Choukri placed his hands flat on the table and leant in. 'But I'm not changing mine.'

'Okay, okay. Tomorrow,' Bulent said, beckoning the waiter over. 'C'mon, let's go.'

As he drove Choukri to his hotel, a three-star affair in keeping with the status of a ship's mate, Bulent pondered the question – *what will you do?*

Playing the international shipowner was fun, enjoying the respect of his peers, the interviews in trade magazines, the seats on panels at conferences. And then he would disappear, leaving people to shake their bewildered heads, thinking they had known him.

Easing his foot off the pedal and slowing for the turn to the hotel, Bulent glanced across at the back of Choukri's head. Tomorrow was Friday, the local weekend. Rashid would not be pleased about interrupting his leisure time to meet Choukri.

Choukri got out of the car and leant down to the window. 'Give me a call, early.'

Bulent turned on to the expressway and checked his watch. It was half past nine. He put his phone in the holder and dialled.

'It's as I thought. He wants to meet in the morning.'

The line went quiet for a few seconds. 'Well don't fucking bring him here. I don't want him here.'

'It's Moritz. Your office?'

'Moritz. Shit! Nine o'clock?'

'Have to be eight.'

'Shit.'

~

Choukri checked the television news in his hotel room. CNN was leading with an Istanbul car bomb that had exploded outside Galatasaray's stadium, just as the crowd were leaving the match. The numbers held his attention for a while, the dead and injured, but faded as his thoughts turned to the wish list. It was still in its infancy but starting to take shape, in his computer and in his mind.

There were three options for the guns' targeting programme – computer download of a target's image, laser guidance and map coordinates. For simplicity, and for the vast majority of targets, he had chosen the last option: map coordinates. For the rest, downloaded images would be used, for which the internet generously offered a multitude of crystal-clear pictures to choose from.

Long after midnight, with his eyelids heavy, he pushed up from the desk and stepped across to the open window. *It has to be Moritz*, he thought, and Bulent had been right. There were plenty opposed to it, and tomorrow he had to deal with Rashid, not his father.

With the warm night air washing over him, he turned it over in his mind. The corporate world held no interest but he understood that, principally, Sharjah Trade and Commerce was a trading house. It dealt in various commodities and also operated manufacturing facilities, a cement works and a chemical plant. In the marketplace the relationship was out in the open. Everyone knew that STC was an important customer for OceanBird. Bulent courted them, serviced the account diligently and conducted all affairs in a textbook fashion. Their contracts were usually legitimate. When they weren't, and should the shit hit the fan, each had a contingency to distance itself from the other. If arms were found in bags of cement, who put them there? Was it OceanBird or was it STC, or were they both innocent victims of something contrived by a third party?

But the father was in his sickbed, close to death, and the son was running the company now. He shook his head, regretting there would be no stories tomorrow of the old man's nostalgia for his youth, the traditions of honour, the feuding and raiding, the bellow of camels, the old Mauser rifles – Turkish relics from the First World War – a few grains of rice and a mouthful of stagnant water, but mostly for a breed of men toughened by hardship. And the glory, especially the glory.

EIGHT

Shortly after nine o'clock on Friday morning, the phone on Dan's desk rang. The caller's voice was unfamiliar. He listened. Thirty seconds later he said, 'Eleven o'clock. I'll be there.' Putting the phone down gently, he sat back in his chair. *Christ*, he thought.

Fifteen minutes before the hour, Dan set off down Bell Street. The rendezvous was only at Alf's, but he was certainly not going to risk being late. As he opened the door, he saw LaSalle was there already, pushing up from a table at the side and stepping across to the counter. He was a good few inches taller than Dan had first thought and, though dressed like an academic, carried himself like an athlete.

His hand enveloped Dan's own broad hand as though it were a child's. 'I understand the coffee's good here.' He smiled.

Dan knew Edmund LaSalle by reputation only: a big beast at the top of the heap, Deputy Director of MI5, though without a specific portfolio, concentrating broadly on strategy and development. He sensed power in everything about him ... understated, underlining. Behind those heavy-framed glasses were clear, perceptive eyes. They were not without a suggestion of kindness, but overwhelmingly they spoke of purpose.

He took a seat at the table, facing him, waiting while LaSalle measured a level teaspoon of sugar, lowered it gently to his cup and stirred twice, clockwise. Dan said nothing, watching, repeating the ritual.

'Rather quaint ...' LaSalle said, a curious smile playing on his face as he pushed an old-fashioned plate of biscuits across.

'This is Alf's,' Dan said. 'He does it his way.'

LaSalle took a sip of coffee. 'I've looked at your Indian Ocean report. What interests me is how you constantly argue against yourself – rather uncommon here – and at every turn present solid factual evidence for a tragic accident. Yet you don't believe it?' he added, looking up.

'They're just facts, and they're only true if you want to believe them.'

'What you choose to believe?'

'Yeah, you've got a choice. There's a fact to back everything up, but only if you want to believe.'

'And you're not making that choice, you don't have that faith. While others take them at face value?'

'Yeah. They've made a choice.'

'And I'm one of them,' LaSalle said, an eyebrow rising. 'Though I must say I understand your argument, which others do too. Though I dare say you don't *choose* to believe that.'

'That's not fair. You've just told me. Why wouldn't I believe you?'

LaSalle smiled. 'But we have to make an analysis, on both facts and supposition. And when the factual argument is overwhelmingly more convincing, which it is here, we must be guided by it.'

He reached across and selected a biscuit. Dan followed his lead.

'I'm not a seagoing man,' LaSalle continued. 'But I find the data compelling – the AIS, the InMarSat distress signals, the other satellite evidence …'

'Me too. But I've been in these places, on these ships, carrying these cargoes. It's too neat.'

'Too pat,' LaSalle mused. 'Besides, won't the Danes do our job for us?'

'Forget Denmark. They just want out. I know the guy doing the report and he's blanking everything. Doesn't want to know. Too emotional.' Dan stopped himself, aware for a moment of place and person, realising his voice had risen, that he'd been leaning across, crowding the space, too emotional in his railing against emotion. 'We weren't there,' he continued, sitting back, lowering his tone. 'We didn't see it with our own eyes. They're just blips on a screen. And they don't prove there's a ship attached to them. There's only a ship there if you want one to be.'

LaSalle snapped his biscuit in half, chewing it slowly, pondering. 'The digital age ... Its grip on otherwise intelligent people ... However, I fear the philosophical implications belong in some other forum, and not here, not today.' He rested the tips of his fingers under his nose, apparently deliberating over the last few words. He glanced at his watch. 'Interesting discussion, Dan, but we must move on. I understand you're in touch with Salim Hak?'

'That's right,' Dan said, wondering where this might be going.

'Good. And what's next?'

'I'm meeting him, Azmi and Nick Pittman this afternoon.'

'Good. I shall want to know everything to date, and everything that transpires between you, Hak and Azmi, and anyone else connected with your discussions. That's everything you say and do, everything they say and do – and your observations ...'

'My observations?' Dan said, tilting his head back.

'Your observations,' LaSalle confirmed, without elaboration. 'And, for reasons too tedious to go into now, I'm arranging a raid on OceanBird in Sharjah. Or I should say, our friends in MI6 are arranging it.'

Dan nearly spat a mouthful of coffee out. He straightened in his chair as LaSalle continued.

'Things have been strained between London and the Emirates and we're trying to rebuild the entente cordial. I was there last week and we reached an understanding with their new head man, and a little joint operation is an ideal way to develop the relationship. So, will that suit you?'

'Too right it will.'

'Good. And you do not mention this to anyone. It may percolate to the surface, procedurally, in MI6. And should that be so, we'll deal with it.' He sighed.

Dan took a sip of coffee. 'And do I know about this?' he said.

'You do.'

'What if they know that I know?'

'Everything has its cost,' LaSalle said, without irony.

'And you'll cover JC for me?'

LaSalle nodded. 'Keep me updated,' he said, reaching in his pocket and pulling out a card. 'Should you need to talk.' He eased his chair back, ready to leave.

'Just one thing,' Dan said. 'Do you believe Al Qaeda's finished, the "big one" a thing of the past, just mopping up now, the lone wolves?'

LaSalle sat back again and smiled. 'You know it's our policy.'

'Yeah, but do you believe it?'

'Let's just say that for the mass of our resources it's prudent.'

'But you think there's still a chance?'

LaSalle smiled again. Perhaps, Dan thought, at his persistence, because there was nothing that suggested he was patronising naïveté.

Eventually he said, 'I'm not closed-minded to the improbable.' He brushed some biscuit crumbs from the table to the plate and looked up. 'I read your file – you're an interesting man. And, as a naval man, you of all people should know about chains of command and their value, so I won't labour the point. In my experience, the only men here who indulge the luxury of ignoring their superiors' orders nearly always have private means or a rich wife. And you,' he added, 'have neither.'

He got to his feet, extending his hand across the table. 'And don't forget, I'm not here to save you from JC, and I'm certainly not here to save you from yourself. Just try to bend to the wind, won't you? In this business we meet a lot of wind and it's mostly strong and foul smelling.'

~

Dan walked along Millbank, gathering his thoughts. MI6 were just one bridge along the river, westward. It was a cold day with a bright sun filtering through the bare plane trees lining the embankment, though it failed to throw clear light on his coffee with LaSalle. The only thing he knew was that it had been both disorienting and encouraging if he put a conveniently self-centred spin on it. Meeting Azmi would be testing enough, without the disquieting feeling he would in effect be spying on a spy, an infinitely more experienced one than himself.

But wherever his thoughts ranged, they kept returning to LaSalle. Could the raid simply be a matter of convenience, as implied, with MI5 and MI6 keen to use it just to help patch up a loveless relationship? *If that's the case, why tell me?* They could just go ahead and, if something was found that incriminated OceanBird, they could tell me later, should they choose to. He couldn't understand it fully but was grateful to simply accept it, feeling it had to be a definite step in the right direction.

Lars was playing on his mind too. Leaving Hull to settle had seemed the best option, but he could not put off the inevitable indefinitely. He hadn't contacted Lars and there had been no word from Copenhagen. And just how, he reflected, should he have pitched such a scenario anyway? How do you move seamlessly from tragic accident to full-blown terrorist assault? What would have been the best way to dismantle an essentially good man's entire belief system and traduce his beloved sea and ships?

Knowing his name would flash up on Lars's phone, he took it as a positive sign when he heard him say, 'Hello.'

'Lars, it was good to see you last week and I'm sorry I had to lay all that on you.'

'Me too.'

'I was wondering, now it's been a while, maybe you've thought about it a bit?'

'Yeah, I think about it, and I don't want to talk about it, okay.'

Dan stood still, staring at the pavement, gathering his thoughts, but Lars beat him to it, adding, 'Don't call me any more about this.'

The line cut.

'For fuck's sake …' Dan sighed, lifting his eyes and meeting the stern gaze of a smartly dressed woman walking a Dachshund.

It was his first visit to MI6. He lingered, putting off the inevitable, his mind switching between the impending meeting and the phone call. *I would have listened to your argument*, he thought. *I would have respected it. But you didn't really have one. All you had was blind faith and extra time to confirm your prejudices.* Taking a deep breath of cold air, he resolved to shut it out and focus on the here and now.

He headed over the plaza to the main entrance, stepping across a security moat, the first of two. The building's creamy stonework and scarab green paint looked sharp in the harsh winter light, redolent of Egypt, a sphinx stretching languorously down to the river, as pleased with itself as a well-fed cat.

At the reception counter an efficient woman – one of three – reassured a civilian who seemed anxious about her first experience of an outré world, fearing that once inside she would never be allowed to leave. Dan presented his ID as though it was routine. One of the receptionists phoned through to Hak and indicated a long row of leather seats across the atrium.

His feet echoed on the stone floor, the sound reflecting from the high ceiling. Letting his eyes drop, he wondered what lay beneath, aware there were numerous subterranean levels housing sensitive departments and data centres.

The space was momentarily quiet. When he'd stepped through the doors, thirty or more people were criss-crossing. Now there were barely a dozen. With sideways glances, he checked them out: civilians, diverse visitors, contractors, MI5 and GCHQ people and two men with an air of Special Branch about them.

Obscured behind some exotic plants to his left were four Africans. Three of them sat stiffly in business suits, marginally apart from the remaining one, who was relaxed and resplendent in silks of green, tangerine and purple, his pillbox hat set at a jaunty angle. Across to the right, a Frenchman spoke in hushed English to a clean-cut American.

After the momentary lull, the atrium was filling again. He recognised a man from MI5, comparing him for a moment with himself, with others, but failing to identify what might distinguish MI6 operatives from their counterparts in MI5.

From behind the security barrier, Hak beckoned, swinging a lanyard in his hand.

'Looks dangerous, but he's really one of ours,' he quipped to the guard.

Dan held the visitor pass over the scanner and passed through the gate with a forced attempt at an appeasing smile, wondering if 'everything', in LaSalle's book, extended to Hak's possibly affected insouciance. But he made a mental note all the same, in case it should prove relevant when reporting his observations.

Hak led the way through the inner sanctum, along a wide, lofty corridor to a row of lifts. The doors slid back with barely a hiss and Dan looked out through a tinted glass wall to layers of terraced geometric gardens, descending to the river beyond.

'Babylon,' Hak said, his eyebrows bobbing, as the lift rose as effortlessly as a hawk on a thermal.

Dan hesitated at a 'Meeting Rooms' sign, on what he had noted was the eighth floor.

'No, this way.' Hak grinned. 'He doesn't trust meeting rooms. Sees spies everywhere.'

'Even here?' Dan said, casting a furtive glance around.

'Doesn't shake hands either. Just give him a nod,' Hak said as they reached the end of the corridor. After a knock at the door, they stepped through to a large office.

Befitting Azmi's status, the fittings were expensive, though the decor was sombre and the bright lighting jarred. *To make people feel less comfortable?* Dan wondered, noting the low temperature and the seemingly careless, though perhaps contrived, way that the mundane paraphernalia of daily life was draped over and around everything. In the blink of an eye he took in dusty and tattered cardboard boxes haphazardly stacked against a wall, a bicycle wheel, and a grubby hi-vis jacket, partly on an expensive leather sofa and partly on the plush carpet. A waste-paper basket overflowed with food packaging, contributing to the musty scent in the air.

A man looking at some wallcharts turned and smiled. He introduced himself with an iron handshake – Nick Pittman, Hak's immediate boss and head of the Pakistan desk.

'And this is Akhtar Azmi,' he added, sweeping a hand towards the window, 'head of the Indian subcontinent – 1.7 billion troublesome souls.'

A small man emerged from behind a mountain of buff-coloured files piled across a large desk. He walked around it without haste and looked up, straight into Dan's eyes, and said, 'How do you do,' with a perceptible nod. 'Thirty-one million more if you count Nepal and Bhutan, which I am always mindful to do.'

Both Hak and Pittman acknowledged Nepal and Bhutan with a nod.

'So,' Azmi said, gesturing to a table at the side of the room. 'You've been with MI5 for a few months now. Settling in well?'

'It's all good.'

'And you're keen on brotherly communication between our agencies?'

'Very much,' Dan confirmed.

'I'm not,' Azmi replied, turning and casting a weary eye at his desk. 'I have ample bloody paper, and so many memos from Miss Clymer. They gave me a present at Christmas,' he added, glancing disdainfully to the floor at his side.

Dan looked down. A box, still in its wrapping, the sealing tape unpicked – a shredder.

'It was Mr LaSalle who put you on to me, I think?' he said, switching the subject.

Azmi nodded. 'Indeed.'

'He's well informed.'

'Of course he is,' Azmi said, matter-of-factly.

Hak smiled across the table, as if to say *don't mind the old man, he's just warming up.*

'One thing before we get started,' Nick Pittman said. 'You know the *Ocean Dove* arrived in Bar Mhar the day before yesterday?'

Dan nodded.

'The customs office sent a man to deal with it, and we haven't seen anything that suggests unusual circumstances.'

'Pakistan customs report to you?' Dan said.

'Not really. We've got an intercept on their server. Anyway, the shipyard asked for a customs officer to be sent and he—'

'When did they send the request?' Dan cut in.

Pittman smiled. 'Twentieth November, I'm afraid – about two weeks before the ship disappeared.'

'So,' Azmi said, opening a hand. 'India lost its guns and they're unhappy. And you lost a ship and you're unhappy. What caused this accident?'

'Accident,' Hak repeated, with emphasis.

'Denmark's running the investigation and it's going to take a while,' Dan said. 'I know about the voyages, the cargo, the way it was packed, how it was stowed on the ship, but not what set it off.'

'Well, tell me,' Azmi said, opening his hands again in invitation. 'Let's hear it.'

'The *Danske Prince* loaded the guns in Varberg, Sweden, came through the Baltic, round the Skaw peninsula of northern Denmark and dropped down to Rotterdam,' Dan said.

Azmi raised a hand to stop the flow. 'And loaded the ammunition in Varberg?'

'The ammunition too.'

'Continue … all the details please.'

'In Rotterdam it picked up two containers of dynamite for one of the iron-ore mines upcountry from Freetown, Sierra Leone. Then there were three containers of small-arms ammo from England for delivery to the Nigerian Army in Warri, and—'

'*Which* port in England?' Azmi said without lifting his eyes, his pencil hovering over a notepad.

'Sheerness.'

'Continue.'

'And the Nigerian cargo was manufactured at one of the old Royal Ordnance plants, now part of BAE – like Bofors.'

Heads nodded at the mention of BAE.

'From Sheerness it went out through the Channel, across Biscay and down the coast of West Africa. First port of call was Freetown. No problems there, in and out in twelve hours. Five days later they arrived in Warri where they sat for two weeks while the Nigerian military screwed up the import processes. It's Nigeria …'

'Shit happens,' Hak said.

'Port Elizabeth in South Africa was next, for fuel and stores, and to load two containers of ammonium nitrate for delivery to Colombo, Sri Lanka.'

The other three all looked up. 'Ammonium nitrate,' Pittman said, making a note in his pad.

The implication of ammonium nitrate was mutually understood. Its principal use around the world was as a fertilizer, but it could be unstable. Dan knew their thoughts were focused entirely on its notoriety as the explosive component of choice in IEDs.

'I'm with you, but the local shipper was South Africa Petrochemical Corporation,' he said, 'and the amm-nit trade out of Port Elizabeth is well known, well regulated and totally legitimate. Accidents happen, but this is meat and drink to SAPET and the *Danske Prince*. They know what they're doing.'

'Knew,' Azmi reflected.

'Knew,' Dan corrected himself. 'I checked the cargo data. The packing and handling procedures were by the book, the stowage on board, the building of bulkheads in the hold to segregate cargoes – it was all correct.'

'But something went wrong,' Pittman said.

'Something did,' Dan said, looking around the table at each of them. 'Now we move on,' he continued. 'The *Ocean Dove*'s voyage started in Jebil Ali, UAE, sailing directly to Maputo in southern Mozambique, which it left on the Monday morning, heading back north again, where its route converged, quite rightly, with the *Danske Prince* at 8 a.m. on Tuesday, but always with the *Ocean Dove* an hour or twelve miles ahead. For the next five days the ships kept pace with each other, with the *Danske Prince* a few miles behind.'

'Is that normal?' Hak said.

'Yeah. They were both on the correct route and ships like to follow other ships—'

Hak looked at him questioningly. 'They do?'

'The data tells you already who's around and where they're going – so you're kinda familiar. And you can pass useful information, like telling the following ship about a hazard in the water, or just tell them to get their fishing lines out for a shoal of something.'

They seemed satisfied with the explanation, so he moved on. 'It's better if you see this on screen,' he said, plugging his laptop into the jack on the desk. He projected an image on the wall screen.

'I worked back from the accident site, tracking both ships from when the *Ocean Dove* left Maputo an hour ahead of the *Danske Prince*, checking the gap between them and specifically when other ships intercepted them. The Mozambique channel is a busy route, so other north and southbound ships regularly passed by. When they left the channel and fanned out into the Indian Ocean there was still plenty of traffic around, but then it became less. So I set a hypothetical target: when was the first time the ships had a two- or three-hour window when no one would intercept them, when no one was within about fifty miles?'

They had all turned to the screen, the backs of their heads to Dan. Pittman was scratching distractedly at his chin. Hak was perfectly still. Azmi shifted his chair and leant in a little more.

'This is the *Danske Prince* and this is the *Ocean Dove*, and these dots are the other ships around them. This is Maputo on Monday. Now watch. Monday, Tuesday, Wednesday, all the time there's other ships that can see them and they don't get any time alone. Same on Thursday and Friday. And now Saturday, late afternoon, what do you see?'

'We see,' Azmi said, without turning, his head nodding.

'You've got the *Topaz* sixty miles south-east and the *Stadt Hamburg* ninety west. The *Prince* and the *Dove* are on their own, at least three hours to themselves, out of sight – and what happened?'

Dan's eyes switched from the back of one head to another. They were still, concentrating on the screen. Hak's thick black hair glinted under the light. Azmi's bald head glistened, the age blotches bright with maroon, purple and black.

'Opportunity …' Pittman speculated.

'For what?' Azmi said, to no one in particular.

Hak turned. 'But we know the two ships were never near each other.'

'That's what the data confirms,' Dan said.

'Sure,' Hak replied. 'And if we don't believe the data, what happened?'

'The two ships were together and they trans-shipped the cargo.'

'And can the data be manipulated?' Pittman said.

'I'm no electronics expert, but it stands to reason it can.'

'Okay, assuming they do this trans-shipment?' Pittman said. 'This is heavy stuff, right – don't they need to be at a port?'

'They're geared,' Azmi said quietly, almost to himself, his head still turned to the screen.

Geared? Dan thought. An interesting use of terminology, remembering something Hak had said in the pub the first time they met.

He picked the point up without comment and elaborated. 'They've got their own cranes. You just put the ships alongside each other and the cranes swing across. Four guns and twelve ammo containers. That's sixteen lifts at about three minutes each, so forty-eight minutes – half that with two cranes.'

'All over in under thirty minutes?' Pittman reflected.

'Yeah, basically,' Dan said, looking around the table at each of them in turn.

It was Azmi who broke the silence. 'And what about the data from the ship itself – the *Ocean Dove?*'

'I haven't seen it yet but it won't be much use,' Dan said. 'Because of its age, it's not required by law to record longer than twelve hours.'

'And that's from when?' Hak said.

'Well, the French were on site early on Monday morning – so Sunday evening?'

'Hmm,' Pittman grunted. 'Completely useless.'

'What about the crew?' Hak said. 'Any suggestion of collusion?'

'The *Danske Prince*? I seriously doubt that. Where are they now, drinking beers on a beach? And then there's the funerals ...'

'Geopolitically. India ... Pakistan?' Pittman mused.

'It's hardly a rogue state getting its hands on nuclear weapons,' Azmi said pithily, scratching his head and frowning.

He turned in his seat, his chin on upturned hands, his narrowed eyes raking Dan's face. 'I don't buy this. The crew of the *Ocean Dove* are seamen, not assassins. And it's stirring up a hornet's nest on my patch and that I will not abide. You're barking up the wrong tree, and besides, it's way beyond Five's remit so why are you and LaSalle wasting your bloody time, and mine? The only one making any sense is your Miss Clymer.'

On that note, he pushed up from the table and shuffled towards his desk, glancing back over his shoulder. 'Keep this strictly confidential. Pakistan and India are …'

Salim Hak and Nick Pittman looked at each other, at Dan, as Azmi sank from sight. In unison they completed his sentence for him. 'A riddle.'

NINE

Rashid took a head-clearing dip in his pool at six thirty in the morning. His villa was on an exclusive estate in Dubai, which boasted a championship golf course, marina and tennis club. Part of his schooling had been in Switzerland, before an MBA from the University of South Florida in Tampa, so the more conservative regime of Sharjah didn't altogether suit him.

A Pakistani maid served breakfast on the terrace. She was sixteen, willow thin, the daughter of one of Hassan Khan's cousins – a relationship that was keeping her virginity intact.

His eyes followed her gently swaying hips as she turned and went back to the house, the tip of his tongue on dry lips. His gaze dropped, her image fading and Choukri's appearing in his mind.

They were both the same age, thirty-two, born within weeks of each other. But Rashid was painfully aware that one of them was just five feet six tall and had a soft paunch spilling over the top of his swimming trunks. But at least today, with his father incapacitated, he wouldn't have to endure seeing his eyes light up at the sight of Choukri.

Bulent's car was already there when he drove his AMG Mercedes into the car park.

'Looking good,' Rashid said, stepping across to where Choukri was standing.

The handshake was crushing. He steeled himself and kept the pain from his eyes, welcoming Choukri like an old friend.

They stood back and ran an eye over each other; Choukri in chain-store working clothes, Rashid in pearly white jeans and a black Dolce & Gabbana shirt with silver trim and buttons.

Rashid apologised with a grin for his inability to operate the big Italian coffee maker in his PA's side room. 'There's a vending machine in reception,' he said, glancing to Bulent.

Bulent raised his hands. 'I've got it.'

Rashid's office was large and expensively furnished. To one side was a meeting area with fluffy white carpeting and black leather sofas around a coffee table the size of a honeymoon bed.

Choukri had his back to him, looking at photographs on the walls. Rashid asked after family and health, receiving a singular 'Fine' to each enquiry. His own father's health was open knowledge and while he hoped for the return of the courtesy, it was not forthcoming.

'Please,' he said, gesturing to the meeting area as Bulent returned from the reception hall, his hands cradling plastic cups.

'It has to be Moritz,' Choukri said, wasting no time.

Rashid sat back. 'Yes, Bulent said that was one of the options you were considering.'

Choukri leant forward and put his coffee down. 'It's not an option.'

Rashid looked across but failed to catch Bulent's eye. His phone call last night had left little room for doubt that Choukri's mind was made up, and he would have welcomed support.

'There are alternatives,' Rashid said. 'They'll work just as well. And besides, we don't have the money.'

'They won't work. I've seen the firing scenarios from Khan, and we have the money. The Emir has pledged it.'

'I don't think the Emir realises the cost,' Rashid said.

'The cost for what?' Choukri said. 'For you? If we go to some other terminal there will be people. They'll see us, they'll phone the authorities within one minute, and five minutes later some hero in another ship will ram us.'

'They want too much,' Rashid said. 'Seven and a half million dollars. Ridiculous. Plus dismantling and packing, shipping, import taxes, reinstallation. And a lot of the plant is outdated technology. It needs updating, so that's another five. You're looking at a fifteen mill project. It's crazy money.'

'Then negotiate. Isn't that what you do?' Choukri said.

Rashid smiled. 'It's not that simple.'

Bulent broke the silence. 'More coffee?'

'No,' Choukri said irritably. 'How much then?'

'Two, maybe three million. No more,' Rashid said.

'And the dismantling?'

Rashid's head wavered from side to side as he estimated the figure. 'Maybe three quarters.'

'So, we pay that and get the price for the plant down to three, maybe four million – all to be paid upfront before they allow us to put the ship in and load the cargo?'

'Yeah, it has to be upfront,' Rashid said.

'We can arrange stage payments,' Bulent added, 'spread the cost of the plant and the dismantling over about three or four months, but everyone will want final payment before there's any talk of the ship coming in and taking the cargo away.'

'Then it's clear,' Choukri said. 'And we have a budget of five million.'

'Which we don't have,' Rashid said, stabbing the air with a finger.

Choukri turned to Bulent. 'How long will the dismantling take, two months?'

'Three will be safer.'

'Okay, so we wrap up the negotiations for the plant by the end of February. The dismantling contractor works through March, April, May, and the cargo will be packed and waiting on the wharf, ready for loading. The ship arrives on a Thursday morning. We take the pilot on board and berth at about noon.'

Bulent was tapping a thumbnail on his teeth. 'Thursday won't work,' he said.

Choukri turned. 'Why?'

'There's no customs office at Moritz. They'll have to send a customs guy to clear the ship and do the crew immigration and so on. And that guy will inspect the entire ship, and the hold …'

'We can deal with him,' Choukri said.

'Sure we can, but he'll go missing and they'll be looking for him.'

'Shit. You're right,' Choukri said. 'Then we arrive on Friday. No one will miss him for a few hours. And the pilot's no problem. He'll go straight to the bridge and won't know what's in the hold. We just put him ashore and say thank you.'

'What if the customs inspection is late?' Rashid said.

Choukri shrugged. 'No problem. If the guy is late or doesn't show up, we just carry on.'

Rashid sat in silence, chewing it over. It sounded so definite and Choukri was brooking no doubt. And he had no doubt that it was going to happen just the way Choukri said it would. There was exhilaration at being part of it. But it was tinged with fear and regret and resentment at what he stood to lose. He had made his pact with the Emir, as had his father before him, and Bulent, and the Emir had made them all what they were today. This day had to come and they all knew it. No amount of wishful thinking would make it go away.

'So,' Choukri said after a while, 'it's agreed.'

Rashid shifted in his seat as Choukri got up, stepped around the coffee table and sat down next to him.

'Make it happen. Go next week,' Choukri said, gripping his arm.

His face was barely inches from Rashid's own, his pupils shrinking to dots. Rashid felt himself squirm but Choukri only gripped his arm more tightly, before letting it go with a flick of his fingers.

'I can't go!' Rashid said, feeling blood rushing hotly to his cheeks.

He pushed up to his feet, pacing about the room and flexing his arm, which he knew would show bruising within the hour.

Behind him, he heard Choukri's level voice. 'Yes you can.'

'I can't fucking go,' Rashid said, his anger rising. He stopped and turned. 'It only puts the price up. What do they think when the CEO suddenly flies in? Ah ha, they want this plant, we have them … This is business – things you don't know.'

Bulent raised a mollifying hand. 'He's right. Better to send Jawad.'

'Precisely,' Rashid said. 'Jawad's a chemical engineer, for fuck's sake.'

'And he's sharp,' Bulent said. 'He's perfect for it.'

Choukri was quiet for a moment before conceding. 'Okay, Jawad can go next week.'

'No!' Rashid snapped. 'He doesn't go next week. He talks to them next week and tells them he's busy with other projects but will fit it in his schedule soon.'

'Besides,' Bulent added, 'it's Christmas, the new year. Nothing gets done.'

'Okay,' Choukri said, getting to his feet. 'But no delays.' He looked about the room at the various doors, adding, 'I've got to take a shit.'

'Out in the hall on the right,' Rashid said, pointing to a door at the side and not to his private bathroom.

When Choukri's back had disappeared through the door and the sound of footsteps had faded, Bulent patted down the air with his hands. 'Be cool, Rashid.'

'Cool? I hope this is the last time I see that fucking psycho.'

'He's just thick-skinned.'

'Skin? That's not skin, that's scales.'

Bulent pushed himself up and stretched his legs. 'Don't part on bad terms. Make your peace. If he thinks there's a weak link, you know what can happen ...'

Rashid breathed out heavily. 'I know. But would that be so bad?' he said, adding an ironic smile.

'Let him know you are with him,' Bulent said.

Choukri came back through the door with fresh coffee in his hands, giving them each a cup before he sat down. Rashid had seen this in the past. With Choukri, if it was carrot and stick, it was nearly always stick, but how the carrot was appreciated when it appeared. He'd seen the effect on others and he recognised how he too was drawn in.

He got up and went across to Choukri, taking the seat next to him.

'Don't doubt it'll be done. It *will* be,' he said, nodding his head and narrowing his eyes for emphasis. 'Now, you leave tonight, but before that you must see my father. He's only got weeks to live.'

'And maybe he'll have a story for me,' Choukri said, his face brightening.

'This afternoon?' Rashid said.

'We'll do that.' Choukri nodded. He paused before adding, 'Now this is important. When I was with the Emir we discussed the lead-up. For some months there will be random operations – airports, streets, clubs, where there's people, where they're relaxing. Europe, the US, anywhere it hurts and gets attention. It will be a distraction and …'

'Keep the security forces occupied …' Rashid said, glancing across to Bulent. Neither of them had mentioned the bomb at the Galatasaray match in Istanbul, among Bulent's own people.

'Exactly,' Choukri continued. 'What they call *lone-wolf* attacks. They think we're weak, only capable of small things. And when the public panics, they must be seen to be busy, so they use all their resources. And while all this is happening they are thinking that we have never been further away. They think it's all in the past, that they are winning … So, the *Ocean Dove* trades on, STC makes plans for Moritz and our brothers around the world make noise. They don't know why, but they know it must be heard in the highest places, and it will.'

He drained the last of his coffee. 'There's something else. People have been asking around in Pakistan. It's just one guy doing the asking.'

'But he's in the way,' Rashid said, allowing his tone to suggest it was a statement rather than a question.

Choukri's head rocked from side to side. 'I don't know too much about him yet. Could be better just to feed him some good news. Our guys know what he wants to hear.'

'And if that doesn't work?'

'Then we deal with him.' Choukri shrugged.

Rashid opened his hands questioningly. 'It's just routine?'

Choukri nodded. 'Sure – the guns, the *Ocean Dove* going to Bar Mhar. They've got to ask …'

'Whose security, the Americans?' Bulent said.

TEN

Dan stepped into the office and handed across a package wrapped in tinfoil.

'Julie's Christmas cake,' he said.

'Thanks,' Vikram smiled. 'You had a good time – did you go to Suffolk?'

Dan looked down. 'No, we didn't make it ...' But then his face brightened. 'Otherwise it was perfect. Did absolutely nothing. A major improvement on last year. And you?'

'Great thanks,' Vikram said, raising a trouser leg theatrically and flashing lurid new socks.

Dan raised his eyebrows. 'Get you. Sexy beast.'

'What happened last year then?' Vikram said.

Dan sat down. 'You know our flat ... We had my mother over with her new boyfriend. Total slimeball. Couldn't hold his drink, pissed by lunchtime and calling me *Captain* – thinking he's very clever. Next thing I know he's in the kitchen and he's got his hand on Julie's arse. You know, up her skirt. And I mean right up!'

His eyes rolled to the ceiling as the image flashed through his mind. The grope was bad enough, but it was the leer and dribble from wine-stained lips that he would never forget. 'So Julie's whacked him and *he's* getting stroppy – can you believe that? And I'm ready to ...'

Vikram grimaced. 'So he had turkey in hospital?'

'It was Christmas.' Dan shrugged. 'My mother was there. Peace and goodwill to all men ...'

Last year's celebrations were a struggle he had difficulty forgetting and, looking on the bright side, a resounding success this year. The only drawback was returning to work. With money tight and enthusiasm for festivity scarce, they had closed the door, done absolutely nothing and seen no one. Julie's parents had won a cruise and Dan's mother had gone away with another new boyfriend.

'You're just like your fucking father,' had been her parting words last year – a father he couldn't remember. She knew they were the worst six words for him to hear. It came as no surprise that they didn't speak to each other until the summer.

Both Dan and Julie had taken some extra time off and devoted it to each other and Phoebe. They had examined the family budget and set a spending cap – no unnecessary outlay until June. A resolution had been made about the unhappy state of their careers. Julie would try to find a way to get paid by her clients and find clients and work that was profitable, and Dan would make a conscious effort to understand, live with, and bend himself to the security service. If one or both of them made no progress, they would be free to start again with something else. This was also to be reviewed in June.

'June,' Dan had said. 'The world will be a better place in June.'

'It will,' Julie happily agreed.

But now it was early January and though the sun may have been shining, it was bitterly cold. From the window he could see St Jude's Gardens, just along Bell Street, where frost was on the ground in the shadows and a handful of early snowdrops clustered around the bases of bare trees.

From a work perspective, not much had happened over Christmas, but he'd taken ten days off and needed to catch up, go through his files and update his correspondence.

'Any news?' he said, glancing round.

Vikram shook his head while he finished a mouthful of Christmas cake. 'Quiet.'

'And?' Dan said, nodding at Richard Nuttall's empty chair.

'Not sure,' Vikram said. 'I think he's seeing his old boss.'

'Figures.' Dan pondered. 'At least I can eat his piece of cake ...'

Vikram turned away. 'Is our team going to be short of a player, and perhaps one more ...?'

Dan shrugged. 'Not my intention.'

'Oh yeah, I nearly forgot,' Vikram said, swinging round again in his chair. He slipped his glasses from his nose, polishing them with a blue-and-yellow checked handkerchief. 'There was something. Just before New Year I was in Thames House, coming out of a meeting. I heard voices along the corridor. JC and someone else. And I thought I recognised the other voice. It was getting loud and I heard your name, and Pakistan and Hak. So I slowed down, stayed around the corner. Anyway, that's all I heard.'

'Loud … like arguing loud?' Dan said.

Vikram nodded.

'And then?'

'Nothing. So I turned the corner and there's JC and LaSalle. They hadn't heard me coming. They both stopped, looked at me, and I just walked past.'

'Did she say anything later?'

'No.'

Dan pondered it for a moment. 'Well, thanks for that,' he said, turning back to his desk.

He checked the AIS website for the *Ocean Dove*'s position. On Christmas Eve the ship had left Bar Mhar for Dubai, arriving on Boxing Day. Using the ship's precise coordinates, he narrowed the location down to the Halliburton wharf in Dubai's Jebil Ali port complex.

It sailed again on 29 December, heading for Balikpapan, Indonesia. The ETA was 14 January, a direct voyage of sixteen days.

Okay, he thought, it completed repairs in Bar Mhar, ballasted to Dubai and loaded a full cargo. It was very likely to be oil-related machinery and almost certainly on Halliburton's behalf, though from time to time third-party cargo passed over their terminal.

Dan had been to Balikpapan, as first officer on the *Astrid* with Lars Jensen as his captain. It was a hotspot for the oil industry, with oil majors and service companies clustered around the giant refinery operated by Pertamina, the state oil company. It was perfectly typical of the kind of trade a ship like the *Ocean Dove* would be active in. So what could he deduce from it? The answer was absolutely nothing.

A picture was forming in his mind of the *Ocean Dove*, its cargo, and the negotiations that led to it being fixed by Bulent Erkan, who he knew from Hugh Pinchon, the shipbroker at the Lloyd's reception, as a 'really short fat guy, all Armani and Gucci and giant Rolex, but a great guy.'

Dan looked at his LinkedIn picture in the file again, trying but failing to connect his own preconceptions with the broker's description. Yes, he was a fat guy, but wasn't that a thin person's face underneath before too much of the good life had taken its toll? The mouth was too small now and the lips too thin, encased in those jowls. And could that be a hint of cruelty in those eyes, or were they just struggling for room?

Mubarak hadn't got around to adding a picture to his profile, but, interestingly, he'd sailed on the *Ocean Dove* when it was owned by Claus Reederie in Germany – as Lars had said in Hull. He'd been its first officer and then its captain. Dan knew there was nothing unusual in officers transferring with a ship when it was sold to new owners. It brought continuity, particularly on the technical side, where a chief engineer may have been on a ship since it was built and knew all its foibles.

And Hassan Khan, CEO at Bar Mhar? He scrolled down. Khan was every inch the marine engineer: neat and studious, keen to list all his qualifications, certificates and appropriate experience. Dan looked through his profile, stopping at Karachi Shipyard, where Khan was proud to say he had led the team responsible for the weaponry installation on the sword-class frigates.

So, there was Khan, a young and ambitious engineer with good qualifications and a solid start to his career at the Gulf Arabian Shipbuilding and Repair Yard. Then he's offered the chance to go home, to Karachi, to a good position. Perhaps he didn't 'lead' the team on the frigates. Perhaps he was responsible for something mundane lower down the chain? After all, it was only LinkedIn, where a licence to embroider was happily exploited by the vast majority of its users. And that was when he went off the rails and became involved with Bofors guns. *Oh yeah?* Really, with his expert knowledge of weapons plastered all over the web ...

Closing the file, his eyes drifted to the window, wishing he was on the *Ocean Dove*. Its tropical outlook was more attractive than outside, where flurries of snow were swirling in the wind along Bell Street.

He swivelled his chair round. 'You said you recognised LaSalle's voice. I didn't know you knew him?'

'I don't really,' Vikram said, turning to face him. 'It's this India Liaison Group thing.'

'Do I know about that?'

'The inter-agency cooperation initiative?'

Dan shook his head.

'I'm on the India Group. JC put me up for it. There's us, MI6 and GCHQ. We had a kick-off meeting after work a couple of weeks ago. Just drinks, informal, you know. And LaSalle was there. He's chairing the India Group.'

'Who else was there?'

'JC, some guys from GCHQ and some others from Six.'

'Some others like Azmi, Salim Hak, Nick Pittman?'

'Yeah. Azmi and Hak. I didn't know you knew them.'

Dan shrugged. 'I got a call from Salim Hak about the *Ocean Dove* and he wanted to meet. And JC was on to me about getting in touch with him.'

'Circles …' Vikram said.

'What do you reckon on Salim Hak?'

'I couldn't really tell you, but I know he used to be field, and a good operator by all accounts. Broke his back in Afghanistan and got captured. Then the Taliban smashed his hand up with a rifle butt. Held him for five months, apparently. Can't have been pleasant,' Vikram added, with understatement.

'No,' Dan said. 'So now he's behind a desk. And Azmi?'

Vikram smiled. 'The old man? Supposed to be something of a legend in the service. But I don't know him.'

'I can't make Hak out. One minute he's staring straight into your eyeballs, and the next he's drilling holes in the floor. All public school and posh "dear boy". You should see him put the wine away, and then he's joking about being a Muslim – but I kinda like him.'

'Azmi's a Muslim too. At least I assume he is. It's a Muslim name, and so's Akhtar. And I don't think he drinks. Only had fruit juice when I saw him.'

'I met him. Bit weird, but clever. Maybe too clever. A hard nut too – doesn't take prisoners.'

'Doesn't suffer fools gladly is the term, I think.' Vikram smiled. 'Oh yeah,' he added, 'and Salim Hak's some kind of international backgammon player. Had to leave early to catch a flight to a tournament.'

'Where was that?'

'Can't remember. Somewhere warm. He joked about it, you know,' Vikram said, eyeing the weather outside disapprovingly and shaking his head.

'Monte Carlo, Rimini?'

'I can't remember. Does it matter?'

'No,' Dan said, turning back to his desk.

Outside, the snow was gusting in the wind, random, haphazard, unlike the information lined up neatly against him. The argument, or, more accurately, the factual data, was firmly against his hypothesis. As he chewed it over, he had to concede it was barely a hypothesis and more simply a suspicion. All he had was conjecture about something that didn't smell right to him. Others disagreed and pointed conclusively to the data. And should he care, he wondered. Clymer had told him he was losing his focus, and looming over it all was the promise he had made to Julie – to make a conscious effort to understand, live with, and bend himself to the security service.

His report to LaSalle was overdue and needed to be sent. It was complete, but he was comfortable with neither it nor with the situation. As for 'observations', as LaSalle had put it, they were somewhere between brief and absent. What, he reasoned, could he read into Azmi, or Hak for that matter? He was finding them both obscurely unreadable and, until he felt he was standing on firmer ground, there was an unwillingness to aim an opening salvo anywhere near his own foot.

The report was clear that he'd withheld nothing from Azmi, Pittman or Hak. All his theories and scenarios had been shared, all their questions answered straightforwardly. They knew what he was thinking without ambiguity. The only omission, from both the report and during the meeting, was any mention of the second voyage being shadowed by the *Ocean Dove*. It hadn't been his intention to withhold it; it was more a case of the right moment failing to present itself. Though now, in hindsight, and without properly understanding if it would prove significant, something was telling him he should be pleased he hadn't disclosed it.

The Christmas break had offered plenty of time for thought, but not sufficient for insight. At times he'd allowed himself the luxury of feeling he might have achieved something. LaSalle had taken an interest and he carried considerable weight. That he had his own agenda was beyond dispute. *But what exactly was it?* Dan gnawed the top of his pen.

One thing was clear. LaSalle wanted information carried to and from MI6 and, for a man in his position, he'd gone to some lengths to select an appropriate vehicle. *Yes, he took a good, hard look at me.* Dan nodded to himself; LaSalle had checked personnel files, argued with JC – and won, of course. Then he'd carefully selected the venue, allotting more time than would otherwise have been reasonably due, *and humoured me.*

But was that strictly true? he thought. Perhaps he had weighed LaSalle wrongly. Perhaps the setting, the tone, offering coffee and a selection of Alf's biscuits with one of the gods, privately, informally, was his trick, to demonstrate how easy it was to make mistakes about people and about caseloads. He would have had every right to sit there, showing little more than disdain for the banality of the proceedings and the tiresomeness of a green case officer who was stepping out of line, but he hadn't. Perhaps it wasn't an act.

At no time had he mentioned the *Ocean Dove* and India or Pakistan in the same breath. Neither had he specifically said the file should be closed, though it was beyond doubt that he knew Clymer's position. Admittedly, he'd been clear he felt the case held little water, but he hadn't said 'bin it'. Dan clearly remembered what he had said. 'I'm not closed-minded to the improbable.' Why would a man who weighed his words as carefully as an Antwerp merchant weighed diamonds leave a door ajar? To encourage me to do his bidding?

His train of thought was broken by an incoming message from Lars.

'We got everything from the French. They wanted to keep it and do the investigation in France. No way we accept that. Tried to call you but missed. Give me a call. I got something for you.'

ELEVEN

'Hi, Jawad, real good to meet you.'

'Please, my friends call me Joe.'

'Okay, Joe, that's great. Let's get you some coffee. Max will be with us shortly.'

Joe took a seat. The meeting room was on the eighth floor. Its windows looked down on a square, half in shadow from the buildings around it. There was a video-conferencing screen at one end of the room, whiteboards on the wall and a dozen plush chairs surrounding a large table. He'd dressed carefully in plain black shoes, black socks, charcoal grey suit, a dark blue tie over a pale blue shirt and a modest watch just showing under the cuff. His hair was neatly cut and he was clean-shaven. The impression he wanted to give was lawyer, surgeon or private banker. In the shaving mirror he'd practised bringing a twinkle to his eye, a twinkle that would suggest a discreet and successful practice in any one of those professions, with clients who trusted him and enjoyed his company.

An oversized white cup and saucer was placed at his side. 'You wanna get chocolate shakings on that?'

'Thank you.' Joe smiled.

The door swung open and a tall man in his early forties swept around the table, his hand outstretched. 'Hi, Max Paulsson. Aaron been looking after you?'

Pumping Joe's hand, he held rock-steady eye contact before taking a seat next to his colleague.

Joe pushed two business cards across the shiny grain. 'Jawad Balal, MSc, BEng, Head of Process, STC Chemical Corporation.'

Two came back in return. He thanked his hosts and picked each card up individually with both hands, reading them in detail before placing them carefully in front of him on the table, face up. Sitting across from him was Max Paulsson, Senior VP Commercial Development, Red Oak LLC. At his side was Aaron Epstein, Lead Counsel and Compliance.

'So, Jawad,' Max said, sitting back and clasping his hands behind his head, 'I've got five minutes and then I'll leave you and Aaron to sort the details out. Tell me about STC.'

Joe smiled, said, 'Call me Joe,' and gave them a short history of his company, its capabilities and aspirations.

'Sounds great, Joe, but I gotta tell you, I'm not keen on your valuation. Aaron brought me up to speed on the preliminary discussions last week,' he said, sucking through expensive dental work.

'The price?' Joe smiled. 'You know how we Arabs love to argue with our friends. Let's leave that for later – something we can look forward to.' He twinkled.

'Over dinner tonight.' Max twinkled back, running his thumbs under his braces.

Joe leant across the table. 'We can conclude and make down payments by end February, dismantle and pack in March, April, May, and ship out in June with stage payments every month.'

'Could be okay …' Max said. 'But I'm not too bothered about timescales.'

It seemed to Joe that it was probably more than okay, more than Max could have hoped for. He sensed that the man from Red Oak was feeling increasingly confident that he had the measure of the man from STC, which could only be a good thing. He also knew the schedule was critical.

'It's a great plant and a great site,' Max continued. 'The city needs commerce and services and great places to live and hang out. We're leveraging global aspirations. You've seen it there – that site's like broken teeth in what will soon be a very kissable mouth,' he said with a leer.

'Progress.' Joe smiled enthusiastically. Sure, he'd seen it. He'd been there last week to inspect the plant. He'd seen the strata of the city change quickly from the window of his taxi, its concentric circles of wealth fanning out wider. The city fathers were extending the good life to all its places, if not all its citizens. Everywhere was to become an attractive space and an idealised place to live, work and relax. The city wanted commerce and services, and heavy industry was to be banished to unseen zones. The Red Oaks were to be encouraged, the Moritz's squeezed. With every minute the taxi had driven further from the city, the decay had ratcheted up. He'd looked from his window at the weather-stained concrete of high-rise blocks, boarded-up shops, graffiti, the growing feeling of torpor, the people becoming fatter. It had seemed ironic that they wore tracksuits – presumably the only things that would fit. Any sign of energy was draining away in the betting shops, pay-day loans, chicken takeaways, money-transfer kiosks and tattoo parlours, where those with no voice could indulge a little self-expression.

And no doubt one day Sharjah would look like this, he'd thought, as would Mumbai, Lagos and Chittagong, and any other city with global aspirations playing catch-up, measuring their progress against the least offence they gave to Western sensibilities.

'More coffee?' Aaron said.

'Please,' Joe replied, getting up and walking round the table, where Aaron was loading fresh beans. 'What's the story behind Red Oak?'

They were an investment fund, Aaron explained, concentrating on prestige residential developments globally, most of which they pre-sold to high-net-worth investors looking for safe havens in places like Vancouver, Paris, Geneva, New York, London or Sydney.

'Developments typically generate revenues of between three and five hundred million,' Aaron said. 'And we've got nearly three billion in funding available.'

'But why are you based here, in Moscow?'

Aaron smiled. 'Ah. The money's mostly Russian. And a lot of the end clients are Russian too. But our European HQ's in London and we've got marketing satellites in Geneva and Paris, and New York of course.'

'Of course,' Joe agreed. 'And so you just bought out old Moritz?'

'Yeah, Max closed it out a while back.' He paused. 'You know, the original Benyamin Moritz fled from Germany in the thirties and set his chemical company up just before the Second World War. And it did well. Then globalisation changed the game and Ben junior gave up the fight. But he's old and no one's coming through the family – a daughter in TV production in California and another one teaching speech therapy to kids in Africa. So we bought it, lock, stock and barrel. And the plant will be sold,' he smiled knowingly, an eyebrow raised, 'and the site redeveloped.'

'That's the way it is.' Joe smiled.

'And you guys can get a ship in the dock there – to load the plant?'

'No problem,' Joe said. 'Our technical people have checked it out.'

'That's good.' Aaron nodded. 'By the way, I meant to touch base with you earlier about your visa for the site visit. One of our supervisory board is some kind of congressman – so he's got all the connections and could've helped smooth it through.'

'Thanks. But it worked out fine,' Joe said. 'We've got friends in the right places too.'

Leaving the meeting at around four o'clock, Jawad went back to his hotel for a couple of hours. If it meant he had to swallow his pride, so be it. Red Oak were unrealistic in their expectations and looking for the kind of sucker that just didn't walk in off the street nowadays, but the risk that they might lose confidence and try to move on to another potential buyer was not acceptable. The deal had to be concluded and he was being suited and booted for sucker of the day. He could clearly imagine the awkward conversations he would have to face over the coming months, with peers in his industry asking why he'd bought a pup.

As he soaked under the shower, he couldn't shake 'leveraging global aspirations' from his mind. Last week, when he had inspected the plant, the security guard had said something on the same lines – about women and drink and pleasure. He had been an entirely different person from an entirely different background, but seemingly he had also been a disciple seeking the same holy grail.

'Yes, sir. We were expecting you,' the guard had said, pulling a cap on to his head and straightening his blue uniform with its Sentinel Security badge on the breast pocket. 'It is so cold. You will take a cup of tea?'

Joe had recognised the accent – African – but not the country.

'You're used to warmer weather?'

'Yes, sir.'

'And where is your country?'

'Liberia.' The guard smiled, his back straightening proudly. 'My home is Monrovia. You know it?'

Joe shook his head. 'I'm sorry, not really.'

'It is named after James Monroe, America's fifth president – our founding father.'

'Monrovia, I get it.' Joe nodded.

'And what is your country?'

'Sharjah.'

'That is where?'

'It's in the Emirates.'

'Like Saudi Arabia?'

'Kind of,' Joe said. 'It's next to Dubai.'

'Ah, Dubai. Where the soccer players go, where you have women and drink and every kind of pleasure.' The guard grinned.

'Yeah, we've got everything.' Joe had smiled, wondering just how the local tourist board would take his confirmation of the women and drink and every kind of pleasure.

~

The hotel desk phoned at six thirty. Outside, the street was dark, the sky glowing orange in the city lights. A limousine was at the kerb. Max was on the phone in the back seat.

'How's your hotel?' Max said, slipping his phone in his inside pocket with a flash of the yellow silk lining his suit. 'If I'd known I'd have put you somewhere smarter.'

'It's fine, Joe said. 'STC's very strict on expenses.'

'But not on chemical plants.' Max winked. 'You like Japanese? We could go to Nobu.'

'Sounds great. I've heard of it. But you'll have to help me with the ordering – and what are those crazy things you eat with?'

'Chopsticks!' Aaron smiled. 'Don't worry, I spent two years in Tokyo.'

'Two years balling geisha girls, now look at him.' Max smiled. 'Made all his hair fall out. What about a cocktail first?' he added, glancing round enquiringly.

'Is there sand in my desert?' Joe said, raising an eyebrow.

'Attaboy … then let's party and do some good business.'

A greeter swung the heavy glass doors open. 'Good evening, Mr Paulsson.'

Black stone lined the bar's floor. The walls were faced with black suede. The counter was twenty metres of black chrome. Behind it, the staff were very blonde, tall and good looking. Sharp silver light bounced from mirrors and glass. Joe thought it looked as if the Arctic had been dipped in black paint on midsummer's day.

Three T&Ts appeared, Tanqueray and tonic, in tall glasses loaded with ice and wedges of lime. Joe looked around, picking up the beat of the music, the heavy bass, the driving rhythm, drowned by the sound of a hundred people. The crowd were mostly young, smartly dressed. There was a heady whiff of money and money seekers blending coolly with arts and music people. The languages were international – Russian, American English, English English, French, and, as Joe's ears pricked up, even Arabic.

'Cool place.' Joe smiled, chinking his glass on Aaron's as Max signed the tab and flirted with the six-foot blonde serving him.

'Yeah, Max and I come here a lot. It's great for babes,' Aaron said.

Joe clocked his diligent groundwork, his probing for the kind of predilections and entertainments a new client may be interested in. Perhaps he'd see Aaron whisper the information in Max's ear later, and earn a pat on the back.

'Yeah, I noticed,' Joe yelled into his ear enthusiastically, playing a low-value card openly.

Max joined them again. 'Dreaming of those beautiful polymers?'

'Yeah, and pipe coatings. I love the smell of pipe coatings in the morning. Smells like …'

Max clattered his glass into Joe's with a respectful nod, completing Lieutenant Colonel Kilgore's line from *Apocalypse Now*: '… Victory!'

Joe recognised the play, the ice breaking, the client dropping his guard with a drink in his hand, willing to shoot the breeze. They ran through their favourite films, quoting lines, reliving the scenes, laughing at the antics, relaxed, easy. People joined them for a few minutes as they passed by and recognised Max, who made sure he collared all the pretty women and introduced them to his new best friend, whose status continued to rise. Hey, meet Joe, he's captain of the Dubai polo team. Hey, this is my friend Joe, he's the Finance Minister of Dubai, he's the prince of a million square miles of oil wells and desert.

Aaron fetched and carried, allowing Max to concentrate on setting the ground rules, getting to know his target and soften it up. Drinks were the prelude. The main event would come later. Now was the time for Max to demonstrate what a great couple of guys he and Joe were, how they shared interests and values, had a common philosophy on the important things in life. As a consequence they could not fail to do business together. To fail would be unnatural, perverse. Should Joe dissent and find himself unable to see it Max's way, it would reveal a moral fault line, expose him as a poseur, unable to hold his place in the real world.

'Okay, let's eat,' Max said, draining his glass and checking his watch in one synchronised movement.

Right on cue, Joe thought. For the last two minutes he'd been anticipating that Max would demonstrate how timing was of the essence and it was time to move on – how alpha guys didn't stand still and react to what was happening around them. They set a fast pace and let everyone know they had more important things awaiting them and could barely afford the time to be where they were now.

'Such a beautiful city,' Joe said, settling into the back of the limo and craning his neck. They swung by the perimeter of Red Square, past St Basil's Cathedral with its minaret towers and spiralling onion domes of blue and white lit up like a fantasy. At the head of the square sat the great slab of the Kremlin, massive and forbidding. Joe widened his eyes, belittled by scale, by place and company, softened up.

The maître d' ran his experienced eye over Max's tailoring. 'I've got the perfect table for you.'

'With perfect service.' Max smiled, slipping some thousand Rouble banknotes in his breast pocket.

Aaron studied the menu and checked Joe's preferences for hot and cold, seafood and meat, explaining the subtleties of sushi and sashimi. Max discussed sake and checked the degree of rice polishing in the Junmai Daiginjô-shu variety, which met with both his and the sommelier's satisfaction. Joe looked about, taking in the scene, letting his hosts know he was suitably impressed.

The crowd was not unlike the cocktail bar set, though the Arctic scene had warmed. This was more boudoir, with blood reds and burnished copper. Across the room a table of eight were enjoying the theatre of a personal chef.

Conversation flowed. Max kept it light with a dusting of anecdotes. The service was slick. Delicacies followed one after the other: white fish sashimi with muso, scallops, crab tempura, black cod. Joe struggled manfully with his chopsticks and overdid the wasabi sauce with the Wagyu beef.

'Wow, hot!' he said, fanning his mouth.

'Ferocious. Like the women here.' Max grinned.

'Yeah, you need to watch that stuff. Water only makes it worse,' Aaron said, topping up his cup with a generous measure of sake.

'No more for me, thanks,' Joe said, right on time.

The waiter hovered a few paces away. At Max's signal he cleared the table and brought coffee, double espressos. Max dabbed his mouth with a napkin and looked across.

'So, you like my plant?'

'I do. But ...'

Max leant in. 'But?'

'I think we are going to end up too far apart on price.'

'What are your ideas?' Aaron said.

Joe noticed the sideways glance that Max gave Aaron, saw the irritation that he'd indicated the price was negotiable so early in the discussion.

Max held Joe's eye, confirming he was the one to talk to. 'We got three valuations from professional brokers.'

'Brokers are brokers – they want the instruction. The market's dropped. Just look at commodities. Our prices have dropped twenty per cent this year.'

'They'll go back up,' Max said. 'We're not talking short positions here. We're talking long term, right?'

Joe conceded the point. 'But no one is investing. I can buy new plant, twice the capacity, twice the speed, half the energy consumption, and all on soft loans. Moritz is inefficient. It's why they've gone and we're here. And it's why you're going to make money developing the land – but from a very second-hand chemical plant? That's not going to happen.'

Aaron started to say something but the flat of Max's hand moved across the table.

'I'm only hearing what you can't do. Tell me what you can.'

Joe drained his cup. 'That's good coffee.'

Max's eyes remained fixed on Joe. He clicked his fingers and pointed to the coffee cup as it chinked back to the saucer. The waiter turned silently on his feet, reappearing moments later with a fresh espresso as Joe laid out his position.

'A lot of the plant is mismatched or needs replacing. Either way, I've got to buy new. The tanks and storage are shot. The linings are gone. I don't need to tell you about the NDT.'

'The what?'

'Non-destructive testing. Ultrasonic, magnetic particle inspection, flux-leak scanning,' Joe said, reeling off terms that were conceivably relevant but unnecessary. 'But we can move quickly, wrap the contract up next month, dismantle in March, April, May, and ship out in June.'

'There's plenty of time,' Max said dismissively. 'We don't get planning till Christmas.'

Joe chose not to dispute the planning approval, which he knew was due in June, having drawn it out in conversation with the security guard at the plant. He put his hands on the table. 'Twenty per cent cash down, twenty per cent each March, April, May, twenty per cent before shipment. A short contract, American law, arbitration in New York –

okay?' he said, looking across to Aaron, who nodded his agreement. 'And two point seven five million.'

Max's eyes rolled. He sat back and folded his hands behind his head. 'Dinner's been great, thanks. You take the bill. I'll take the tip.'

Joe pushed his chair back. 'Excuse me a moment.'

There was no need to hurry. It was not as if he was leaving a hot date to go cold on him. The more time he could give them the better. Let Aaron bring some unimaginative and unambitious reasoning to the proceedings. Max liked money. Aaron liked neat contracts with partners who performed quietly.

He took a cubicle in the lavatory – not for the sake of modesty – reasoning that Max had probably seen a movie where the alpha male clinches the deal in the bathroom.

The water in the basin was warm, the towel cool and soft. He washed his hands, splashed his face, checked his teeth and straightened his tie. Looking good, he thought. He even managed to hide the surprise from his own face at how sober he felt. The Lebanese were relaxed about alcohol, with a bar on just about every street corner. No one had asked where he was from, assuming he was a generic Arab, and when pressed would be exposed as a lightweight trying to be sophisticated, a man of the world, Westernised.

'Okay,' Max said, as Joe resumed his place at the table. 'Aaron's pointed out some leverage for me on your schedule. I'm gonna say five and you're gonna say three. Then I'll say four and you'll say three point two five. So let's agree at three and a half million.' He held his hand out across the table.

Joe smiled and reached across. 'Done.'

TWELVE

Dan stepped across the cobblestones at the back of the building. A gabled window flashed in the sunlight, the brickwork glowing orange against a thin sky. Icicles hung like musical notes from the guttering. He rubbed an eye. Getting up at three in the morning in late January and catching a six o'clock flight was not his preferred start to a winter's day.

'It was the stables,' Lars said, approaching a low block at the back of the courtyard.

They entered a long room, brightly lit, modern and functional, at odds with the carefully preserved exterior. A row of tables stretched along one side. Facing them, a grid section was marked on a wall. Dan recognised annotations on it. He lingered at the tables, his eyes sweeping over a coil of rope, a bucket, a shirt, a binoculars case and other items, all labelled and numbered. Further on and drawing his attention were fragments of wood. Some were quite small but others were substantial, up to a metre long. He looked across to Lars.

'Not sure yet,' Lars said, anticipating the question.

Moving on to a laboratory section, Dan stared down at an instrument.

'A spectrometer,' Lars said. 'We got everything we need.'

A woman turned in a chair at a workstation tucked in an alcove at the far end. She stood up and walked across, smoothing her tartan skirt.

'Melissa Lopez,' Lars said, making the introductions.

She offered a warm, firm handshake. 'Hi. Lars tells me you were navy,' she said, her hazel eyes glinting as she swept a mass of dark hair over one shoulder. 'We'll be speaking the same language then.'

Lars rolled a cigarette and went out to the yard, leaving them to get better acquainted. They worked out they had probably been on the same US–UK exercise in the Arabian Gulf a few years before.

'So, after college I served nine years and then joined the agency, which is coming up five years ago now,' she said. 'Navigation's always been my thing.' She paused. 'Lars is feeling a bit awkward about … you know.'

'Yeah, we talked on the phone. It's okay. We go back a long way.'

'He told me. Whatever …' She smiled. 'Anyway, he asked me to take a closer look. I haven't got a clear opinion, or even a hunch,' she added with a knowing look. 'I've just gone for the data and a double-check. So, you wanna see what I got?'

They sat together at her desk. Melissa brought up images on the screen and explained the processes. 'I took the course and cross-referenced it to the confirmed satellite positions, excluding all areas the ships didn't have the speed to reach – so we know they weren't there, right? I ran it for twenty miles from the location, and this is what I've got.' She pointed to the screen. 'See this blur?'

Dan narrowed his eyes. 'Can you enlarge it?'

She shook her head. 'Not with this.'

'But later?'

'Maybe,' she said. 'Look, come and see it in context,' she added, getting up and walking over to the wall grid.

'Here's the location and here's the next twenty miles. And the blur comes up here.' She tapped a finger on the grid. 'It's precisely in line with the *Ocean Dove*'s route. If you calculate the timings, the blur's moved at an average twelve knots. I just can't be sure about the time stamp on the image. By all my deductions it should be accurate – but I can't guarantee it.'

Dan turned and looked around the room, assembling the details in his mind. Lars was standing by the row of tables, looking at him quizzically. Dan hadn't heard him come back in from his smoke. The satellite coverage was patchy. At the precise time and at the precise location, nothing had passed overhead. There was no confirmed image of either the *Ocean Dove* or the *Danske Prince*. That was definite. All he had was a blurred image of something that was too small to be the *Ocean Dove*, but was on its route and moving at the same speed. The image was eight miles ahead of the accident location and, if he accepted the unconfirmed time stamp, it was precisely where the *Ocean Dove* should have been.

'An anomaly in the image?' he said, turning back to Melissa. 'Some sort of atmospheric interference?'

She turned her nose up. 'I don't buy that.'

'You got any ideas?' Dan said, turning to Lars.

'There's something there. But you guys are the experts.'

Dan blew his cheeks out. 'Yeah.'

'You know, at first,' Lars said. 'I just didn't ...' He stumbled for the words, his eyes dropping before lifting them again. 'And I still don't know what I believe. But what I'll do now is a proper investigation and I'll do it my way – and a little bit your way. But you gotta prove it, right.'

'Can't ask for more,' Dan said. 'And I'm grateful, for everything.' He looked around the room and gestured to Melissa, acknowledging her presence and the fact that Lars could easily have contrived to keep them apart.

Lars had phoned him a few days ago and gone some way towards explaining his scepticism in Hull. Dan had apologised, accepting he could have handled his side of it better. Earlier this morning, over coffee, Lars had gone further, speaking of the shock in Denmark and the government minister, new to his post, who wanted it cleaned up quickly – *clean* being the operative word.

Dan turned back to Melissa. 'You said you might be able to enlarge it?'

'It's possible, I think ...' she said. 'But the only equipment powerful enough is back home, and it'll take a while.'

~

Dan had a window seat on the flight back to Heathrow. There was an empty blackness over the North Sea with neither moon nor starlight, without horizon or reference point. He closed his eyes and thought about Melissa, wondering where her blur was going to fit into the scheme of things.

It was Clymer's responsibility to monitor every case. If someone failed to raise or update something, she had to revive it and demand action where appropriate, either to further the case or close it. So far, to their mutual satisfaction, he had kept quiet and so had she, until the last Monday meeting.

'So, the Bofors file. That's closed now?' Clymer had said.

'No it's still open. I sent you an update.'

'You did?' she said, scrolling through her inbox and adding, with a roll of her eyes, 'If it's important you must highlight it.'

'Anyway, I found out that the *Ocean Dove* shadowed the second shipment of Bofors guns in July.'

'What do you mean by shadowed?' she said, keying his dashboard and putting it up on the main conference screen for everyone to note.

'The second shipment went down West Africa and when it passed Angola the *Ocean Dove* came out of Soyo port and stayed on its tail for two weeks.'

'On its tail?'

'Yes. Twelve hours behind.'

She studied the screen, her brow furrowing. 'It's clearly dragging your score down. Twelve hours – that would be out of sight, wouldn't it?'

'About a hundred and forty miles away.'

'So it's hardly shadowing?'

'Well, in shipping terms it's relative. And there's something else. On the final voyage, when the *Danske Prince* disappeared, the two ships had been together for five days, but it was only on Saturday afternoon they found themselves alone with no other ships around. It was the first window of opportunity.'

'Opportunity for what?' Clymer said, the creases on her forehead deepening, before countering his suppositions with words like 'conjecture', 'coincidence', and 'perhaps'. Eyes around the table switched between the two of them and, during one particular silence, everyone's concentration broke at the sound of a pencil snapping. 'Show me,' she added, gesturing behind her.

Dan got up from the table and ran his hand over the wall map, explaining the ships' routes along the coastlines and through the Mozambique channel to where they eventually split from each other in the Indian Ocean. His efforts to draw a difference between coincidence of geography and the trading patterns of ships, and the very same ship being bang on the spot five months later met only with a terse 'unproven' or 'I don't buy that'. It was the same with the six days leading up to the *Danske Prince*'s disappearance and the 'window of opportunity' on the Saturday afternoon.

With an impasse the inevitable consequence, Clymer overcame it by turning her back and moving peremptorily to the next case, leaving Dan standing by the map with an isolating walk back to his seat.

'Can you give me two minutes when we wrap up?' Dan said, pulling his chair out, his tone neutral but his voice loud enough to drown others.

Clymer looked along the table, the tip of her tongue probing a new shade of lipstick, a curious beige that didn't match her hair, eyes or clothes, though she seemed pleased with it.

'Can it wait? I've got an eleven o'clock,' she said.

'Two minutes?' Dan repeated. He'd expected the prevarication, the reflex of letting everyone know that her time was precious and meticulously planned.

'If you must.' She nodded.

When the meeting closed, Dan picked up his things and walked round the table, sitting down in the seat next to Clymer's.

'You've got my report and I want a conclusion, and so do you,' he said.

Clymer leant back in her chair, her body language telling him that she noted his directness and tone.

Dan leant in closer. 'I know you don't fancy this, but I do, so I want it sorted. Your calendar says you're free at two o'clock on the tenth.'

Vikram had been waiting for him on the steps outside Thames House.

'Done,' Dan said, sweeping past.

'And a leap to where?'

'Dunno,' Dan said. 'And I don't care.'

In the corner of his eye he saw Vikram stop. He could feel the eyes raking his back as he strode over the paving slabs. From behind he heard, 'Yes you do. And that's the problem, you care too much.'

'Let's get a coffee,' Dan said, without looking back.

They stood outside Alf's. The east wall was out of the wind but in the sun, which was surprisingly warm.

Breaking the silence, Vikram raised a sympathetic eyebrow. '"I'm a team builder – it's what I do …"' he said, laughing at his weak impression of Clymer. They laughed harder when Dan tried it, his own effort even worse.

'And thanks for your help,' Dan said, referring to the report Vikram had helped edit. 'You know, sorting out my punctuation.'

Vikram took a sip of coffee and licked the froth from his lips. 'It's better than you think – or maybe not as bad.' He smiled.

Dan had worried about his written English ever since the shock of comparison with the other navy officer cadets. It was true, he did tend to steamroller through form and structure. But he worked hard at it and felt no shame, merely accepting it wasn't one of his strong points. Not long after they had first met, Dan had shared his doubts with Vikram, and Vikram had told him that as far as he was concerned, his acknowledgement and acceptance of it seemed to mark him as intelligent, perhaps even confirm it.

'Funny thing was,' Dan said, 'when I left I realised she hadn't said a word, not one. It was just me doing the talking. I said I wanted the meeting and that was it. Then I just picked my stuff up and fucked off.'

Vikram looked at him. 'Wait till you see her.'

'True,' Dan had said, knowing he needed to get his case thoroughly rehearsed, factually. From a personal perspective, he regretted the argument was becoming obscured and less about fact as it was about will.

Disembarking at Heathrow, he checked his messages. A new one caught his immediate attention.

We need to meet. There's been developments.

~

The next morning, Dan took his usual route to the office from Westminster Tube station, across Parliament Square, around the back of the abbey and along Great Cuthbert Street. It had snowed in the night and frozen hard in the early hours of the morning.

The road was rutted and ridged. Cars and vans edged along cautiously to the muted sound of ice crushing beneath them. The pavement was alternately crisp under snow or thinly iced and slippery where well-intentioned efforts had cleared it from entrances.

He blew into his hands and looked up; a woman in a dark blue overcoat was a dozen paces ahead, picking her way gingerly towards him. She skidded to a halt, the coat-tail swaying around her legs. With a jerk of her head and a gloved hand shooting out to the railing, her startled eyes fixed on a point over Dan's shoulder.

It was barely a scream, more a cry of shock, but he clearly heard her a split second before the sound of a racing engine registered. It was directly behind, not off at an angle in the road, and it was coming hard at him. The tyres were biting for grip, shrieking as they lost and found it again.

His head spun round, his hand heaving on the railing as he sprang into a leap. Half over the rail with his head staring down and legs flailing in an arc, he felt the low retaining wall shudder beneath. Sparks flew in the corner of his eye as metal ground against brick and rail. Something solid, a bonnet or a windscreen, rammed into the sole of his foot and spun him round. He pivoted on the rail and crashed down in a heap on the other side.

With his face half buried in snow, he heard a dull thud, a sharp gasp and the sound of an engine accelerating and the crashing of gears. It took a moment to gather himself, mentally and physically. By the time he'd pulled himself up, the van was fishtailing down the road and slewing into a side street.

Everything hurt, but he knew in an instant that nothing was broken. He hobbled the few short paces along the railing to the gap. Just shy of the entrance the woman in the blue coat lay in a tangle, a leg skewed at an obtuse angle. Red was already vivid against snow white.

Dan knelt at her side. She blinked hard, lifting her head a shuddering inch, trying to look along to her feet.

'No,' Dan whispered. 'Stay still.'

There were voices over his shoulder, a man and a woman crossing the pavement on the other side of the road, the door to their office open behind them.

'Go back,' Dan yelled, raising a hand. 'Call an ambulance! And bring blankets.'

He took his raincoat off and eased it under the woman's head, muttering encouragements and running his eye over her, smoothing down the blue coat that had risen up over her knees. There was blood on her face but it was superficial, perhaps grazed against brick.

The people from the office appeared at his side, four of them now, a man and three women. There were no blankets but they had brought coats. One of the women was kneeling at Dan's side, holding the shaking gloved hand at the end of the blue sleeve.

Dan looked back along the path. There were tyre tracks in the snow stretching back twenty-five metres. He looked the other way, searching his memory for everything he'd seen and heard in those brief seconds, closing his eyes for a moment and trying to lock in the images.

It was a typical street, neither a thoroughfare nor a rat run. The buildings were red-brick Victorian and tall, four or five storeys, some with semi-basements, most with a low wall and black iron railings. There were trees, but not all along, and not where it had mattered. There were permit-parking bays on the other side of the road and no-parking signs on his. The woman in the blue coat might have seen precisely where and when the van mounted the pavement, he thought, but as he looked down at her trembling face, he knew now was not the time to ask.

He glanced around. The man from the office was looking along the road too.

'Did you see it?' Dan said.

He shook his head gently. 'Only heard. I looked up when I heard. My desk's by the window,' he said, turning and pointing. 'And the guy's just gone and run away. God help us.' He sighed.

'The guy?' Dan said, looking him in the eye.

The man raised his hands. 'I didn't see. I'm just, you know ...'

It was an interminable wait. Time limped by like a beggar as Dan knelt in the snow, racking his brain for something meaningful to say to the woman on the ground, who was shivering from fright, pain and the cold. After what seemed an age, everyone turned at the sound of a siren at the top of the street. One of the women from the office stepped into the road, waving her arms.

~

Vikram heard feet on the stairs. They were slower than the ones he was expecting. He looked up as Dan walked through the open door, his eyes dropping to the torn trousers and bloody knee.

'Couldn't get me a coffee?' Dan said, flinging his raincoat down.

Dan was in his boxer shorts when Vikram returned, peering over a shoulder and running a hand across his grazed back. He sat down, flexing a leg out and turning the ankle left and right, up and down. 'It's bigger than the other one, all swollen,' he said, looking up and taking a sip of coffee. 'A van ... Great Cuthbert Street. It just came up the pavement. I got over some railings but a woman wasn't so lucky. She's in an ambulance. Got hit hard, I think. Not good. Not for her ...'

'An accident?' Vikram said neutrally.

Dan blew his cheeks out. 'I guess. The driver didn't hang around.'

'What, hit and run?'

Dan nodded. 'Just fucked off up the road.'

Vikram looked at him. 'Here. Get up. Let's have a look at you.'

He stepped around Dan, running his eyes up and down. A large patch of bruising on the shoulder and back was starting to show, with another by the hip. His knee was scraped raw and there was grazing on a hand. And an ankle was discoloured and puffed up.

'You look okay, but you should get it checked out – go over to

Thames House,' he added, meaning the in-house medical centre.

'I'm all right,' Dan said, slipping his shirt back on and pulling his torn trousers up. 'Wish I could say the same about that poor woman.'

'And don't forget, it has to be reported,' Vikram said, raising an eyebrow.

Agency protocols were clear. Any personal incident of any nature had to be disclosed, however commonplace it might seem to the individual involved.

'Yeah, I know. I'll sort it out later.'

THIRTEEN

Jawad helped himself to coffee in Bulent's office. 'Moritz is going well,' he said. 'We'll sign next week and then the contractors start dismantling.'

'Have you appointed one?'

'Not yet, but I sent them a letter of intent yesterday. They're cool. And you?'

'The same,' Bulent said. 'Just waiting really. I can put the *Ocean Dove* into Bar Mhar for fitting out any time.' He paused. 'What's it like, this Moritz place, you know, for the guns?'

Jawad looked away for a moment before answering. 'Well, I'm no expert, but I'd say it's perfect. There's nothing there, just the river.'

'Will we get the time?'

Jawad weighed it. 'That's the question, isn't it. But I think so. And is anyone really looking at us with all that going on? Anyway, people see what they're conditioned to expect. They see something but can't rationalise it – our brains are preprogrammed to expect one thing and unable to believe or process what we actually see. They won't see the ship ...'

Bulent took a mouthful of coffee and sat back. 'I hadn't thought about it like that but I guess you're right. There's just one thing,' he added, getting up from his desk and stepping across to a map on the wall. 'We can't risk Suez. There's no way of knowing what might happen in the canal. Sometimes they just look at the documents and wave you through. The next time they give you all kinds of shit.'

He pointed to Pakistan and ran his finger over the map, tracing the route.

'Don't we have friends there?'

Bulent shrugged. 'Sure, but that's someone else who needs to know, and someone who has to be on duty the day we transit. You know what the canal is to Egypt, all politics and jealousy. Do we risk that?'

'No,' Jawad said. 'I guess we don't. Does Choukri know?'

'Not specifically. I mean I haven't discussed it, but he must be thinking the same.'

'Well, it's news to me, so you'd better make sure,' Jawad said. 'In fact, better make sure everyone knows. It could throw all the schedules out.'

'Right,' Bulent said, a smile spreading over his face. 'Can't Rashid deal with it?'

Jawad grinned. 'Great idea. Anyway, I put all the Moritz stuff in a report for Choukri. First thing I hear from him: I need more, give me all the details. All underlined.'

'Exactly,' Bulent grunted, mimicking Choukri. 'I spoke to him the other day and got my balls chewed off. He was in a right fucking mood about something.'

Jawad acknowledged with a shake of his head.

'Fancy Nobu tonight?' Bulent said.

Jawad turned and laughed.

Bulent gave him a sideways glance. 'I said something funny?'

Jawad came over and sat down. 'Sorry,' he said, 'it's just the Moritz guys, or I should say the Red Oak guys. They took me to Nobu in Moscow and it brought it all back. It's strange, but I think those wankers made my mind up for me.'

Bulent eyed him questioningly.

'They're some kind of investment fund, hedge type thing. There's two of them. One's the bull, a real hand-pumper, strutting his stuff, slick as snake-shit and totally insincere. He's fabricated a personality from the pick-n-mix box, self-help books and copying other people. And he's crap at business, doesn't understand it like we do – and that's a worse sin! And me? I'm just a rag-head fresh out of the desert. So I can't be on his level. I can't ever reach it. And I shouldn't even dare think about it. The other guy, the contracts guy, he's small in every way. He hasn't got a personality but he'd like one, and the bull is his ideal. But in reality the bull's only a steer, all horn and no balls, a wannabe baller. I think he was raised in a field next to the bulls, looking over the fence, copying the moves and picking up the lingo, you know …'

Jawad looked up. Bulent's elbows were propped on the desk, hands folded under his chin, his head still.

'So they took me to a hip bar where the beautiful people hang out and poured drinks into me,' Jawad continued. 'Then we went to Nobu, where I struggled with the chopsticks and burned my mouth with this strange wasabi stuff.' He flicked a hand disdainfully. 'So, we've eaten and we get down to money, and I pay too much, and he thinks it's too little. And so what. The price is worlds apart and we're worlds apart, literally. They say globalisation has shrunk the world, turned it into a village, but from where I was sitting it couldn't have been more different, more remote. These guys have retrenched. They're not reaching out. They only look inwards. It's all win-win for them and people like us just don't count. We have no needs, no rights. It's their right to have everything. They look at you but they just don't see you.'

Bulent sat quietly, nodding his head. After a while he said, 'I know. That was me, in Germany – their good little Turk. I didn't exist really.'

'It's just money, isn't it,' Jawad said. 'It's the only thing they care about and the only thing that holds them together. Society, family? Every doorway has a homeless person, every bit of skin is covered in tattoos. There were two security guards at Moritz, just struggling immigrants from Liberia doing the only kind of shitty job they could get. Anyway, one of them, a nice guy, he didn't know Sharjah but he'd heard of Dubai, where the footballers go, and where we have "women and drink and every kind of pleasure". And to him, that's civilisation, and "everything" is presumably everything money can buy. Just some poor African, but he's soaked up the Western ideal, and he's right. Look how Dubai's been bent into a shape they can approve of. What have we done? Why did we do it? Why do we need their approval?'

Jawad looked across but it seemed that Bulent was not inclined to break the silence. He felt he understood why – that his experiences would have resonated with him. 'So I'm off Nobu for a while,' he added, raising an eyebrow. 'Could murder a lamb kebab though.'

'Kebabs it is,' Bulent said, his expression brightening as he clapped his hands together. 'And fuck those wankers.'

'Yeah, we're going to.'

~

But before a kebab supper, Bulent had to get on with some work. After discharging in Balikpapan, the *Ocean Dove* had ballasted to Singapore and loaded a cargo of accommodation buildings – a workers' camp for an LNG project in Mozambique.

The ship was arriving that evening and he needed to keep it employed. Profit at the end of the year was of academic interest. The paramount reality now was for cash flow, until the ship returned to Pakistan for fitting out.

From Mozambique it was going to ballast up the coast to Mombasa, Kenya, where he'd already fixed some steel reinforcing bars, another low-paying cargo. There were mitigating reasons for fixing the steel out of Mombasa. Firstly, the cargo was destined for Umm Qasr, Iraq, which would bring the ship back to the Arabian Gulf, close to home, close to local sources of cargo, where his contacts and marketing were stronger. Secondly, Mombasa was an ideal base for a crew change. Communications were good, flights and hotels plentiful and cheap, the prices driven down in an irony that was not lost on him by fears of terrorism that had driven the tourist dollar away.

There was another task before leaving the office. Opening his email and pulling the keyboard across, he began typing.

'Dear Mr Khan,

I have received very worrying reports from the Capt. of the Ocean Dove. The recent work you carried out at the yard is proving to be totally below standard. Attached are the relevant photos. As you can see, welds have broken and cracked and steel plate is lifting and buckling. So far, the work you have done to other ships in OceanBird's fleet has been entirely satisfactory. I have no explanation for these problems. I can only suggest it is down to substandard materials and workmanship. This is costing me serious money! I expect you to put this deficient workmanship right at your entire expense and at a time when it is convenient for me to schedule the ship into Bar Mhar. I sincerely hope we can settle this matter quickly and that your yard can continue to be the yard of choice for the OceanBird fleet.

Best regards

FOURTEEN

Dan left the office and turned his collar up. The recent cold front had brought a biting east wind in its wake. He wasn't feeling particularly inclined to bend to it, as had been recommended, but he made a conscious effort not to confront it. He checked his watch and walked faster, trying to build some heat. It was six thirty and his rendezvous in the pub was in fifteen minutes.

He'd suggested they should meet at the same place as before, but it hadn't gone down well. Pity, he thought, the Guinness was good. Now he had to find the Coach and Horses in a mews behind Vincent Square, Westminster, which he assumed would have a cellar full of Merlot.

'Hezbollah?' Dan said, setting his Guinness down on the bar.

'She changed her name, married him, and it was all a long time ago.'

'But still?'

'Everyone's got a past.' Salim Hak shrugged. 'So our friend Khan married a Palestinian and at one time she was mixed up with the local scene. So what, the folly of youth? Look at our politicians – half of them were card-carrying commies – and some of us were caught dealing dope when we were thirteen.'

'Ouch,' Dan said.

'Mere details,' Hak commiserated.

'And the Indians found this – but we've no record?'

'Our paper trail's dead,' Hak said. 'Azmi picked it up from them and they got it from Shin Bet. There was a bit of a share out – he told them about your specialist knowledge and suspicions, and now, inevitably, the fuckers want to do something about it.'

Dan considered it for a moment, realising that if Shin Bet, the Israeli internal security agency, had provided the information, it was probably accurate. 'And you can't let that happen?'

Hak frowned. 'What, India running wild in Pakistan? Azmi won't have it.'

'So you'll set it up? And then share the intel with them?'

'Guess we'll have to,' Hak said resignedly, running a hand through his hair.

Dan finished the last couple of inches of his pint and turned to order another round. The pub was quiet, with only an elderly landlord sitting on a stool at the back of the bar. The scattered customers were equally quiet and of equally advanced years, but they seemed at home and comfortable on the faded green-and-peach banquettes, minding their own business, rheumy eyes staring off somewhere into the middle distance, careworn faces unflatteringly lit in the glow from reproduction carriage lamps. Strange choice of Hak's, Dan thought, completely at odds with the first place they had met.

The wait for the landlord's attention was welcome. It gave him a chance to collect his thoughts. His case was vulnerable and would quite probably be shelved if JC got her way. LaSalle was setting up a raid on OceanBird and now Hak and Azmi were seemingly obliged to do the same in Bar Mhar. And he was effectively being relegated to bystander on a case without merit that senior people were concerning themselves with for reasons they implied were little more than procedural.

'And you don't trust the Indians?' Dan said, handing across a large Merlot.

The corner of Hak's mouth curled up with distaste, though not at the wine. 'I don't trust anyone. Except you, of course.'

'Of course,' Dan agreed. 'So when's all this going to happen?'

'Leave it with me.' Hak shrugged. 'I've got a guy, he's perfect for it.'

'And another thing,' Dan said. 'You know they're likely to take the file from me without a handover to your side ... JC's already told me she wants it closed. It's not exactly domestic security, so I guess it stands to reason?'

Hak conceded the point with a gesture. 'And have you closed it?'

'No. I've got a meeting with her. We'll see …'

Hak raised an eyebrow and took a large swig of wine. 'Good luck with that,' he said. 'Then we should be glad we've opened our own file.'

So, Dan thought, his pulse quickening as the implications fell into place. Hak, with Azmi's albeit reluctant blessing, would set up a raid on Bar Mhar. He remembered Azmi's dark warnings of stirring up a hornet's nest on his patch – something he couldn't abide. Coupled with LaSalle's OceanBird initiative, both ends would be covered now. It was real progress, yet Hak didn't seem to know about the Sharjah raid and something was holding Dan back from broaching the subject. His reticence was tinged with something that felt like regret, but as he chewed it over, it wasn't taking much to brush any guilt away. Whatever Hak was doing, there was a sense of agenda about it. LaSalle's position was clear and now something was telling him that Hak, and perhaps Azmi, were working their own channels too – and working him.

'What's all that?' Hak said, breaking the silence and nodding at Dan's upturned hand on the bar. For the past minute he'd been absently picking at a scab across his palm. 'Been scrapping again?'

Dan smiled. 'This? No,' he said, self-consciously looking down and dropping his arm to his side. 'The ice the other morning … Stupid van came off the road. I got out the way but some woman wasn't so lucky. Went to see her in hospital – broken hip, compound fracture of the thigh. Nice woman, solicitor.'

'Nasty business. At least she's well placed to handle the compensation claim.' Hak added blackly.

'Not really – the driver fucked off.'

'I see …' Hak took a mouthful of Merlot, his eyes darkening and remaining on Dan. 'Did you get a look at him?'

Dan shook his head. 'Happened too quick, behind me. Reported it though. The uniforms are dealing with it and Perkowski's taking a look – do you know him?'

'Know of him. We've got the same at our place,' Hak said, referring to MI6's internal security, which was also handled by ex-Special Branch operatives.

'The Danish report I sent you – does it throw any light?' Dan said, shifting the subject.

Hak weighed it for a moment. 'Interesting. But not really.'

'Okay,' Dan said. 'And the raid, who else will know about it?'

A sharp look from eyes the colour of Guinness provided the answer.

FIFTEEN

Dan arrived early for the meeting, signed in and went straight up to 4F, one of the cubicles on the fourth floor. A single light lifted the gloom in the narrow room. Outside it was grey and overcast and a light drizzle speckled the window at the end. Heavy-duty carpet tiles lined the floor below grey partition-board walls. A faint murmur of voices was coming through them from a neighbouring room. In the middle of the floor was a grey melamine table, empty, surrounded by a chair on each of its sides. He checked his watch. It was 1.50. Then he looked at the table and chairs, gauging which seat held precedence, opting for the one under the window facing the door. He sat down with his back to the door and opened his file, setting it out in front of him on the table.

At precisely two o'clock the door opened. Clymer took in the room at a glance and walked around Dan, standing over the table, leaning in, her hands spread flat on the surface.

'So, my three o'clock has been called forward to two thirty.'

Okay, have it your own way, Dan thought. 'No problem,' he said.

Clymer smiled. 'I'm glad you scheduled this meeting one to one. Gives us a chance to … chat.'

'That would be nice.' Dan smiled back. 'Perhaps we'll have time at the end.'

Clymer blinked first. 'So.'

'You've read my updated report?'

'Well,' Clymer said, a forced half smile of apology on her face. 'I only had time to speed read it.'

'And from speed reading it, what action do you recommend?'

She brought her hands together under her nose, her head tilting to one side. 'It changes nothing. Close the file.'

'Just like that. No threat, under any circumstances?'

'You haven't made the case.'

'I said as much. I made it clear there's no proof, but that's not the point. I see potential for threat. That's what I'm saying.'

'And I don't,' Clymer said, pressing her hands down firmly on the table. 'Close the file. Do something productive. There are so many challenges.'

'And what about LaSalle, doesn't he expect something from me?'

Clymer stiffened. 'He's not your concern, and …'

'But wasn't it you who chased me up about getting in touch with Hak?'

'You need to address yourself to this team.'

Dan turned away, knowing that looking at her would only increase his frustration and push him closer to saying something he would regret. He wanted self-control to argue it through. He'd told himself there were two things to be avoided: a slanging match and a battle of wills.

'Okay, I understand, but what I don't understand is why you don't want to back me,' he said, his voice moderated.

'It's not that I don't—'

'But it is,' Dan cut in. 'You're not even passing it on, just closing it, dead.'

'There's nothing solid to pass on.'

'I know it's not solid. I've shown it isn't solid. So can't we just leave that alone?'

'Fine,' Clymer said.

'But this is the thing. This is what gets me. I'm supposed to be an expert. My opinion is meant to count. It's why I'm here, isn't it? I understand the file might not be for us, but I don't understand why you think it's not something for MI6. My judgement says there's a potential threat, that none of this adds up.'

'And mine doesn't.'

'And yours is based on?'

Clymer's face pinched. 'So, let's try to look at this objectively. I'll give you my reasons.'

Dan sat back, opening his hands, inviting her, nodding in agreement, allowing her the option to interpret his gesture as apology if she wished.

'Firstly, there is clear evidence, accepted by all the other experts, that your ship was nowhere near the other one. Fact. Secondly, the potassium nitrate exploded.'

'Ammonium nitrate.'

'Ammonium nitrate. Secondly,'

'Thirdly.'

Clymer's face pinched again. 'Thirdly. Who's behind this? No one's this organised, this well-resourced. All the evidence points to disintegration within the terrorist organisations. They're left with nothing but random attacks. Look at it, Amsterdam, Toulouse, Ohio, the Istanbul football stadium, the Madrid concert, and all the others. Fourthly, if terrorists want guns, there are plenty available in collapsed regimes – Syria, Libya, Yemen and so on.' She paused. 'So, lastly, this satellite analysis – I mean, involving our American friends. You're losing your focus, your effectiveness. I'm building a team here, a good team. It's what I do. And I need you to think hard about how you can be part of it going forward. Are we clear on this?'

Sure, Dan thought. It's perfectly clear. It's clear you're unwilling to think beyond narrow limits, actively subscribing to the pushing of a status quo, a feel-good that the war on terror is being won, the feel-good your pundit and politician friends have a deep need to believe when they reassure the public. You want me to be part of this cosy group-think, inside the collective, so when you're wrong, everyone's wrong together. It's what you call teamwork and leadership.

He was tired of arguing, tired of the pointlessness of it. Why argue with someone who didn't want to know, with someone against whom you couldn't win anyway? He'd made his argument in his report, both for and against his own hypothesis. He'd covered the comparisons with ordinary field artillery, which as Clymer had said was lying around waiting to be picked up like windfalls in an orchard. What annoyed him most was the assumption the battle against terrorism was more or less won, amounting to little more now than the mopping up of individual cells and lone wolves. The political wing of the service was pushing the scenario. Their promotions depended on it. If they could convince their masters they had completed the current job, there was only one sensible option: promote them to somewhere new where they could work their magic again – an advisory role at the Home Office or the UN, or managing some sort of institute for some sort of strategic study. The private sector were suckers for war heroes, too, especially when use of intelligence could be demonstrated.

Dan knew he was picking his ground unwisely, but he couldn't help himself. 'I don't buy it, this idea we're winning,' he said. 'I don't know for sure that Al Qaeda, Daesh or ISIL or whatever we call it is on the bones of its arse. No one knows that.'

Clymer sighed. 'And you know better after, what is it, nine months? I take advice from people who've dedicated their lives to this service. Ten, twenty, thirty years of knowledge. I listen to them and so should you,' she said, colour flooding to her cheeks.

But I do listen and I can see your exasperation rising. I listen to you spinning it to suit those you want to please. You know what they want to hear, that their tax billions are amounting to more than 'we can't be sure'. They want to hear we're winning and they want it presented with positivity, which you do convincingly.

'Okay,' Dan said. 'I'm putting it in writing, official request to open a case, with full assets.'

'And I will reject it officially, *in writing.*' She leant in closer. 'So, I think we need to schedule a meeting with HR. Perhaps we'll all benefit from a re-evaluation of our situations going forward.'

~

When Dan got back to the office, Vikram was at his desk. His back was to him, his eyes on the screen. Dan said nothing as he settled down in his seat. A moment later Vikram's chair turned.

'Well?' he said. 'How did it go?'

'I fucked it up.'

'You sure?'

'You weren't there. You didn't see how I fucked it up.'

He would have been content to brood, but Vikram coaxed it out of him. By the end Dan was glad of reliving it because Vikram didn't see it quite so badly, but he too was perplexed by the re-evaluation with HR.

Dan nodded at Richard Nuttall's empty chair.

'You don't know?' Vikram said.

'No.'

'He's resigned. It's in your inbox.'

'Bingo,' Dan said, opening his email.

Nuttall's message was to both of them. He was going back to DHL. His old boss had seduced him, or perhaps it had been the other way around. Either way, he was going to be their new Executive Vice President – Strategic Land Services Europe.

'Strategic?' Dan pondered. 'And how exactly do you leave MI5?'

Vikram shrugged. 'I think it's complicated.'

'I didn't pay attention, you know, at the start.' He paused, thinking. 'JC was in a bad mood, so I guess she knew about him?'

'Must have done,' Vikram said, his eyes drifting upwards. 'Sea, land and air,' he mused. 'Land has slipped. The tide in the sea is turning and it's starting to look as if she's going to be left with just air – up in the air …'

'Won't look good on her CV – us three were her idea,' Dan said. He paused, waiting to catch Vikram's eye. 'And I said I'm putting it in writing, full assets.'

Vikram sat back. Both of them knew what that meant. An official request, in writing, ensured it would have to go through the process. There were established procedures. Senior management would have to review it. JC would have to involve her own boss. Flesh might be winkled from shells. Private agendas might not remain quite so private.

As Dan looked at Vikram, gauging his reaction from the lines spreading across his forehead, he wondered what breed of cat he might have let out of the bag and what others would have to say about it, particularly LaSalle.

He turned back again and scrolled through his files to the *Ocean Dove*. It would be quick and easy to close it. There was a tangible benefit. The case was currently a negative, dragging his score down. It could rise with a single click, should he so choose, should he do what Clymer wanted him to.

'By the way,' Vikram said. 'I took a call from Perkowski. You need to get back to him – what's happening there?'

'Dunno,' Dan said without turning round. 'The only good bit is JC didn't mention it. Suppose she forgot …'

~

An hour later, Dan stood on the platform at Westminster Tube station. The cacophony of announcements, the cloying scent of fast food, the flurry of pigeons surrounded him, commuters brushing by with unseeing eyes locked on private missions. His own disengaged eyes were drifting vaguely into the distance. Across the rails, a man in a raincoat looked in his direction. It took a while for his attention to register, but then Dan realised he knew him. He was someone who had come out of Monday's meeting room at ten o'clock when he was going in, someone whose greeting should be discreetly acknowledged. What would the guy be thinking – never mind, the poor chap's had a hard day and there's a problem on his mind that evidently must be kept warm and taken home? Dan managed a nod a moment before the guy's train came rattling along the platform, the cold backwash shutting him out from the back of his mind and filling the void with more self-examination.

The image of the van driver refused to leave his mind. It was only a single freeze-frame; a long-peaked cap pulled down low, big-framed sunglasses, a thick beard, possibly false, filling every last bit of face. The face was set in a single expression that failed to express regret or panic or ineptness, a single expression that spoke only of resolve.

He'd walked the street countless times, gauging the precise location from all angles – no street furniture, no trees, no nothing, just forty metres of uninterrupted pavement, with a low kerb … How often do you get that in London?

He felt alone, a minority of one, his mind returning to the same fundamental questions. Why did he still think he was right? What had he got that everyone else hadn't – a better brain or an overdeveloped imagination fuelled by an overt ego and a latent fear of ordinariness? Was that why he had taken the job? Were others seeing through him? Were they way ahead and he was far behind? Had he actually found his right level – a small fish in a big pond? Why couldn't he just go with the flow? Wasn't that what Julie and he had discussed?

Thoughts were becoming more outlandish. He could leak something to a subversive rag. They were well known to him, with their journalists hanging around the local bars, their ears cocked.

And what about an anonymous email to Bulent Erkan?

Danske Prince, Bofors guns, Ocean Dove, Bar Mhar. All being watched ... A sympathiser.

A London Tube station was not an ideal place to have a crisis of confidence. Luckily, the train arrived, snapping him from his introspection. The doors hissed back and a blast of hot air greeted him. There was a seat, still warm. The man next to him was engrossed in a spy novel. *Naturally.* At least someone hasn't lost his sense of humour. And he clearly knew he needed to hang on to his own.

'Is it good?' he said.

The guy looked around. 'Very. You should try it.'

'I've read some of his others,' Dan said.

'They're very realistic, aren't they?'

'Oh yeah, very.'

'Ah, my stop,' the guy said, closing the book and standing up. 'He really knows about espionage and the security services and stuff.'

Dan smiled. Lucky him, he thought; it's a good job someone does if we want to sleep peacefully in our beds.

SIXTEEN

Bulent was putting the phone down when Jawad appeared in the doorway.

'Look at this,' he said, pointing to his screen.

'Our modelling analysis for the next eighteen months indicates now is the optimum time to sell the Ocean Tern *and assign the funds to the agreed ongoing investment strategy.'*

It was an email from the Network's financial management company, Alpine Capital Partners in Zug, Switzerland, with a copy to their Dubai office.

Bulent knew it wasn't advice. It was an instruction. The euphemistic 'ongoing investment strategy' was actually a liquidation. The *Ocean Tern*, a sister ship to the *Ocean Dove*, would be sold, though the market would be led to understand this was just to enable OceanBird to move up and invest in newer and larger ships.

'What will you get?' Jawad said, helping himself to coffee.

'Three and a half. I've just spoken to Hugh Pinchon – you remember him, from our London brokers? He was out here last year.'

'Yeah.' Jawad nodded. 'And that's three point five million towards the Moritz costs. We'll get the same message at STC soon. I'm sure there's half a dozen parties already doing their due diligence. Sovereign wealth funds and venture capitalists will all be contenders to buy us.' He paused and smiled. 'STC's attractive, poised to grow, and the acquisition of the Moritz plant is a major step towards new markets and revenue streams.'

'Smart investment.' Bulent grinned. 'Just hope the buyers have got a good crisis-management team.' He stood up, a hand outstretched as though he was holding a piece of paper, a prepared statement, pretending to read it. 'We assure our valued stakeholders and partners that STC remains committed to its ethical charter. Health, safety, environment and community are part of our core values and vision, and we will conduct a rigorous internal enquiry to ensure we never again blow the fuck out of ...'

Jawad shook his head. 'Sick bastard.'

'It's the company I keep.' Bulent sat back in his chair and turned towards the window. 'Do you think Choukri knew how the Emir was going to balance the books?'

'Did he need to? The Emir said he'd get the money and that was good enough.'

'Yeah, probably.'

'And where's the *Ocean Dove* now?'

'Left Mombasa on Thursday for Umm Qasr.'

'And then?'

'Don't know. Ideally I need about eight weeks' local trading, so I'd better get my finger out.'

Bulent looked across the files on his desk. The first thing he needed to do was to reply to Khan, who had rejected his claim for the faulty work carried out on the *Ocean Dove*.

After sending a strong message he turned to the matter of the next contract for the *Ocean Dove*. It would shortly be available for employment in Umm Qasr, Iraq, and the market was quiet. He checked through his records. There were no requests for feeder ships to work in the Gulf. There were virtually no requests for anything. Feeder work would be good. It was simple, clean, and usually under contract to a reliable partner, one of the big container lines, like CMA CGM, whose certificate Lieutenant Boissy had admired on the bridge.

Nothing at the moment, he thought, *but it's a fast-moving game and tomorrow is another day.* He prepared a message to send to his push list.

'*MV* Ocean Dove. *Open in Umm Qasr 4 March. Prefer intra-gulf trading. Pleased to receive your proposals.*'

~

Jawad had enjoyed the coffee and the exchange of news, but there was plenty of work of his own to get on with and the prospect of instructions coming from Alpine was looming. He chewed it over in the lift down to his own office. The sale of the *Ocean Tern* matched the outlay for the Moritz plant. In addition there were the costs for the contractors to dismantle and pack the plant, around three quarters of a million dollars. Then there was the funding the *Ocean Dove* would need for its final voyage – fuel, port costs and other running expenses. Key people from OceanBird and STC incurred an administration burden too – flights, new identities, accommodation and so on.

The potential sale of STC would bring in an even larger chunk of money, though he realised that it was merely the beginning. There were huge gains to be made from shorting the corporate stocks and indices that would suffer directly from the attack, and conversely from backing the stocks and indices that would benefit. There was no getting away from the fact that he was excited at the prospect and impressed by the strategic thinking. It seemed outlandish that when all was said and done, the Network would show a colossal profit. How was it, he reflected, that the Emir could sit in his counting house, pat himself on the back and say, 'And I made money on it too, a veritable fortune, thank you.'

SEVENTEEN

Edmund LaSalle strode towards the door, stopping a few paces short of his guest and briefly dipping his head in greeting.

'I thought we'd eat in,' he said. 'You sit here – much the better view.'

The fifth-floor stewards were used to discreet lunches and welcomed what were usually more generous tips. The meeting table in LaSalle's office had been transformed with a piece of crisp linen, cutlery, glasses and a spray of seasonal crocuses and snowdrops. The walls were oak panelled under an ornate plasterwork ceiling. LaSalle stood at one of three tall windows looking down over the river, his hands clasped behind his back as he gazed out. Akhtar Azmi stood at another, his hands likewise.

'I'm sending this Bofors business across the river. But not to you,' LaSalle said, his eyes following the progress of a single scull as it skimmed downstream with the tide.

Azmi turned to him briefly before resuming his contemplation of the South Bank. 'And leave me between India and Pakistan?'

'Which you are more than capable of,' LaSalle said, gesturing to Azmi, both of them turning at the sound of a knuckle on the door and the squeak of a trolley wheel. 'The beef's usually good,' he said, picking up a jug of iced water and filling Azmi's glass. 'The crux of the matter is neither India nor Pakistan, but Sharjah – if there's anything to Brooks' supposition. What did you make of him?'

'I don't like him.'

'I rather do.'

'Bloody trouble. Not our type.'

LaSalle smiled. He also thought better of drawing a comparison with the arm Azmi frequently threw around Salim Hak's shoulder. He knew the defence anyway. He'd heard it many times before. Hak had suffered. He deserved their indulgence. And it was always bookended with 'He bloody well does what I say and I don't bloody well ask more from any man.'

'I rather like Brooks' instincts and I think he's precisely our type,' LaSalle continued. 'And we might find our answer in Sharjah. India did not frustrate its own shipment and, if Pakistan is involved, it's only subsidiary. Either the *Ocean Dove* has a crew of seamen or a platoon of highly trained killers. If they're seamen it was an accident. If they're not, we have our link – to whatever it is we have to identify. Was it an accident?' he added, looking up.

'Of course it was.' Azmi sighed, waving a hand dismissively. 'Your bloody man's just pushing an agenda. He's new, the taste of drama. A bloody fantasist, I mean, this assassination attempt with a van ...'

'Your words, not his,' LaSalle countered neutrally. 'But wiser heads must prevail.'

'When the ship arrived in Bar Mhar it was cleared by Pakistan Customs, all perfectly normal, all arranged well in advance. He told you?'

'He did,' LaSalle said. 'And I ran the names through the databases. Nothing registered.'

'We did too and everything was clean. So why are you wasting your time on this? Ridiculous. Give it to Hak. He'll clear it up.'

'There I must disagree with you. And I'm perfectly satisfied this is not some petty intrigue between India and Pakistan.'

'No,' Azmi agreed, 'it's not. And I don't need to remind you that it's never petty,' he added stiffly. 'And now India's threatening to take matters into their own hands – on *my* patch.'

LaSalle picked up the dish of beef and offered it across as a peace offering. He understood Azmi's position, how his life was dominated by the mutual distrust between India and Pakistan. He felt some sympathy for India. Pakistan was virtually their own country. At least it had been, though it seemed its ownership now was very clearly in Azmi's proprietorial hands. And he knew only too well that the last thing anyone wanted was a hotbed of activity in one's own territory.

The waters became muddied. Priorities were sidelined. Too much time was spent spying on spies.

'I'm sure you will make them see the error in that,' LaSalle said reassuringly.

'But why are you, of all people, going at this head-on, straight to Sharjah?' Azmi said. 'It's not your style.'

LaSalle shrugged. 'It's less than ideal, I agree. But fences need to be mended,' he said, referring to the historic problems with the UAE.

He reflected on the situation for a moment as Azmi tucked into the beef. All sides agreed the root of the problem lay at the feet of MI6's Gulf section, where a new broom was heading the department now. LaSalle had recently been with her and other colleagues on the same joint-services mission to Abu Dhabi, where they had met the UAE's new head of security and agreed he was a shrewd operator they could all do business with.

'And Brooks, he'll keep his nose out of it?' Azmi said.

'As far as I'm aware JC's told him to close the file. But somehow I doubt it,' LaSalle added matter-of-factly.

'Bloody trouble,' Azmi muttered.

The steward returned to clear the main course, moving around the table without drawing attention to himself. LaSalle eyed the cheese board at his side. The Stilton looked good, the yellow mottled and earthy, the blue veins blackening, the crust properly scabby. Mindful of his guest, the prospect of a glass of port was only a fleeting temptation.

'But Brooks, he's of no consequence – is he?' LaSalle said lightly, his head cocked to one side. 'He seems to have got under your skin.'

As Azmi offered no more than a scowl, LaSalle sensed now would be opportune to fill the silence. 'There we are then. I'll do the handover and I sincerely hope it's the last either of us hears of the matter.'

A reply came quickly. 'You'll do the handover?'

'Just some minor details I want to add – nothing really.'

EIGHTEEN

Late winter was a quiet time of year. Friends were on diets, off the booze and shoring up their finances after the festive overspend. Dan was babysitting at home. He had been keeping his head down and so had Julie, though she was going out for the evening with an old girlfriend from university.

Striking a high note, the think tank paid their outstanding account and increased Julie's workload. She'd felt a personal responsibility for it, as if her own selfish indulgence risked the family finances and stability. It had hung over her like a cloud, but then the sun had broken through and Dan felt the reflected warmth. Perhaps their Christmas resolutions had cleared the air and reinvigorated them both.

From a work point of view, he had kept his word and knuckled down. The security protocols he'd helped to introduce on passenger ferries were showing results already. His own contribution had drawn praise from more than one of the other agencies involved. It seemed ironic to him that nothing he'd done had been due to any specialist knowledge and was little more than common sense. But the team earned plaudits internally and externally – to JC's undisguised pleasure.

Keeping the *Ocean Dove* in the background, he'd realised the less said about it and the more he was seen to be getting on with other matters, the better it was for everyone, and hiding behind the unofficial licence issued by LaSalle would only have been antagonistic.

Julie smiled. 'I'm looking forward to this evening.'

'Do you good,' Dan said.

'By the way, how's your ankle? You don't seem to be limping any more.'

Dan looked down and stretched his leg out. 'Hundred per cent.'

Julie nodded. 'What's that?' she said, peering over his shoulder as she passed behind the kitchen table.

'Just some website.'

'Backgammon? You don't play, do you?'

He glanced round and shook his head.

'So what's the interest?'

'It's just something at work. Some of the guys, you know?'

'Online gambling … a new vice to go with the drink and drugs?' She winked.

'Yeah. I've only lost six hundred quid so far this week,' Dan said, grinning and turning round. 'Seriously, it's not that sort of site. It's for professionals. Come on, you're going to be late. All that time in the wardrobe – but you're looking good.'

Julie smiled. The friend she was meeting was a journalist on a style magazine and she had a critical eye.

'How many ways can you spell Mubarak?'

Julie looked at him, her expression clearly suggesting she had no idea at all what his question meant.

He tried another. 'Why does a senior bloke purposely crap-up his office? Smart place, expensive stuff, but he's littering it with junk. And it's dirty – won't let the cleaners in.'

'I don't know,' Julie said with a shrug. 'Who?'

'Azmi, head of India at MI6.'

'And he's Indian?'

'Yeah.'

'Perhaps he's an ascetic,' she said, turning and heading across the hall.

'A what?'

'Look it up. Use that D thing I got you. And don't say "crap-up". It's so … ugly.'

'How do you spell it?' he called after her.

At the sound of the front door closing, he reached across for the dictionary, eventually finding the entry. After looking at it for a while, the only conclusion he could come up with was *maybe*. If Azmi was an ascetic, it still didn't throw any useful light on the thrust of his original question.

Putting the dictionary away, he turned to an email he'd received a week or so before from Lars. He'd read it thoroughly, more times than he could remember. It was close to a hundred pages, padded with preambles, protocols, biogs of investigating teams, pictures of ships, maps and cargo lists. Once again, there were photographs of the missing seamen, including the boy who had so narrowly missed his eighteenth birthday.

He flicked through, going over old ground. Only a limited amount of debris had been recovered from the accident site and he'd seen it with his own eyes on exhibit tables at the Danish Maritime Authority. There were two lifebelts and a hard hat, each marked with the ship's name. DNA analysis confirmed with ninety-nine per cent accuracy that the hat belonged to the chief engineer.

The mate of the *Danske Queen* had sailed previously on the *Danske Prince* and had long admired the captain's binoculars case – made from a distinctive leather with an elaborately tooled clasp. He confirmed the case was certainly Captain Pedersen's.

There was a residue of blood on the elbow of a shirt. It had belonged to the second engineer. His wife confirmed he suffered from eczema and was apt to scratch it, especially around the elbows.

Dan sighed. It was hard to concentrate on such details while his mind insisted on returning to the timber fragments. The explanation was too neat, too logical. He shook his head and scrolled on.

Lieutenant Boissy was routine and anodyne, raising his head above the parapet with an opinion just once – to praise Captain Mubarak and the *Ocean Dove*'s crew. Well, he thought, what could he expect to read here? There was little chance of a line starting: 'Then to our surprise we discovered four cases of Bofors guns and twelve containers of ammunition …'

Captain Mubarak's own statement was logical and comprehensive. He was evidently intelligent and a man of feeling, Dan thought. All his actions were correct by any code he might be judged by – humanity, professionalism or the code of the sea. There was nothing new to glean. He and his crew were the only witnesses. They were plausible witnesses. They added authoritative weight to what was appearing to be the accepted, and acceptable, assumption.

The further he read, the more it seemed to want to head in a certain direction. To call it a whitewash would be too strong. But it had a clear tone. Perhaps the authors were unaware of it. Perhaps they would be disappointed to hear they were giving that impression – to at least one particular reader in London.

The report closed by stressing its findings were preliminary and no conclusions could be reached at this early stage. The investigation was ongoing. But he had to conclude his case seemed to be weakening. What would his colleagues think, especially Clymer? They would repeat their argument. The incident's cause was clear. Where was his defence going to come from? 'But,' he said to himself, out loud, with a shake of his head, 'that timber's not right.'

He closed the file and logged into the AIS website. After Mozambique, the *Ocean Dove* had steamed north to Mombasa and was now showing an ETA in Umm Qasr, Iraq, for the end of February.

From the amount of time the ship spent in Mombasa, he concluded it had been loading. *So, well done Bulent Erkan, how clever of you.* He knew that a ship was supposed to earn its money on a trip *to* East Africa, where outward cargoes were scarce, and anything a ship could load out of Mombasa was generally thought of as a bonus.

Though he knew his face only from LinkedIn, the overriding image in his mind was of a really short, fat guy, all Armani, Gucci and giant Rolex. He turned, gazing absently towards the window. I'd like to meet you, Bulent. That would really be something. I want a good look at you. I want to know what you're capable of. Are you a front for some sort of terrorist group, and who are they, what are they? Or are you just a thief, a modern-day pirate, stealing to order, but for whom? Who are you really, Bulent Erkan?

Just before ten o'clock, he closed the laptop and reached under the sofa. Julie was going to be home by eleven. Just a small one, he thought, pulling the weed box out and starting to roll a joint. A few draws, Dennis Bovell on the headphones, in bed by the time Julie got back.

He was tamping down the roach when his mobile rang.

'Hi, it's Melissa. Not too late, I hope? I've just got the analysis back and I know you wanted to hear right away.'

Dan nodded as she ran through the processes before reaching the conclusion.

'It's a what?' he said, the joint crushing to dust in his fist.

NINETEEN

The *Ocean Dove* was nestling at a berth in Jebil Ali, Dubai, closing its hatch after the cranes had placed the last bulldozer on the bed of a waiting trailer. Umm Qasr had come and gone without incident and, as a bonus, the ship had fixed some construction equipment being demobilised from a contract in Iraq. It was only half a cargo and it had paid badly, but it was better than nothing.

It was Saturday, 12 March. Just before noon Choukri took the Metro into Dubai, where the line ended, before hailing a cab to complete the journey to Sharjah. Saturday was a normal working day, the first of the week. Everyone was at work.

In Bulent's office, Choukri pressed his hands flat on the meeting table. They were still dirty from supervising the unloading, a fingernail torn at an ugly angle, the bandage around it stained.

'Gabon? No fucking way!' he said. 'Don't even think it.'

Jawad, Bulent and Rashid looked at each other, then at Choukri.

'So we'll take the feedering,' Bulent said.

'Exactly.'

Bulent had two employment options for the ship. One of them was a cargo to Gabon. The voyage would take them south around the Cape and up the coast of West Africa. The schedule would be tight, without any hitches. Choukri was not prepared to risk languishing in Africa while they tried to find a suitable cargo to reposition the ship back in the Indian Ocean, in Pakistan, where nothing was going to stop him from keeping his appointment with Khan.

There was also some feeder work, but it was only for thirty days.

'A month's work. Then we find a cargo to India or Pakistan,'

Choukri said, turning to Rashid and making sure his irritation was clear in his voice.

Rashid had backed Bulent's argument for the Gabon cargo, pointing out it paid better – acting the role of the astute businessman. Choukri could accept Bulent's default position would always be to do what was best for the ship. But Rashid, what did he know about ships and why should he care? He just wanted to hear his own voice and find some higher ground to look down from. Jawad, Choukri noted, kept his own counsel until asked and didn't hesitate to back the feedering.

'Okay. We do the feeder work,' Rashid said, as though he was chairing the meeting.

'Of course we do,' Choukri said. 'What are you thinking – or not thinking? We're so close now I can almost smell it and you're pissing about over a few dollars. And yeah, I've got the date from the Emir. It's all approved.'

Choukri leant back. The reaction around the table was clear. They sat in silence, knowing what it meant – that the Network's planners and strategists had completed their studies, their modelling of the human and financial costs, the impact on the victims' and nation's psyche, and the long-term prospects on the long and tortuous road to recovery.

'And what does it look like?' Jawad said after a while.

'Like everything we can dream of,' Choukri said, nodding to himself. 'Thirty, forty thousand, maybe more ...'

'Dead?' Bulent said.

'Dead.'

'And injured?'

'Hard to say.' Choukri pondered. 'A quarter of a million – we can only hope ...'

Eyes dropped to the table. Further questions were redundant.

'Anyway, what's happening at Moritz?' Choukri said, looking across to Jawad.

'It's good,' he said, straightening in his seat and clearing his throat. 'The contractors are doing well. Everything's on schedule.'

'And you?' Choukri said, turning to Bulent.

'Same. The agents are lining it all up, the customs, the stevedores, everything.'

'Exactly.' Choukri nodded.

'There's one thing,' Rashid said. 'We were wondering what we're going to be doing, where we go, you know … No one's said anything and we'd like to stick together, us three.'

Choukri affected to listen as Rashid went through the lack of information and the vagueness of the instructions they had received. His eyes switched to Bulent and Jawad, who exchanged an uncomfortable glance. Neither of them looked in Rashid's direction, distancing themselves from his use of 'we'.

'But you're going in the morning?' Choukri said.

'Yeah,' Rashid said, 'but …'

'What more do you need?'

'We'd just like to know. Where, what, you know.'

Choukri shook his head. 'They know you. They know what you can do. You'll go where they need you.'

'But you don't know where that is?'

'No,' Choukri said, surprised that it was assumed he might. He also made sure there was a conciliatory tone in his denial, meant for Bulent and Jawad, letting them know that he understood Rashid was speaking for himself and not for them.

To placate Rashid, Choukri turned and said, 'You'll all be fine. I was going to talk to you about it anyway. Let's have two minutes together at the end.'

Jawad broke the silence. 'You know STC has been sold?'

'No?' Choukri said.

'Venture capitalists in Singapore. They've got an office here in Dubai. Thirty-five million.'

'Dirhams?'

'Dollars,' Rashid said, his tone reproving.

Choukri pondered, but ignored the slight. 'Capitalists … so much …'

'The completion date's set for the first of the month,' Jawad said. 'So if we want to get paid you'd better not arrive early at Moritz. We want to hold the money – they can hold the baby …'

'And buyers are looking at the *Ocean Tern* in Djibouti next week,' Bulent added.

Choukri nodded. 'Khan's doing well. He's going to be ready.'

The feeder contract was good news. Choukri was keen to tell Mubarak and the crew, who would be particularly pleased. It was comparatively easy work, carrying containers for a big shipping line to and from the smaller ports that the big ships didn't call at – feeding containers to and from the mother ships. They'd be given a set rotation of ports in the Arabian Gulf and stick to a strict schedule, always knowing where they would be on a given day. It was routine, which could be dull in the long term, but it would also be a welcome break. As a bonus, it was three days before they were due to start, in Fujairah, which meant shore leave.

'By the way,' Choukri said, 'I got the Danish preliminary report. They like the IED. They're buying it.'

'It was worth all the trouble – getting the right stuff,' Jawad said, nodding his head.

'You got the report from India?' Bulent added.

'Exactly. But I also got it from London, where everything is …' Choukri said, scowling, his voice trailing off.

'Is what?' Jawad said. 'Problems?'

Choukri shook his head. 'Nothing. I got it covered.'

Bulent pushed up from the table. 'Just give me a few minutes. I need to reconfirm it with the brokers.'

Choukri turned to Jawad, his eyebrows raised questioningly. 'Can you just …'

'I'll get a coffee,' Jawad said, leaving Choukri and Rashid alone.

Choukri turned to him and leant across the table. 'You shouldn't have sent those messages.'

Rashid shifted uncomfortably in his seat. 'I just wanted to make …' he started to say.

'You shouldn't have done it,' Choukri repeated, before raising his hands and patting down any response in a calming gesture, his voice soothing. 'You don't have to worry. Your talents are known. They know this. They need people like you, leaders, business leaders, people with special talents. I don't know where you will go or what you will do there, but I know they need you.'

Choukri had only received a summary of the messages from his contact in the Network, but he knew they had broken every kind of protocol. The coffee was cold and bitter. He swallowed a mouthful of it to mask the unpleasant taste of both his previous words and those still to come.

'We don't always get on, Rashid, but I know you and they know you. Everyone knows what you can do. We need money, and who could be better? You do things I can't begin to understand. You know things I will never know. Who is more valuable? You are. Not me. So just wait. Be patient. Trust your brothers as they trust you. Okay?'

Rashid sat back, his chin lifting a degree higher with each of the honeyed words. Choukri looked at him, trying to summon compassion to his eyes as contempt spun through his mind, expecting Rashid's first impulse, fortunately suppressed, would be to acknowledge the accuracy of his eulogy and add weight to some of the finer points. But, luckily for both of them, it seemed another voice within was telling Rashid to be quiet.

Choukri stood up and extended his arm across the table, careful not to crush the soft hand that met it. 'Please, will you ask Jawad if he has two minutes for me.'

When Rashid's back disappeared through the door, Choukri swirled his tongue around his mouth, reached for the coffee cup and spat into it.

While Bulent made his calls and sent confirming emails, Choukri sat alone with Jawad, going over his plans of the Moritz terminal, studying the sketches and photographs, comparing images on Google Earth, adding to his own mental picture of the layout and location.

'And the main building?' Choukri said.

Jawad thumbed through the dossier. 'Here,' he said, showing him the relevant photos. 'It's pretty rough now – pigeons in the rafters, broken windows, bird droppings on the floor.'

'When I stand on the jetty and look across the river, what do I see?'

'Straight across you've got the warehouses and workshops. Behind that are the exhibition centre and airport. Then upstream is the fuel storage depot.'

Choukri nodded. 'North-west.'

'Mainly west. Only a little north.'

'Exactly. And downstream, this development place with the bar?'

'It's four hundred metres away. There's a creek on the plant's eastern border, then the development. It's angled to look away from Moritz – no one wants to see it.' He shrugged.

'And the bar?'

'I had lunch there – not a bad cheeseburger. It was winter, quiet, but it's busy in the summer. There's a big terrace on the river. It's a typical bar-meets-diner-meets-speakeasy kind of place. Wooden floors, brick walls, black-and-white pictures of Buddy Holly and Marilyn Monroe, Cadillacs and transatlantic liners – you know.'

Choukri acknowledged, though he was uninterested in the hospitality industry's generic design and marketing concepts. He continued to turn pages, collecting his thoughts and honing his perception. He'd studied the maps and charts, plotted GPS positions, measured degrees, minutes and seconds. He knew the location better than anyone. But he hadn't been there and felt a gnawing hunger to experience it. 'Here, in the old gasworks,' he said. 'The trees will have grown by summer?'

'But not tall. It's scrub, just wasteland.'

'Okay,' Choukri said, returning to the pages and muttering about electricity substations and exhibition centres. After a while, he pushed the report to one side. 'So, the position's strong. We're exposed to the open river, but on one side we've got the creek and the old gasworks on the other. At the front of the site there's a steel fence and the main building is between it and the ship. And it's abandoned, no one there, just two security guards – and our ship on the berth ...' He paused, lifting his eyes and adding emphatically, 'This is the place.'

As they wrapped up, Choukri nodded to himself and said 'good job', with no indication of whether he was referring to the generality of the discussion, the accuracy of Jawad's plans, his handling of the Moritz acquisition, or simply everything.

Jawad's reticence was rewarded when Choukri added, 'We can use more like you,' glancing across and then down at his bandaged finger. 'Fuck. Trigger finger,' he said, again with the hint of a smile.

Bulent's head appeared around the door. 'Done,' he said. 'Fully fixed. Thirty days feedering.'

'Exactly,' Choukri said, getting up and gathering his things without a backward look.

~

The crew had heard the news by the time he arrived back at the ship. Snoop and Assam were already on the quay, scanning the horizon for the taxi they had ordered.

'We're taking Faisel. Gonna get him laid by a big fat mamma. She's gonna sit her onion on his face and piss all over him, yeah,' Snoop said.

'And what does Faisel say?' Choukri said.

'He doesn't know,' Snoop said, crossing his eyes.

'He'll need his anorak.' Assam grinned, poking his tongue out and shaking it about.

Choukri looked up to the bridge where Mubarak was leaning on the wing rails, gazing down sceptically.

'Don't get arrested,' Choukri said, wagging his bandaged finger at them before turning to the gangway and calling out. 'No, don't get *him* arrested.'

He made his way up to Mubarak. They exchanged knowing looks as a couple of others joined Snoop and Assam on the quay. There were footsteps on the stairs below and Faisel appeared on the gangway.

'So,' Mubarak said. 'Fujairah on Wednesday morning, six o'clock on the berth. Is he still a virgin?'

'Probably. Four rotations, seven-eight days each, thirty in total,' Choukri said, his head rocking as he made the rough calculation.

Mubarak turned, eyeing the quay sceptically. 'I hope his anorak is waterproof ... What's an onion?'

TWENTY

Bulent heard shouting through the open door to his office. He could see the far side of the open-plan main room but not the reception. The words were confused, different voices, all of them competing with the mobile phone at his ear and the dirty joke a broker was telling him. 'Call you back,' he snapped, tossing the phone on the desk.

He took it in at a glance. The uniforms were black, paramilitary, fatigue trousers tucked in boots. Belts were festooned with guns, radios and various items jangling on chains. There were more than a dozen men. All of them were carrying riot sticks. His eyes flashed around the room, seeing three distinct sets of insignia. He recognised the Sharjah police badges but not the others.

Uniforms moved from room to room. One guarded the entrance. OceanBird's staff were at their desks, sitting back and touching nothing, their arms folded across their chests as men reached across them to switch phones off and shut down computers. The bookkeeper screamed when a baton crashed down on her desk and a man barked, 'Sit still.'

'What the f—' Bulent started to say as a piece of paper was thrust at him. He glanced down. The national crest was familiar. The signatures, each obscured with official stamps, were not. The word 'warrant' was clear enough.

'Quiet,' a man shouted, before reading from a laminated card. 'When you are told to, you will place all mobile phones, tablets, laptops or other devices on your desk, either owned by you or by the company. And then when you are told, you will file out to the corridor where you will wait for further instructions. You may not speak to each other.'

Bulent drew breath and started up again, waving his arms about. A tall man turned, his polo shirt filled mainly with muscle. A large gold tooth flashed in his mouth. Bulent didn't see him raise his hand but he plainly felt the jab of strong fingers in his chest. He sensed gold-tooth was in charge. The uniformed men frequently looked in his direction, seeking a nod or the signal from a finger. But, across the room was another standout character, observing with an air of detachment.

He was dressed in a traditional robe, his head covered with a keffiyeh, his eyes concealed behind dark glasses. Standing no more than five feet six in his sandals, he was in his early thirties. Bulent recognised the Gucci logo on the frame of his sunglasses, and that the length of his robe indicated a family of prestige, no doubt with connections to the royal household.

The sunglasses dipped towards an open door. 'Your office?'

Bulent nodded. He turned to the uniform at his side and, receiving a gesture to proceed, followed the robes swishing across the floor, the sandals squeaking.

The robes folded themselves comfortably into Bulent's chair and a hand gestured to the guest seats at the front of the desk.

'Your company, Mr Erkan, is being investigated for tax irregularities.'

'We're clean,' Bulent said, incredulous. 'Always on time and—'

A pair of small hands rose soothingly. 'I'm sure that is the case so there will be nothing to worry about.' The dark glasses cast around the office and a finger flicked the chromium click-clack balls on the desk. 'It's just routine.'

'Routine? I've got ships to run …'

'It's only a matter of a few days,' the man said lightly.

'With no communications?'

'In an hour you can go downtown and pick up some more computers and phones.'

'Great.' Bulent huffed.

'The building has Wi-Fi and I understand IT prices are more than reasonable at the moment. And then there are very good bargains to be had in the souk.'

'Yeah, brilliant.'

'It's all there,' the man said, gesturing to the piece of paper that Bulent realised with surprise he still had in his hand. 'And please don't leave town other than in exceptional circumstances, for which you may apply for permission through the appropriate channels. How is the shipping business now?'

'Bad. And getting worse by the day.'

'Oh dear. I'm sorry to hear that. But this will all be over soon,' the man said, rising from Bulent's chair. 'Shall we,' he added, indicating the door.

Bulent stood by the window in the main office. Below him, in the car park, a hire truck's tail lift loaded with stacker crates started to rise. The office shelves were clear of files. Fluff lay in uniform squares on the carpet and climbed the walls where filing cabinets had stood. Screens and keyboards sat on desks, the cables strewn haphazardly, connected to nothing. The men in uniform watched on, leaving the way clear for others. Noting the open attaché cases with foam pockets for screwdrivers, wire trimmers and aerosol sprays, Bulent assumed they were mostly IT technicians. Through the main door he could see his staff lined up along the corridor, their restless eyes avoiding contact with both their colleagues and the security officers.

As the bookkeeper dabbed her cheeks with a handkerchief, the man with the gold tooth handed him another piece of paper, a receipt for OceanBird's records and equipment.

'Thank you,' Bulent said through gritted teeth, putting it down on an empty desk with barely a glance.

'You're welcome,' came the reply. 'Have a nice day.'

~

The hire truck pulled out of the car park first, followed by a pair of minibuses. The man in the robes and the one with the gold tooth were the last to leave. The robes settled into the back of a Mercedes, a phone at his ear, the door held open for him by gold-tooth before he got in the front with the driver.

'We'll be back at the depot in twenty minutes,' the robed man said, continuing his phone conversation. 'The guys will drain the computers first and the transfer will be with you shortly.'

'Was there anything unusual?' the caller asked.

'No …' The robed man pondered. 'I don't think so – but let me just check.'

He leant forward and exchanged a few words with gold-tooth before sitting back.

'No, nothing,' he said. 'My men have done this often enough to know when people have something to hide.'

'Understood. Was Bulent Erkan there?' the caller said.

'Yes. But he didn't say much apart from having to send instructions to ships and other operational stuff – the usual complaining …'

'Okay. I'm looking forward to seeing the results, and thank you for everything.'

'Not at all, Mr LaSalle. It's my pleasure.'

~

Jawad was up from his desk the moment he saw Bulent step through STC's door. He hurried across and shepherded him back to his office.

'I came up,' he said, 'but some big fucker with a gold tooth told me to piss off.'

'Yeah, he was in charge. And some guy in a high-status dishdash. Did you see him?'

Jawad shook his head.

'Tax,' Bulent said, handing the warrant to him. 'That's what they said and that's how they acted.'

Jawad sucked through his teeth and scanned the document. 'You remember what Choukri said about some security guy asking around in Pakistan?'

'Yeah, I remember, but that's Pakistan. And weren't we going to feed him what he wanted to hear?'

'Sure,' Jawad said. 'Maybe he didn't like it.'

'Maybe. Look, they emptied the safe and I've got to go downtown and get some computers and shit – you got five thousand?' He paused. 'Then I'll have to tell Choukri.'

TWENTY-ONE

'We go now,' Choukri said, pushing Mubarak's crossword to the side of the chart table. He smoothed a calendar down and rapped it with a stiff finger.

Mubarak looked at the date, at Choukri, before nodding his head.

The *Ocean Dove* had been sitting off Fujairah for six days and despite Bulent's efforts there was no prospect of a cargo or employment. It had reached the point where, if he had fixed something, the ship would be delayed for fitting out at Bar Mhar.

Choukri stabbed the date again. 'It gives us a few days to play with for bad weather or problems. We must go now.'

He counted out the days and looked round over his shoulder. Faisel and Assam, Cookie and Snoop, were standing expectantly on the bridge in an arc. Each of them met his eye with a solemn blink or a pursing of lips. Snoop turned to Assam, failing to catch his attention as he stared ahead, his jaw muscles flexing on a wad of khat.

Today was Sunday, 17 April. Bar Mhar was less than a day away. If they allowed ten days in the yard they would be on schedule, with something in hand for delays or bad weather. They could time their run to arrive on the dot, on the particular Friday. And it had to be a Friday, the equivalent of Sunday in the Gulf.

Returning his attention to the calendar, his hands spread on the table, he stared at the date and quietly repeated the word 'ten' to himself.

'Faisel,' he said, glancing round. 'Send this to Bulent: "for sake of schedule we should leave now for repairs in Bar Mhar."'

More of the crew had gathered on the bridge. They stood in silence, nodding to themselves and looking around for confirmation. Faisel sat at the communications desk and keyed the message. They all wanted activity. It meant the end of the build-up. Sitting off Fujairah was just compounding the frustration. If Bulent had fixed a quick cargo or some kind of short employment for the ship, it would have been a disappointment, another delay to the inevitable.

Choukri drummed his fingers, glancing up every few seconds, his impatience rewarded when Faisel turned sharply, his eyes wide.

'Well, read it out,' Choukri urged.

Faisel peered at the screen and read: 'I was thinking the same thing. Please go ahead.'

Within minutes the funnel was coughing darkly and the throb of the main engine could be felt through the bridge floor. From the bows came the clanking sound of the anchor chain, the capstan heaving it through the guides.

Mubarak adjusted the helm and pointed the bows east as Faisel radioed the traffic control centre in Fujairah. It was merely a courtesy – outward clearance formalities had already been carried out and the ship was free to go whenever it wished. Gulls on the crane masts squawked their protests and took to the air as the ship got under way, circling the wake for scraps.

Choukri switched the light off in his cabin at three o'clock in the morning. Until midnight it had been his shift on the bridge, a busy shift. His eyes had tired, his mind slowed, but he had still managed to find three hours for the wish list.

He slept late into the morning. It was gone nine o'clock when Cookie brought a plate of waffles and eggs and the maple syrup bottle to the bridge. Iran's southern shoreline had slipped by in the small hours, merging seamlessly into the Makran coast. They were out of the main shipping lanes, with just minor coastal traffic and the odd fishing boat to deal with, which was no more than routine on a clear morning.

'How are we doing?' Choukri said, pushing his plate aside at the chart table.

'We're doing well,' Mubarak said. 'Two hours to Bar Mhar.'

'Exactly,' Choukri said, sitting back and taking a sip of coffee, content that all was well, content the ship was in good hands and keeping to his schedule.

Tariq had the helm. Mubarak was perched on a stool at the side of the console with coffee and his crossword.

'Echelon?' he said. 'Tariq, is echelon an English word?'

Tariq's eyes searched around and he shook his head. 'Esherlong? I didn't hear it.'

Mubarak chewed the end of his pencil. 'Never mind. It's French – the rung of a ladder. A hierarchy? It fits, and it must be. I'll look it up.'

Just before noon, the main engine slowed for the turn into the bay and the approach to the shipyard. Linesmen were on the jetty to meet them, Snoop and Assam at the rail waiting to throw ropes. Mubarak observed from the wings, calling out instructions through the bridge door.

'Hotter than before,' Choukri said, his hands resting on the wing rail, looking down as men hooked mooring ropes over bollards.

'It is,' Mubarak agreed, running a finger through his glistening eyebrows.

'I checked the forecast. It's good for the next week and there's no sign of the south-west,' Choukri said, referring to the south-west monsoon, the tropical storms that sweep the Arabian sea and northern Indian Ocean from June to September.

'By the way,' Mubarak said. 'There's a message from Bulent. He's delayed on the road but should be here by six o'clock.'

Ten minutes later, Choukri walked across the yard towards the main building. The door to the office opened and Khan came down the steps, pointing to the main workshop. Choukri turned towards it, meeting him a minute later.

'All is good?' Khan said.

'Exactly.' Choukri smiled, shaking Khan's hand. 'We're ready.'

There was a fresh glint in Khan's eyes. It suggested he shared his eagerness and wanted to seal their commitment.

'My guys are going to make a scale mock-up of Moritz over there,' Choukri said, nodding across the yard. 'No problem? They need to practise the drill.'

'Makes sense,' Khan said. 'And there's plenty of room,' he added, sliding the workshop door open and ushering Choukri in.

They made their way through to the back, to a wall of containers. Khan opened the doors of one of the containers and stepped inside, walking to the end and out through a secondary door cut into the steel. It opened out into a chamber, a replica of the *Ocean Dove*'s hold.

Choukri stood at the doorway, looking down the workshop – the hold – taking in the scale and the detail. At the far end was a single Bofors gun, mounted on its plinth across a web of steel beams, with a walkway above. Ducting was laid across the floor connecting the gun to power and water supplies. At its side was a huge revolving carousel. On the floor were chalk marks in a variety of colours, denoting different materials and functions.

After a while, Choukri stepped forward, his eyes switching left and right.

Khan beckoned. 'Let me show you,' he said, leading Choukri around the gun for a full turn.

'See these,' he said, tapping a foot on some heavy I-beams. 'These go across the width of the hold, and I've increased the size of the rubber mountings. A cargo ship is not built the same as a warship. The vibrations and stresses, the fatigue, are greater. And these,' he added, 'are my shell cassettes. Designed them myself and made them here. They work just like a spring-clip in a handgun, though the spring is electrically powered. Here, give me a hand.'

Choukri found a good grip on the carousel and put his weight to it, looking up as it towered over him. Between them they managed to do no more than rock it a little on its well-greased bearings.

'Sixty tonnes of shells when it's full,' Khan said. 'I've stress-tested it for wear and metal fatigue. Taken it to bits, put it back together again. There's no sign of weakness at all. Same goes for all the guns,' he said, turning and looking back down the workshop. 'Each of them was unpacked, put on their mounts, tested, and then dismantled and repacked again. Do you want to see it working?'

Choukri's eyes widened. 'It's possible?'

'Sure,' Khan said, stepping across to a laptop and plugging a lead into the back of the gun. On the side wall was an electrical control box. He pulled the lever down. A low hum came from the gun.

'The programme is a dummy, fifty imaginary targets split into five groups of ten, each shell to be placed a hundred metres apart. Here,' he added, 'you do it, but keep your eye on the barrel.'

Choukri stood at his side looking down at the screen. Khan pressed a key to disable the ammunition feed, then another which brought up the target list. He hovered his finger above a key and nodded to Choukri.

'The Russians did this?'

'Yes,' Khan said, looking questioningly at him.

'It's all done?'

'It's all done. It's perfect.'

'Okay,' Choukri said, pressing the key.

The background hum increased. There was a high-pitched whine and a hiss of hydraulics as the gun swung around. The barrel came up a few degrees, depressing like a piston with each of the ten rapid but more or less silent shots. Then it swung in another direction, the barrel dipping this time, followed by another ten fast pumps. Again, it switched its aim and repeated the process until all five targets and all fifty – dummy – shells had been launched. Each target had used up three seconds. The entire process was over in fifteen.

'My God,' Choukri said, standing back and staring.

'Did you see it,' Khan said, 'the way the barrel makes a minute adjustment for the hundred-metre spread? You can just see, you really can.'

'I couldn't make it out,' Choukri said, shaking his head.

'No, neither could I at the beginning. At twenty-five-metres spread you can't see it. Not at fifty, not at seventy-five, but at a hundred you can, just. It's so fast.'

Choukri sat on the floor, drew his knees up and clasped his arms around them, his eyes raking the gun, happy in his contemplative silence. Khan stood quietly to one side, leaning his back against the wall.

Minutes passed before Choukri shook his head softly and looked across to him. They talked through processes for a while, of things that still had to be done, such as programming the wish list.

'I must bring the chief engineer and his crew here. Four o'clock?' Choukri said.

'Sure. I'll go through everything with them. All the drawings are on disk too,' Khan said, looking around at his creations, nodding to himself as Choukri followed his gaze, keen not to miss a single detail.

As they got up to leave, Khan patted his pocket and took out a small box the size of a cigarette pack. 'I nearly forgot. These came for you.'

TWENTY-TWO

'You're quiet,' Vikram said, swinging his chair round and considering the back of a motionless head on a hunched neck, staring at a screen. For the past half an hour he'd heard nothing but sighs and random mutterings – 'steelwork', and 'no way,' and 'fuck it'.

There was no answer. He turned back to his desk, hearing footsteps clomp towards the door. A minute later, a cup of coffee was put down at his side.

'Take a look,' Dan said, gesturing to his empty desk before stepping across to the window.

The room was quiet as Vikram read.

'Well,' he said, coming to the end and looking round. 'Seems pretty clear to me.'

'Yeah, too clear.'

Vikram's eyes screwed up. 'Can't you just let it go?'

'I know,' Dan said.

'Do you? I think you got off pretty lightly. LaSalle's been nothing but fair – you do see that, don't you?' He paused. 'Okay, JC's been a pain in the arse, but ...'

'Yeah, yeah. I hear you.'

Vikram shook his head. The words were clear enough. Believing them was another thing.

'Come on, I'll buy you lunch,' he said.

They walked down Bell Street in silence and though Vikram wanted to break it, every thought that crossed his mind had the empty ring of platitude about it. He bowed to Dan's greater knowledge of the subject but not to his attitude, though he had a sneaking regard for how he stood up for what he felt was right. It was probably this, he thought, that

LaSalle saw merit in. Without flattering himself that he knew LaSalle, what little he did know led him to feel that he was above the ordinary considerations of mortals like himself, having one sole ambition, or ideal – what was best for the security of the country. LaSalle evidently respected Dan's opinion. He also, evidently, thought he was wrong in this case. The mere fact of it bolstered his own opinion. But, once again, it was only data, though it was hard data, hard evidence, which fell in line with every other piece of evidence and data. It also fell in with Dan's stock refrain of it being 'convenient' and 'too neat'.

'It's just paper,' Dan said as they walked along.

It didn't sound like either a statement or a question. It seemed to Vikram that he was simply giving voice to a private thought. 'What's just paper?'

'What they got from Sharjah. Just paper. Copies of emails, accounting, letters. And still no one's been on the ship or the shipyard. It's just paper.'

Vikram nodded without commitment, relieved that the interruption of opening the door to Alf's gave him an excuse not to reply. He slipped further from the hook when Dan's mobile rang, though he felt sympathy at the caller ID which was waved in front of his eyes.

'Yes, Jo, I'm just out at lunch with Vik,' Dan said.

Vikram ordered for both of them and sat down at a table while Dan dealt with the call. He heard him agree that the chain was clear and picked the point up when Dan joined him.

'The chain of emails between Bulent Erkan and Khan,' Dan said. 'They started in January, Erkan complaining and Khan passing the buck. But now the *Dove*'s back at Bar Mhar for repairs to the repairs – more steelwork for the steelwork. And Khan's paying. He's pissed with it, but …'

'And you knew the *Ocean Dove* was back at Bar Mhar anyway?'

'No,' Dan said facetiously. 'I haven't been checking. I've been getting on with productive stuff – for the team.'

'Absolutely,' Vikram said, with equal insincerity. 'And in addition to the solid reason for the *Ocean Dove* going back to Bar Mhar, there was nothing else to suggest, well, anything …'

Dan shrugged. 'So OceanBird came up clean. Just a normal hard-working company. We know Bulent Erkan's shagging a girl from the duty-free shop when he's not booking hookers on his phone. We know they keep a lot of cash – but cash and ships aren't exactly strangers. And when the rest of it comes in, we won't find anything there either.'

OceanBird's communications were a priority. All the phone, fax and email logs had been checked and the contents examined. The long job of sifting through paper files was going to take a while yet, handled by local security operatives and a team from MI6's Gulf section sitting in a warehouse in the UAE. Experience was already telling everyone that it too would draw a blank.

Vikram left it at that, dropping his eyes to the coffee Alf had just put on the table. Further comment would serve no good purpose. He sympathised with Dan's position. The disappointment was palpable, the brave face understandable.

'And it's due to sail this weekend,' Dan said after a while, glancing absently out of the window. 'Back to honest work, earning a crust.'

'Like you. Like JC just reminded you.'

'Like JC just reminded me,' Dan agreed. 'And talking of reminders, I'd better drop LaSalle a line.'

Vikram was intending to leave early for the weekend just after five o'clock. As he cleared his desk, Dan took a call on his mobile. From his tone, Vikram sensed the caller had something of interest. He was pleased to hear enthusiasm in Dan's voice, but the feeling went decidedly flat when he heard him say, 'Okay, Salim, six o'clock.'

'What are you doing now?' he said.

Dan turned in his chair. 'It's nothing. A Friday night drink. Just a couple of details to wrap up. Two pints and home.'

'Why don't I believe you?' Vikram said. 'He's bad news and you should know it.'

~

It was a clear spring evening. The sun was low, picking out sprays of daffodils in iron grills at the feet of the plane trees. With a few minutes to kill, the slightly longer route along the river offered a chance to stretch his legs and pump some fresh blood into his tired mind. He was also apprehensive, subconsciously delaying his arrival at another new pub, the Brigadier Munro, behind Eaton Square, one of London's wealthiest enclaves.

The outcome of the OceanBird raid was difficult to accept and, while his heart was pinning its hopes on Salim Hak, something was telling his head not to. Salim Hak. Did he like him? Or was he just patronising him because he was useful? Did he need to like him? The notion of pity felt wrong. Was Hak damaged goods – as the water-cooler gossip had it – or fighting his demons the only way he had found so far? Azmi probably knew him better than anyone and was quick to defend his corner. Was that because Azmi was the kind of man who stood up for the effective operators in his team, regardless of the less well-informed opinions of others, or was it guilt, because *he* had sent him on that fateful mission into Afghanistan? On both counts, he conceded, he simply didn't know. He turned it over, drawn back to usefulness, which also begged the question: just who was more useful to whom?

No, he thought, there was no clear answer. Hak was impossible to categorise, probably flawed, enigmatic, but compelling. He drank like a fish but never slurred his words, nor was he indiscreet. He stuck to salient facts and, Dan had to acknowledge, there was an object lesson for himself in that. And, he was more experienced and knew the game much better than he did. It was something he realised he shouldn't lose sight of.

Hak was already at the bar, his back to him. He didn't turn but Dan could see the ornate mirror across the back wall was providing him with a commanding view.

'Pint of Guinness and another large Merlot,' Hak said as Dan arrived at his side. He reached into his pocket before flicking his eyes to an empty table over by the far wall. 'I've got to make a call. Take a look at this,' he said, handing some papers across.

'Good news?' Dan said. 'I need some.'

'You'll be the judge of that.' Hak shrugged. 'Bad day?'

'I've known better …'

After handing some cash to the barman, Hak turned back to him. 'Anything specific?'

'Just the usual shit.'

With a dip of his shoulder, Hak set off towards the door. Through a window, Dan saw him check up and down the street before crossing over and disappearing into a shadow.

The table Hak had indicated was now taken. Dan looked around the noisy bar. The crowd were young, well heeled, the accents taking him back to his days at the staff college.

There was an empty table at the far end. He sat with his back to the wall and smoothed the pages out in his hands. The report form was an official IsC document. The agent and mission were identified by code words and reference numbers. Today's date was at the top. It was countersigned by Azmi and, Dan realised, it shouldn't have been out of the office.

He read it through quickly in one go, taking in phrases – Makran Highway, three nights in the cliffs, minimal security, *Ocean Dove* repairs, gained access to, access to, Bulent Erkan, access to … After a second reading he folded it slowly and slipped it into his pocket, tilted his head back and closed his eyes. The scrape of a chair made him sit up straight.

Hak's elbows were on the table, hands together, fingers propped under his nose. There was a studying silence before he leant in.

'But the good news is there's nothing going on there,' he said.

Dan shrugged. 'Good news?'

'Bit bloodthirsty, aren't we? No terrorists. No Bofors. No threat. Isn't that what we want?'

'Yes,' Dan said, opening his hands in reluctant acceptance. He took a long drink from his pint and settled the glass down gently, allowing a respectful silence to pass in acknowledgement of the greater truth: there was no threat, and it was what they all should want.

'It's just the … disappointment, I guess,' he said. 'I'd hoped, you know.'

Hak merely nodded, though it seemed to Dan there was understanding in his face.

'And the waiting ... it was early Feb when we set this up, and now it's mid-April.'

Hak held his hands up. 'These things take time, dear boy.'

Yeah, Dan thought, *everything likes to take its time*. The delay in the OceanBird raid was understandable. There was delicate ground to go over, new protocols, the building of trust in the rekindled relationship. In Pakistan, why hadn't it just been a case of Hak and Azmi getting their heads together, allocating an agent to the job and issuing the order? But he saw there was nothing to gain from pressing the point. The report was clear. He ran the facts through his head again, accepting them but still probing for an omission or inconsistency.

'So Erkan was there for just one night?' he said, tying it in his mind to the OceanBird raid.

'He arrived on the early flight from Dubai,' Hak said. 'The yard sent a car for him, an ancient Toyota with a blowing exhaust. Khan did not send his own car and driver. It sat on the yard all day – so what does that tell you?'

'That he wasn't an important visitor.'

'Precisely. Just some irritating client.'

Hak drained his glass and looked round at the bar before turning back. 'My man was in those cliffs for three nights. He watched by day and slipped down to the yard by night. Virtually no security, just one old fat guy in a shed who never went out. He saw everything – and all it amounts to is a ship in a shipyard being repaired.'

Dan nodded. 'You're right. Except, was he your man? It isn't the guy you told me about.'

'Azmi's man,' Hak said, sportingly conceding a point. 'I'd lined my guy up, knows the ground, experienced. But when Azmi disagrees ...'

And again, generously, he left the silence that followed to hang, allowing time for Dan to go through his thoughts. After a while Hak put his open hand over the table. Dan reached into his pocket and returned the report to him.

It had been thorough. Dan had a picture of Azmi's man in his mind's eye. He could see him motionless in the cliffs by day, binoculars trained on the yard and ship, a darkly dressed figure moving silently through the shadows by night, in the offices, the technical drawings on Khan's desk, in the warehouses and workshops, the steel plate cut, labelled and laid out ready for installation. The ship's gangway raised every night – something he knew was a correctly noted detail, a detail of procedure carried out regardless of any perceived notion of security in an isolated and remote shipyard. And then there was the optical probe, slipped into an empty hold via a ventilation duct at the side of the hatch coaming – once again, a clearly noted and technically accurate detail. And the panels cut out from the hold floor precisely where Erkan's photographs had illustrated the buckling and deficient welding. It all had such a ringing finality.

'He knows about ships, this guy?' Dan said.

'Does he?' Hak said, neutrally.

'It's nothing. Just the language he used,' Dan said, noting and weighing Hak's uninterested reply. He considered some of the points again before turning back to him with a sigh. 'And I suppose you heard about my whale?'

'I heard.'

The sympathy in his tone was a comfort. Melissa Lopez, back in her laboratory in the USA, had concentrated on the blurred satellite image. She had considered anything that could conceivably have been in the water – packs of timber, shipping containers or other cargoes washed from the decks of freighters, flotsam and jetsam, ocean waste, submarines and, of course, small boats. All had been discounted for various well-reasoned grounds. Finally, with input from the Oceanography Institute and some orca experts, they had narrowed it down to a whale.

'You know they swim at twelve knots in dead straight lines and migrate in those waters at that time of year,' Dan said, shaking his head. 'Right shape, right size, mostly black, bit of grey, bit of white ...'

Hak merely nodded his head and set his empty glass down on the table. He looked up. 'When I was new to this I had a serious down on a guy in Lahore. Everything that went through there was going straight out the back door. I was convinced it was him, and—'

'And you made yourself a pain in the arse and you were wrong.'

'I fucked up his career and lost the service a good man. The smell – my smell, clung to him.'

'Are you patronising me?'

'Are you patronising *me*?'

'I asked myself that on the way over here,' Dan said, with a conciliatory smile.

'Me too,' Hak replied lightly.

Dan smiled again. 'We don't know each other, do we? But I guess you know more about me. I don't know where you live, if you're married, children, where you're from. I know you had a bad time in Afghanistan, but everyone knows that. And you went to Cambridge and you're some kind of high-class backgammon player, going to tournaments in places like Rome and Ravenna.'

Hak frowned. 'Never been to Ravenna, or Rome. Mean to, one day.'

'Rome or somewhere. Vikram told me.'

'Rimini?'

'Yeah, Rimini. That's the one.'

A wry smile of resignation spread across Hak's face. 'Not my finest hour. Out in the first round. Some devious Egyptian, I think. May the curse of the pharaohs be upon him.'

'Bad luck,' Dan said, swallowing his surprise at the prospect of the Egyptian conceivably being Mubarak.

'Luck?' Hak said with distaste. 'It's never luck.'

Dan looked down at Hak's empty glass. Too right, he thought. It's never luck. The raid on both OceanBird's offices and the shipyard had left him with nothing but stark confirmation of his own misjudgement, his fallibility. Forget luck. Luck had not come into it. He had been wrong. Others had been right. Every route was emphatically blocked. There was nowhere to turn on this doubly disappointing day, except he could choose to follow Hak's lead; there was always drink and the thought of it had rarely been more appealing.

TWENTY-THREE

Choukri looked around the table. There was only one subject at dinner that evening in the *Ocean Dove*'s mess. The demonstration of the guns in the warehouse had made an indelible impression. He could sense the crew felt lifted, their confidence bolstered, see the animation in their faces. Doubts were justifiable. The hijacking of the *Danske Prince* had been an undoubted success, but it was only a memory now, a long time ago, last year even. Euphoria evaporated quickly, leaving a void that long periods at sea only dulled further. They had planted a seed under dead ground but there had been nothing to see. Now it was sprouting, ripening into flower, and soon it would burst into fruit.

The chief engineer and his team had stayed late with Khan, going over technical details. Now they were debating among themselves about power sources, rates of flow and grades of lubricating oil. It was the kind of disagreement Choukri wanted to hear, unlike the one across the table.

The mess was crowded this evening, rows of bodies cramped along both sides. The window was near him but the room was becoming hot and airless.

'I murk him, yeah,' Snoop said. 'Glock and soft nose, back of the head, real close.'

Assam sneered. 'No way. He's mine.'

'Then I do the toy cops, yeah,' Snoop countered, jabbing his spoon in Assam's side for emphasis.

Assam scowled at the ice-cream stains on his shirt and swung an elbow, catching him squarely in the ribs. 'Motherfucker!'

Snoop's head jerked up, appealing across the table. 'You saw that! I get them, yeah. Don't I?'

Choukri stared at him before switching his eyes to Assam and returning to his mangoes and ice cream. The engineers went back to their technical data, Snoop and Assam to their bickering.

'A well-fed crew is a happy crew.' Cookie smiled, leaning against the doorway.

The next morning, Khan's engineers and the crew were back at work early. Electricity hummed, welding torches flashed into life, sparks flew, the process under way.

Assam had prepared a couple of lists for the practice run, one for the material and another for the physical stages. The mock-up of the terminal had taken shape. There was a clear outline of the main building with stones laid out for the walls and oil drums for the door openings, all set eighty metres back from the quay, just as it was at Moritz. He'd given his team their instructions and they knew their individual roles.

Choukri stood on deck and pressed the stopwatch button. 'Go.'

The men worked in relays, carrying everything by hand across the hold, through the access door, along passageways, up flights of stairs, down the gangway to the jetty. The sun was overhead, the day becoming hot. Assam ran from point to point, checking, cajoling. One of the men stumbled on the stairs. A clammy hand lost its grip and a package bounced down the steps.

'Cunt!' Assam yelled, sweat arcing in the air as he shook his frustrated head and stamped a boot down. 'And now you're a dead cunt. And I'm a dead cunt if I'm anywhere near you!'

The materials were on the jetty. Now it was time for the oil. A hose was connected to a fuel tank manifold and run over the side. The man to receive it was not in place on the jetty. Snoop leant over the rail and cursed as the linesman ran down the bouncing gangway.

Choukri pressed the stopwatch. 'Now take it all back and start again.' He let his expression say the rest: there would be no point any of them asking what time would be good enough.

Assam looked at Snoop, back to Choukri.

'But boss, there's people getting in our way,' one of the crewmen moaned.

'Just like on the day,' Choukri said.

Snoop's head slumped. There was a cut on his cheekbone, his chest heaving, sweat running down his forehead into blinking eyes. The Dogg's tongue was almost hanging out.

'Can we use the basket, boss?' he panted.

A smile crept from the side of Choukri's mouth. 'Please,' he said, sweeping his hand as if he were inviting him in for tea.

As they trooped away wearily, he leant his hands on the rail and looked out over the yard, his mind switching to the targets' coordinates, the wish list. In the main office a team of clerks were in a side room with copies of it. He had briefed them carefully the previous evening with Khan. They worked in pairs. One called the numbers in a quiet steady voice while the other typed. The pairs were in sync with each other, filling the spreadsheets quickly. Each hour they stopped and reversed their roles. Every two hours they exchanged with their colleagues and started checking, one looking at the list, the other reading out the numbers.

He had dismissed the option of laser targeting. In some instances photographic images were appropriate, but the vast majority were just map coordinates, long sequences of numbers expressing degrees, hours, minutes and seconds. It was repetitive and tedious work but they were good clerks and prided themselves on their accuracy.

Stepping back across the passageway, he peered down into the hold. Once the guns were fitted in the ship there would be no point in maintaining the weapons cache behind his bunk. The crew had racked out one of the ship's storage containers and a couple of men were transferring everything – Kalashnikovs, Glock pistols, rifles, ammunition.

'Hey, careful with that,' he called, as one of them handled a particular rifle. 'That's special.'

~

Just before six o'clock, Hassan Khan walked down to the ship and followed the sound of voices until he peered around the mess door.

Mubarak rose from his place and beckoned him in, signalling to those seated next to him to move up and make room.

'Cookie,' Mubarak shouted. 'Bring coffee and your pistachio cake for Mr Khan.'

Choukri moved from his usual place mid-table to sit opposite Khan, and poured him a glass of water.

'Hmm, this is so good,' Khan said.

Cookie beamed at the doorway. The table was quiet. All eyes faced west, watching a man eat cake.

'Cookie makes it for us when we've been good. So we don't get it often, do we, Assam?' Mubarak said, raising an eyebrow.

The crew laughed, easing Khan's self-consciousness. He took a mouthful of water and pronounced the cake the best he'd had. The crew nodded their appreciation.

'So,' Khan said, his eyes switching between Choukri and Mubarak. 'We're ready on shore.'

Choukri gestured to Faisel. 'Get the hatch open,' he said, continuing around the table and allocating roles – crane driving, rigging, lighting, shore labour.

One by one the crew left the table. Those without a specific task joined them, to assist their mates.

'So,' Kahn said, pushing his chair back. 'Shall we?'

Two trailers were alongside the ship. The hatch was open, the hold bathed in orange light spilling out ethereally to the jetty. A crane lowered slings to the first packing case. Choukri climbed onto the trailer and checked the shackles. The crane took the weight of the gun slowly, inching from the trailer bed. Hands guided it, reaching upwards, eyes watching anxiously as it rose and swung gently over the hold wall before descending from sight.

When all four guns were on board, lined up at the side of their bays, the crew unpacked them. By nine o'clock it was done. Khan watched with satisfaction as the men stood back and looked at the transformation of their ship, permitting themselves a reverential touch of the guns' smooth grey paint as if it were the coat of a sleeping tiger.

TWENTY-FOUR

Dan signed in and took the lift to the fifth floor. The carpet in the high-ceilinged corridor felt soft underfoot, the light switches metal and shining. Colours were less utilitarian than other parts of the building. There was a studious hush. Some of the doors were closed, some open. Glimpses into offices gave a hint of people and place on a floor he hadn't seen before.

He found the meeting room and went through the open door. A large polished table was in the middle of the floor. Panelled walls stretched to a tall, ornate ceiling. On the far side were three lofty sash windows overlooking the river. One side of the table was unoccupied. He took it in at a glance, his place obvious, but he waited to be told. At the end by the door was a woman in her forties. He thought he recognised her, along with the younger woman at her side. He assumed they were both from HR but couldn't place them with certainty. Clymer was sitting next to her boss, David Myles, whom Dan had only met briefly. Bookending the table was Edmund LaSalle.

Clymer leant across and poured Dan a glass of water, saying nothing, a concerned smile playing in her eyes. Nice touch, he thought.

LaSalle hadn't taken his eyes off Dan from the moment he stepped through the door, though he'd said nothing and hadn't acknowledged him.

David Myles opened the meeting. 'You know why we've called you here?'

'I think so,' Dan said, without elaboration.

He hadn't gauged the tone yet and knew it was usually better to let the other side talk. Was this a discussion forum, a rebuke, a firing, or something else? He'd expected Clymer to be accompanied by perhaps one or two HR officers. David Myles' presence was understandable too, but LaSalle?

'So, let's get up to date,' Myles said, his head cocked to one side. 'You met with Jo and she instructed you to close the file. Subsequently you put in a written request for an operational case, which she denied in writing, and repeated her instruction to close the file. And as at this morning it's still open.'

Dan's eyes flicked around the table. Five heads, all still, all waiting for him. He sat back. 'Yeah. I'd been meaning to.'

'Let me tell you, our reaction is no different from Jo's. We've reviewed the file, found no case to answer and sent it over to Six – and that's it,' Myles said, looking across questioningly.

'Okay,' Dan said, adding no more, realising what Myles had just said – that he'd sent it to MI6. It contradicted Clymer. She'd said the file was to be closed and there was nothing solid to send over. Had she changed her mind or been overruled by Myles, or could it have been LaSalle? He glanced along the table but failed to meet his eye or, for that matter, to detect in his expressionless face the merest flicker of recognition for what Myles had just said.

Clymer straightened her back and spread her fingers across the table. 'So, I followed the file with interest, supported it, supported Dan. He's been very passionate about it and put a lot of good work in, but it reached critical mass and, as we all know, I made my decision. But, I truly believe he didn't mean any harm.'

Dan had avoided eye contact with Clymer, though she was directly opposite him. His attention had been on LaSalle, who was keeping his own counsel. Now his gaze lifted, his eyes narrowing as Clymer left the last word of her eulogy, 'harm', to hang.

'I don't think there's any question of motive,' Myles said. 'But there have to be consequences, and all this after receiving written instructions from your line manager once due process and case review had been completed. You can see we are obliged to take this most seriously.'

'I do.'

Myles looked to his left. 'Rosemary.'

The senior HR woman tidied the edges of some sheets in a folder and took a sip of water. 'A disciplinary caution will not be marked in your file and no further action will be taken at this stage, though we trust you understand that we unanimously feel a caution would be warranted. After discussion, and taking into consideration certain unusual influences,' she said, pausing and looking in LaSalle's direction, 'we have jointly concluded that for everyone's benefit, and yours particularly, a six-week suspension is appropriate, which will be marked in your file as a sabbatical – a paid sabbatical.' She paused again, her head tilting to one side. 'We recognise you've been under considerable stress lately and feel sure the break will do you good – a chance to recharge the batteries. Do you have any questions?'

Dan limited his response to a single, 'No,' sighing inwardly. *Stress? Spare me the bullshit HR sanctimony, will you …*

Myles left Dan's terse reply to settle before picking things up again. 'I hope that will close the matter,' he said. 'How are things generally, how are you settling in? I hear you've been implementing very effective new protocols in the ferries.'

'Yeah, that's been … interesting. And everything's fine.' Dan nodded.

Rosemary from HR cleared her throat. 'I understand you were involved in a pub brawl just before Christmas, in the Queen's Head.'

'What? That's bollocks! I didn't start anything, I stopped it.'

'No one's suggesting you did, but would it not have been wiser to walk away? The service manual is quite clear about compromising positions.'

'Look. It was nothing. Vikram bumps into this guy, spills his drink. He's apologising but the guy won't have it, calling him a Paki and getting set to spark him, so I stepped in. And nothing happened.'

'Spark him?'

'Punch him.'

'But how could you know? Had he said something?'

'Lady. Please. I just know, all right? I come from there. The guy had the look …'

Dan could see she was taking offence, feeling patronised. He was grateful for LaSalle's intervention when she drew breath and leant in to reply.

With his hands spread across the table, LaSalle coughed once and looked up. 'Can we move on. If you don't mind, David, would you?'

'Jo's transferring in early June,' Myles said. 'She's going up to run Home Office Liaison. We haven't confirmed who will replace her yet. It's still in process.'

Clymer was looking at her phone, scrolling through messages. She lifted her eyes to meet Dan's.

'I'm pleased for you,' he said, though the pleasure was all his own. HOL was an important role and a major step up. It would come with an office on this very floor and a key to the government's door. He made a quick calculation in his head. Today was 20 April. His return would dovetail precisely with her departure. No prizes for guessing who had pressed for the six-week period, he thought.

'I'm looking forward to building the team,' Clymer said.

'It's what you do,' Dan said, looking away and fleetingly catching LaSalle's eyes, which were quietly smiling.

'If there's nothing more, I—' Myles started to say.

LaSalle leant in. 'I'd like a word with Dan.'

Clymer looked up the table. LaSalle was perfectly within his rights, though procedurally it was irregular. And he clearly meant a private word.

'So, I want it on record that I do not appreciate this continual undermining of my position,' she said. 'I cannot tolerate my authority and judgement being compromised.'

LaSalle held his hands up. 'Your protest is noted. And with respect, Jo, we've been through this.'

David Myles held the door open as Jo Clymer gathered her things together and filed out, without looking at either LaSalle or Dan, leaving the two them alone.

'A variety of emotions are running through my head – bemusement, frustration, disappointment. But foremost is anger,' LaSalle said, leaning across the table, his jaw muscles twitching below the ears. He ran his eyes up and down Dan, quartering him like a hawk, before eventually turning away and letting out a long and exasperated sigh. 'Do you take me for a fool? I simply do not know what to do with you. Simply do not know …'

He turned back, his head shaking from side to side, teeth clamped together, eyes locked on Dan's. 'Why can't you get it into your thick skull? You are to leave this business alone.' His voice had risen to a crescendo before subsiding in frustration. 'How could you possibly imagine I wouldn't learn of your incursion in Bar Mhar? Hak is another matter, and thankfully not my problem. But you? On any other day you'd be straight out of the door without a moment's hesitation – or regret,' he thundered.

Dan could accept the hesitation. The regret was hard to take. Everything was collapsing. His case was gone, his colleagues deserting him, and the person he looked up to most in the service was plainly washing his hands of him. 'My wife told me I'm a bonehead over the weekend,' he said. 'My colleagues haven't got time for me and JC gave up a while back, and I don't blame her. And I've made myself look stupid in your eyes.' He paused, looking down before lifting his gaze once more. 'This case has crushed me. I mean really crushed me. Friday night? That was closure. It was all dead ends. OceanBird – dead end. Bar Mhar – dead end. And I had a shit weekend, and I was a shit to my wife. Now it really doesn't matter because it's over, and I know it.'

LaSalle sat back in his chair, folding his arms and studying Dan's face.

'Everywhere I turned,' Dan added. 'Everything I thought was wrong turned out to have an answer, a believable answer. It made sense, you see, and now I don't believe myself. I don't trust myself. I've fucked up big time.'

He lifted his eyes, keen to gauge how the stream of consciousness he had poured out was being received across the table. LaSalle had sat up again. He was leaning forward, a finger absently stroking his nose.

'Do you know,' he said. 'I think I believe you this time.'

'Was it Azmi?'

'Was what Azmi ... who told me? Never mind.'

LaSalle pushed up from the table. His tall frame was silhouetted in the middle window, his hands on his hips as he rocked on his heels. The chair creaked when Dan stood up but there was no movement at the window. Taking it as his cue, he stepped across, taking up a position at his side, the pair of them looking down on to the river.

'One thing you must understand,' LaSalle said, without turning, without acknowledging the person at his side, 'in this business, there are always angles and perspectives, levels and subsidiary levels. And they're always linked and they always develop exponentially. They evolve like brewer's yeast – though their end product is rarely palatable.'

He turned, catching Dan's eye and nodding in the direction of the river. 'You see that barge. It's simply taking waste to a processing plant. The man on the barge, the one in blue, he's seen something and reported it. In its own right it's important, but meaningless in the greater scheme. Our bargee friend, and quite possibly whomsoever he reports to, are unaware that Special Branch is investigating a minister who awarded a contract to unsavoury elements in the waste-disposal business, whose seemingly legitimate enterprise is a mere laundry for their lucrative activities in the drugs trade. These people also own a string of nightclubs, where the wild son of the minister rubbed up with the wrong crowd and compromised himself – and his father. And the deeper Special Branch delves, the more they uncover. The cocaine comes from Colombia but is routed via The Gambia, so our friends in MI6 are involved, who find the Gambian logistics is managed by a Belgo–Turkish enterprise that is already under investigation by Interpol. Then, as an aside, it's discovered that our waste-disposing drug distributors are also wholesaling to Belfast, where the trade is controlled by the IRA, who are partially paying in firearms, which our waste disposers are selling to Bosnians in Luton, who are connected with ... who in turn are connected with ... And before we know it our yeast will mutate once again and only God understands, only He knows how it will develop and what it will breed. We mortals can but try to contain it, in part. In part ...' he repeated, turning and holding Dan's gaze.

I know what you're waiting for, Dan thought. *You're waiting for the last sign of reluctance in my eyes to be replaced with acceptance. Fine, you can have it …*

~

The south-facing tables outside Alfredo's were bright with sunshine.

'And a rum. A large one,' Dan said.

Alf put a hand on his shoulder. 'Bad news, son?'

'Dunno. Good and bad, I think. But probably mostly good …'

It seemed the only way to look at it. An unofficial caution. That was all. And six weeks' paid leave. But it was freighted with disappointment.

Weak, he thought. Piss weak. David Myles had said there would be consequences. Really? In the here and now there were none. Long term or career-wise? Maybe. Perhaps that was what he had meant. Perhaps it summed up the service, which was the greater disappointment. Somehow the edifice was crumbling before his eyes. It was supposed to be an elite institution. He'd pinned his hopes on it – and on proving to himself he was worthy of his place in it.

Alf put the tray down, looking on solicitously, his white coat hovering by the table.

'It's okay, Alf,' Dan said, glancing up with a smile.

The coffee was strong and hot, the rum intensifying the heat as it coursed through him. All his life he had faced consequences. Now he felt like a protected species, unaccountable. As a child he'd regularly felt the flat of his mother's hand. More often it had been whatever she happened to be holding at the time. The estate and borough he'd grown up in were harsh places to step out of line. There was no escape from consequences in the navy, from above and from contemporaries. At sea, in command, the penalties were even greater, because one set one's own. These new ground rules felt uncomfortable, the protection unearned.

And now Clymer was to be promoted – because she wasn't up to it at this level? No, don't get cocky, he reflected, accepting there was plenty he didn't know. But could that really be how the service dealt with discipline? He shook his head. Surely not. Fuck it. He sighed. Two things seemed clear. Either his imagination was running ahead of itself or there was something he wasn't quite getting. He drained the last of his coffee and resolved he had only one thing to do: go back to the office and close the file. Play the game. Although there was an option. He could put it into cold storage. It was more or less the same thing, but it would leave a faint pulse in the case's veins.

Whichever direction his thoughts took, they kept arriving back at LaSalle. *Surely he protected me*, Dan thought. Left solely in the hands of JC, Myles and HR, it could only have gone one way. Yet there he had been, softening the blows. Why had he done that? Because ultimately it was all his own fault and he'd owned up to it? Or was it because they still had unfinished business together, regardless?

Yes, LaSalle had bollocked him, loudly. That was clear, Dan thought. But how quickly he'd thrown a blanket over the flames. He remembered LaSalle glancing over his shoulder from the window, his gaze drifting to the place at the table occupied a short while before by Jo Clymer. 'We can't all be perfect,' he'd said. 'And nearly all our best people have a degree of – difficulty.' *Was that a reference to me*, he wondered, *or his own younger self?*

And the anger. Had that been at the ruination of a vital and promising case? No way, he thought. Or had he been piqued at the absolute letter of the law, his law, not being followed? And whatever his private agenda was, how would his own withholding of the information about the Bar Mhar raid have been critical? Dan looked around, pondering, trying to find some connections, a finger pinging the empty rum glass.

In the corner of his eye he became aware of a figure. Coming down the street from the north was a man. Was this the same guy that went up about ten minutes ago? The jeans and the bomber jacket were registering in his subconscious, as was the unobtrusive walk. He lifted his eyes as the guy approached, watching him closely, provocatively. The man passed by without reaction and turned the corner.

Dan got up from the table. At the junction he watched the leather back disappearing along the embankment. About two hundred metres away, the man stopped and spoke to someone coming in the opposite direction.

Two minutes later Dan nodded and flashed the ID in his wallet. 'Excuse me, sir. The guy in the bomber jacket just now. What did he say to you?'

The man looked Dan up and down and took half a pace back. 'Er, nothing. He was looking for Talbot Street ...'

'Foreign accent?'

There was a shake of the head. 'No. Nothing. Maybe northern?'

~

'And that's it, just some kind of informal caution,' Julie said. 'And six weeks, doing what?'

'That's what they said.'

'And it means what, three strikes and out, or ...?'

Dan shook his head. 'Dunno. I'll ask Vikram.'

'Just as it's going so well,' Julie said, her eyes narrowing.

'Is it? I'd been keeping it in. but ...'

'Hiding it from me.'

'I wasn't hiding it, but anyway, at work it's out. And I know it hasn't done me any good.'

'*Us.* It hasn't done us any good.'

Dan opened his hands, pleading guilty. 'Us.'

'So come on, tell me something,' Julie said, her voice rising.

'There's a file, okay. JC was telling me to close it and walk away. But I saw a threat and she wasn't interested.'

He reached across, covering her hand with his own, but it brought no response. 'You remember before Christmas when Lars phoned, the Danish ship sank? That's what it's about, and it's been going on since then. Anyway, I forced the issue and was told to close it, but I didn't, and then I put in a written recommendation for a full case, which JC rejected – in writing. Then she told me to close the file again.'

'And you didn't.'

'No. But I have now. Well, sort of. It's in cold storage.'

'Cold storage?'

'It's an official status. It's okay.'

Dan recognised the look in her eyes, the tone of voice, the body language. Her threshold for bullshit was low, usually signalled by creases in her brow, and he realised that he was getting dangerously close to it.

'You're not taking any of this in, are you,' she said, her eyes running up and down, her forehead showing pronounced lines. 'You're just getting in deeper.'

He didn't reply. She looked away before turning back to him. 'So it was just you and Clymer, and she's being what – emotional about it?'

'Not really,' Dan said.

'And the facts back you up?'

'Not really.'

'Oh, for fuck's sake, Dan.'

'They didn't want to listen.'

'No, you listen for once!'

'Don't bollock me. What do you think? You're the PR expert. What's best for us?'

'So it's my problem then?'

'No.' Dan sighed. 'It's my problem.'

'So she's got the facts on her side and you're the emotional one. And then you undermine her. Brilliant. You think that works?'

'It's my watch, my conscience, that's all.'

'Your conscience. Your watch.'

Julie pushed her chair back noisily from the table. He looked up at her bristling back as she fiddled with things on the worktop, moving jars and bottles about distractedly, scraping them across the surface, clunking one into the other.

'Other people were involved,' Dan said. 'LaSalle, you know, I've told you about him, the deputy director.'

She turned in an instant. 'Deputy director – of the whole of MI5? You didn't mention that.'

'It's okay. I told him what he wanted to hear – smoothed it over.'

'*Smoothed* it over?' she said, stretching the word out. 'Yeah, right …'

'It's okay. He's from Suffolk,' Dan said, nodding to himself before realising the pointlessness of what he'd just said.

'Suffolk? Fuck Suffolk!' Julie cried, flinging her hands up, her shaking fists hovering with exasperation over his head.

'But what if I'm right?'

'Oh yeah, there's always that,' she said, before sighing with what she referred to as his full name. 'Dan Brooks no argument.'

He opened his mouth but quickly closed it again, feeling no response was probably the right response.

'Look, you bonehead,' she said, reaching down and shaking his shoulders. 'No one will want to work with you. How can your managers deal with you?'

'JC's going. Been promoted.'

'It's not her. It's the next one and the one after that.'

'But what if I'm right about this?'

She rapped a knuckle on his head before smoothing the hairs down with the flat of her hand.

'What am I going to do with you?' she said, staring down.

'But what if I'm right?'

'Stop saying that, will you! You think you're the first? It's not about being right.'

'What is it then?'

'It's about … It's about the way things work.'

'Is it? Look, I don't know what to think. One minute I'm in the shit and the next minute some senior guy is pulling me out of it – for reasons I can't explain. And he's some kind of impressive dude. Brain like a supercomputer. But he's also human. And he had three cautions on his file when he was younger. He's something else … got a big place in Suffolk,' he added. 'Family's been there five hundred years. It's got a moat – can you believe that, a moat.'

'I can,' she said. 'But I'm not going to speculate about someone I don't know – even if their roots are in Suffolk and their ancient family seat is moated …'

She stood in silence, staring down for a moment and turning with a flourish. Dan listened to the sound of heels on the kitchen floor, along the hallway, the bathroom door slamming shut. He knew she understood and he knew she could never accept it.

And what if he were right? What sort of man would she be left with, he wondered? A compromised man, like so many of the others she worked with every day – the ones she advised how to compromise themselves to their maximum benefit, to their mutual benefit, because, after all, she got paid for it. Why not split their duties as husband and wife. She could walk with the money and he could stand on principle, one offsetting the other, with both consciences assuaged. Wasn't that what a marriage was all about, balancing the metaphorical books?

Deeper still, he knew what lay at their foundations, what underpinned them, what they had built from. It was ground they had been over before. He knew her questions, and the answers she gave herself. *Why did I marry this man? Because I love him. Can I change him? Not really. Do I want to? Not really. What would I think of him? He wouldn't be the man I love.* But more importantly, what would she think of herself? It was this she would find the most troubling. From his side, he always kept it short and simple. He wouldn't change a thing about her. And it was true.

TWENTY-FIVE

'No, I'm tired and I'm pissed off,' Bulent said. 'Bar-fucking-Mhar … Complete waste of time. All the way there and all the way back, just to have him spray me with a mouthful of pizza and grunt "Exactly, I knew all about it." And he lets me bang on for about twenty minutes before he says it.' He shook his head and ran a hand over his cheek, picking at a bite-scab under a two-day stubble. 'I'm going home for a shower and a sleep.'

Jawad ran his eye over him. 'Well, you'd better ease up on the coffee.'

Bulent looked down at the mug in his hand, blinking distractedly. 'You should see it. Arsehole of the world. Nearly all the way to Iran. Dead shit all over the road – camels, goats, cows, and the flies and fucking mosquitoes. Hassled at every police and army roadblock, and I've got a driver who only speaks Urdu or whatever it is, and a clapped-out old Toyota that stinks of exhaust fumes.'

Jawad listened patiently to his ranting, knowing it would burn out quickly. Yes, it had tired him and offered no opportunity to experience the finer things in life, but to his own mind it had not been a waste of time. It had served a very meaningful purpose.

Well,' he said. 'At least we know we're one jump ahead.'

'There's that,' Bulent conceded.

'And he knew the raid was coming?' Jawad continued. 'He knew the date and time, but didn't warn us – so we'd act more naturally?'

Bulent threw a hand up. 'Yeah, just that. He knew there wouldn't be anything incriminating so he let it go right ahead. And it wouldn't surprise me to find out he was behind it … well, maybe. He kept banging on about how important the emails between OceanBird and the yard were – you remember?'

Jawad remembered well enough how Choukri had emphasised the importance of a plainly visible dispute over shoddy workmanship. 'It was an insurance, that's all. A good insurance, but only in the unlikely event of some sort of raid happening.' He shook his head. 'But he had a hand in it? No. I don't buy that.'

Bulent's face screwed up. It seemed to Jawad that he was clearly of the opinion that Choukri was capable of anything. He sat back, chewing over some of the other things Bulent had told him, trying to put everything in order and perspective. He was surprised at the reach and depth of the Network's intelligence. They had people everywhere, he knew that, but he was shocked to imagine the levels they had penetrated to.

The information in Choukri's hands was coming straight from the top. At every stage, starting with the Danish Maritime Authority report, they had known what their opposition was thinking and doing. The security services had established that the first opportunity for the *Ocean Dove* to intercept the *Danske Prince* with any degree of privacy had been late on the Saturday afternoon. They had considered the trans-shipment scenario and examined the satellite imagery. Fortunately, the frames were heavily blurred and the artfully disguised RIB had been dismissed as a migrating whale – as intended. The dhow fragments were found to have been impregnated with SAPET's unique ammonium nitrate formula, and every available piece of tracking data proved conclusively the *Ocean Dove* had not been within a dozen miles of the accident – until it went to help.

Just one person had formed a dissenting view and everyone had dismissed his opinions. It all seemed to boil down to this one guy. Bulent had evidently been unable to find out which security service he worked for – while implying that he suspected Choukri knew but wasn't prepared to divulge it. The guy was ex-navy and he'd served time on merchant ships, which meant he'd been able to look at it all with an informed eye. But he was new to the security services and no one was backing him. They believed the facts and the data, the facts and data that Choukri had so painstakingly contrived.

'And the guy making all the trouble was taken off the case even before the raid?' he said.

'That's what Choukri said,' Bulent replied. 'And the case itself is low priority now – just some sort of political football they're kicking around.'

'You think he's CIA?'

'Guess so. The London office? But I don't know for sure. The satellite and whale people were definitely American. And like I said, he told me loads of stuff about him, but not who he is.'

'It's weird. A guy in his thirties, married with a baby daughter, ex-navy, ex-freighters, chasing a guy in his thirties, married with a baby daughter, ex-navy, ex-freighters …'

'It's totally fucked up,' Bulent said, pausing. 'And Choukri *liked* it. He didn't say it but I could tell. He liked it all right.'

Jawad pondered the symmetry, the parallel lives. Choukri had a target and it wasn't necessary. It was personal, matching himself with his own mirror image, wanting to know who the better man was. If the guy's case was effectively dead, then why bother? The threat had passed, but Bulent was clearly under no doubt that this guy was still figuring largely in Choukri's sights.

'Why keep it up?' Jawad said. 'He's not a problem any more and it will only draw unnecessary attention. The fire's gone out so why go back and pour petrol on it?'

Bulent didn't reply, the look on his face expressing the words for him: *you know Choukri.*

And on top of all this, Jawad realised, in a matter of days the Network's intelligence had established that the security services considered OceanBird benign. The raid had unearthed nothing of relevance and, informally, they were spreading the word that interested parties should not hold their breath. They had wasted their time and money – except for the fringe benefit of furthering relationships in the Emirates.

He exhaled. 'And now we've got an open road ahead of us.'

~

At seven o'clock on Saturday morning Choukri was standing in the forward end of the hold, looking back over the guns towards the bridge. All four of them were installed in a uniform line, ammunition carousels at their sides, barrels pointing over his head, synchronised to the millimetre. The main fitting out had been completed the previous evening, leaving the final coupling of hydraulics and electrics, cable protectors and walkways for today. There was even a folding table, a command centre, hinged in place on the hold wall.

Each gun placement was identical, but it wasn't stopping him from checking where one had a small red cable, the next did too. His eyes switched from gun to gun, his boot shuffling a hose across the floor to match the line and angle of its brother. He turned at the sound of a hold door creaking on its hinge.

It was Khan. Under his arm was a laptop. He smiled and started across, picking his way carefully, taking time to inspect his men's work. 'Like it?' he said, looking around.

'I don't have the words,' Choukri said, reaching a hand to a barrel, allowing his touch to express his admiration. He shook his head. 'It's the quality. I just never imagined.'

'The men have done a good job,' Khan said.

Choukri looked at him. 'It's your work.'

'But your vision.' Khan patted the laptop. 'The target programming is in here,' he said. 'But we have to go through the manual procedures, how you can stop for a minute if you need to, then fire independently.'

'We do it now,' Choukri said, impatient.

'It's better later,' Khan said. 'It's all a process. The men need to see it too.'

'Okay,' Choukri nodded reluctantly.

It was cooler in the hold today, but also more sultry in the listless air, which refused to move. The sun was there somewhere, trying its best to break through, held back by a blanket of hazy cloud. The morning's work had seen the steel-mesh walkways bolted in place, pipes and cables connected and neatly clipped along the undersides. There were signs at every junction box for 'on' and 'off' or 'do not switch off'. Each gun placement was identical down to the last detail, the size, colour, and sequence of cable and hose.

~

After lunch, Khan wiped the back of his hand across his forehead as the men settled into position in front of him. At the front was the chief and his engineers, Choukri, Faisel, and four mechanically adept crewmen – one to each gun. Mubarak stood to one side. At the back were Snoop, Assam and the rest of the crew. The command table was folded down with the laptop open on top.

The covers had been removed from one of the guns, its inner workings laid bare. Khan explained the components, how they interacted with one another and how they should be cared for, pointing out the lubrication points and the quantity, frequency and type of oils and greases.

'They're beautifully made, they're robust, and they're new,' Khan said. 'They won't be any trouble if you follow procedure. But we have to keep them in perfect condition. My main concern during the voyage is damp and humidity. Don't forget they're designed with seawater in mind. They're well protected, but we don't want to leave anything to chance, eh?'

The chief nodded, his eyes turning to four dehumidifiers that had appeared during the morning and were lined up to one side against the hold wall.

'We'll do a test run now. And pay attention to the maintenance areas I've identified,' Khan said, lifting a finger to one of his engineers who was standing to one side by the main power box.

He pulled the switch. The hum of the guns cowed the crew into silence, their ears cocked, eyes staring.

'Choukri. Will you please. You remember the sequence?'

'Exactly.' Choukri stepped across to the table, adjusting the angle of the laptop screen. 'Now?'

'Now,' said Khan.

All four guns leapt into action, without sound suppression in the hollow shell of the hold. They were dry runs with neither ammunition nor explosion, but the crew shrank back, their faces apprehensive at the barrels pumping in unison.

Khan basked in their reaction as the men slowly regained their composure, turning to one another, exchanging wide-eyed looks and blowing out their cheeks.

'Okay, again,' Khan said. 'And close attention this time.'

He nodded to Choukri who keyed the sequence. The chief leant in. All eyes were fixed on the guns, but not Khan's. His were roaming the faces of the men, relishing the charged atmosphere.

With the second demonstration complete and the crew's undivided attention, Khan drew them closer, pointing out key features and technicalities. The chief was learning fast and able to answer many of the crew's questions himself. Khan stood back, looking around, catching Choukri's eye, exchanging a glance of satisfaction over his protégé.

Khan turned to the men and called them across to an ammunition carousel, explaining its processes and how each shell was fed in turn, where pinch points and jamming might occur and how to overcome them. After a while he backed away, leaving them in the chief's hands to practise their routines.

Choukri beckoned Khan over, the two of them looking on with pride. The men were working well together, encouraging each other and delighting in their progress as they got to grips with it.

'No problem there,' Choukri said.

'No problem at all.'

'And now the manual procedures,' Choukri said, gesturing to Faisel.

Khan switched the laptop on and set the programme to the start page, explaining every feature, tab and drop down, moving the cursor around to all of them in turn. Each gun had its targets preloaded. For simplicity, just one click would trigger them all from the start through to the end and, at any time, a gun could be deselected and fired manually, before another click would put it back into automatic sequence with the others.

Choukri and Faisel leant in, their eyes following every move. From time to time they took over the controls and duplicated what Khan had just shown them, practising the routines, building their confidence.

The system had a sound logic and an absence of abbreviations and techie buzzwords. Each tab gave a detailed description of what it would do. Nothing had been left to guesswork or assumption.

Choukri lifted his hands and turned to Khan. 'It's perfect. Easier than booking an airline ticket online.'

Khan beamed in delight before checking his watch. It was late in the afternoon. The shells in the demonstration carousel were lifted out and taken back to the storage containers. It would be the crew's job during the voyage to fill the carousels. Two hundred and forty tonnes of ammunition needed to be carried by hand from the containers.

With the last of the packing up completed, the men filed out of the hold, leaving just Khan, Choukri and Mubarak. Above them the hatch was rolling into position, the steel panels rumbling and clanking in their guides. Then there was quiet, just the whirr of dehumidifiers, one between each gun and its ammunition carousel.

'It's up to us now,' Khan said, glancing to each of them before turning to look down the hold, the guns looming ever more powerful in the thin light, their shadows magnified, spread across the floor, climbing the walls. 'Did you ever truly believe we'd reach this point?'

Choukri turned to him, his face set. 'I did. And I truly believe we'll reach the final one. This I believe.'

'I sometimes wondered, but I do now,' Mubarak said, his eyes becoming cautious, almost pensive, as he looked around. 'It seems inconceivable that no one has stirred, not a soul. Or are they watching us now, up in the cliffs or orbiting the atmosphere. Is there a squadron of ships out there below the horizon, the Americans, the French, British, Dutch. Perhaps the Russians and Chinese too, in solidarity – can the world really be asleep?'

TWENTY-SIX

Dan opened the curtains and let the sun in. It was ten o'clock on Sunday morning. He'd been up since six with Phoebe and it was now time for Julie to greet the day. She rolled away and pulled the covers over her face. He turned them back and guided her hand to the cup he had put on the bedside table.

'The park before lunch?' he said.

'After a bath.'

'I'll take Phoebe now. You come when you're ready,' he said, stepping across the hallway to the bathroom and running the taps.

Getting used to a sabbatical was difficult for both of them. Dan had made himself as useful as possible, avoided the pub and kept the weed box in check. Having time for Phoebe was proving rewarding, though sometimes taxing. He was having to come to terms with the guilty truth that it could also be boring. So far, the time on his hands had not caused any friction at home and he was grateful for that.

He let the pram roll ahead with a 'Wheee!' Phoebe repeated it with excitement. She was picking words up quickly, using them randomly and pronouncing them in a way that was difficult to understand, but was definite speech. For every word she knew, or thought she knew, there were ten more she understood. Unsteadily but enthusiastically, she had been on her feet for a couple of months now and was fast becoming a real walking, talking, living person.

With a foot absently rocking the pushchair, he settled down on a park bench and checked his messages. The *Ocean Dove* was on his mind, but resisting the temptation to meddle was taking precedence. All he knew was that its current destination was South Africa and there was nothing contentious he could read into that.

There was still an urge to check the AIS, OceanBird's website and various information sources, but he knew he had to be seen to be playing the game. Nine months in the service had been long enough to appreciate that they had the resources to monitor him and probably would. He realised and accepted that he did not have sufficient knowledge of the system to circumvent it. As part of his remit he subscribed to countless shipping news wires and trade sites, but he was careful to avoid anything that could be interpreted as pushing the bounds of credibility. Taking a general interest was one thing. Specific searches were another.

Jo Clymer had suggested he should use his free time wisely. As patronising as it was, he clearly remembered her tapping her nose darkly, before adding, 'So don't be tempted …'

Nothing new had arrived from Copenhagen, which didn't surprise him. Besides, the full report into the *Danske Prince* wasn't expected for months and it was unlikely fresh information would come to light.

Now it seemed the only real option was to try to let it wash out of his system. It was easy to say and proving difficult to live with. Brighter moments hinged on LaSalle, a man he accepted he could not read properly, but someone who was surely his ally. At least he hoped that was the case. He'd lost count of the number of times he had turned their discussions over, trying to recall every word and gesture, interpreting them afresh, examining each nuance from a new angle, giving them credence where none was necessarily due.

At low points, he wondered if he had indeed lost faith in his own judgement – the bitterest aspect to deal with. 'Let it go,' he would unconvincingly tell himself, repeating the mantra aloud whenever he found himself drifting back to perspectives, angles, levels and subsidiary levels.

But certain perspectives, angles, levels and subsidiary levels still worried him. The look Hak had given him when he had asked who knew about the Bar Mhar raid was still clear in his mind. The implication was plain. It was a foundation stone of the security business: those who needed to know would know.

There was no hiding from it. Deep down, he knew his reticence had been motivated in part by self-preservation. The correct course would have been to report to LaSalle immediately, regardless of what Hak had implied. And what exactly had he implied – that if Dan wanted to play with the big boys, he'd better observe the big boys' rules? Saving face with Hak, someone he both put his trust in and instinctively mistrusted, was bordering on shameful. He should have disclosed it. In the marrow of his bones and bone-headedness, he knew it.

A couple of weeks into his sabbatical, Dan had called LaSalle, who made time to meet him, though not at Alf's. The coffee wasn't quite up to standard, but LaSalle managed to organise a plate of biscuits.

'But the facts,' LaSalle had said. 'From the size and nature of the timber fragments, the deduction is they were ship's timbers and very probably from a dhow. The sizes were consistent with the supposition and so were the round holes – the dhow builders' traditional peg fixings. One fragment was made from two pieces joined together by pegs, which more or less confirms it. Moreover, the planking indicated trauma, from impact and explosion, and detailed tests confirmed both. Chemical analysis established that fragments of paint and hull coatings embedded in the timber were precisely the same as the types used on the *Danske Prince,* and minute traces of steel were consistent with the type and grade of plate used by its shipbuilding yard. The outer faces of the timbers were encrusted with typical marine matter, organisms *and* detonated ammonium nitrate, so it's clear the explosion did not come *from* the dhow – the force of it went *into* the dhow, from the outside. The only conclusion is that the dhow made contact with the *Danske Prince* and suffered the consequences of one of the ship's cargoes exploding, the ammonium nitrate, for reasons unknown. The impact of the explosion was substantial and in close proximity, which corresponds with where the ammonium nitrate was stowed on the *Danske Prince.* The cargo was close to the waterline at the bow, presumably the point of impact. It makes no sense for the ship's stern to collide with the dhow, and contact along either side is equally unlikely. If that had been the case it would have been a glancing blow, with significantly less impact. It has to be the bows. That alone makes sense. And the precise chemical composition of the traces of ammonium nitrate match precisely with the formula used by SAPET. So there is no reason to doubt it was their product, though I grant you there is also no suggestion as to the how and why. No human traces were found at the accident site, so the dhow was presumably unmanned, and nothing associated with a dhow was found either, no net or sail fragments, no fittings or equipment of a type either a dhow or its crew might reasonably have, indicating everything was washed from it and lost to the sea a long time ago. The dhow may have been waterlogged, partially submerged, difficult to see – and it may have been in that state for many months or years.'

Dan sat there perfectly still. His eyes were fixed on LaSalle, who had spoken for two minutes without drawing breath and without referring to notes.

'From the size and scale of the timbers,' LaSalle continued, 'the dhow was unlikely to have been less than twenty metres long. It was of heavy construction, ocean-going. The principal timber was acacia, with traces of mangrove. Traditionally, the only dhow builders surrounding the Indian Ocean who use acacia are from Yemen. India uses native teak from Kerala, as do the yards of the Arabian Gulf who import it in large quantities. In East Africa, particularly Zanzibar, coconut is the preferred material. So everything points to a dhow built in Yemen, but there's nothing to suggest it remained there. Dhows are bought and sold. It could have changed hands many times without a single record of any transaction. Putting an age on the dhow is impossible. The fragments were carbon dated, but that sheds no light at all on when the vessel itself was built, merely confirming the age of the timbers.'

Now he paused, looking across as if to say *It's all complicated, it's all imprecise, unknowable and unprovable – do I need to go on?*

Not really, Dan thought. There was nothing he could add and nothing had been overlooked. Having lived with and churned over every last detail for so long, had LaSalle missed even the slightest nuance he would have pounced on it. But the best he could manage was to pick up the tone. 'The Danes made enquiries in the dhow communities and coastguards, hospitals, charities,' he said. 'It could be months before there's clear info. They might have to go back a long time, and the further they go the more unreliable the information's going to be. The dhow could have been drifting for years.'

'That it could.' LaSalle nodded. 'And then there's the compelling data. So I regret, Dan, there is an inevitability to all this. The ship hit a dhow and the cargo exploded – and that should be the end of the matter.' LaSalle took the last biscuit from the plate and snapped it, offering half across the table. He pondered for a while. 'Tell me, do you know Captain Ahab?'

Dan thought for a moment. He knew the name, but couldn't place it immediately with a ship or shipowner and certainly not with the *Ocean Dove*. 'No ...' he said, cautiously.

'*Moby Dick*. The obsessed Ahab. Obsessed with his great white whale.'

Dan frowned and sat back. 'That's not fair,' he said, looking away, annoyed with himself, annoyed at confusing a literary captain with a literal one, and annoyed at exposing who he was. Everyone knew about the whale now. At the final Monday meeting before his suspension a wag had said, sotto voce, 'Thar she blows,' to general amusement all round. But, as he raised his eyes again, he could see that point scoring had not been on LaSalle's mind.

'The word "fair" is never far from your lips,' LaSalle said. 'You seem to set great store by fairness in our unfair world. And no, it's not fair, but people will associate you with the analogy. And if you hang on to it like a dog with its bone, I'm not sure they'll be without justification.'

'I hear you.'

'Good.' LaSalle nodded, crunching the last morsel of biscuit. 'And how's your lady solicitor?'

'Out of hospital and mending.'

'That's good to hear. And Perkowski's tidied it up?'

'I wouldn't quite say tidy. Seems we've got a skilled car thief who's skilled at avoiding CCTV – but just a crap driver, apparently.'

'So it would seem,' LaSalle said. 'Well, time has passed. Perhaps we can assume it's concluded itself satisfactorily.'

Dan nodded, though not wholly in agreement, more in hope, and as he had noted himself, the past few weeks had seen him less cautious, less suspicious, less inclined to start at sudden noises or question strangers in the street about other strangers.

It wasn't difficult to understand LaSalle's push for conclusion, for no logical case to answer in the fate of the *Danske Prince*, no threat from the *Ocean Dove*, no one trying to terminally remove his obstacle of a presence. Now was an opportunity for a fresh start, for a rewarding career. Yes, it was understandable, and LaSalle certainly wasn't a well-intentioned uncle advocating the long-term goal of a secure government pension. That was wide of the mark, he realised. It also felt like a disservice to even venture there.

The memories were fading, replaced with awareness of the here and now, the tantalising primacy of the future. He turned sharply as Julie appeared at his side, shaken from his thoughts.

'How's my daughter?' she said, looking down into the pram before sitting beside him.

'Happy,' he said, gathering his wits. 'See how I've got the sun on the lower part of the blanket but not on her face.' He smiled. 'I'm getting good at this.'

Julie's eyes narrowed. 'Not bad. You're a fast learner – at some things.'

'But slow at others,' he said. 'And I'm sorry,' he added, holding her eye. 'I'm sorry I've been such an arse lately.' He nodded to himself, staring down before looking back to her. 'I saw LaSalle again, and he was clever about it ...'

He felt her shift a little closer to him. She didn't know LaSalle – referring to him as the Suffolk man, the father figure that Dan was so impressed with – but she'd let him know that while she understood she was reluctant to share his faith.

He turned to her, shaking his head. 'It all just kinda spun out, got complicated. I was just, I dunno, getting lost, I suppose. I guess I was out of my depth. I thought I knew what was going on, but I didn't, and I couldn't tie the ends together, and everything just kept getting looser, just slipping away. But I wouldn't let go. Couldn't let go ...' he added, as Julie put her hand in his. 'I told LaSalle this business had crushed me, really crushed me. And it was true, sort of. But it's the system, their system that crushed me, not the facts, not the evidence, not because I accept I was wrong – he can think what he likes …' He shrugged. 'But worst of all,' he said, pulling his head back and looking directly into her eyes. 'Worst of all …'

'Don't doubt yourself,' she said, squeezing a little tighter. 'Not over the big things. I don't.'

He looked out from the bench over the park, seeing nothing, content in the closeness of the silence and Julie's presence by his side. There was a feeling of lightening, an unburdening of weight over the guilt for his actions professionally and, even more so, personally. As tension loosened in mind and body, he thought he might finally begin seeing through the haze to the other side, to a bright blue yonder. But as much as he tried to reach out to it, his mind kept returning to the unshakeable belief that something about the *Ocean Dove* stank.

Julie turned to him. 'I've been thinking. Perhaps we should go to Suffolk.'

The joy of those few short words was almost physical. He could feel them coursing through him like endorphins. It was something he'd hoped to hear her say but had not pressed. Friends had recently inherited a cottage on the Suffolk coast from an elderly aunt. Though basic and isolated, it was in a glorious position and they could have it for a fortnight. At first, Julie had resisted the idea, arguing carefree sabbaticals rather than constructive work were indulgent. They had only seen pictures of the cottage, but the garden with its fruit trees and a path over fields to the beach looked so inviting. The future held uncertainties and a day like this only served to reinforce the imperative to press on, with hope, to have confidence in the long term. Their six-month plan would come to an end soon, so why not bookend it with something refreshing?

'We can go together at the beginning for a long weekend and I'll come back here from Tuesday to Friday to get some work done,' she said.

'Then you can stay all the next week at the start of June,' Dan said, checking the calendar on his phone. 'And when you're back here I can get on with some things.'

By way of thanks and a payment in kind he had offered to help sort the place out, give the garden an overhaul and do some odd jobs.

'Phoebe can watch you from under an apple tree,' Julie said.

Dan lifted his shoulders from the bench and peered into the pram. 'I'd like that. It might be her first memory.'

'Like the boy at school …' Julie said.

Dan turned to her. He nodded, remembering.

There had been a boy in his class who always went to Suffolk whenever there was a holiday. With luck, other children may have got a day at Canvey Island, but not Dan. Suffolk had come to be some sort of ideal. He had no idea where this boy went – to a caravan, chocolate-box cottage or five-star hotel. It hadn't mattered. What counted was that he went, and perhaps now their daughter's first memory would be sweet compensation, something precious he had not been able to have.

'Suffolk,' he said.

'Suffolk,' she repeated. 'An end to all this.'

TWENTY-SEVEN

Choukri was on the wings, sweeping his binoculars over Algoa Bay, South Africa, a natural horseshoe forty miles across. To the east was a sandy shoreline and what looked like wilderness beyond. On the west were the industrial ports of Coega and Port Elizabeth, where the *Danske Prince* had loaded ammonium nitrate and the *Ocean Dove* had sailed straight past. Port Elizabeth appeared benign today, with its familiar outline of port cranes in the foreground and tall buildings flashing sunlight from glass behind.

It was just after 09.00 on Tuesday, 10 May, sixteen days after sailing from Bar Mhar.

Through the open doorway he heard a familiar voice.

'Good morning, Algoa Bay. This is Captain Mubarak of the *Ocean Dove*. We're dropping anchor at the bunker station.'

'Good morning, Captain. We were expecting you. Please contact the suppliers on channel 14. They'll be listening.'

A call for fuel and stores in Algoa avoided the usual formalities. The ship would remain clearly offshore by some miles, without troubling the customs and immigration authorities. A small tanker would come out, tie up alongside and pump fuel in. The same arrangement was made for ship's stores, which would arrive by supply launch. Offshore in a sheltered bay was quick and easy and, more importantly, it was without inspection or prying eyes. Choukri lowered the binoculars and nodded to himself with satisfaction. Algoa Bay had been identified carefully, one of the few facilities of its kind on the *Ocean Dove*'s route.

Bunkering offshore was all well and good as far as the crew were concerned. It required more or less the same input as being in port.

Replenishing the stores was another matter, and their arms were aching after days of carrying ammunition. Two hundred and forty tonnes of shells had to be transferred by hand from the storage containers at one end of the hold to the carousels at the other, a distance of fifty metres to the furthest gun and twenty to the nearest. They had started with the greater distance, reasoning the work would only get easier, but the benefit of their logic still seemed far away. Heavy weather near the equator had stopped work for three days. Squalls and a driving wind had seen the ship pitching in troughs, the crew unable to keep their balance, searching for the next handrail as they moved about. Choukri had been pleased to learn the forecast for the next seven days promised fine weather.

The bunker vessel manoeuvred alongside. Lines were thrown down, some to secure the ships together, others as lead lines to attach to the fuel hoses, which would be hauled up and screwed into the manifolds of the ship's fuel tanks.

It was business as usual with all the courtesies. The chandler's clerk enjoyed coffee and Cookie's pastries. The bunker technician's eyes lit up when Mubarak slipped a bottle of whisky in his bag.

'Not bad,' Mubarak said, glancing at his watch before looking across to Choukri.

It was five hours since they had dropped anchor. Now they were under way again.

'Next stop, Moritz pilot,' Choukri said. It had a definite finality to it.

Faisel gripped the console, concentrating on the horizon before looking around, first to Choukri, then Mubarak.

Breaking the quiet, Mubarak said, 'Take her out to twenty.'

The international convention on territorial waters was set at twelve miles from the shoreline. Beyond that, at a clear twenty miles, a ship could feel secure from interference.

Choukri turned the figures over in his head. It would be nearly two hours before they were twenty miles offshore, approaching four in the afternoon. It would leave little time for ammunition shifting.

'Okay, no ammo today,' he said, looking over his shoulder as cheers came from the wing door behind him. 'Double shift tomorrow,' he added without a smile.

They were in whale country now, where the Indian Ocean met the Atlantic. Some had been seen off the port bow in the early light that morning, perhaps a dozen, but too far away to identify. Great white sharks were not uncommon either. Cookie had been told to take extra care when he hauled up his fishing lines in the mornings.

For the next two days the ship would head due west under the tip of Africa. At breakfast time on Thursday morning, after rounding the Cape of Good Hope, the rudder would turn and point them north.

Choukri knew how the weather was set for the next week, but the future prospects were troubling him.

'Let's check the long-term forecast again,' he said, glancing across.

Mubarak looked up from the console. 'We did do it last night, remember …'

They logged into the weather-service website, a studious quiet on the bridge as they ran through the voyage scenarios, independently making their own calculations according to speed, distance, wind and current, and the unknowns that only experience could prepare for.

Mubarak leant in at Choukri's side as they studied the meteorological charts. It all looked good, the winds minimal, currents steady, sea temperatures as expected, and in a week's time they would enter a high-pressure zone that was expected to remain constant.

'And here,' Choukri said, running a finger over the screen, scanning the chart out in the middle of the Atlantic and looking for signs of trouble in the fickle coastal weather systems along America's eastern seaboard.

Mubarak nodded his head. 'No problem there.'

'Exactly.'

~

Most of the crew were in their cabins. Only two were on the bridge:

Faisel manning the helm and Mubarak staring down at the crossword, his upturned hands under his chin.

He put his pencil down, glancing around.

'What's that,' he said. 'Do you hear it?'

Faisel's eyes searched around in concentration before he eventually shook his head.

'It's like a vibration. The prop shaft?' Mubarak added. 'There, it's louder now.'

After a few moments a smile spread across Faisel's face. 'Okay, it's music ...'

Mubarak shook his head and returned to the crossword, satisfied that the equilibrium of his ship was under no suspicion. A minute later, he pushed the paper aside, the corner of his mouth twisting. Coming up through the deck was a steady bass note, its unwelcome vibration competing disharmoniously with the only vibration he wanted to hear – the contented heartbeat of an efficient vessel running smoothly and making good progress.

Faisel stole a glance from the corner of his eye as the volume cranked up, accompanied by both top notes and an additional rhythmic thumping.

Mubarak slipped from his chair, pacing around agitatedly and staring at the bridge floor. He tossed his head towards the stairs.

'Get down there and find out what the bloody hell's going on.'

Standing at the console, checking the readings, the sound increased once more. Now he could hear men's voices and catcalls, and barely hear or feel his own ship. A message came into the communications monitor. He saw it flash on the screen but didn't hear the ping.

Faisel was back a minute later, the smile on his face reassuring and partly relieving Mubarak's irritation.

'Yesterday, when you filmed us ...' Faisel began to explain.

The pieces fell into place. Mubarak had been on the wings, looking down through the open hatch to the chain gang ferrying ammunition to the carousels. After a while he'd started to film it. A couple of hours ago, Snoop had asked to borrow the phone and had transferred the footage to his computer, setting it to music, running through his namesake's back catalogue until he found a match of rhythm and time.

There had been symmetry in the crew's movements when Mubarak watched them, like some bastardised line dance, the men stepping in sequence, three paces in one direction empty-handed, three back again cradling a shell like a baby. After days of practice they had settled on a rhythm that worked seamlessly, each man in sync, spread equally apart in a line from container to carousel. They knew the pace, shifting one way to receive, then the other to offload, repeating their steps like machines.

Faisel beamed, extending a hand to the door. 'You've got to see it!'

With a knowing shake of his head, Mubarak made his way to the stairs, descending to the crew deck. Staring along the corridor, the dance and the music was clear in an instant. He glanced down, surprised to see his own foot tapping, his amusement rising as the crew became aware of him and turned the heat up, repeating the moves, camping them up with a flourish and chanting the hook in the soundtrack.

Snoop's head was banging. 'That's kickin' tight!' he yelled, the beat in perfect time with the chain gang's motion, a line of the crew in the cramped passageway, three steps forward, three back, their arms swaying under the imaginary weight of shells. The volume was at maximum, the men shouting, their faces animated, their boots crashing down in symmetry.

Mubarak threw his head back. It was good to laugh. It had been a while since the last time he'd felt his ribs ache.

Turning unobtrusively on his heels, he slipped up the stairs to the bridge. Through the windscreen, the bows ploughed a steady course towards a setting sun that was streaking the horizon in great belts of orange, coral and pink. He looked at the majestic colours for a moment, a wistful smile creeping over his face. Below him, the unfamiliar vibrations of the ship from music and the thumping feet of a happy crew filled him with optimism.

TWENTY-EIGHT

Jawad pulled into the yard and parked next to Bulent's car. He checked his watch. It was five thirty in the morning. As he got out of the car, Rashid pulled in behind him.

Rashid came over, greeting the two of them cautiously. They waited together, saying nothing. The sound of an engine revving in the street had them all turning nervously.

'Not us,' Bulent said as the car sped up the road and turned out of sight.

Jawad thought about the instructions they had all received – report to the office car park at six o'clock with their passports, phones, personal computers and one travel bag. There had been nothing more, no destination, no plan.

He looked around the deserted car park. It was Friday, the weekend, the offices closed. Bulent had told him that all of OceanBird's people were to be moved. They were a small team and they were all complicit. At STC it was another matter. Only a handful were Network insiders. The majority of the two hundred and fifty staff worked innocently at their careers, particularly the new venture-capitalist owners, who were only now beginning to get their feet under the table. They had owned the company for nine days and were excited at the prospect of the Moritz plant arriving in Sharjah at the end of the month for recommissioning.

'You got any better idea where we're going?' Rashid said.

Bulent shook his head. 'Not really.'

Jawad looked across. Why speculate? he thought. Some people might be flown out to the far corners of the world, while others would perhaps go overland, perhaps into the vastness of Saudi Arabia, though no one knew where. They had simply been given times and meeting points and, very evidently no one else had been told to assemble at the office car park at 6.00 a.m.

'The baggage weight limit means tourist class,' Rashid added, the corner of his mouth turning up at the prospect. 'We should go business at least.'

Jawad eyed him, scraping his foot on the ground as though he'd picked up some tourist-class shit on his shoe. But he said nothing, knowing Rashid wouldn't understand anyway.

'If you think about it,' Bulent said. 'It stands to reason we'll be held somewhere today, a safe house or something. If the *Ocean Dove* has to back off for some reason and take another run at it in a few days or whatever, we can all be back behind our desks tomorrow as if nothing happened.'

Makes sense, he thought. 'What time is it on the *Ocean Dove?*'

'About two,' Bulent said. 'The pilot will be on board at six.'

'And then?'

'Four hours to the berth.'

Jawad looked down, shuffling a piece of gravel contemplatively with his foot. The Moritz terminal in winter was vivid in his mind. He wondered what it would look like today, in summer.

They all swung round at the sound of tyres coming over the pavement. A pair of Mercedes van taxis with blacked-out windows pulled across and stopped on either side of them.

Three men got out of the back of the nearest van. Its side window lowered, revealing a heavyset face staring coldly at them from the passenger seat. A gold tooth flashed in the morning sun.

Jawad froze, his heart pounding. He turned his head, meeting Bulent's haunted eyes. They were filled with an unequivocal confirmation – my God. Sharjah police!

'Passports, phones, laptops and car keys,' Mr Gold said, nodding to a man who was stretching a holdall open. 'Now!' he barked, when no one moved.

Jawad's legs were slow to respond. He stepped across and fumbled on the ground. When the holdall was full, hands clamped roughly on his shoulder and bundled him through the van's passenger door. He got in, sliding across to the far side, followed by Bulent and Rashid. Two men occupied the jump seats behind them.

The convoy pulled out of the car park: his own Audi, Bulent's Porsche and Rashid's Mercedes, followed by the two taxi vans. Slowing for the interchange at the end of the street, the cars switched lane but the vans stayed where they were.

'Hey, the airport's that way,' Rashid said petulantly.

No one answered. *For God's sake, shut up*, Jawad thought, not daring to speak, his eyes staring resolutely ahead.

Rashid turned in his seat, his eyes darting. 'Where are we going?' he demanded, giving Gold's shoulder an impatient jab.

There was no response. Rashid gave him another prod and this time Gold swung round but said nothing, his scowling eyes and raised finger speaking for him.

The outer fringes of Sharjah slipped by. They were heading east into the sun, on the main coastal highway, the sea on their left and the desert to the right. Jawad looked over his shoulder. There was a flash of white as the driver in the van behind smiled. The passenger in the front remained expressionless behind dark glasses. Across the back seat, lit clearly by the low sun, were the outlines of two more men.

He tried to rationalise the overload of information, to set some sort of order. If the authorities had rounded them up at six o'clock, they must also have everyone else, including the Network's logistics people who were handling the escapes. It seemed inconceivable that this was some sort of eleventh-hour breakthrough. The nonchalance with which they had picked them up suggested they had known for a long time, confident the drama of helicopters and squads of soldiers would be unnecessary. On the contrary, it had been low-key but pinpoint. They knew their targets were just three unarmed businessmen waiting for a ride. How long had they known, he wondered – a month, six months, a year? Waiting until the last moment was smart, he thought. It allowed the net to widen. But just how deeply had they penetrated? Surely not all the way to the Emir?

In the corner of his eye he could see Bulent's stony face. Words were not required. He knew exactly the same thing would be racing through his mind – if the security services knew so much about them, they would know everything about the *Ocean Dove*. There was a stark image in his imagination: a cargo ship on blue water, an armada of naval vessels circling it, jet fighters screaming overhead, helicopters lowering men in balaclavas. Smoke and flames were pouring from the shattered bridge of the *Ocean Dove*, its decks littered with cartridge cases and the bloody bodies of the crew where they had made their futile stand against an overwhelming force.

The van slowed and turned onto a track into the desert. For the next twenty minutes they bumped along slowly before the track crested a dune and petered out into a flat plain of grey grit. The ground beneath them was smooth, their speed increasing to what felt like a steady sixty, plumes of smoky dust streaming behind.

In the centre of the windscreen, in the shimmering distance, there was a shadow on the ground. They were heading straight towards it. Jawad couldn't make out what it was, gauge their distance from it or judge its size. It could have been as small as a sheep or as big as a truck, but it was the only thing to be seen in the featureless landscape. He pressed his knee against Bulent's and looked ahead.

Ten minutes later the engine revs dropped and they slowed to a halt. Mr Gold stepped out and slid the door back on Jawad's side.

A wave of burning air swept over him as he swapped air conditioning and carpeting for sand and grit. The other van pulled up behind and the men got out, stretching and looking around. One of them spat in the dust and he heard him say 'Faswat-at-ajuz' – the hag's cunt.

So that's where we are, he thought, turning and looking again at the shadow thirty metres away – just a mound of earth, a windbreak for an old dried-up well. Now it made sense. He'd heard of this place, loosely of legend, though evidently real enough now. The nomads spoke of it in stories a hundred years old, already poisoned and putrid, full of dead goats and the victims of tribal blood feuds.

Standing there in the middle of nowhere, in dead silence, with the plain stretching to the horizon, he became aware that the other men had shifted away, leaving them to one side, alone. They were in a line, exposed. Gold walked across, a pistol in his hand.

He stopped a few paces from them, his feet planted, looking each of them in the eye. In front of Rashid his penetrating stare dropped momentarily, his head shaking with disappointment.

Jawad shifted his head a fraction, glancing from the corner of his eye at the darkening crotch in Rashid's grey trousers. A simple truth flashed through his mind. Everyone connected with the Network and the *Ocean Dove* was to be summarily executed. There would be no trials and no publicity. The public did not need to know how close they had come to disaster. Tonight they would sleep easily in their beds once again. Standing in the desert, his bowel muscles working overtime, legs locked back to disguise the shaking, it seemed so obvious.

Two shots rang out. Rashid spun backwards. He was twitching as Gold walked across, reached down to an ankle and dragged him across the sand. At the side of the well he heaved at Rashid's belt, carefully finding a dry grip and bending him over the lip, his head down the well, backside in the air, legs dangling.

Gold slipped the wallet from the back pocket, pulled an arm out of the well and twisted a ring from a finger and a watch from the wrist. He reached down again, grabbed a handful of hair and yanked his head up, putting a bullet in the back of his skull. With a cursory glance at shattered bone, he let the head flop before reaching down to Rashid's feet and tipping him headfirst into the hag's cunt.

Shoving the pistol in his waistband, Gold leant his hands on the wall and peered down for a moment, swatting at an angry mist of flies, his face screwing up as the disturbed air rose from the well. Then his back straightened. He turned and looked across.

Jawad's stomach churned at the stench of rotting and decay that had drifted over from the well, the flies buzzing at his sweating face. His feet were rooted to the spot as final and silent prayers raced through his mind.

'You two. Back in the van,' Gold said.

Jawad sat in silence. They were alive and it seemed they had a chance of remaining so. Gold offered no explanation and he didn't dare ask for one. The other van was leading. When they reached the highway it turned west towards the city. Their van turned east. No answers were sought and none were given.

After a while Gold turned. 'His father died last night. There was nothing to be gained from telling him. And you? You're going on a dhow cruise.'

Gold turned back. He'd said his piece and it didn't appear that he was inviting discussion.

'But you're Sharjah police,' Bulent blurted. 'Some kind of special security?'

Gold looked over his shoulder. 'It's just a day job.'

The driver's eyes flicked to the rear-view mirror. 'Relax,' he said. 'Now that was a man, but the son? Don't even think about him, no good for anything. But you two are, and soon you'll be balls-deep in Indonesian babes.'

He smiled over the last few words. At his side, Gold's head was nodding in agreement.

The relief was palpable. There was no reason not to believe in the future – any future. Jawad felt confident enough to risk a question.

'You seem to know a lot, about everything?'

'For the last two years I've known every time you farted,' Gold said. 'And I'll know for the next two as well.'

There was no good reason not to believe him, he thought. They had to be the Emir's men, part of the internal security system. It was rarely discussed, but such a group had to exist. It was taken for granted that it did. They might number thousands around the world and if they knew everything about him, they would know about Rashid, who hadn't been killed for fun. If it had been stage-managed for their benefit, it had certainly been effective. However, it still left the main question, why Rashid?

'Unhinged,' Gold said. 'Firing off stupid messages to the Emir about his own importance and how he could do things better. Too risky. Especially now the old man's gone. What he was really looking for was a way out, so we gave him one.'

Jawad turned to Bulent. 'Indonesia in a dhow – it could mean weeks at sea? We'll be out there and they'll be searching. Do you think we'll know what happens?'

From behind the wheel the driver said, 'You'll know.'

'The whole world will.' Gold nodded.

TWENTY-NINE

Choukri was at the head of the ladder to welcome the pilot on board just before six o'clock on Friday morning. They lingered for a moment, taking their bearings, the pilot pointing out landmarks to the shore before leaning on the rail for one last look out to sea.

'Going to be a glorious day,' he said.

The low sun was flashing like crystal on the water, blazing a celestial path from the horizon to the hull of the *Ocean Dove*.

'Exactly.'

Faisel stood up when they came through the doorway. 'Pilot on bridge,' he announced.

Captain Rowley was tall, though grey hair, a gaunt appearance and metal-framed spectacles couldn't disguise a twinkle in his eye.

Introductions were made and he went through the preliminary safety checks, familiarising Mubarak and the bridge crew with the route on the charts, general procedures and when he would like to take his breakfast. The pilot was in charge and the crew would carry out his orders, though as ever, it would ultimately be Mubarak's ship.

'And with your permission,' the pilot said.

He had effective control now, checking the helmsman's inputs, monitoring the instruments, adjusting speed and course and periodically taking his binoculars to the wings for a visual check. Mubarak gave the crew reassuring nods, observing and reconfirming with the pilot, each referring to the other as Captain.

Tariq had control of the helm, repeating each instruction aloud before carrying it out. After a while Rowley turned to him, a quizzical look on his face.

'Is that a bit of a Birmingham I'm hearing?'

Tariq smiled. 'Yeah, it is.'

'And where am I from, son?'

Tariq pondered for a moment. 'Lancashire?'

Choukri stiffened as a look of horror shot across the pilot's face.

'Yorkshire, please … You tell 'em, son,' the pilot said, throwing his head back and laughing, chuckling to himself as Tariq explained his good-natured – and well taken – faux pas.

For the first hour they were in the open sea before turning into the estuary, which was now beginning to narrow. The low outline of the Isle of Grain was to one side, Canvey Island to the other. The wide mouth tightened further as they slipped between Gravesend and Tilbury. It was more like a river now, sinewy in its twists and turns by Grays and Greenhithe.

Cookie brought the pilot his breakfast, scrambled eggs on toast, which he ate standing up at the console, observed by some of the crew from the corner of their eyes. Assam and Snoop were stealing glances at him through the open doorway, like vultures circling the lame.

'Yours?' Rowley said, his eye drawn to the crossword on the console.

'It's from your *Observer* newspaper. I download it every week,' Mubarak said. 'Do you do it too?'

'No.' Rowley smiled. 'Partial to a sudoku though.'

'Shame,' Mubarak said. 'Eight down's giving me a bit of trouble.'

Choukri looked around. The sun was shining and the pilot was happy. Choukri had told Cookie to prepare his special scrambled eggs, the ones with the subtle addition of a little Parmesan cheese and a dash of Dijon mustard. They always went down well with visiting officials. Nothing was out of place or giving rise to disquiet. He knew pilots liked to work with a well-maintained ship and a professional crew who responded accurately to instructions. On top of that, a little courtesy and charm went a long way.

Regardless, Choukri was taking nothing for granted, underplaying his role on the bridge, conscious he was Mubarak's subordinate and not the mission leader. Tariq had stepped outside for some air. It looked as though the crew were quizzing him.

They received no proper reply as Choukri called Tariq back and substituted his presence with his own. 'Move along,' he said quietly, motioning with his eyes to Snoop and Assam.

Faisel had the helm now. Captain Rowley saw him looking ahead at the graceful arc that spanned the river and filled the windscreen.

'The Queen Elizabeth bridge,' he said, glancing at his watch. 'We're making good time. We'll be there in an hour.'

'And the Rotherhithe Tunnel underneath,' Tariq added, looking up to Rowley, who acknowledged his lack of local geography with a kindly smile.

'Dartford Tunnel, son.'

Emerging from the bridge's shadow, to the left was the Littlebrook power station with the Purfleet container terminal on the opposite bank. The river snaked around Erith and Rainham, the tide turning and the mudflats receding, the landscape industrial with dull grey piping and shining white storage tanks. The sun added an autumnal gleam of russet to rust along the waterfront, broken in places by a little greenery, a patch of scrub grazing or a park. Here and there a church spire rose in the background or a finger pier jutted out into the river.

'Reduce speed one knot,' the pilot said.

'Reduce by one,' Faisel confirmed, the engine note subduing, the vibration through the floor smoothing.

The Thamesmead housing estate slipped by to the left, brownstone and uniform. On the facing bank was the Ford car plant. Rounding the next bend, ahead of them was the London City Airport and the twin piers of the Woolwich ferry bookending the north and the south banks. A mile further was the Thames Barrier and, just minutes beyond, the Moritz terminal.

Everywhere was becoming familiar. Choukri recognised places from his research, the detail embellished by the pilot's commentary. The names were important. He felt his pulse quickening. When they passed through the Thames Barrier he mentally checked his estimations. A spring tide was due in two weeks, an unusually high one.

'Marvellous piece of engineering,' the pilot said.

Choukri shook his head. 'Exactly. To hold a tide like that …'

The *Ocean Dove* began its approach, edging towards Moritz. They were already facing in the right direction, making it a straightforward manoeuvre to berth alongside, little more complicated than pulling in and parking at the side of the road.

Tariq was on the radio to the Vessel Traffic Service, advising them they were starting their approach.

'We have you on screen,' VTS confirmed.

Men were on the quay, linesmen employed for the day, or more accurately for about fifteen minutes. After securing mooring ropes to bollards they would be free to go home.

Set back from the waterside was the dismantled plant, packed and ready for shipment. Two thousand tonnes of machinery stretched across the terminal. The contractors had completed their contract and laid the cargo out in regimented rows, in sequence for loading. Some was in wooden cases and crates, some in containers or neatly bundled pipework. Storage tanks, vessels and columns rested on supports at the back. It covered an area close to the size of a football pitch, forming a protective barrier between the ship, the main building and the outside world.

Captain Rowley followed Mubarak and Choukri down the gangway. 'It's been a pleasure,' he said, shaking their hands in turn. 'Are you going to load now? I can see there's plenty to do.'

'We've got a day's work first to prepare the ship,' Mubarak said. 'We start on Monday.'

The linesmen's foreman stepped across to them, gesturing to his men standing by their minibus.

'Are we done, boss?'

'All done,' Choukri said. 'We'll see you again on Wednesday after completion of loading.'

As the van pulled away, Choukri saw a man heading towards them from across the terminal, weaving his way through the banks of cargo.

'Sorry, bit late,' the man said, introducing himself as the customs officer. 'I'll do the crew immigration first and then the ship, starting in the hold.'

'This way, please,' Choukri said, ushering him towards the gangway.

Mubarak pulled out two chairs on the bridge. The ship's documents and the crew's passports and seamen's books were laid out neatly on the chart table. The customs man scrutinised each in turn and made entries on a laptop. He was a little guy, about forty-five, pinched, nervous, with a shaky hand. He was also punctiliously slow.

'Okay, Captain. I'll leave my stuff here if that's all right?' he eventually said.

'Of course,' Mubarak said, extending a hand to the door.

~

Assam led the way down to the hold, the customs officer behind him with Snoop bringing up the rear. At the well of the stairs he opened a doorway and went into a dimly lit passageway. After a few paces he stopped, turned the handle of the hold door and flicked the light switches. The customs officer and Snoop followed him in, all three of them allowing a moment for their eyes to adjust to the light.

The customs man turned his gaze along the hold and stepped forward automatically, before hesitating, his mouth open. 'What the f—'

Assam's fingers tightened around a cosh in his waistband and brought it down on the back of the customs officer's head in one swift movement.

Snoop prodded the prone figure with his boot. There was no response. He turned and went across to the weapons store.

'And some rags,' Assam called out.

There was neither sound nor motion from the floor as Snoop grabbed the man's collar and lifted, shuffling rags under the head with his boot before stepping to one side, raising his arm and looking at Assam.

'No way, man,' Assam said, taking the Glock from his hand and striking a pose.

'Okay, got it. More flava, yeah,' Snoop said.

Assam screwed his face up. 'That's still so fucking lame. Bust him like this!' He snatched the gun again, but this time he squeezed the trigger, twice.

Snoop spun around and brought his boot crashing down. 'Motherfucker!'

The word spat from his contorted mouth as Assam blew over the end of the silencer and raised an eyebrow. They both turned at the sound of footsteps behind them, their faces straightening.

Choukri looked at them, at the crumpled body on the floor, at the rags oozing blood into old grease stains. 'It's done?'

Assam nodded.

'Then stop fucking about and clear it up!'

There was no time for bickering. Assam dragged the body to an empty container and dumped it on the floor. Head and rags had become separated. Snoop put his boot on the rags, prodding them along the blood trail before kicking them into the container.

~

Choukri checked his watch as he stood on the wings. It was just before eleven. Below him the hatch was rumbling open. Just one panel would be raised, leaving a gap large enough for the crane to lift the explosives through. The chief was rigging a pump for the fuel oil and Choukri could see Tariq crouched behind a stack of pipework on the terminal, keeping an eye on the security guards in the hut. The pilot's taxi had been and gone. The back of the linesmen's minibus had long since disappeared up the road, and no one was going to miss the customs officer for hours. The terminal was theirs.

'Just look at it,' Choukri said.

'I am,' Mubarak said. 'But I don't know if I believe it.'

There was barely a cloud in the sky. The wind was slight but it was there. Importantly, it was coming from upriver, from the west, over the top of Canary Wharf and the City of London, the beating hearts of the financial community.

'What a thing,' Choukri whispered, staring upstream to the south bank where the Shard Tower reached to the sky like some fantastic love child of the pyramids. His eyes swept back to Canary Wharf in the foreground, looking up and down the towering edifices of banks and financial institutions. And if that wasn't enough, looming behind it was a second tier, the City business district and its landmarks, the Gherkin, Tower 42, the Leadenhall building. Across the river a plane was taking off from the City Airport as flags fluttered from the roof of the Excel Exhibition Centre.

He stood and stared. There was a sense of disbelief, as if he could reach out and touch it all from his front-row seat.

Behind him, on the bridge, Faisel and an engineer were setting up scanning equipment – receivers to monitor the security and emergency service channels. There were two laptops, one for television, the other for radio. The BBC were running a cookery show and the radio had picked up Capital FM. The plangent guitar of the Isley Brothers' 'Summer Breeze' was drifting through the open door. Punching the palm of his hand, he snapped from his thoughts and turned to the equally silent Mubarak.

'Okay,' he said. 'In one hour it's noon. We have time. We keep our focus.'

He stepped back to the bridge and grabbed the binoculars. Across the creek the old gasworks had sprung into bloom with soft green leaves in its birches, lilac and purple pokers in the scrub buddleia. Downriver, the deck was filling at the bar where Jawad had enjoyed his cheeseburger. People were lounging in deck shoes and shorts, sandals and spaghetti straps, sunglasses on heads, drinks in hands. He panned over to the electricity substation on the opposite bank, upstream to the fuel storage depot, then back to the bar. At five hundred metres individual faces were clear in the powerful lenses. Lips were moving, chatting and laughing and ordering another round.

Letting the binoculars drop around his neck, he stretched his hand out, his fingers spread. There was no trembling. He realised with finality that he felt nothing now.

Choukri made his way down the companionway. On the quay, the explosives team looked at him anxiously, eager to put their Bar Mhar drills into practice. There was an apron of free space extending twenty metres from the quay to the first row of cargo, a working area for the loading operations. Devices were to be placed among the crates and cases, with the less effective ones nearest the ship. Some of them were just smoke bombs, for show. He ran his eyes over everything, checking it was all correct before motioning with a flick of his head.

'Then get to it.'

Tariq's voice came over the walkie-talkie, reporting the security house was quiet.

With Snoop and Assam, Choukri threaded his way through the banks of cargo. Tariq was fifty metres in front of them, concealed behind a stack of piping.

'Nothing happening up there …' Tariq said.

Choukri looked ahead before quizzing him on the layout inside the security hut, which Tariq knew from escorting the pilot to his taxi. He wanted to know what would be immediately in front of him when he stepped through the door, where the counter was, the gap around it, the desk and the easy chairs for the guards.

Tariq knelt and sketched it out in the dust as Choukri glanced up to Assam and Snoop, making certain they were taking it in.

Both guards were in their seats when Choukri opened the door.

'Good morning. Beautiful day,' he said, stepping forward with Assam and Snoop close behind.

'Yes, sir,' the guard said, starting to rise from his chair.

'Exactly.' Choukri smiled. He was already filling the gap in the counter when he pointed to something on the back wall and took a step towards it.

The guard turned to see what had caught Choukri's eye. A cosh came down on the back of his neck followed in an instant by another heavy thud to his skull. The other guard had barely stirred from his book when Assam sprang at him and lashed three rapid blows to his head.

'Still alive,' Snoop said, crouching on the floor at his side before scrambling across to the chair and tugging at uniform buttons. 'This one too, just.'

Choukri pulled the washroom door open. 'In here,' he said.

The first guard was dragged by the legs. Assam reached down to the man's belt, yanking his trunk and head across the threshold, leaving his legs propped up against the back wall.

Snoop tipped the slumped figure of the other guard out of the chair, unlaced his boots and threw them in the direction of the washroom. Assam kicked them through the door. The blue trousers were already down when Choukri rolled the body over and Snoop pulled the jacket off – with its Sentinel Security badge on the breast pocket.

Assam pulled the man across before standing to one side, a hand on the door frame, the toe of one boot cocked on the floor behind his standing leg.

Snoop raised the Glock.

'Two each,' Choukri said.

The back of one head was exposed, the other buried. Blood peppered the wall with the second shot. Snoop put his boot on a hip and shoved, exposing the inert body below, face up, an eye just beginning to open.

Assam closed the door, shoving hard against a socked foot jutting into the room.

'Don't forget the cap,' Choukri said as Snoop gathered up the uniform.

Choukri stood at the fence. The road outside was quiet. He checked his watch. It was eleven twenty. They walked back quickly to where Tariq was still hidden.

'Put these on and get up there,' Choukri said, handing him the guard's clothes. 'When the guns start, come back.'

The explosives crew had laid the charges in the cargo and were waiting for Choukri. On the ground beside them was the fuel hose, ready to be threaded into the main building. Next to it was a holdall with the crew's computers and phones.

'They all there?' Choukri said, prodding the bag with his boot.

There was a nod of confirmation.

'Set them at the heart of the fire. They must be incinerated.'

When he stepped back onto the bridge, Mubarak and Faisel were adjusting the ship's ballast and trim, making sure it was sitting just so, at the correct angle, not down at the stern, up at the bow or listing to one side. The gun crews were in the hold, removing covers, connecting power lines and checking everything. Above them, the chief was monitoring the oil pump, the hose pulsing as fuel surged through it.

Out on the river a tug chugged by towing a barge loaded with construction materials. Its crew, to a man, looked in their direction. Commercial ships like the *Ocean Dove* were a rare sight this far up the river, beyond the Thames Barrier. They no doubt found it a novelty worth seeing, but were too far away to pick out any detail. A dredger had gone past earlier heading upstream, a string of refuse barges in the opposite direction. The majority of the traffic was small scale, mostly yachts and pleasure boats.

Assam's voice came over the walkie-talkie. 'Shut off the pump, Chief.'

All the devices were set in place and the building soaked in fuel oil. The floor conveniently sloped to the centre, to a drainage channel designed to catch runaway chemicals. The men had blocked it with rags and now it was a foot deep at the centre, glistening like treacle.

Choukri watched a launch go by. His concentration was on the fuel storage depot and a window of opportunity. He would have preferred a little less attention from the river, though the sniper rifle was silenced and, by the time it had worked its trickery, all eyes should be resolutely upstream.

Mubarak checked his watch. 'Noon in twenty minutes.'

'Okay,' Choukri said. 'Everyone in the hold.'

Choukri walked around the guns, the tip of his tongue between his teeth, checking, moving on, hesitating and checking again. The command table was hinged in position. He put the laptop down and plugged it in, tweaking the connections and arranging the run of cables just so. The crew assembled in ones and twos, standing in a semicircle, still, expectant, every eye fixed on his slightest movement. Barely a sound crept through the open hatch panel. They were in the heart of London but they could have been alone.

Everyone knew the roles they had been assigned. The second engineer in the engine room. Mubarak on the bridge. Snoop and Assam on the terminal to set the explosives off and defend it from the land if necessary. The chief at the guns. A man on the hatch machinery. Faisel at Choukri's side.

'You've got the gangway,' Choukri said, his eyes on Cookie. 'If they come for us, and if Snoop and Assam don't make it – you pull it up.'

Cookie looked across at the two of them, his face creasing in apology. Neither met his eyes. They were concentrating on Choukri, who turned and extended a hand to Mubarak.

The captain stepped towards the guns and got down on his knees, facing east. The crew followed his lead, prostrating themselves as Mubarak began to recite:

'You would know the secret of death.
But how shall you find it unless you seek it in the heart of life?
The owl whose night-bound eyes are blind unto the day cannot unveil the mystery of light.
If you would indeed behold the spirit of death, open your heart wide unto the body of life.
For life and death are one, even as the river and the sea are one.
In the depth of your hopes and desires lies your silent knowledge of the beyond.
And like the seeds dreaming beneath the snow your heart dreams of spring.
Trust the dreams, for in them is hidden the gate to eternity.
Your fear of death is but the trembling of the shepherd when he stands before the king, whose hand is to be laid upon him in honour.
Is the shepherd not joyful beneath his trembling that he shall wear the mark of the king?
Yet is he not more mindful of his trembling,
For what is it to die but to stand naked in the wind and to melt into the sun?
And what is it to cease breathing, but to free the breath from its restless tides, that it may rise and expand and seek God unencumbered.
Only when you drink from the river of silence shall you indeed sing.
And when you have reached the mountaintop then you shall begin to climb.
And when the earth shall claim your limbs then shall you truly dance.'

THIRTY

The crew rose from their knees. Choukri embraced each of them in turn, looking into their apprehensive faces, his eyes inches from their own, willing the transference of his inner resolve through the strength of his hands that were gripping their shoulders.

He looked around as they set about their tasks. In the weapons' container, Assam was handing guns out through the door, Kalashnikovs with multi-round drum magazines. One for Cookie and a bag of magazines, two for the bridge, one each for himself and Snoop. Others to be placed at the ready around the ship.

At the head of the stairs he checked the bridge before stepping out to the wings. Below him, on the main deck, a crewman was standing by the hatch machinery waiting for his signal. Cookie propped his rifle out of sight and swung the guard rail open for Snoop and Assam, their guns trussed up like a parcel in the legs of an old pair of overalls. Halfway through the sprawl of cargo they found a protected position with a clear line of sight to the main gate and security house. Snoop looked back and raised a hand.

Choukri turned back to the bridge and pulled a chair across. 'Sit,' he said. 'Jam yourself against the door and keep still.'

Faisel sat down, facing out. Choukri grabbed another chair for himself and lined it up behind, shifting a little to one side to achieve the correct angle before resting a rifle barrel on Faisel's shoulder.

Mubarak stood to one side, his binoculars raised as Choukri zeroed the telescopic sight.

'See anything?' Choukri said.

'Two workmen on the right, halfway back,' Mubarak said.

'I've got them.'

The fuel depot was on the opposite bank about six hundred metres upstream. Seven tanks faced them in a line with two more rows behind.

'I'll take the far left tank, the middle and the right, in that order. Two shots each.'

'Okay,' Mubarak said.

Choukri pulled the gun back, a German DSR-1 sniper rifle. He leant it against a table and reached for the pack of incendiary shells that Khan had given him in Bar Mhar, lining them up ready for use.

The radio DJ said there was just enough time for one more song before the midday news. The TV chefs peered anxiously at the oven door, the backing music rising portentously. Would the soufflé rise or fall? Stay tuned and find out after the commercial break.

Choukri went outside for one last check, looking upstream and down. It was clear in both directions. He stepped back inside and nodded to Mubarak, holding his eye. 'Give the order.'

Mubarak stiffened. 'Open the hatch,' he said into his walkie-talkie.

The words sounded sweet to Choukri. It was the signal the crew were all waiting for, that he had been waiting for, the years of planning coming together with three short words.

Resuming his seat behind Faisel, he nestled the barrel on his shoulder.

'Breathe easy.'

'There's two workmen walking towards the back,' Mubarak said.

'Okay, I see them. Tank one, about a metre up, dead centre. On my count, three, two, one.'

His finger squeezed. The nail had regrown, stronger than before. The rifle gave the slightest of jumps. He worked the bolt for the next round as Mubarak trained his glasses on the workmen.

'One of them has looked up,' Mubarak said. 'Okay, he's carrying on now.'

Through the telescopic sights Choukri could see two dark jets spurting onto the concrete apron.

'Middle one,' Choukri said.

Mubarak counted the tanks from the left out loud. 'Hit,' he said, followed by another. 'Hit.'

In seconds there were six holes in the tanks. Choukri reached over for the incendiary rounds as Mubarak kept his binoculars on the workmen.

'Now they've really heard it,' Mubarak said. 'Go for the far-right tank.'

One or two out-of-place *dings* might have seemed acceptable, but six had put the men on their guard, pacing about, looking around. Choukri had them in his sights again. They were advancing towards the front, speculating on what they had heard. He shifted the rifle and trained it on the tanks.

The first one's safety label said Jet A1, aviation fuel for the City Airport. A streak of yellow zipped across the apron. Time stood still for a moment, the workmen freezing before turning and running in the opposite direction. Flames were taking hold, merging, when two thousand tons of fuel exploded with an earth-shattering boom. A fireball shot into the clear blue sky. Shock waves set off sirens on both sides of the river, the smoke thickening, heading downstream on the breeze.

Choukri sprang from his chair and went out to the wings.

'Snoop, Assam. Do the building,' he said into the walkie-talkie.

There was no reply. He repeated the message, his eyes raking the terminal.

Snoop's voice crackled through. 'Here, boss. We couldn't hear you. It's the noise!'

'Do the fucking building, now!'

'On it, yeah.'

Choukri hurried down the stairs to the hold, striding across to the chief, who looked at him questioningly.

'We're doing good,' Choukri said, giving him a reassuring nod.

The chief's head twitched as another crack ripped through the air, the echo bouncing around the hold walls. The sound was close. Choukri glanced up. It had to have come from the Moritz building, confirmed by a dirty black cloud that was spiralling across the ship from the terminal.

At the command table, Choukri's finger hovered over the laptop. He stared at Faisel.

'Give me the order.'

'Do it!' Faisel said. 'Do it now.'

The guns hummed into life, the turrets swivelling, barrels lifting. They fired short bursts of twelve shells each, a dozen for the fuel depot and a dozen for the O2 Dome, Excel Centre and City Airport.

The crew leapt back at the sound. The guns were unlike anything they had heard before, like metal on metal, or piledrivers hammering into the ground. Choukri considered them for a moment, pleased they weren't alarmingly loud, their noise disguised and confused by thunderflash bombs on the terminal and explosions on both riverbanks. In these bizarre scenes they would surely pass as nothing unusual.

Mubarak's shoulders were hunched over the wing rail when Choukri came back up from the hold. He stepped out, standing silently at his side, taking the scenes in. On the far bank an inky mushroom cloud erupted into the atmosphere as shells rained down on the fuel depot. Tanks collapsed like tin cans as thousands of tonnes of noxious liquids sprang into flame, spewing a blanket of smoke over the river, advancing on the *Ocean Dove*. Acrid clouds were rising from the oil in the Moritz building and smoke bombs on the quay, drifting over the ship, cloaking it in a fog. If the ship was visible at all, it would appear to be just another victim and the last thing anyone was looking at, or for.

Just down from the tank farm, three planes outside the airport terminal lay twisted and burning. Fire was raging through the main building; Choukri figured they must have hit the kitchens or a gas main. Mubarak handed him the binoculars and jabbed a finger in the direction of the Excel Centre.

Though he'd never set foot in the place, Choukri knew it intimately. The long hours researching targets for the wish list, the tired eyes, the myriad details and endless map coordinates were now concluding. He'd studied Excel's website and knew they were hosting WorldPower, a gathering of the global power-generating industry. From the convenient link to WorldPower's own website, he knew it would be studded with board directors from GE and Siemens, ABB and Mitsubishi, politicians, lawyers, consultants and two thousand delegates. He'd programmed the first shells to hit the Customs House railway station behind the centre. The second wave was for the reception area, the third for the exhibition hall. A split second later the fourth salvo would hit the main conference chamber, where he knew Nigeria's Energy Minister was going to deliver the closing keynote speech at noon – three minutes earlier.

Mubarak stepped back a pace, brushing Choukri's side. 'My God …'

Swinging his glasses round, he focused on the spot where Mubarak's startled eyes were now locked. East-facing windows in Canary Wharf were darkening as people clustered to them like flies, the horror unfolding in sequence along the river in a line downstream, the uproar of the fuel depot, the Dome, the Excel Centre and the airport as another fuel tank exploded.

The Network's planners had gamed the reaction, their Impact Assessment Team anticipating and preparing for all scenarios. The briefing had been clear, and Choukri clearly remembered it all. He knew precisely what would be happening in those office towers – knew it was no different from Baltimore to Baghdad, from Kiev to Kabul. Human reaction was always the same.

The IAT's analysis had run to three hundred pages of schematics, engineers' reports, structural animations, psychological assessments, archive footage and witness and survivor statements. It covered both the technical and the human sides: the screams, the tears, the soiled underwear, the disbelief, the wide-eyed exclamations with the mouths remaining open.

Competing urges would be racing through minds that were refusing to reason. Could it be an accident at the fuel depot that had spread downriver? But that old industrial works on the south bank was blazing too? It couldn't be terrorists on a beautiful day, on this scale. And when it did happen, it was in another part of the world and they watched it on TV. They weren't supposed to be part of it. They stood in their thousands transfixed at windows, staring, hands gripping colleagues at their sides, unable to believe they might be under attack.

From his vantage point on the wings, Choukri saw the sequence unfolding in his mind's eye. Thousands of hours of meticulous research and planning and interminable numbers tapped into spreadsheets were culminating in barely an hour's chaos. He was infinitely more familiar with the city than a native, could picture every target, the objective of every single shell. He understood what was happening, what people would do and say and think, or be unable to think. He could see and feel it, even taste it – the bitterness of acrid smoke on his lips, the palls gusting on the breeze, drifting into and out of his line of sight, twisting to a wall of black on his right and a clear blue passage to Canary Wharf.

He stared in awe at the shells hitting their targets, a split second between each explosion, raking the glittering edifices from top to bottom, descending from the twenty-fifth floor, the twentieth, fifteenth, tenth, fifth, with each salvo ending in ten shells at the base of each building where they would attack the engineering systems, lifts and sprinklers, blocking the ground-level emergency exits.

It was four minutes after noon. Shells rained down on Canary Wharf, the line of towers along the waterfront belching smoke. Flames were leaping from gaping holes as masonry, steel, glass, desks and bodies cascaded to the ground. Floors and stairways were collapsing, lifts trapped mid-floor, the buildings losing power and water pressure, the sprinklers unable to cope.

Devastation raged across Canada Square and Bank Street, Cabot Square and Churchill Place, in the offices of HSBC and Citigroup, JP Morgan and Credit Suisse, Bank of New York and Barclays. Security computers were sending automated alerts to the emergency services and the public's calls were crashing the systems as fire crews, ambulances and police cars scrambled in every direction. Some people would be running for cover. Some would be filming on mobile phones. Many would be lying dead or injured. The shattered edifices of Canary Wharf stared forlornly down, flames licking, shattered glass and twisted steel, cladding ripped, hanging like torn flesh from their sides.

The walkie-talkie at his belt squawked.

'Come down,' Faisel's voice urged.

At the command table, Choukri's eyes were fixed on the firing sequence, the targets scrolling to the end – the end only of the list of

Canary Wharf's targets. He reached across Faisel and pressed pause, glancing around the hold.

The chief was moving from gun to gun, running a hand over a barrel or carousel, checking hoses, monitoring gauges. The gun crews were looking anxiously in his direction. An eerie silence fell around them. Their ears had become accustomed to the cacophony of a thousand sirens and alarms, thunderous random cracks and deeper rumblings further away.

'Okay?' Choukri shouted across.

The chief gave him a thumbs up.

Choukri turned to the next set of targets. Downriver was the Thames Barrier and the electricity substation and, just beyond on the north bank, Tate & Lyle's sugar works at Silvertown. Further along still were military barracks, the Royal Horse Artillery and the Princess of Wales' Royal Regiment at Woolwich and the Purfleet container terminal.

He held his hand out flat, staying Faisel who was poised over the keyboard, his finger hovering.

'When you see me up there,' he said, pointing to the wings, 'keep it going. Keep the momentum. Then get straight back on the main programme.'

He turned and ran along the hold to the door. The downriver group was important. They were targets in their own right, but they were also diversions. The more that was happening around them, the less they would stand out.

Purfleet was too far away to see, obscured by the urban sprawl. Woolwich was only two miles away, close enough for him to make out the trails of smoke behind buildings in the foreground. The first shots had been aimed at the farther targets, the last to the nearer. In rapid succession, like sticks of bombs dropped from a plane, the shells came down on the sugar works, the Thames Barrier and the electricity plant.

In the steel box of the hold, the only guides had been sound and the sky above the open hatch, at first clear and blue, then streaked with smoke, before choking in swirling blackness. Now the breeze was settling, the huge clouds from the fuel depot rising higher and drifting downriver. The south bank was clearing, the midstream too, the north bank shrouded as thirty image-guided shells smashed into the Thames Barrier's central piers and the power and control towers on the banks.

Choukri stood transfixed for a moment before turning back to the bridge. 'Anything yet?'

Tariq shook his head. 'Nothing.'

'No mention of us at all?'

'Just confused talk. The police, the fire guys, whatever.'

'And nothing on TV or radio yet,' the communications engineer said, glancing around his screens.

'We're six minutes in, and still nothing,' Choukri said. 'Won't be long …' He turned and looked out through the bridge windscreen. 'They know all right. Over there, in Canada Square. There's a newspaper, the Daily something. They know.'

Behind him, the first news trickled in – *we're getting reports of a fire in East London at a fuel depot by the river …*'

~

At 12.07 the guns turned west again. An infernal rain hit the City business district, image-guided for the landmarks, in degrees, minutes, and seconds for others. It swept down Fenchurch Street and Leadenhall, along Cornhill and Cannon Street, up Gracechurch Street and Bishopsgate, homing in on the institutions: Lloyd's, the Stock Exchange, the Old Bailey, the Guildhall and the Bank of England.

High up at windows in Tower 42, the Walkie Talkie, the Gherkin and the Leadenhall Building, the horror of Canary Wharf was repeated as steel and glass peeled away and crashed to the ground in biblical showers. The concourses thronged with people going to and from meetings, to lunch, to meet friends or just soaking up the sun on a bench. At street level they were still unaware, the pavements bustling, taxis pulling in for pickups, lines waiting for buses. When the first wave hit, they stopped in their tracks and looked up, moments before cascading debris cut them to shreds.

Some stood traumatised, rooted to the spot. Others ran. Crowds surged into underground stations in an unequal meeting of tides, sweeping all before them, massing at barriers in a frenzy of ribs cracking like twigs and lungs compressing in the stifling heat, in the foetid stench of vomit and piss and shit.

Along the river the bridges were picked off in sequence: Tower, London, Southwark, Millennium, Blackfriars. Waves of shells fell on City Hall, the Globe Theatre, Guy's Hospital and the Tate Modern. The newspaper offices, *The Sun* and *The Times* at London Bridge and *The Financial Times* at Southwark all received personalised press alerts. The *Daily Mirror* in Canary Wharf had already received theirs ahead of the competition. All the media were alerted, the commercial radio stations clustered in Leicester Square, the ITV centre by Waterloo, the BBC in Portland Place, CNN, Fox, Facebook, Twitter.

Seventy-five shells clawed at the pristine skin of the Shard, glinting like a jewel in the sunlight, a deadly rain tumbling down to the crowded piazza as it shed its coat of jagged glass.

The carnage advanced upstream. A train on Hungerford bridge slowed for Charing Cross station, shuddering and peeling sideways. Its front carriages toppled into the void, twisted and mangled in the water, the mid-section left dangling, the tail hanging on for dear life.

Passengers on the Millennium Wheel, London's eye on the city, had booked their tickets and waited patiently in the queue, determined that nothing was going to spoil their day in the sunshine. A minute after noon, those at the top experienced a bird's-eye view of the fuel depot. At first it had been pure spectacle, shocking but curiously thrilling, before it turned to morbid fear three minutes later when the blazing skyline seemed to advance towards them.

At nine minutes past noon they were screaming and on their knees. A spoke lashed out from the hub. The wheel lurched but carried on turning. Another shell hit the base of a support leg and the other leg bent in a struggle against unequal weight, the metal creaking and groaning, beginning to topple.

Pier decking flew into the air as the base of the wheel smashed down, crushing and submerging a tourist boat tied alongside. A hundred metres out in the river the top of the wheel sent a bow wave of water crashing over the embankment, knocking down fleeing people like skittles.

The shelling continued its demonic march westward, up Fleet Street and Holborn, St Paul's and the Strand, through Lincoln's Inn and the Royal Courts of Justice. It spread north, along Oxford Street, up to the stations, King's Cross, St Pancras and Euston, to Lord's cricket ground, where England had just taken four Sri Lankan wickets for eighty-nine and were looking forward to lunch.

Salvo after salvo crashed into Oxford Street every thirty metres, into Selfridge's and Topshop and H&M. Trays of watches and rings littered the street outside a jeweller's, a bus on its side, a burning taxi in a shop window, the dead and the dying strewn on the pavements. In the frenzied scramble a foot punted a severed head into the road. No one knew or cared if it had belonged on a shop mannequin or a woman's neck.

The tide swept through Covent Garden, where crowds had thronged around musicians, jugglers and people-statues, an out-of-tune busker and three graduate cellists from the London Academy. On it strode, in the teeming streets of Soho, into Leicester Square, along Shaftesbury Avenue to Piccadilly, fanning out to St James's and the Mall.

Outside the American Embassy, protesters dropped megaphones and police abandoned surveillance cameras, for once finding common cause. The gilded eagle on the roof soared into the air, the entire building shaking, the bombardment pounding down.

On it swept, down Park Lane, south to Buckingham Palace, south to Westminster and Parliament, where a full house was in debate and anxious to complete a bill before the summer recess.

A thousand shells a minute rained down on specific and random targets, the utilities and telecoms, residential and leisure areas, institutions, museums and petrol stations, houses, shops and offices. Fire took hold, sweeping from building to building, the security systems failing, the water pressure dropping, the roads blocked by collapsed buildings, splintered trees, mangled cars and buses, and it was still only 12.12.

~

'We did good,' Max Paulsson said, licking cappuccino froth from his lips and scrolling through his emails. 'Here's the message,' he said, handing his phone across.

'Hi Max. I hope this finds you well. Come down to Moritz on Monday to see the ship loading. Meet me there and I'll buy you and Aaron lunch! Best regards, Joe.'

Aaron Epstein was sitting at the meeting room table in Red Oak's Berkeley Square offices, adding up some figures in a sheaf of documents. With the last stage payment received on their account a few days ago, the two of them had arrived in London yesterday for the regular monthly management meeting.

'Storm?' Epstein said, cocking his head to one side as handed the phone back.

Max went across to the windows. They faced west, into clear blue sky.

'Weird,' he said. 'I hear it but I don't see it. Sounds real close, like thunder.'

He shrugged his shoulders and looked away as most of a tree outside their offices came through the glass.

THIRTY-ONE

'I knew Suffolk would be a winner.' Dan smiled, one hand on the steering wheel, the other giving Julie's knee a squeeze.

He checked the mirror. Phoebe was sleeping peacefully on the back seat. She'd walked on the sand, paddled in the sea, dozed under an apple tree and eaten her first ice cream. It had been the sweetest week of her life.

'Shit …' Dan said. 'Look at that.'

The traffic on the M11 was backing up ahead, just as they were enjoying an easy journey in the sunshine. They had left the cottage intending to be home at lunchtime, do a supermarket run in the afternoon and have a relaxing weekend before Dan reported back to work on Monday. The DJ had just played 'Summer Breeze' and reminded everyone to get the barbecue things sorted out.

Smoke had been faintly visible on the horizon for the last couple of miles, and a minute earlier the signal on the radio had disappeared. There hadn't seemed to be any reason why he should connect the two. Fields can catch fire in summer and radio signals can weaken in hot weather. He'd dismissed both as inconsequential.

The motorway had climbed steadily for the last mile before levelling out on a plateau. It looked down over the eastern fringes of London, a familiar waypoint, of fundamental change, one moment an idyll of farmland and wheat, transformed at the crest of a rise into the shimmering towers of the city, spread out in the distance like an architect's model.

Dan stamped on the brakes. Julie stretched a hand instinctively towards the dashboard as the car jolted. The traffic ahead had stopped. Car doors were hanging open. People were in the road and on the hard shoulder. The scene was impossible to take in at a glance – where to look first, where next. They were seven or eight miles from Canary Wharf and a dozen from the City, but it was all too easy to identify. Smoke and dust were rising in a biblical pall, a dark backdrop for the vivid flames licking from individual buildings and entire districts.

Dan veered across to the hard shoulder. Julie twisted round anxiously to the back seat, one hand on his leg, her fingernails digging in.

He yanked his seatbelt free and leant across, gripping her arm.

'I don't know,' he said. 'Stay here. You're safe here.'

She nodded her head distractedly before he jumped out and ran to the boot, tossing a pram and a deckchair out and tearing at a bag for his binoculars.

There was a signal on his phone, three bars. LaSalle's card was in his wallet. The number went straight to voicemail. He pressed send again, and again. This time it answered.

'It's Dan Brooks. I'm on the M11. I can see all across London. What's going on?'

'I think we're under attack.'

'What kind of attack, car bombs, what?'

'From above. We've been hit. Six is hit. I can see them from the window.'

'What does it sound like. What can you hear?'

'It's like a—'

The line cut. Dan checked the screen and pressed redial. Nothing. No voicemail, not even a pre-recorded message about network coverage, just a blank.

He opened Julie's door and leant in, looking into her eyes. 'It's some sort of attack. I don't know. I lost the line. We're okay here. It's okay.'

Her eyes were flicking between his own and the scene ahead. It was the same all around with people circling between cars, looking away, looking back, staring in vain hope that something was playing tricks with their imagination. The traffic on the northbound carriageway had backed up and stopped. Engines were switched off. A disturbing silence was falling.

He squeezed Julie's shoulders. 'Stay here. Give me a moment.'

His binoculars were powerful, too powerful for what he was being forced to witness. Chains of fire, dust and smoke were advancing uniformly across the city. He looked on, horrified, fighting to suppress emotion and summon a detached logic, the calculation of numbers, timing, distance, line and route, rate of fire.

LaSalle had said they were under attack. It appeared to be coming from the east, spreading west. A pattern was emerging. The radius was difficult to estimate but he plucked at ten miles and swept his glasses east. The Dome he recognised, and the towers of Canary Wharf.

Guns, range ten miles, rapid fire, coming perhaps from the river. *Can it really be true?* It seemed too fantastic. Bofors guns, four of them, on a ship, a ship like the *Ocean Dove*?

There was a background hum in the air. It had been there since they arrived. His subconscious had dismissed it as superficial, the drone of a combine harvester or a farmer topping a meadow. But now it had changed tone, attracting his attention. He looked across the fields where a line of pylons stretched into the distance. Rising up from them was a helicopter, a power-line surveyor. It had broken its rhythm and pulled up to take a look at a safe distance from the wires, hovering, with the windscreen pointing in his direction.

He ran back to the car and jumped in. Julie was still in the passenger seat, but now she had Phoebe in her arms. The area around them was cramped, the cars abandoned haphazardly. The engine revved as he lurched back and forth, turning to face the fields and bumping up the verge. The front of the car had lifted, its headlights pointing up. He pumped the flasher.

'What are you doing?' Julie said.

'The helicopter. I'm signalling.'

'Why?'

'I've got to try.'

'Try what?'

'This. Everything. It's my case, it's happening … C'mon,' he urged, switching to Morse code. 'Look at me, look at me!'

Helicopter pilots were often ex-military, he reasoned, and though his Morse was rusty and very likely the pilot's as well, it was all he had.

He repeated the same message, again and again. *'SOS MI5. Come to me.'*

The nose of the helicopter dipped. It started to descend, dropping steeply. Dan knew he had to do something, but what exactly? There were two imperatives. The first was to stay with his wife and daughter. The second was to go. He still had no idea which to choose, but having attracted the pilot he realised he couldn't lose him now.

'Just wait here,' he said. 'One minute.'

He ran round the car and scrambled down the bank, vaulting the fence and sprinting out into the field, trying to put distance between the crowds on the motorway and the helicopter. The pilot was unlikely to land if he thought he was going to be mobbed. A glance over his shoulder reassured him. People had turned to look, but he was no more than a sideshow.

The pilot opened the door and pulled his headphones down. Dan ran under the blades and leant in, staring into a pair of sunglasses between a shaved head and a goatee beard.

The words came out in a rush. 'I'm Dan Brooks, MI5, we've got to get down there.'

'Down there?' the pilot said. 'Looks like a fucking war zone to me.'

'It is! I'll explain on the way.'

'You got ID?'

'Course I got ID!' Dan said. His head dropped. 'Fuck it! Left it in the car. It's terrorists on a ship. Four stolen Bofors guns. They're down there in Docklands. They've got a nineteen-thousand-yard range, so they must be there. We've got to find them! Are you really making me run back for my fucking ID?'

'Bofors guns. Nineteen-thousand-yard range?'

'Four of them. Sold to the Indian navy and lost from a cargo ship last Christmas. But not lost, hijacked, before the ship was scuttled.'

'You ex-forces?'

'Navy. Lieutenant commander.'

'Okay, we go.'

Dan turned his head towards the road. 'My wife and daughter. They're in the car.'

The pilot turned to the line engineer sitting next to him. 'Could be risky down there ...'

'And you'll wait here,' Dan said.

The pilot nodded. 'Don't hang about.'

Dan ran around the front of the helicopter and pulled the engineer out. He was not a young man and was unused to running across farmland on a hot day. A minute later they were over the fence and he was shoving him up the embankment.

Julie was standing by the car. Her eyes switched between Dan and the city over his shoulder. He could see in her face that the shock was subsiding, her rational mind returning.

'You'll be all right here. Just wait for me.'

'Do what you have to,' she said.

~

Dan looked at his watch. It was 12.27. 'They must be somewhere near the Dome. Start there and then downstream.'

'Four minutes and we'll be there,' the pilot said. 'I was army. Tom Bergen. My Morse is a bit slow – but I got there in the end.'

Dan smiled. 'I was counting on it. Nice to know you, Tom.'

Bergen glanced across. 'I took a good look at you before I let you in here,' he said, the hint of a cautious smile on his mouth. 'You didn't look like a nutter, I couldn't smell booze, and that's a military watch on your wrist. And you knew your Morse and said *yards*.' He nodded, confirming it to himself. 'I've been on exercises with your lot so I know what Bofors are, and anyway, your guess of what's going on down there was just about the same as mine.' He paused. 'And arguing about it in a field wasn't likely to be something I'd look back on with pride ...'

Dan raised his eyebrows. 'Thank fuck for that,' he said, turning to the dashboard and scanning the dials and gauges in front of him. 'I'll try the radio – channel 16.'

Bergen nodded. It was a standard marine setting, an open channel that all ships were required to monitor.

Dan knew the risk. The *Ocean Dove* was likely to be listening. They might take it as a warning and think again, or they might increase the pace. He pressed the speaker switch.

'This is Dan Brooks. I'm a government security officer and I urgently need information on a ship, possibly called the *Ocean Dove*, with the name OceanBird painted in big letters on the hull. Has anyone seen a ship like this in London yesterday or today? Over.'

The radio stayed quiet. As he reached up to repeat the message, a voice came through.

'Hello, mate. This is the *Jane. G.* We're a tug doing the council rubbish run. I saw that boat this morning, don't know its name but it had that bird down the side and a picture on the funnel. We was down near Purfleet and he was coming up. What the fuck's going on? Over.'

Then a new voice cut in. 'This is the *Kew*, Port of London pilot launch. We took a pilot out this morning at 06.00 to the *Ocean Dove*. She was going to be berthed at the old Moritz works. Over.'

'What's Moritz and where is it? Over.'

'It's a closed-down chemical plant on the river with its own berth, about one mile upstream from the Thames Barrier. On the south bank. Over.'

'Thank you. Over and out.'

As Dan looked through the windscreen searching for landmarks and checking his bearings, Bergen was already a step ahead.

'Got it, south bank, one mile west of the barrier,' Bergen said.

The scale of the horror was unfolding graphically. On their right was Canary Wharf. A little way behind it, the City business district. In his headphones Dan heard Bergen exhale and whisper, 'Fuck …'

The river was mostly obscured by smoke but Dan was still able to track its twists and turns. Below was the smouldering Excel Centre, to his left the Thames Barrier, its neat line of pillars now as irregular as a mouth with some of its teeth kicked out. A mile upstream on the south bank and dead ahead through the windscreen was a smoking industrial site. It had to be Moritz.

~

Tariq yelled from the bridge. 'The radio. Channel 16. They're on us. Some government security guy.'

Choukri spun around on the wings and ran in. 'What do they know. What exactly?'

'This guy was asking if anyone had seen the *Ocean Dove* in London.'

'And what did they learn?'

Tariq's eyes widened. 'The pilot boat said we're here!'

Choukri lifted his walkie-talkie. 'Everyone. They're on to us. Watch the river and sky!'

Mubarak was out on the wings, his binoculars raised. 'Helicopter!'

Choukri dashed out to him, leaning over the rail, checking around. Down in the hold, all four guns were still pumping a thousand rounds a minute, the carousels turning, the barrels too hot to touch but still working to maximum efficiency. Across the quay, he saw Assam and Snoop crouching among the cargo on the terminal, training their Kalashnikovs on the helicopter.

~

Something clicked in Dan's mind as the scene unfurled below him.

'Look at it,' he said, 'where Moritz is, the way the smoke's moving right over it on the breeze, south-west. It's the perfect hiding place. It's fucking genius.'

'Doesn't the smoke get in the way?' Bergen said.

Dan shook his head. 'The guns are programmed. They don't need to see.'

'Shit. I was thinking we can blow smoke over them with the blades, blind them.'

'No difference,' Dan said.

'So what *can* we do?'

'Find them. Make sure.'

'Wish this was my old gunship – fully armed …' Bergen said, shaking his head. 'I'll go west round the back,' he added, yanking the controls into a dive, swooping in a low arc through the billowing haze from the fuel depot.

There was a break in the smoke as they fanned out over the river. The *Ocean Dove* was clear for a moment alongside the wharf, it bows pointing west and its hatch open.

'Bastard!' Dan cursed; the four grey boxes lined up in the hold were all too clear, their barrels pumping.

A familiar voice came over the radio. 'LaSalle calling Dan Brooks. Over.'

Thank you, God. Dan had been praying someone would be monitoring the open channels, someone like GCHQ, and that it would filter back.

'Brooks here. I'm in a helicopter over Docklands. It's the *Ocean Dove*. It's moored in the river and firing.'

'A helicopter?'

'Don't ask. Have we got assets?'

'We have assets. Coordinates please.'

'One mile upriver from the Thames Barrier,' Dan said. 'South bank. The old Moritz chemical plant.'

~

Choukri's eyes alternated between Tariq and the radio as the helicopter cut across their bow four hundred metres upstream. The sniper rifle was propped at his side.

He steadied it against the door frame, the cross hairs on the helicopter's windscreen, switching from the guy in sunglasses to the one next to him – the one whose mouth was moving. He breathed out, feathering the trigger before yanking his head back, his eyes widening. 'You!' he spat, recognising Dan's face from the dossier he had on him. 'Why couldn't you just die when you had the chance …'

By the time he'd sighted the rifle again, the helicopter had dived low and right. He'd missed his shot. 'Fire! Fire! Take that fucker out!' he yelled into the walkie-talkie.

The helicopter windscreen was pointing away, a flank exposed as it careered over the old gasworks. Snoop and Assam let rip with automatic fire. Cookie scrambled across the hatch to the landward side, concentrating his aim on the tail rotor. A hail of bullets clattered into the back of the fuselage.

Choukri dashed to the wings as the helicopter dipped from sight beyond the plant, masked by acrid smoke billowing from the roof of the main building.

~

With the engine dying, Bergen pulled back on the stick, trying to find enough altitude to autorotate to the ground on the blades.

'There!' He pointed. 'Hang on.'

They were losing height, the engine unable to give power, dying in a fit of spurts.

An eerie silence fell as Dan stared down at a patch of green surrounded by houses. It was quickly replaced by wind howl, the blades autorotating and slowing their fall. Bergen heaved at the controls, the cabin swinging from side to side.

Dan felt his spine jar and the air rush from his chest as they thumped into a flower bed, the blades lashing a parked car like a can opener.

'You okay?' Bergen said, turning to him.

Dan nodded. 'Think so,' he croaked, his lungs refusing to breathe.

A seat belt clicked and Bergen clambered out. Dan's breath was returning. He took a gulp and tried his door. It didn't move. He pulled himself over Bergen's seat, unclipping a fire extinguisher at the side of it.

'Here,' he said, as flames licked around the engine bay and exhaust ducts. Bergen yanked at an access panel and fired it, his face turned away, eyes shut tight.

Dan walked about for a few paces, his hands gripping the base of his spine. He looked around, getting his bearings, working out the route to Moritz. From the smoke rising over the houses in the distance, he reckoned they were about five hundred metres away.

They had landed in a cul-de-sac, a cluster of semi-detached houses around a green. A single road pointed in the direction of the river. People crept from their houses, looking around anxiously, a smouldering helicopter in a flower bed just one more bizarre sight on a surreal day. The quiet was unnerving, the only sounds distant, rumbling and booming like thunder behind faraway hills, the air filthy with a noxious stink and bitter taste.

'You coming?' Dan said.

'Too fucking right!'

At the top of the road was a staggered junction. They turned left and then right, continuing north at a fast jog. The roads were lined with cars but no one was about. At the end was a patch of waste ground with the Moritz works on the far side, a hundred metres up on the left.

'It's all happening now,' Bergen said. He raised his eyes, his chest heaving, sweat beading his forehead. 'Look.'

Arcing around the terminal was an Osprey, a hybrid plane-helicopter, a type used by the SAS. It disappeared from view behind them, not far from where they had abandoned their own.

Dan edged along a wall and parted some leaves in a bush, a fingertip brushing against fence wire. The *Ocean Dove*'s bow and the top of the accommodation block were visible, the rest of it hidden behind stacked cargo on the terminal. The guns had stopped firing but the ship was still there, with smoke coming from its funnel.

'Could be getting ready to leave,' he whispered.

The fence stretched along the road. Three quarters of the way down were the main gate and the security building. He looked diagonally across the yard towards the river. There were choices – the main gate, over the fence from where they stood, or down the side of it by the creek. Waltzing through the main gate was a non-starter and there was open ground to cross if they climbed in now.

'If we get down the side, there's cover in the yard,' Dan said. He looked along the fence that ran down to the river on Moritz's eastern boundary. The ground was thick with brambles and nettles. A steep bank tumbled down to the creek. But it was cover. 'They could have people on the terminal.'

'They could …'

Fifty metres in, Dan stopped and pushed back some undergrowth at the fence. Light summer clothes offered little protection and his bare arms were trickling blood, a thorn wedged in a dripping ear. 'Bit more,' he said.

Behind the fence were storage tanks shielding them from the ship. They crouched motionless, eyes scanning the terminal for any sign of movement, checking shadows, ears cocked. A black plume gusted towards them from the main building, a lick of flame crackling from a shattering window.

'Looks clear,' Dan said.

Layers of barbed wire topped the fence. Dan ran an eye over it. He needed to get up, over and down in one quick movement – and perhaps back again even faster.

Bergen pulled his shirt over his head and handed it across. Dan put a foot in his cupped hands, another on his shoulder, spread the folded shirt over the spikes and swung across, wincing as barbs gashed his palm and a thigh.

When Bergen was over they started to make their way along the terminal, a few steps at a time, slipping from crate to packing case, stopping, checking, before moving on. Dan peered gingerly around the side of a shipping container, his head shooting back. He raised a finger to his lips. A leg was stretched out on the ground, the sole of a boot upturned.

He crept back around the other side. The leg was attached to a body, face down, blood on the back of the head. It was motionless, no sign of breathing, a Kalashnikov on the concrete. Stepping silently, Dan picked the gun up and reached behind until he felt a hand taking it. Blank eyes stared up as he rolled the body over, an exit wound the size of a pool ball gaping in the forehead, the mouth open, a green slime dribbling from it.

Glancing round over his shoulder, a shadow flashed and a length of steel piping crashed down. The Kalashnikov clattered to the concrete, followed by Bergen.

Dan sprang to his feet, gauging the relative distance between the gun and the pipe-wielding guy, who was evidently doing the same.

It was equidistant, half wedged under Bergen, and the man had a four-foot piece of pipe in a vice-like grip. Dan's eyes flashed around, checking his ground, looking for a weapon; he was surrounded by metal in an alley of shipping containers, with only the smoke-filled sky above. He could back away, or go forward, and that didn't feel the better option.

The eyes staring at him were narrowed. Dan saw they held an animal quality and no fear. There was something else in them, something he could only sense: that they recognised him. They were set in a resolute face on a powerful body, which sprang at him.

He yanked his head away. The pipe swept past his eyes with a whoosh in the air, clipping the top of his shoulder and clattering against a container with a hollow bang. It was immediately followed by the sickening crack of a hard fist connecting with his mouth and nose. He launched himself forward, his head back, his neck muscles uncoiling as he planted his forehead into a cheekbone. The man crashed against a container, side-stepping in an instant as Dan waded in but missed.

A voice crackled on the walkie-talkie hooked on the man's belt. 'Choukri, where are you?'

The call didn't bring a flicker to the man's eyes. He leapt forward, and this time he connected. Dan felt air surge from his chest as the pipe slammed into his ribs. He staggered back but the man was on him like a cat. The pipe rattled on the ground as a strong hand ripped at his throat and a fist rained blows to his head.

Dan raised a leg and stamped down, aiming for ligaments around the knee. His foot brushed by. In an instant he knew his opponent was as quick as he was strong, and there was relish for the fight in the face that was inches from his own. Slamming his opponent backwards, Dan lost his balance, bringing them both down in a writhing tangle.

They tumbled out of container alley onto the open terminal, still locked together. *This guy's going to kill me*, Dan thought, *he wants to do it and he can do it.* He knew he had the fight of his life on his hands, a fight for his life. The swollen veins on the temples were inches from his own face. He could smell the breath, feel the calloused hand crushing his windpipe.

As he shifted his weight, the side of the man's head banged into his cheek. With a lunge, Dan opened his mouth wide and bit down, his teeth clamping on something solid. Locking it in the side of his mouth, he heaved up with his legs, shaking his head like a dog with a rat.

Dan spat out an inch of bloody flesh and tissue as the man staggered back, bellowing in pain and fury. A few paces separated them; enraged eyes stared at him. The end of the man's nose was torn clean away, a torrent of blood running into his mouth, down his chin and splattering up from the hard ground. He exhaled a shower of crimson droplets, his chest heaving as he drew breath, readying himself.

There was a haunting emptiness in Dan's mind. All that remained was adrenaline and an instinct that he had one or maybe two seconds before his opponent closed in to finish it, to finish him. He saw the tension build in the powerful body in front of him until it froze with a jolt.

A puff of concrete dust leapt at the man's feet, followed by another that ricocheted with a whine and a sharp ding as it buried itself in something metal. The man stared down with a start. It shocked Dan too, his heart pounding, and it shocked his brain into motion. He tried to think. Someone was shooting and it couldn't be coming from the *Ocean Dove*. A third shot crashed into the concrete an inch from the man's boot.

In the blink of an eye the man turned and disappeared behind a stack of packing cases. Dan lurched forward, his eyes darting wildly. The assailant was nowhere to be seen. Taking deep breaths he tried to compose himself, running his hands over his sweating face. He glanced down – his palms streaked red. There was the foul taste of bile rising in his throat, mixed with blood. *Come on,* he urged, slamming the flat of his hand down on a crate. *Bergen!* He shook his head, spat, and ducked back into container alley.

Bergen was conscious, propped up against the wall of steel.

'You okay?' Dan said, crouching at his side.

Bergen wheezed. 'What happened?'

'You got hit with a pipe.'

Bergen lifted his head slowly. 'You don't look too clever.'

'I met your pipe man,' Dan said, running his eyes over him and feeling for the pulse in his neck. He looked down into his eyes, checking the haze was starting to clear. 'Back in a moment.'

A few steps away at the end of the line of containers, he edged his head out. 'Shit!'

The *Ocean Dove* had slipped from the berth and was turning midstream, pointing its bows downriver. He looked up sharply as two shadows swept across the terminal, whipping up a biting cloud of dust. Closing his eyes for a moment, he heard Bergen's voice. 'Apaches!'

The *Ocean Dove* was broadside to the helicopters when they raked it with 30mm cannon rounds. Dan clenched his fists as steel tore from the *Ocean Dove*'s superstructure, the drone of high-powered engines fading as the Apaches banked downriver, replaced by the bark of automatic weapons from the ship, blazing away from the wings and deck.

~

Mubarak had sent a crewman to the bows to cut the mooring lines. Bolt cutters were already in position. With no linesmen on the shore or time to operate the winches, a quick cut was all that had been needed. With a squirt from the thruster, the bows had swung out as the engine speed rose. On the main deck, Snoop and Tariq poured fire into the oncoming helicopters. Cookie was at their side, one leg knelt down, his gun barrel resting on rags slung over the rail.

'Where's Choukri!' Mubarak yelled from the bridge. 'We need the sniper rifle on the pilots!'

Snoop's head snapped round as he changed an ammunition drum on the wings.

'Isn't he with you?'

'He went to find Assam on the terminal, and then cut the stern lines,' Mubarak shouted. 'He's here somewhere.' He grabbed his walkie-talkie again. 'Choukri! Choukri!'

THIRTY-TWO

Dan looked across the terminal. It seemed clear, but he slipped the safety catch from the Kalashnikov just in case.

'I'm just going to check,' he said, glancing down to Bergen.

The Apache gunships were ducking behind the smouldering pillars of the Thames Barrier.

Zeroing the missiles, he thought.

In a synchronised movement both helicopters emerged from behind the pillars, hovering just above the river, before launching laser-guided Hellfire missiles. Four slammed into the accommodation block and four into the bows at the waterline. The Apache on the north shore swung up and veered away, skirting through smoke, heading upriver and trapping the *Ocean Dove* in a pincer move. Another four missiles skimmed upriver. The ship lurched sideways, the second Apache lining itself up behind, its missiles smashing low into the stern at the rudder and steering gear. More erupted in the back of the accommodation block. It was difficult to gauge what was happening as smoke and flames shot out through shattered steelwork, the ship drifting towards the south bank, its bow dropping.

In unison, the helicopters rose and closed the gap from both ends, raking the accommodation and walkways with a stream of cannon fire.

Dan could see the ship had lost steering and power, but there could still be men alive, below decks. They would be armed, perhaps rigging the ship with booby traps or explosives to scuttle it. The bow was grounded at an angle in the shoreline mud. The tide was turning, running out, picking up pace midstream and forcing the stern towards the shore, holding it fast. The ship was wedged, its superstructure smoking, blackened by fire, pockmarked with jagged holes.

'Fuck it!' he spat, punching a packing crate. 'Why am I here? I need to be there!'

He made his way back to check on Bergen, who was sitting up now.

'Stay here. Stay quiet,' Dan said, putting the gun down at his side. 'I've got to get a closer look.'

Bergen nudged him and flicked his eyes skyward. 'F-16s! Yanks. Where's the bastard RAF?'

Picking his way through rows of cargo, Dan crawled to a mound of earth at the side of the terminal. The ship was about five hundred metres downriver. There was no sign of activity on board. Above him, the sky was filling with the thunderous sound of criss-crossing jets bouncing from bank to bank. More helicopters had appeared, some of them civilian looking. One of the Apaches was holding station above the *Ocean Dove*. The other was herding random helicopters away, probably news crews, he thought, and the Apache above the ship seemed in no hurry to go any nearer. It could be running thermal imaging or waiting for backup.

The feel of steel on the back of his neck froze him to the spot. It was replaced in an instant by a boot, stamping down and grinding his face into the ground as hands wrenched his arms behind his back. Another hand grabbed the back of his head and pulled him up by the hair.

'Who the fuck are you?' a black balaclava with a Glaswegian accent spat.

'Dan Brooks. MI5,' he spluttered, his mouth filled with dirt, the taste of blood on his lips.

'We heard about you on the way up. That bald cunt back there with you?'

They let go and stood back, their guns trained on him. Dan got to his feet, wiping dirt from his eyes and spitting blood and grit. 'Why? What have you done to him?'

The shoulders below the balaclava shrugged.

Bergen was slumped with his back to a container, his eyes unfocused. Blood was running down the side of his head. It was a fresh wound.

Crouching down, Dan lifted Bergen's chin.

'He'll be all right,' one of the men said.

Dan turned and glared. 'This bald cunt's got concussion and thirty minutes ago this bald cunt was inspecting power lines in his helicopter. He's been shot down by terrorists, beaten with a steel pipe and now he's had a good shoeing from the SAS – so call for a fucking medevac!'

The Scottish balaclava turned to another balaclava. 'Make the call.'

'And stay with him and secure the area,' Dan added. 'And get me on that ship, now!'

~

Dan ran back across the terminal to the main gate with six SAS men.

'What do I call you – Jock?' he said.

'Every other cunt does.'

At the gate they turned east along the road and then down a side street towards the river. There was a small wharf for launches at the head of it and, a stone's throw away, the *Ocean Dove*.

'What's the situation?' Dan said, looking upriver to the bows, where ropes were hanging down to the shallow water.

'My lads are on it, working their way through. They're all dead so far,' Jock said, breaking away and speaking into his mouthpiece. 'That's the all-clear. Eleven dead, one just alive,' he added.

'Fourteen!' Dan said, remembering the crew list from the reports Lars had sent him. It was the standard figure for a ship of its type anyway, and the same as his *Astrid*. 'There's fourteen crew. One dead on the terminal, so there has to be thirteen on the ship. And make sure the one who's just alive stays alive. We need him.'

Jock went back to his mouthpiece, issuing orders for another sweep. The men on board were adamant they had accounted for everyone, but they started again.

'And what about up there,' Dan said, looking west. 'In London?'

Jock blew his cheeks out. 'It looked like fucking hell when we flew over. I dunno,' he added, shaking his head.

'Is anything working? I've got to speak to my people.'

'It's all fucked. That's what we heard. Couldn't get jack out of no one on the way up. No sit-rep, nothing. Never seen nothing like it.'

Dan contemplated the prospect of an SAS man never having seen anything like it. After a while, he broke the silence. 'I left my wife and daughter on the M11.'

Jock turned to him, the cold blue eyes warming a little. 'Your pal. He'll be all right.'

'He's not my pal. I found him and his helicopter by the side of the road. He's one of yours, army, I don't know what, but a helicopter pilot. I was navy,' he added.

'Fucking matelot ponce! Should have known.' Jock laughed. 'Look, I'll have comms set up in a few minutes. See that blue door there.'

'Can you patch me through to Thames House?'

'Sure. If they're up and running.'

They waited. Jock's mates were on the *Ocean Dove*. Planes and helicopters swept over the river – RAF, army, navy, even an American heavy transport. The Apaches had backed off and disappeared from view. High above was what appeared to be a cordon of helicopters, a circle of dots a thousand feet up, holding position, keeping prying eyes away.

Time was precious. Before long they would be swamped by Special Branch, police, and every imaginable agency. Getting on the *Ocean Dove* before the rush was paramount.

He glanced at his watch. It was one o'clock. And Julie. What about her? God. There was no signal on his phone. He showed it to Jock.

'I think it's working in some places, but not around here. Need to go out a bit further.'

He was just about to ask if the comms behind the blue door could patch him through to a mobile phone on the M11 when Jock turned to him.

'Eleven crew dead. One alive. And there's one more, some customs guy. There was ID in his pockets.'

A rope ladder unfurled over the bow. Dan waded out, the water up to his waist, his feet squelching in mud that was doing its best to suck the shoes from his feet.

He swung over the rail to the walkway. A pair of bolt cutters were lying on the deck at the side of a mooring winch. A short length of rope was hanging from the drum.

'Clean cut,' he said, picking the end up and inspecting it. 'No time to wind, just cut.'

The passageway along the side of the hatch was littered with spent cartridges. Cannon rounds from the Apaches had mangled the rail and hatch walls. At the head, by the entrance to the stairs, was a body in yellow overalls. It lay face up, staring. Dan crouched down and ran his eyes over the man. There was no insignia but his sleeves were rolled up over burly forearms, the back of his hands and wrists pockmarked with burns and scar tissue.

'The cook,' he said.

'Aye?'

He knelt down and took a picture on his phone before moving on to the accommodation block.

The bridge had taken five missiles and was barely recognisable, blackened and smouldering, strewn with shattered glass, gaping holes in steel, the console blown half away, the air filled with the bitter smell of explosives and burning. Three bodies lay on the floor, their uniforms scorched, torn and bloodstained. There was just enough remaining of their insignia to identify rank and function.

Two balaclavas were at the side of one of the bodies, whose head was on the lap of another man, cradled in his lifeless hands.

'The second officer,' Dan said, looking into a pair of limpid eyes that were staring up at him. Soft lips parted in gasps, blowing weak little bubbles of blood and saliva. His shirt was in tatters, his chest torn open.

'Looks like a fucking choirboy,' a balaclava said. 'Heart's still going, you see? And he keeps saying something.'

Dan knelt and put an ear close to his mouth. 'Shoe, shewk, shoot, shootie?' he repeated, his eyes narrowed in concentration. 'What do you think?'

'Dunno. Can't make it out,' the balaclava said.

Underneath him was an older man, unrecognisable, with one side of his head blown away. The contrast was startling as Dan put his foot into the raw and bloody mess and eased him over, revealing an untouched side, a cultured face with an almost serene expression.

'The captain. Mubarak maybe, but I've never seen his photo.'

'And this one?' Jock said, looking questioningly at a Sentinel Security uniform and easing a finger away from the trigger of a Kalashnikov.

One of his colleagues shrugged. 'He was blasting away. So I had to slot the cunt.'

'There's Sentinel signs at the gatehouse,' Dan said.

'Aye, I saw 'em,' Jock said, looking to one of his men. 'Check it out.'

'Okay,' Dan said, crouching again. *It's true*, he thought, looking down at a face that wouldn't have been out of place next to an altar. 'This choirboy's got to live. Can your guys handle it?'

'Aye, and the medics are here in two minutes.'

Dan took pictures, close-ups of their faces, before stepping out to the wings. There was a body in yellow overalls in a pool of spent cartridges. The overalls were open to the waist over a Snoop Dogg T-shirt.

They made a search of the ship, accounting for all the bodies, photographing them, noting rank and position. There were three in the engine room: the chief engineer, second engineer and one more – a motorman or oiler. One was on the port-side stairs, one by the forecastle and others in random places, but no short fat guy in Gucci and Armani with a chunky Rolex on his wrist. Dan was not surprised, but was still slightly disappointed.

'I've never seen anything like this,' he said, standing very still in the hold, his eyes darting along the precision line of guns, the carousels, the cable feeds and walkways. 'Look at the engineering, these shell racks, like automatic feeds. Look at the scale of it, the work that's gone into it.'

At the end of the hold, a little fold-down table with a laptop on it caught his attention, as did the impatient shuffling of feet next to him.

'Here, give me a hand,' he said, pulling his shirt over his head and using it as a glove on the power lead. 'Lever the plug with your knife.'

Jock slipped a blade behind the plug and teased it out. Dan closed the laptop, slipping it between the folds of his shirt.

At the stern of the ship, behind the accommodation block, were the aft mooring winches. The starboard ones were all stowed. One on the port side was paid out over the side of the ship, the rope hanging loosely in its guides, the end dangling in the river. He pulled the rope up and looked around.

'Clean cut again,' he said. 'But no bolt cutters ... Now the guy who was supposed to cut the line here, like the one at the bow, could have shinned down it to the river and cut it there, and ...'

Jock leant over the rail, his pale eyes scanning the banks.

'How long does an aqualung last?' Dan said.

'An hour, if you stretch it.'

'So he's got a bag, an air tank, flippers, mask.'

'Aye, maybe. But could have been stashed down there already.'

'Yeah, why not,' Dan said. 'When it was leaving, I couldn't see the stern from where I was on the terminal. So he swims at three miles an hour with three knots of current. That's six miles. If he'd landed at Moritz we'd have seen him, right? Could be on either bank. Could still be in the water ...'

'Could be fucking anywhere.'

'And we haven't found the chief officer, the mate. Has to be him. Fuck it,' Dan said, realising that of all the dead bodies he'd photographed, not one of them had the end of their nose missing.

'And he's got a nose wound – a bad nose wound ...'

'How bad?'

'Bad. I bit it off.'

An eyebrow lifted, but no comment was made. Jock spoke only into his mouthpiece, telling his people to spread the word quickly and start a sweep search.

'And why just him?' Dan said.

'Rat deserting the ship?'

'Not that. There has to be more. But what's so special about just him?'

Back in the accommodation block, Dan looked up and down what had once been the corridor in the crew quarters. The dividing walls had been blown away, the panels charred, remnants of belongings scattered. By a process of elimination he was pretty sure he was standing in what had been the mate's cabin. The bed tipped over by the remains of a dividing wall had to be his.

He righted the bed and stripped the sheet carefully, starting at the bottom, folding it in on itself, following the same process with the pillowcase. When he got up, Jock was standing to one side, looking on.

'We've got the bodies of the others,' Dan said. 'Easy DNA match. But this one, I'm not letting this get compromised.'

'It's your party. But if anyone asks, I've seen a laptop and now a sheet ...'

~

Behind the blue door was a terraced house. Stairs led up from the hall with two rooms to the side knocked into a lounge–diner. At the back was a kitchen with steamed-up windows where a retired couple were making tea in relays.

'There you go, darling,' the woman said, as an eye in a balaclava winked and crooked a little finger daintily from a nice bit of floral Crown Derby.

The door opened. A black balaclava carrying a heavy rifle stepped in. He went across to Jock and said something. They both turned to look at Dan. The new pair of eyes smiled.

'Do I know you?' Dan said.

'Don't reckon you do,' a soft west-country voice said. 'But I know you – seen you from that tower block overlooking the terminal.'

'Okay, got it ...' Dan nodded, the bullets ricocheting at Choukri's feet falling into place. 'Why didn't you shoot him?'

'You was doing okay.' The man shrugged, tapping a boot against Jock's. 'Best I could do was let him know, like. Anyway, I couldn't. You was standing right in the way, mate.'

'I told him to stop fucking about and do the both of you.' Jock laughed.

'Thanks a lot,' Dan said, 'And the other one, by the containers, that was you?'

The guy nodded.

'Well, I owe you. Thanks,' Dan said. 'And there was green stuff coming out of his mouth …'

'Khat. Saw it in Yemen last year.' They quietened when the lady of the house came in with another tray of tea and sandwiches. As she turned and left, Dan said, 'Can you send someone up to the terminal? There's a bit of evidence I forgot.'

Jock's arms folded across his chest as Dan explained what had happened. Eventually, he shook his head. 'And my guy's going to get down on his hands and knees, fingertip search in the dirt, and he'll find it – the end of this cunt's nose …'

'Yeah. Where I spat it out.'

The comms-man got through to Thames House. A minute later they found LaSalle.

'There's twelve dead,' Dan said. 'Plus one still alive but in a bad way, and one missing. There should be fourteen crew. The missing one is the chief officer, the mate.'

'Okay,' LaSalle said.

'I think he's slipped over the side into the river. Could be anywhere now. He's got a forty-five-minute start on us.'

'Right.'

'Can you get on to the PLA and …'

'PLA?'

'Port of London Authority. They can tell you who the ship's agent is and the agent will have the crew list, with names, passport numbers, everything.'

'Okay, we're on it. Can you get yourself in here?'

Dan turned around.

'We'll be out of here in about ten,' Jock said.

'In about half an hour,' Dan said, ending the call and looking at Jock. 'Via the M11?'

The signals man tried to raise Julie and another cup of tea was put in Dan's hands, with a corned beef and pickle sandwich.

He felt guilty at his hunger, eating in silence, staying away from the window, unwilling to look. He was soaked from the waist down, his legs and shoes black, hands and arms cut, lip split. The inside of his thigh had been gashed by barbed wire, a rib was cracked and his nose was broken. But it meant nothing to him, absolutely nothing, compared with what he knew lay upriver in a ten-mile radius from where he was drinking tea in a very English way, served by a very English woman whose parents had no doubt talked nostalgically of the blitz. Her father had probably worked on the river or the docks before they became airports, exhibition halls and global financial centres. It was touching to see dust rings on the sideboard; she had evidently got her wedding china out specially. At his feet was a trail of dirt he had trodden into the carpet. He looked up apologetically, meeting a forgiving smile.

'Another cup of tea, darling?'

'No thanks,' he said.

But he did ask if he could clean himself up at the kitchen sink. A mirror propped on a shelf told him his face was a mess. The hot water felt good, though it made his nose bleed again. He stuffed some kitchen roll in a nostril and checked the swelling around an eye. As he dried his hands the signals man called out, 'I've got your missus on.'

Closing the blue door behind him, a single glance told Dan they had got on board the *Ocean Dove* just in time. The road was jammed with cars, vans and trucks, the wharf swarming with flashing blue lights and every colour of uniform.

The Osprey was in a school playground. When he stepped on board, Tom Bergen was there already, asleep in a seat. The SAS were going to take him back to Hereford with them.

One of the balaclavas met Dan's eye and handed him a tattered crisp bag, the colours and writing faded. 'Best I could do.' The man shrugged. 'It was just lying around.'

Dan looked at it, carefully folded, seemingly empty. Then his fingers rounded on something small, something fleshy. Holding it gingerly, he slipped it in his pocket.

THIRTY-THREE

The balaclavas were removed when the Osprey was airborne. Dan had no interest in their faces. His own was pressed to the window. The route to the M11 only skirted the fringes of London and he was painfully aware it would get worse when they flew diagonally over the city to Thames House. Up here, for the time being, he knew he was being spared the rawest detail, detached, looking on from a distance.

The suburbs were still green but the city's core was black. Smoke was rising from square mile after mile. Flames licked from tall buildings, some of them still all too recognisable. From landmark buildings, the greenery of parks, bends in the river, he was able to identify specific areas, the devastation from Canary Wharf to the City, across the West End, up to North London, out to Kensington and Chelsea, all along the south bank.

There was so much detail to take in. Looking out over it, he realised that detail was inconsequential in the greater scheme – and there was most definitely a greater scheme. The guns must have been fitted in Bar Mhar, he reasoned, when Azmi's man had said it was innocently receiving repairs to its steelwork. But who had lied – Azmi's man, Azmi, Hak, or all three of them? And had the agent been Azmi's man, or Hak's? He only had Hak's word that Azmi had overruled him and hand-picked the guy himself.

He thought back to the last information he had, when the *Ocean Dove* had sailed from Bar Mhar, making calculations in his head. Pakistan to Port Elizabeth was about fifteen days. From there up to West Africa was around another fourteen, then a dozen more to London. So, about forty days, with a few days in hand for bad weather, the possibility to speed up or slow down and a day to bunker en route. And that would necessarily have been somewhere discreet, somewhere offshore? He racked his mind. Of course, Algoa Bay, an easily forgettable element of the Port Elizabeth complex, with its discreet offshore facilities. The schedule fitted together perfectly – to arrive today, on Friday, 10 June.

But it had just been a voyage, a mere component. Once again, he realised, it had all been part of a meticulous greater scheme. A shudder ran down his neck, thinking about how far back it might all stretch, perhaps many years, perhaps to the very foundation of OceanBird itself, a company that had quite possibly been set up with one overriding objective.

He shook his head, mindful of the here and now, the imperative of the moment. Without having to give it a moment's thought, he knew there would be time enough over the coming days to examine every last detail. The more he considered it, the more he realised it was going to be a harrowing exercise, delving not only into the who, what and why of their enemy, but into his own performance too.

The pilot had Julie's GPS position from her phone. Dan could see the scene on the motorway was unchanged. Lines of blocked traffic stretched into the distance and to the junction with the similarly static M25 ring road.

He hurried up the embankment to meet her, trying to make light of the look of horror in her face as she waited at the fence.

'Look at you!' she cried, tears welling in her eyes as she ran her fingers lightly over his cuts and bruises.

Jock's men made a fuss of Phoebe when they boarded – a much-needed comfort of hope and purity for cynically hardened men. Tender fingers stroked her cheeks, fingers that had squeezed triggers less than an hour before.

It had taken only minutes to get from the river to the motorway. In merely a few more they would be at Thames House, and Dan knew they would be dreadful minutes for Julie. The scenes below were harrowing and so far she had only seen them from a distance.

Coming in over London she turned away from the window, drawing her legs up and burying her head in Dan's chest. 'But what if

I'm right?' she said softly, her fingers digging into him. He remembered the argument, remembered his words, remembered her dismissal. But he said nothing, only hugging her more tightly.

He looked over her shoulder at the faces around them. They had seen horror before. They had sensibilities that were inured and defence mechanisms that deflected through black humour and euphemism. There was a good-looking woman with them in a summer skirt that had ridden up. But there was no banter. No one caught his eye. The cabin was silent. Grim, unblinking faces were set at the windows.

To the left was Canary Wharf and below them the City, gusting in and out of sight in the palls of dust and pillars of smoke. Southwark and the river, its bridges shattered; the Millennium Wheel half submerged; a thread of train hanging from a bridge; a trail of havoc stretching west into the distance. Dan lost count of the number of shells that had hit the Houses of Parliament, now obscured by the billowing smoke coming from its gaping rooftops.

They put down at the roundabout on the north side of Lambeth Bridge. Thames House was fifty metres away, just across the road.

Jock opened the Osprey's door. 'When this is over, you and the bald cunt, we'll see you in Hereford at the regimental dinner. Good luck, pal.'

Bergen slept on and Dan couldn't begrudge him. No one should be forced to see this. It was better for him to wake tomorrow afternoon and gaze at flowers in the sickbay garden. Perhaps later he could try a look at the television news.

Phoebe was under Dan's arm, bedding and a laptop under the other, a chunk of bloody nose in his pocket. They picked their way across the road, Julie gripping him tightly. He glanced to his side as she gasped; the acrid stench of burning flesh, the charred remains of a bus up against a wall, the blackened and macabre bodies still in their seats, petrified in time. A motorcyclist was flopped over a low wall, one of his legs on the other side of the road, still pitifully in an armoured boot. And two schoolgirls, satchels on their backs, wrapped in each other's arms in a twisted heap. Bloody corpses lay uncovered where they had fallen.

It had looked bad enough from the helicopter, but at street level it was appalling. Dan's eyes darted around as they crossed the pavement. Dazed survivors sat in confusion, staring blankly at nothing or looking pleadingly at him. Many were unrecognisable, all looking the same, their ages and sexes indistinguishable, their clothes, faces and hair plastered in the same uniform dust of grey and brick pink, streaked with blood red. A tall man tottered in one direction and then another, his upper clothes torn from his body, a thick wedge of metal sticking out from a bloody shoulder.

The traffic was still, the way blocked with burned-out vehicles and splintered trees. Only people moved, on the pavement and in the street, hurrying with buckets, bottles of water, tearing the clothes from their own backs for bandages. There was an eerie quiet, of incoherent mumbling, low wailing, the gasps of the dying. Alarms had played out, sirens switched off.

Smoke poured from the upper levels of Thames House, the reception doors a gaping hole of buckled steel in the frontage, the floor covered in glass, masonry and dust. Staff were trying to help people on the street, but like everyone they had their own problems.

Bodies lay in the rubble, some staring vacantly, others with makeshift covers over their faces. People were shouting, calling for water and bandages. A woman knelt at the side of a wide-eyed man, tearing the sleeve from her blouse and binding it around the stump of his fingerless hand.

A shoeless leg poked limply into the passageway as Dan and Julie made their way along. But it was the other leg, with a distinctive shoe on its foot, that caught Dan's attention. The woman was lying on her side, most of the hair on the back of her head burned away. Dan knelt and gently turned her. He blinked hard as Jo Clymer's eyes stared up at him. Her face was blackened. There were blast-burns to the side of her head and an ear was streaming blood. He felt her pulse. It was still strong, though her head was shaking and teeth chattering as words – 'What, how? I do, how, me, me' – spluttered incoherently from her mouth.

Dan's face was close to hers. He ran his hands gingerly over her neck, across her shoulders, down her back and sides, checking for shrapnel and broken bones. 'No, no,' he said quietly, looking down into her eyes. 'You did good, Jo. You did good. Be strong. You can do it. You can do it.'

Julie was on her knees at his side. He glanced round to her. 'This has to come out,' he said, lifting a torn and blood-soaked blouse. A shard of glass the size of a door wedge was sticking out from under Clymer's ribs.

'Push hard when it's out – here,' Dan said, handing her one end of Phoebe's shawl.

Julie nodded, her eyes darting between Jo Clymer and Phoebe, who was propped against the wall at her side, her eyes closed, her chin on her chest. Thank God for small mercies, Dan thought.

He wrapped the other end of the shawl around the razor-edged piece of glass, pressed Clymer's shoulder to the floor with one hand and yanked with the other. Behind him, at the end of the corridor, there was a familiar voice. He looked round distractedly.

'What is it? Julie said as she stemmed the flow of blood.

'Up there.' He nodded. 'LaSalle. I've got to see him.'

'I'll be okay. Go then,' Julie said, turning back to Jo Clymer. 'I'm Julie,' she added. 'Lie still. Don't worry. I've got you.'

LaSalle broke away from the group he was talking with. He ran his eye over Dan's dishevelled state and the bundle under his arm but said nothing. He led the way across the floor.

'How bad is it?' Dan said.

'Beyond bad. Everything's out. We've set up an emergency command room at the back."

'Casualties?'

'I don't know. Thousands. Tens of thousands … the emergency services can't move,' LaSalle said, turning into a passageway and pushing a door open.

There were a dozen seated around a table and about the same number on their feet. A man was writing bullet points on a whiteboard, words like HM Queen, PM, Americans, lockdown. Two men in military uniforms were standing to the side, one an army colonel, the other in RAF blue. None of the faces were familiar.

'Listen up,' LaSalle said, rapping the table. He put a hand on Dan's shoulder and pushed him forward, gesturing that the floor was open. 'This is Dan Brooks. He'll debrief us.'

'The one that got away, this is his bedding,' Dan said, putting it on the table. 'And this,' he added, reaching in his pocket, 'is the end of his nose.'

'His nose …' someone said.

'I bit it off.'

The guy nearest to Dan sat back, averting his eyes.

'And this is the guns' control computer.'

He plugged his phone into the conference screen, scrolling through the camera roll, pointing each body out, the captain, the chief engineer, the one who was still alive.

A stocky red-headed man raised a bloodstained hand. 'He's been flown to Sidcup hospital. Special Branch are watching him.'

They all looked on in stony silence at the photos of the guns. Dan ran through their type, range and capability. The arithmetic of just under a thousand rounds a minute was chilling.

Breaking the silence, Dan said, 'Have we got the crew list?'

A woman in half-moon glasses shuffled some papers and pushed a sheet across. Mubarak was the first name and photo on the list, fifty-four years of age, Egyptian. So that's him, Dan thought, once a silhouette on LinkedIn, now a bloody mess of dead flesh.

The next name belonged to the first officer, Choukri Belabas, thirty-two, born in Algeria. It was clearly the face he'd buried his teeth in.

'He's the one we're looking for,' Dan said, explaining the sequence of the severed mooring lines. 'And we mustn't forget the nose when the description is circulated,' he added. 'It'll be almost impossible to hide that.'

Dan turned back to the list. The next name was Faisel Ibn Bhakri, the second officer. He looked at the photo of the choirboy who was still alive, remembering 'Shoe, shewk, shoot, shootie.' Now that, he thought, could just have been Choukri …

LaSalle leant forward, his hands together, fingers drawn up under his own nose, one of them probing it subconsciously. 'Check the clinics and backstreet doctors. If he was in the river with a wound like that, there's a risk of, what is it, septicaemia?'

'Tetanus …?' was offered, along with 'Weil's disease …?'

'Check it all, every connection, every prescription for medicine,' LaSalle said, glancing at a man taking notes along the table.

Dan looked around the table, unsure if he was supposed to continue, feeling he'd given them everything he could already.

LaSalle put his hands together under his chin. 'And why does he get off the ship? Why only him? What's so special about him?'

He was thinking aloud, rhetorically, but it didn't stop the others from looking to Dan for answers. In the shell-shocked remains of their office and city, their silence asked the same collective question – how did you come to fail so miserably in your duty? A pair of cold eyes, a shade lighter than RAF blue, raked him from head to toe, wordlessly asking, aren't you the specialist? Half-moon glasses perched disdainfully on the tip of a sharp nose – but you're the case officer?

The red-headed man burned with disbelief. 'But damn you, man,' he said out loud, his strained voice cutting through the silence. 'You must know! You've studied this ship, backed by all our resources!'

Dan took an involuntary step back from the table. *But I did know*, he thought, a burning flash of anger welling up inside him. *I made my case and you overruled me*. He wanted to say it out loud, to shout it, but could only clench his fists at his side, his haunted eyes turning imploringly towards the door.

LaSalle slapped the flat of his hand on the table and pushed up to his feet. 'We're done here,' he said, grabbing Dan's arms and bundling him out, the door slamming behind them.

In the corridor, LaSalle's hands were still gripping him. 'That was not intended,' he said, looking him directly in the eye. 'I apologise.'

Dan had no interest in an apology and no inclination to either acknowledge or accept it. The words had cut straight through the bone to the nerve. Was an apology even warranted, he wondered, feeling he was far from entirely blameless. 'The raid on Bar Mhar,' he said. 'Did you see the report, the outcome?'

'I didn't. But it was evidently – negative?'

'It was.'

LaSalle considered it. 'And this was shortly after our own enterprise in Sharjah failed.'

'I got it on the Friday night in the pub with Hak. Does it matter – *did* it matter?'

LaSalle shook his head. 'On balance? No. I would have been obliged to accept it at face value too. But you were identified as trouble early on. They played you. The matter was sure to die once you stopped shouting from the rooftops, and with unsatisfactory outcomes in both Sharjah and Bar Mhar, your loss of interest was inevitable.' He paused, a frown spreading over his face. 'Particularly with my pressure and wholly regrettable counsel …'

'Could I have done more?' Dan said. 'Could I have done better?'

'I'm asking precisely the same of myself. In your case? No. In my case? Without a shadow of doubt.'

Dan wanted to say he was relieved, but as he tried to put his own involvement in some kind of order, he realised that in all this devastating disorder, his own role or conscience or pride had no meaning any more. 'Hak played me?'

'I don't think so. Unwittingly, perhaps.'

'Who then. It can't be Azmi, can it?'

LaSalle looked at him resignedly. 'I regret that must remain for some other day, for some other people. You were simply caught in the middle.'

'And, in Sharjah, you were just looking for a reaction, from someone, trying to draw something out?'

There was no reply, just a wearied expression and downcast eyes. Dan was shocked to think that parallel forces had run alongside him. The IsC – MI6's Indian subcontinent section – had long been known as an itch that was impossible to scratch. He was shocked to think that his own file amounted to little more than some kind of catalyst in a joint operation to cut out its cancer. LaSalle had mentioned him initially to Azmi and Jo Clymer had encouraged him to contact Hak, no doubt at LaSalle's insistence. That had surely been the root of the heated words between the two of them that Vikram had stumbled across in the corridors of Thames House. His own file had become lost, the potential threat overlooked, subsumed by some greater prerogative.

And when the reckoning came, which surely must be soon, Dan would remember to let those other people know about his own misgivings, about 'geared' ships, about 'hatch coamings' and those who claimed no knowledge of the sea and ships. Looming at the front of his mind was the meeting with Azmi, Hak and Pittman, and how he'd told them everything he had known or suspected, and crucially, what he hadn't known and couldn't prove. And all the while, had Azmi known every damn detail already, with the crafty old bird drawing his case out of him like shallow water in a pitcher, dropping the pebbles one by one?

'Has Azmi got shipping experience?' he said, looking round at another crafty, though wounded animal.

LaSalle turned, surprise on his face, surprise at such a question at such a time. 'Azmi? I think he used to go as a boy. I believe his father was something in the national shipping line.'

'Then he probably wrote the field report,' Dan said. 'And there was no agent, no raid on Bar Mhar.'

'Quite possibly,' LaSalle said neutrally. He checked his watch. 'Come on, we have to go.'

Dan looked back over his shoulder. Julie and Phoebe were in the building somewhere, perhaps still at Jo Clymer's side, but that had been twenty minutes ago. 'I've got to get my wife and daughter home.'

'Not yet, I'm afraid,' LaSalle said. 'I'm due at Number Ten at two thirty and you're coming with me.'

Dan spun round in disbelief. 'What, and take one for the fucking team?'

'Someone usually does,' LaSalle said.

THIRTY-FOUR

They set off from Thames House at a fast pace. Downing Street was under a ten-minute walk, but it was already twenty-five past two. The scale of devastation increased as they approached Parliament Square. Every step had to be planned, zigzagging between road and pavement, going round or over the harrowing debris.

As Dan collected his thoughts, he realised there was no time to stop, to look or to help. In many ways it was a welcome if guilty release. He'd seen the Houses of Parliament from the air. At ground level it was visceral. It did not improve when they crossed into Whitehall, where government buildings had evidently been a priority target. His nose twitched at the pervasive smell hanging in the air, a rotting dampness on a hot and dry day, musty and acrid.

'What do I call her?' he said.

'Prime Minister,' LaSalle said, looking round and running an enquiring eye over Dan, his strained breathing, his uneven gait.

'Broken rib, I think,' Dan said.

LaSalle nodded. 'Just speak plainly, how you see it, how you saw it. It's not you who's going to take one for the team – let me worry about that,' he added resignedly.

At the head of Downing Street, the security officers stepped in front of Dan, looking him up and down suspiciously. Luckily, one of their number was a regular from the Diplomatic Protection Group, who recognised LaSalle and waved them through.

The door to Number Ten opened to them from the inside, its blast-proof steel casing twisted and charred, but intact. The windows to the side were blown in. Fragments of curtain fluttered in the breeze. The inner hall was filled with people. A tall man at the back caught

LaSalle's eye and gestured over the heads of the throng to a staircase at the side.

As they made their way up, a man coming down at a good clip brushed against one of the framed pictures lining the walls. Dan stretched a hand out to steady it. The face seemed familiar, a portrait of an earlier Prime Minister.

They entered a long room with a table to seat at least thirty. The tall man gestured to a pair of chairs and LaSalle tugged Dan's shirt downwards.

He sat, his eyes restlessly casting around, recognising only a few people in the room and one in particular, a tall, imposing woman midway along the table with her back to the equally imposing fireplace. He noticed that she was sitting in a different chair from all the others, the only one in the room with arms. Nearly every place was taken, with a similar number of people finding standing-room only, lining the walls behind their bosses. Taking the surroundings in, he was intrigued to see the table was shaped like a boat, broader in the beam and tapering fore and aft. Somehow it was reassuring, as though he was on familiar ground.

In the cacophony of competing voices, LaSalle cupped a hand to Dan's bloodstained ear.

'The cabinet room,' he said. 'And that's C, Annette Vogel.' He indicated a woman immediately on Dan's left, the Chief of the Secret Intelligence Service, or MI6. 'The Foreign Secretary, her boss,' he added, his eyes shifting across the table to a pinstriped suit and steel-framed glasses. 'And the Home Secretary, our boss,' as a sharp-featured redhead hurried in and took a seat two places along. He continued around the table, mentioning names, the head of Special Branch, minister for this, minister for that, General so and so … 'The seating is by precedence. The Chancellor should be there.' He frowned, indicating across the table. 'His injuries are severe. Very severe, I gather.'

More suits and uniforms were arriving by the minute, filling the few remaining seats and standing two or three deep around the walls. Not everyone was smartly turned out, but most were. There was evidence here and there, torn clothes, cuts and bandages, and no shortage of haunted eyes. It eased Dan's concern about his own appearance. LaSalle reached across the table and filled two glasses with water, gesturing to him to drink.

At his side C, Annette Vogel, made no approach. The swelling in his left eye had half closed it and he dared not turn his head to her overtly.

A hand tapped on LaSalle's shoulder. He rose and walked around the table to the fireplace and crouched down, his head close to the Prime Minister's. They spoke for some moments. She shifted in her seat, her face lifting, clear blue eyes focusing along a strong nose. Dan met her gaze for a moment, her eyes narrowing in concentration, head nodding. LaSalle stood up and started back to his seat as a man at the Prime Minister's side rapped the table and shouted, 'Order!'

Heads turned expectantly to the fireplace, the rumble of voices subsiding. Dan's heart was beating hard, the ache in his side rising in step with it, his mind veering between the here and now and Julie back at Thames House, tending the wounded, doing what she could. His concentration was broken by a finger tap on his thigh and a familiar voice whispering, 'The unadorned truth.'

The Prime Minister looked around the table in the hushed room.

'The blackest of days,' she said, hands gripping the arms of her chair, knuckles whitening. 'And the blackest for more than the plain reason – as it seems there is only one person here who knows what the hell has happened to us. So, Mr Brooks, would you kindly explain.'

Dan made to rise but LaSalle's firm hand held him back. He drew a deep breath, deciding to speak to the hushed rulers of the land in the only manner he had learned was effective – as if addressing a navy crew.

His voice was strong but not strident, carrying to all quarters of the room. He chose his words carefully, taking his time, the straightforwardness of his language and delivery adding a chilling clarity. And they listened, like junior officers and ratings, trusting his words, trusting him, in absolute silence and stillness, without even a squeak from the packed floorboards around him.

He started where it all began, just before Christmas in the Indian Ocean, sparing little detail, the power of the guns, the engineering, the depth of organisation behind it all, though he was careful to tread lightly over areas he didn't fully understand – the subtexts of LaSalle, and C, sitting quietly next to him.

His phone was connected to a screen at the end of the room. Those standing before it squashed themselves to the sides. Reaction to the pictures was muted. Eyes instinctively turned away from the faces of the *Ocean Dove*'s dead, but returned to them in an instant with rapt horror and fascination. Images flashed before them, the ship, hold, guns, firing computer, death.

The Prime Minister's eyes dropped to the table, her head shaking softly from side to side.

'And if I understand this correctly,' she said, lifting her face. 'You were on the motorway, returning from disciplinary suspension – euphemistically a sabbatical?'

Dan nodded. As the Prime Minister's eyes raked the ceiling, he shifted his gaze around the table, meeting sombre faces, all staring directly at him.

'Good God,' the Prime Minister said, lowering her gaze. 'And you both knew of this threat for six months and did absolutely nothing about it – Edmund, Annette?'

LaSalle leant forward. 'As soon as there is an opportunity I will, of course, submit my resignation.'

The Prime Minister's eyes switched questioningly to C. They were not met.

Dan couldn't quite bring himself to look to his side. In nine months' time, the Director General of MI5 was due to retire. LaSalle should be stepping into the role. It was understood within the services and had the blessing of both the Home Secretary and the Prime Minister and many around the table who knew him.

'Your integrity is beyond doubt, Edmund,' she continued. 'But I fear we will need you more than ever in the coming months.'

Fear? That could be taken two ways. She'll need him, but with regret?

'So, we're hunting two things, a man with half his nose missing and the organisation behind him, the identity of which we have absolutely no idea.' She paused, looking across the table as if in hope of a contradiction, which was not forthcoming. 'I suggest you both,' she added, looking at LaSalle and C in turn, 'set up a joint task force with one single mission – to catch these bastards. I don't care what it is called, who runs it or what it will cost. I simply care about one certain outcome. It will succeed, quickly and ruthlessly.'

There was a stirring to Dan's left. 'Perhaps, Prime Minister,' C said, 'this might be an appropriate time for Mr Brook to take his leave – before we enter sensitive areas beyond his grade ...'

'What? And deny ourselves the only one among you with the bloody balls for the job? Absolutely not!' the Prime Minister thundered, her eyes drilling glacially into the visibly shrinking C.

Her attention switched to LaSalle. 'Your first task is to find a leading role for Mr Brooks,' she said, emphasising the 's' that C had carelessly mislaid. 'He is a man I can do business with and our enemies will regret doing business with. For God's sake promote him, five grades if you must, just damn well do it.'

A voice was heard along the table. 'Hear, hear.'

Other matters were discussed. A minute for this, a minute for that – social order, emergency services, hospitals, the pound. Questions and answers pinged across the table. People rose at intervals to leave and implement their tasks. A minister with responsibility for customs and border security issued instructions to aides ranging behind her. A deputy police commissioner broke away to speak into his radio. A general peered at a map and discussed deployment. From time to time, people appeared at Dan's side, seeking additional information or clarification.

Dan saw the Prime Minister rise from her seat and make her way a few places along the table, leaning in to a discussion. There were a dozen other huddles, new people arriving, others leaving, voices competing. He lost sight of her as his attention switched from one cell of activity to another, figuring out who was who and who was doing what, the extraordinary business of government on an extraordinary day.

A hand came to rest on his shoulder, the unmistakable touch of a woman. He turned, getting to his feet sharply. The hand remained there lightly. Her eyes ran over him, head tilting with sympathy, the tip of her tongue playing contemplatively over her lips as she considered the face inches from her own. Dan stood still, remembering his face in a mirror at a kitchen sink in a blue-doored terraced house, with his split lip, crooked nose, bloodstained ear and puffy, half-closed eye in a bed of purples, blacks and mottled yellows.

'Come and see me next week when the dust has settled,' the Prime Minister said, glancing around pensively and adding with a sigh, 'regrettable choice of phrase ... I want to make sure I understand all the implications and I know I can count on you for straight answers.'

She tilted her head back a little, making sure she had his attention. 'Meanwhile, I thank you. And your country thanks you.' She paused, her expression warming. 'I understand you have a wife and baby – she's a lucky woman – so I won't detain you.'

In what seemed a matter of seconds, Dan found himself down the stairs and standing outside in Downing Street. Between the wail of sirens in the distance, he thought he could hear sparrows chirping. There was relative peace and a warm sun on his back as he tried to gather his thoughts.

It had all happened too quickly. Leaving Suffolk in the morning he had been in two minds, grateful for the time there but increasingly wary of Monday's uncertain return to work. In the space of hours, the world, his world, had jarred from its axis. He realised he couldn't think of it as vindication. Vindication didn't even begin to enter it. Who could possibly want to be proved right about such appalling events?

But the slate was clean. He could start afresh and there was a hunger already, a burning desire to see it through. He knew it had to conclude with but one ending and that he must be part of it. He had the backing of the Prime Minister and the combined resources of MI5 and MI6, and somehow, in a few short hours, it had all become far less daunting than he had ever dared imagine it could be.

Staring into the Prime Minister's face, saying nothing, he'd felt a curious mix of energy coursing through him. There had been an urge to wrap his arms around her, for his own emotional comfort, for their mutual comfort, for his own safety and security and concern for hers, for solidarity and their joint purpose. Demons had been released. In the space of seconds he'd felt pressure rise as a torrent and subside as catharsis. A strange and frightening inner strength was surging through mind and body.

He shook his head and looked away as the black door opened again. LaSalle had stayed a moment for a private word with the Prime Minister.

'She's something else,' Dan said, walking across to him.

'A very splendid and formidable woman,' LaSalle said, before adding wistfully, 'We used to date at Cambridge.'

Dan turned. 'So you ... know her?' He put his hands up immediately, realising the implication. 'Not like that, obviously ...'

LaSalle smiled. 'You did well in there. Very well. C won't last a week. First-rate politician but second-rate mind. And they've never got on. As for me, well?'

'Are you really going to resign?'

'I will certainly press my case. But you'll need help, which I owe you. Perhaps you'll find something for me, as a consultant, pro bono of course. Free of charge – in the public good,' he added, anticipating the question.

They passed through Downing Street's gates into Whitehall. Ahead of them was the Cenotaph memorial. LaSalle stopped and looked up, whispering the words carved in the stone: 'The Glorious Dead.'

He turned to Dan. 'We have no idea what we are up against. It means years – and this,' he said, his foot flicking a shard of glass to the gutter, 'this is merely the beginning. Don't doubt yourself, just trust your instincts. So, are you ready?'

'I am.'

EPILOGUE

Sunday, 19 June
Printed in Manchester

THE SUNDAY TIMES

Matt Ritchie, Features Editor.
Zoe Zalewski, Home Affairs.
David Rice, Charles Ankomah,
Lucy Parsons.
Additional material: Reuters, AP,
AFP, our correspondents.

Eight days have passed since a terrorist ship sailed into the Thames and wreaked devastation in the United Kingdom's capital city, eight days that have revealed the scale of horror and devastation.

As world leaders prepare for a service of remembrance taking place in London next Sunday, tributes continue to flood in from across the globe to those that lost their lives. An internet book of condolence has been signed by over one hundred million amid an outpouring of grief and outrage, the numbers rising daily as the site struggles to cope with unprecedented traffic.

The death toll continues to rise as legions of survivors battle their injuries. At the time of going to press officials have revealed that the number of dead now stands at 41,523 with a further 236,752 recorded as injured. As time passes rescue workers are acknowledging there is little hope of finding further survivors among collapsed buildings.

The Sunday Times and its sister newspaper, *The Times*, have agreed not to individually report the names and identities of those who have died. We will instead publish a separate supplement to be updated each weekend over the next month, where we will pay our own particular tributes to the men, women and children who lost their lives so brutally.

In this vibrant and diverse city that is so often held as a global beacon of style, creativity and achievement, there is no corner of the community that has not lost leading figures, from politics to industry, public service to the arts, fashion to academia, across science and the media and music and sport. In the Queen's address to the nation last Saturday, she spoke of 'The cloud that has descended of such darkness that it threatens to shut out the light forever,' before defiantly stating that 'This will never be.'

The Queen and the Duke of Edinburgh were in Windsor at the time of the attack. They swiftly returned to London, surveying the damage to Buckingham Palace and comforting staff before touring the streets in the afternoon. All official engagements were cancelled as the royal family worked tirelessly during the week, visiting stricken areas and lifting morale with their presence. A doctor in Hyde Park's field hospital choked back tears as he told our staff reporter how the Queen held the hand of a critically injured man who was not expected to last the night, but by morning was showing positive signs of recovery. 'It was just her,' he said, 'just by being there.' And medical staff have been quick to point out that the Duchess of Cambridge has become a more or less permanent presence in the children's wards.

Fire across the city is now under control and buildings have been made safe from immediate collapse. Access to many areas has reopened while the centres of the City financial district and Canary Wharf remain restricted to structural and demolition teams. Gas, electricity and telephone supplies have been reconnected. The underground is now providing a full service and buses are running again with amendments to a large number of routes. Main-line stations are operating with the exception of Charing Cross; the Hungerford Railway Bridge is still out of commission and Tower, Blackfriars and Westminster Bridges remain closed to vehicles but are open to pedestrian traffic.

Hospitals damaged in the shelling have reopened and Hyde Park, Green Park and Battersea Park are closed to the public amid a sea of tents – field hospitals on an unprecedented scale, with operating theatres, casualty and recovery wings, staffed by military and volunteer staff, many of whom have travelled from across the nation and from around the world. One volunteer is Katje Rasmussen, a twenty-seven-year-old nurse from Aarhus in Denmark. 'I was to go on two weeks' holiday on the Saturday, so I came here. What else could I do?' she said, echoing the stories of so many around her.

Many roads and individual lanes have been prioritised for relief traffic and there are numerous diversions around restricted areas and unstable buildings. But the city is moving and working again, with commuters and workers taking to walking and cycling and many reporting they are able to get to and from work without difficulty.

In Essex, Stansted airport is closed to passenger and commercial cargo flights and will remain so for an indefinite period as it adjusts to its role as a primary relief centre. Major airlines have diverted to Heathrow, Gatwick, Luton and Birmingham and have assured customers that all pre-booked tickets will be honoured. Across London to the west, RAF Northolt has similarly been adapted to a relief role, as have the seaports of Tilbury and the Isle of Grain where large areas have been set aside for the upcoming reconstruction.

At 3.30 p.m. on Friday, 10 June, when the Prime Minister declared martial law over central areas of the capital, she also accepted the White House's offer of American troops to be deployed under British officers. A US government spokesman confirmed on Friday that up to twenty thousand servicemen and women are now on active service across the capital as property is protected, order restored and people begin to go about their daily business once again.

In the field hospitals and the streets, American voices are heard everywhere, part of the massive aid project immediately sanctioned by the President in Washington. 'Just clear your airports,' he was reported to have said. 'I'm sending everything you need, everything I've got.'

From around the world offers of help continue to pour in at such an overwhelming rate that officials have been swamped and forced to delay acceptance, while global airports report record traffic as expats and relatives rush to return for funerals, to care for the injured and to offer their help. Consular staff in British delegations are working flat out to process applications and fast-track key workers with essential skills. Thousands of other volunteers are arriving daily by plane, by ferry and the Channel Tunnel or by their own ships, like the armada that left the Netherlands. Hundreds of Dutch marine engineering and construction workers loaded specialist machinery and supplies on ships and barges and sailed from Rotterdam last Saturday. 'The North Sea oil business is dead and I've got men sitting at home and equipment doing nothing on my yard,' said Wouter Den Polder, fifty-two, boss of a specialist offshore contractor. 'No one asked if they were going to get paid,' he added. His company is just one of the many Dutch specialists who took it upon themselves to come, while their fuel bills were waived by Royal Dutch Shell who filled their vessels shortly before departure.

Engineering staff at the Thames Barrier said they are working round the clock in a race to repair the barrage before a high tide on

Thursday that is threatening to swamp large tracts of the city.

On Monday the Prime Minister moved swiftly to announce a new cabinet position – Minister for Capital Rehabilitation. The post has gone to Geoff Bates, a rising backbench MP who was a construction engineer and project director in the private sector before entering politics. The role carries wide-ranging executive powers across the entire spectrum of government and public service as the nation seeks to deal with the aftermath of the atrocity. It has set up operations in Victoria and formed a steering committee across the military, police and emergency services, NHS and key public services and private contractors.

This is a government without a home, temporarily housed in London's Olympia exhibition halls after the Palace of Westminster, parts of Downing Street and various Whitehall buildings were severely damaged. The spaces have been partitioned and communications installed, with a debating chamber, executive meeting rooms and a press facility. Early indications suggest it is working efficiently and internally it is still intentionally referred to as 'Westminster'.

In Westminster and throughout the capital, work has continued non-stop since noon on Friday the 10th. Emergency workers have toiled around the clock to restore services, shore up buildings, clear rubble and deal with unexploded shells. All leave across the public sector has been cancelled, with the numbers boosted by retired workers volunteering their services.

It has been the same in the private sector, where there is a mood of quiet determination to bring normality back to the city. Shops struggled to open on Saturday the 11th, but some did, with evident pride, and many more were doing business again on Monday. It was the same in offices, as employers reported staff arriving early for work, often when there was no office to go to. And due to safety concerns many were unable to get close to their buildings. In the City and Canary Wharf it was particularly painful for those who had survived. One who did make it in, only to find his building cordoned off, was Lee Wickens, twenty-three, a money broker from Ilford. 'They sent me out to the sandwich bar a minute before it all happened,' he said, looking nervously across Canada Square. A few metres from him a senior manager was standing by a placard with his company's name and logo, trying to take a roll call and trying to console, in a scene repeated across the open space, where thousands of people were gathered in huddles around makeshift signs.

It was a typical Friday in June, a day bathed in warm sunshine as people went about their daily business, at work, with friends and with family, making plans for the weekend. The offices and shops were full, the windows open or the air conditioning working overtime, and the prospect of an early or extended lunch break must have been appealing. At noon some had left already, lingering for a breath of fresh air or hurrying to meet friends or business associates.

And at noon the terrorist ship opened fire. At first it concentrated on targets close to where it had moored at the former Moritz Chemical Company's south bank wharf, located a mile upriver from the Thames Barrier. Fire was directed at BP's Westley Farm fuel depot, the 02 Dome, Excel Centre and London City Airport. Then it turned to Canary Wharf and its financial centre before switching to downriver targets, Tate & Lyle's Silvertown sugar works, military barracks in Woolwich, the Purfleet commercial port, a Silvertown electricity substation and the Thames Barrier.

At 12.07 it turned again, this time concentrating fire on the City business district before extending across London, up to Regent's Park and Lord's cricket ground, the main-line stations of King's Cross, St Pancras and Euston, sweeping west up Fleet Street, through Covent Garden, Soho, Piccadilly, Mayfair, Kensington and Chelsea and along the south bank from Tower Bridge to Lambeth. And this was just the first wave, which ended at 12.12, the first of three.

From information *The Sunday Times* has been able to piece together, it is clear that targets were assiduously researched and no single facet of London's life, commerce or culture was overlooked or spared. In the financial centres of the City and Canary Wharf, most of the major banks have been critically wounded, along with the Bank of England and the FCA regulatory body. Both Lloyd's and the Stock Exchange expect to be closed for a minimum of three months. Across the visual media, the BBC, ITN, ITV, Sky, Fox and CNN were all hit during the bombardment, with the comprehensive assault continuing in the written media, where *The Sunday Times*, *The Times*, *The Sun*, *Financial Times*, *Daily Mirror*, *The Guardian* and *The Daily Telegraph* were all hit, along with the commercial radio hub centred around Leicester Square.

Places of worship across the Christian and Jewish faiths were singled out. Five Central London synagogues were attacked, including the Westminster and West London synagogues and the UK's oldest located on Bevis Marks in the City financial district. Westminster Abbey, St Paul's, and all the historic Hawksmoor churches were hit with varying degrees of damage.

Public bodies and public services were targeted, with both the Royal

Courts of Justice and Lincoln's Inn suffering damage, along with every London hospital within the guns' infernal range. City Hall was damaged so severely that engineers have closed it completely and hopes are fading that the building will ever be reopened. The Palace of Westminster suffered serious damage, which has caused both houses to seek temporary homes elsewhere, with the House of Commons relocating to Olympia and the House of Lords to the Earl's Court exhibition centre.

London's infrastructure, transport network and essential services and utilities were all separately picked out in the bombardment along with close to fifty city centre petrol stations, from where fire spread rapidly and was a severe challenge to the already stretched emergency services. All the city centre river bridges were damaged, together with overpasses on major traffic routes, the Central London traffic-light control centre, and main-line stations with their associated maintenance depots and control rooms. Essential gas and electricity supplies were severely disrupted with damage reported to distribution facilities, pipelines, and phone masts and relay centres in the telecoms sector. Engineers struggled initially to shut off supply and subsequently to reopen it safely, but at the time of going to press all the leading utility companies are reporting a full resumption of service. Reports

suggest that ambulance depots and police and fire stations were priority targets during the initial phases of the onslaught, as part of the terrorists' bid to hamper their response and effectiveness.

Specialist areas of the police and security services received concentrated attacks, to New Scotland Yard, Special Branch and the Counter Terrorism Command – or SO15. On the south bank of the Thames, MI6 and its sister security service, MI5, on the opposite bank a few hundred metres from Westminster, both came under sustained attack. More generalised military units, including the MOD in Whitehall and Central London barracks for the many Guards' regiments, also came under concentrated fire.

Completing the already harrowing circle and further evidencing the clear strategy of the terrorists to wound mind, body and soul, London's great cultural icons fell victim to the onslaught. The Tower of London, the Royal Opera House and Sadler's Wells, the Royal Albert Hall, the Globe Theatre, the Royal Festival and Queen Elizabeth Halls, the great galleries of the Tate Modern, the National Gallery and National Portrait Gallery, the Royal Academy and Courtauld, together with the great museums of Science and Natural History, the British Museum, the Planetarium and Victoria and Albert, all suffered structural damage and untold loss to precious works of art, relics and artefacts.

The pattern was repeated across the sporting fields: at Lord's Cricket Ground and the Oval; the Crystal Palace National Sports Centre; at Chelsea Football Club's Stamford Bridge and West Ham's London Stadium; and at London's visible symbols: the Statue of Eros and the Albert Memorial; the Millennium Wheel, still partially submerged in the Thames; Nelson's Column, still stretched out across the pavements of Trafalgar Square; the Monument – to the Great Fire – toppled into neighbouring buildings and blocking Fish Street Hill in London's EC3 district.

And everywhere the shells fell, there were people. They were ordinary Londoners and they were visitors, our guests. They were also politicians and public servants, Nobel Prize winners, best-selling authors, Premier League footballers, Oscar winners, platinum-selling musicians, international cricketers, television and radio presenters, prima ballerinas, virtuoso instrumentalists, Bafta winners, industry leaders, Grand-Prix drivers, Pulitzer Prize winners, diplomats, Olympic medallists, fashion designers, film directors, artists and poets.

From eye witness accounts, CCTV footage and mobile phone videos, it is clear that as the shelling advanced across London it paused and concentrated its wrath on specific targets. As it marched up Fleet Street and the Strand, shells dropped singly before twenty-five were delivered with pinpoint accuracy to Goldman Sachs' headquarters, ten to St Bride's church and twenty-five to the Savoy Hotel. Elsewhere, the pattern was repeated, the shelling evenly spaced in generalised areas and heavily concentrated on preselected targets, all of which were chosen with chilling precision. In the financial districts the leading banks and trading institutions were singled out. The American, Israeli and French embassies suffered varying levels of damage, with the US facility in Grosvenor Square receiving the heaviest onslaught. The French residential community in South Kensington appears to have been a priority target, with comprehensive damage to its streets, shops and services. The Jewish residential community, concentrated mainly in more northerly regions of the city, escaped serious attack as a result of what appears to be no more than the consequence of being out of range of the guns, though synagogues within range were targeted along with the diamond and jewel trading centre of Hatton Garden. Flagship stores – Harrods, Harvey Nichols, Fortnum and Mason, Liberty, Selfridges and couture centres in South Molton Street, Knightsbridge and Sloane Street, were similarly picked out.

In their analysis of the

patterns, leading sociologists have identified the specific levels of research that were employed in the selection of targets. 'It's profoundly chilling to think how they studied us, learned our habits and knew our whereabouts,' said Dame Mary Drummond, Director of Sociology at the London School of Economics. 'Not only did they target our economy, our culture and our national psyche, they knew in precise detail where our leading figures might be, in the hotels favoured by celebrities, restaurants like the Ivy, the arts and media clubs – Soho House and The Groucho Club and the establishment clubs of Pall Mall.' And as another leading commentator added, 'It is one thing to know the financial centres of Canary Wharf and the City, but is something else again to pick out individual companies and office buildings of the hedge fund and investment community clustered around Berkeley Square.'

Leading ballistics experts have informed *The Sunday Times* how the terrorists were able to do this, advising that each individual shell was capable of being coded with its own unique target, either by being programmed with precise map coordinates, a photographic image, or laser guidance.

London is now burying its dead, caring for its injured and counting the financial cost. A spokesman for the BBA (British Banking Association) said last week that though there has been a catastrophic loss of staff and dealing rooms are out of action, business is still ongoing through satellite and overseas branches, and sentiment among customers is coming down strongly on maintaining trade. However, the situation in the insurance and reinsurance sector is markedly more sombre. Philip Walters, Chief Commercial Officer at Lloyd's, said, 'We have only just started to quantify the scale of claims, but it seems clear that the model is fundamentally broken on a global scale.' His views were echoed by a leading broker. 'Just where is the money going to come from to settle claims? The ramifications will be felt for decades.'

Realistic estimates have been in short supply during the week and figures ranging from five hundred billion to five trillion pounds have been circulating in the markets, amid further complications posed by the status of the attack. Insurance experts have said that it is unlikely to be designated as an act of war, and is more likely to be classified as terrorism, which can often be both a grey area in insurance contracts and a specific 'add on' that many policyholders will not have defined and paid for.

Financial regulators across global markets are cooperating on forensic analysis, where shorting of vulnerable indices and companies has been identified, particularly in the insurance sector. Patterns are emerging of a trading surge in the days leading up to the atrocity that suggest massive bets – or shorts – were placed against the decline in value of insurance stocks. Estimates vary, but the gains are thought to run into the hundreds of millions. One insider commented: 'It seems to have gone around the world markets, comprehensively spread against global and domestic players – basically a hedge against all insurance companies wherever they operate.' Another said, 'Insurance has had its challenges, but global sentiment suggests it's got through the worst, stabilised and looked set for steady trading over the next couple of years. So to bet against it now is counter-intuitive.' More worrying for the authorities is the implication that suggests prior knowledge of the attack and its consequent effect, but, as yet, no details are emerging of who placed the trades, or their verified scale.

Globally, the reaction has been largely of the deepest and most profound shock, with crowds holding vigils at British embassies around the world where they have laid flowers and other tributes. Churches of all denominations have held special services and reported record attendances. The Pope held a service of remembrance in St Peter's Square last Sunday and will do so again today as the world reflects on the scale of loss. Funds continue to pour in from thousands of donation sites and pledges from foreign governments and the UN.

Not everywhere was the attack met with grief and sympathy. Islamic strongholds in Iraq, Syria, Yemen and Somalia celebrated long into the night of Friday the 10th. In Iran the authorities were initially slow to quell the exuberance amid a cacophony of car horns. Crowds of young people took to the streets across the Islamic world, but their mood was not reflected across the breadth of their communities with many dismissing them as 'hotheads', and others openly crying 'shame'. The authorities in Saudi Arabia were quick to impose a robust police and military presence, where celebrations were quickly dispersed. Across North Africa from Morocco to Egypt the scenes were largely repeated, only for crowds to melt away as security forces moved quickly to establish order. In France, inner-city Paris, Lyon and Marseille saw cars set on fire in Muslim areas, though police and riot squads were quick to move in. Elsewhere across Europe the mood was more subdued as tensions rose and residents stayed in their own areas where they felt more secure.

Domestically, tensions were high in Britain, where vigilante mobs gathered on the edges of Muslim communities only to be met with a strong police and military cordon. Community leaders from both sides have largely dismissed the actions as born of frustration rather than a clear intent to seek retribution, though many Muslims are concerned, staying close to home and hoping that time will give the charged atmosphere time to settle. The looting in the West End on Friday afternoon and the early part of the evening that appalled so many people is now seen by many commentators to have been overestimated. Officials say the scale is lower than previously thought and concentrated among a small number of groups who acted swiftly and opportunistically. When martial law was declared on Friday and soldiers fired warning shots, eyewitnesses reported that suspects were quick to retreat.

Politically, a consensus was quickly reached, with opposition MPs pledging a willingness to keep political considerations in the background and the government opening its committees and action groups to cross-party membership. 'We need a government of talent now, not of political loyalty,' said one MP – a view echoed across Westminster last week.

But there are questions that need to be answered, questions from the opposition, from government, from the public and the global community. As the initial shock begins to subside, the fundamental questions in every mind are: who did this and how did they do it? To answer part of this we need to go back to just before Christmas last year.

On Saturday, 5 December, a Danish freighter, the *Danske Prince*, was in the middle of the Indian Ocean. In its hold were four Bofors guns and forty thousand rounds of ammunition for delivery to the Indian navy. At 17.20 its distress beacon was picked up by the InMarSat organisation and a rescue attempt was launched. The first ship to respond was the *Ocean Dove*, a freighter owned by the OceanBird Shipping Company of Sharjah, United Arab Emirates. Early on the following Monday, a French frigate arrived to coordinate the search-and-rescue attempts.

Signals and satellite imagery showed the *Ocean Dove* had been between ten and twenty miles from the *Danske Prince* when it blew up and sank with the loss of its eight-man crew. It now seems these signals were manipulated. Only speculation can suggest where the *Ocean Dove* actually was and how it lured the *Danske Prince* to its fate. But it seems clear the *Ocean Dove* 'acquired' the guns and ammunition and was instrumental in the sinking and likely murder of the *Danske Prince*'s crew. No bodies have been found and there is no clear evidence, but sources close to *The Sunday Times* assure us there is no suggestion of collusion between the ships and this is not an avenue of enquiry the authorities are pursuing.

At first, the *Ocean Dove* was not suspected of any involvement in what appeared to be a tragic accident at sea – it even received plaudits from the international shipping community for its efforts to aid the *Danske Prince* in its apparent distress. The next morning it sailed for Bar Mhar in Pakistan, where it is thought to have unloaded its stolen cargo. For the next four months it traded as a regular cargo ship in international waters, before returning to Bar Mhar in April where it is thought the guns were fitted in its hold before a voyage around the southern cape of Africa to London.

International security officials were swift to raid the offices of OceanBird in Sharjah, its sister company STC (Sharjah Trade and Commerce), and the shipyard at Bar Mhar, where all key officials of the companies had already vanished, leaving behind scores of bewildered junior staff who are now held in secure locations and assisting the authorities in the ongoing enquiry.

STC is suspected of acting as a key intermediary in the scheme, by buying the defunct Moritz Chemical Company plant from US property investment fund Red Oak LLC, which had acquired the company and its site for development. In a further twist, the two leading executives from Red Oak who negotiated the sale were both killed during the bombardment of the investment community clustered around London's Berkeley Square. Though usually based in Red Oak's Moscow office, the pair had travelled to London for a management meeting. Security experts suggest that though STC paid around USD 3.5 million for the plant and its dismantling and packing for shipment, it never had any intention of taking it back to the UAE for recommissioning. The financial outlay was purely part of a subterfuge, specifically to enable the ship to moor at an isolated location as close to Central London as possible.

International arrest warrants have been issued for OceanBird's CEO, Bulent Erkan, a thirty-six-year-old Turkish national; Rashid Al Hammadi, thirty-two, CEO of STC and a UAE national; Jawad Balal, thirty-two, a Lebanese national and head of process at STC's chemical subsidiary; and Hassan Khan, forty-four, a Pakistan national and CEO of Bar Mhar Marine Engineering Company.

At 6 a.m. on Friday the 10th a pilot boarded the ship off the Kent coast and guided it to the Moritz facility. The pilot, who does not wish to be named and is recovering at an unnamed location, has expressed his deep shock at the unwitting part he played in the dramatic events. 'There was nothing suspicious about them. The crew seemed so normal, friendly, good at their jobs. And it was a well-run ship.'

His comments have been repeated by all those who were connected with the OceanBird Shipping Company, STC and the Bar Mhar shipyard. There is profound shock and bewilderment in their respective industry sectors as suppliers and customers recoil from the enormity of events, unable to match the actions of the alleged perpetrators with their impressions of them on a daily basis. Once again, the world is dismayed at the prospect of terrorists living clandestine lives in plain sight, often as well-liked and respected members of their communities.

A little after 10 a.m. the *Ocean Dove* moored at the Moritz dock. A customs inspector had travelled to the disused facility to clear the ship and deal with the crew's immigration formalities, an innocent official going about his work, who was found murdered on board by the SAS troop who subsequently stormed the ship a few hours later. His fate was tragically mirrored by two security guards manning the gatehouse at the Moritz works.

It was now noon and the terrorists had the facility to themselves. They had prepared the ship and they were ready to fire, which they did at precisely 12.00. The last shell was fired at 12.39 as two Apache helicopters swooped down and attacked with automatic cannon rounds and Hellfire missiles, killing some of the crew on board and crippling the ship, which drifted out of control until it ran aground a short distance downstream. Experts estimate that the four guns mounted in the

Ocean Dove, which in combination can fire almost a thousand rounds per minute at a range of nearly ten miles, had fired in excess of 38,000 rounds by 12.39.

By now an SAS squad had arrived on the scene, who boarded the ship and fought running gun battles with the remaining crew. No injuries were sustained by the SAS, but the entire crew of fourteen aboard the *Ocean Dove* were all pronounced dead shortly after one o'clock. With no survivors, the task facing the security services is further hindered as they grapple to understand the atrocity and trace its ringleaders. 'If just one of them had survived – we could sweat him,' a Special Branch counterterrorism officer said with regret.

The ship has been refloated by salvage experts and towed to a secure facility at Rochester, where it is undergoing an intensive forensic examination. The names and nationalities of the crew have not been released through official channels yet, though information is circulating freely on the internet.

The *Ocean Dove* is a typical cargo ship, a hundred and fifteen metres long and capable of carrying five thousand tonnes of freight. Its owner, OceanBird, also owned a sister ship among its fleet, the *Ocean Tern*, which was sold in March to new owners in Singapore. The sale is now seen by many as a straightforward money-raising exercise to fund the acquisition of the Moritz plant and the *Ocean Dove*'s journey to London. OceanBird, through its hard-working and respected CEO, Bulent Erkan, had built a reputation within the shipping community. Erkan was well known and well thought of in Hamburg and Rotterdam, where he had spent many years working with established shipowning companies, building his networks and knowledge. In London, OceanBird was represented by BDN, a listed company and one of the largest shipbroking services in the global market.

Four floors below OceanBird in a typical Sharjah office building was STC, a trading house with separate manufacturing plants producing cement and chemicals. The company had been built up by Saeed Al Hammadi – father of the CEO, Rashid Al Hammadi – over the preceding thirty years, and was seen as a pillar of the Sharjah business community, as was Al Hammadi himself, who enjoyed close links to the ruling family and a fearsome reputation for tenacity. Sidelined by a heart condition eighteen months ago, he handed control to his son. We also understand, by coincidence, Saeed Al Hammadi died in his sleep on Thursday, 9 June, the night before the attack. His son, Rashid, is said by those who know him to lack his father's grit, but was nevertheless seen as a capable if less than inspiring leader of the company.

Working under him and heading STC's manufacturing capability, was Jawad Balal, who flew to Moscow shortly after the new year to negotiate the purchase of the Moritz plant. A week before his trip he had travelled to London to inspect the machinery. Aged thirty-two, born and brought up in Lebanon, he is well known in the Gulf and wider industry circles and had been tipped as a rising star.

It is also known that barely ten days before the attack, STC was sold to venture-capitalist investors from Singapore, who have effectively acquired a worthless shell. A spokesperson said: 'In good faith we made an investment in a respectable company. How could we know they were cynically cashing-out ...'

The fourth fugitive is Hassan Khan, boss of the shipyard in Pakistan and once again a respected figure in his field. It is suspected that it was his engineering skills that enabled the *Ocean Dove*, a typical freighter, to be converted with such devastating effect into what effectively became a fighting ship. Unnamed sources have revealed that ingenious engineering modifications were carried out to the ship, the Bofors guns and their loading mechanisms.

What evidently links these four is their positions of influence, their qualifications – all are degree educated – and their ability to operate in plain sight. What is not clear is how they organised themselves. Could it be that they independently cooperated in a scheme of their own design, or is there a deeper link to an umbrella organisation? If there is, it has yet to be identified. Tellingly, no plausible body has yet come forward to claim responsibility for the attack. How did these four men organise themselves, independently or as part of a wider conspiracy?

These are among the questions facing the security services and the government as they struggle to come to terms with the catastrophic failure firstly to detect the threat of attack and then subsequently to deal with it. It was 12.39 before two Apache attack helicopters arrived on the scene and 12.52 before the first RAF fighter jets appeared – fully five embarrassing minutes after American F-16s swooped through Docklands.

Security insiders speak of a confused response that saw a breakdown in basic communication and chains of command, systemic failures in the government's HITS (High Integrity Telecommunications System) and MTPAS (Mobile Telecoms Privileged Access System), and ultimately in the COBRA crisis-management centre (Cabinet Office Briefing Rooms) which was established to spearhead the government's management and response to incidents of this nature.

Seasoned observers and former officers of the security services have spoken of the intensity of the running battle now raging between the nation's security pillars. One former officer, who requested anonymity, said, 'It seems a junior MI5 officer picked up the *Ocean Dove* months ago but couldn't get his superiors to take his suspicions seriously. Then the file was shelved and passed to MI6, who did little about it.'

At 2.30 on Friday, the Deputy Director General of MI5, Edmund LaSalle, and one other man as yet unidentified but noted by Downing Street press observers to be in a dishevelled state from injuries he presumably sustained in the attack, were seen arriving for a high-level meeting at Number Ten. They emerged without comment shortly after three o'clock.

Insider rumours also speak of the actions of an off-duty operative from MI5 commandeering a helicopter close to the M11 motorway, identifying the *Ocean Dove* at the Moritz plant and coordinating the security response from the air. As one former senior officer said, 'If that's true, it's an unimaginable indictment on the entire security apparatus across government, the security services and the military.'

Questions are also being asked as to why the UK does not have a ship-security programme, similar to the one America introduced in response to the 9/11 attacks. Foreign cargo vessels en route to US ports are obliged to give advance notice of their impending arrival, for the Department for Homeland Security, working with the US Coastguard, to vet potential security risks and where appropriate physically inspect ships at predetermined locations offshore, before clearance to proceed to a port or ports is granted.

Eight days after the UK suffered its worst loss of life in a single day since the First World War, questions remain unanswered. Who are these people that wreaked havoc among us? How were they able to do it? Why were we so incapable of preventing it? These questions will reverberate through our society for generations to come as we count the cost of our losses, mourn our dead and rebuild our city.

In all the bewilderment and pain, there is only one clear fact – this *dove* did not come in peace.